# BOURBON SUMMER

## A Bourbon Canyon Novel

## WALKER ROSE

LE Publishing

When my former best friend invites me to her wedding —to my ex-boyfriend—I panic and blurt out that I have a plus-one. Worse, I say it's my boss. And he hears every word.

Tenor Bailey is one of the owners of Copper Summit, the bourbon distillery where I work. Let's just say announcing we're "dating" isn't the kind of thing that earns employee-of-the-year honors. But to my surprise, Tenor agrees to play along. Now we're selling our very fake relationship to this tight-knit small town—and trying not to blur the lines in the process.

Fake dating Tenor comes with unexpected perks: home-cooked meals from his mama, picture-perfect picnics, and sleepovers—in his guest room. Except for that one time I had too much bourbon and ended up in his bed. Oops.

The more time we spend together, the more I wish this wasn't all pretend. But Tenor's been hurt before, and he's convinced love isn't in the cards for him. By the time our bourbon summer ends, I'm afraid my very real feelings will leave me with a broken heart.

# CHAPTER ONE

Ruby

It was Friday night, and I had a mandarin bourbon smash in front of me and a semi-crowded bar behind me. The goblet glass was pretty, filled with ice, muddled mandarin, bourbon, orange liqueur, and bitters. It looked like a hard orange creamsicle. Perfect for summer. Only I wasn't drinking it; I was photographing it.

I swiped to a different undertone on my phone and clicked. Then clicked again. I took a few more shots. Then I put a mandarin next to the glass and went through another round of shots.

"Need a model, Ruby?" one of the regulars called from a few tables away.

I smiled over my shoulder. "I can't afford you, Jason." The older farmer was in his forties, but his kids were my age, in their midtwenties, and he treated me like I was one of their lifelong friends when I'd only met his girls once.

"I'd cut Copper Summit a deal."

I laughed, but inside, I sighed. I'd been suggesting more candid photo shoots. Less-formal sessions, preferably with Baileys involved. After all, the family owned and ran Copper Summit Bourbon Distillery.

*But Junie's the face of Copper Summit* was the response I'd gotten from my boss the two times I'd brought up using others for more informal social media posts.

Junie Kinkade had been the face of Copper Summit since she was old enough to legally work for a spirits company. She was also a wildly popular country singer, which helped drive sales. Her audience loved what she loved, and she loved Copper Summit bourbon.

But . . . the brand could do with a refresh. At least online.

I wrapped up my photo shoot and took the mandarin bourbon smash to Jason's table. "On the house."

His mouth dropped open. If there was one thing Jason loved, it was trying all the new cocktails. "Thank you, Ruby. You're one in a million."

No, I was not. Not at all. Just ask any of my exes. "You're welcome."

I went back behind the bar. Instead of using my phone to stalk the social media accounts of Copper Summit's competitors, I used the tablet we took payments on. I looked more official and less like I was fucking around online while working. But really, I was working while working.

Outside of my day job at the distillery, I picked up a couple of evening shifts each week in the tasting room to give the illusion I had a social life. I laughed with regulars and tourists, and then I drove back to Bozeman and my empty apartment. No one had to know that if I hadn't been working, I'd have been home in bed, scrolling through my phone or reading a book like I did the other five nights of the week.

Movement beyond the front wall-to-wall windows caught my eye. I did a double take.

No.

Not tonight. Copper Summit was my safe space. I got to have a career I loved, one that fit my wallflower lifestyle, and I got to have a social life on the nights I worked the bar.

This environment was a judgment-free zone. So why the hell was my ex-boyfriend in the parking lot, my ex-best friend in tow?

That man had judged the hell out of me.

Oh no. They were walking in.

My heart rate crept up. No, no, no.

Brock Gibson had always mocked my social media marketing position with Copper Summit. Now I was also bartending—which I loved—but no doubt he'd act like I'd hit my head on each rung on the way down the corporate ladder. His words ran through my head, as fresh as the day he'd said them.

*I just want more, Ruby. I don't want to watch the world go by, and you're always buried in your phone. Or in a book. And when we go out, you complain. We can't keep trying to mine a well that's gone dry.* The pitying look he'd given me when he'd said that was still crystal clear in my head. Probably because I relived that humiliating breakup conversation every day since it had happened.

I kept telling myself that at least this time he hadn't given me the *I need a break* convo. Or the *it's not you, it's me* cliché he'd given me the time before that. This time, he had said it was most definitely me.

He hadn't been the first guy to dump me for similar reasons.

They were almost to the door. When had Brock and Cara Simonson started going out? Right after our breakup? Had she been the reason for his sudden disinterest in me? Did they giggle about how unexciting I was? How predictable?

I was frozen, my gaze glued to the big picture windows that lined the exterior wall of the distillery. Brock and Cara. Cara and Brock. In my workplace. The two people who had made me feel the worst about myself. Brock opened the door for her.

*Please go into the main distillery.*

They wouldn't. It was almost eight in the evening and the distillery had been closed for two hours. Only the bar was open this late on a Friday night.

Cara smiled wide at him, flinging her long, glossy blond hair over her shoulder. She mouthed *thank you* and blew him a kiss. My stomach churned. They looked like they were perfect for each other.

Brock entered behind Cara, a big, indulgent smile in place. He used to aim that grin my way. But when his gaze landed on me, his expression morphed into shock. Cara was laughing and pointing to an open table close to the counter when she noticed his expression. She followed his gaze right to me.

My breath stalled. I did not want to do this, but I was the employee. It was my job to greet them. "Welcome to Copper Summit," I said woodenly, smoothing my hands over my bright-yellow skirt. I'd paired it with black, chunky shoes. The white socks went with the white dress shirt I'd tied at my waist. The sleeves were rolled up. The tag had called it a boyfriend shirt and I had bought it just for that. A boyfriend shirt for the tragically single girl.

I looked like a school kid compared to Cara and her wide-legged gray slacks and magenta blouse with a goddamn ruffle that should look ridiculous and not sophisticated.

Her smile didn't fade. It grew broader. The gleam in her eyes turned predatory. Or was it the glow of the neon signs for Copper Summit bourbon on the wall next to her?

"Oh my god!" Her rich voice carried across the din. "Ruby Casteel? It's been forever."

People stopped chatting and watched us. Did they see a train wreck about to happen? Was I the stranded motorist who couldn't move her car off the tracks while they gaped at the locomotive bearing down on her?

"How are you?" That voice. That high-pitched tone. That nasal whine. Her casual yet hurtful comments in school threatened to pour back.

Like when I'd gotten a knit sweater I loved with my own money. *Ruby, that color really washes you out, but I guess with your skin tone you don't have many options.*

Or when I'd debated trying a sport. *Yeah, you shouldn't go out for volleyball. Riding the bench is just a waste of time.*

Then there was the morning I'd worked for an hour on my hair to impress a boy in history class. *That natural curl in your hair could be so cute.*

She blinked at me, waiting for a reply. If I didn't know her better, I'd say she was actually happy to see me. But I remembered how she used to smile when we met up at the playground versus when we passed in the hall in middle school.

"Cara, hi. I'm well," I managed to squeak out. "Hi, Brock."

She threaded her arm around my ex. "Ohmigod. Do you two know each other?"

I tilted my head and waited for his answer. No way was I telling Cara I was that man's ex. She either knew or she was going to find out from him. I'd learned long ago that it was better to keep my mouth shut around Cara Simonson.

Brock nuzzled her hair. "Remember, I told you about her," he murmured. He pinned me with his bright blue gaze. "Hi, Rubes."

I hated that nickname. My dad called me Rubes and I tolerated it from him. Otherwise, it sounded too close to "Pubes" and Cara had thought that was hilarious, calling me Pubes for all of eighth grade.

Before I could correct him, Cara gasped. "*That* Ruby? I had no idea." She laughed. "Small world. I never see you around, but you were always a wallflower."

Brock nodded, and irritation sparked in my gut. I was not a— Eh, yes I was.

I had never been the life of the party. I'd have to go to a party first, and I wasn't the fun-loving, innately sexy girl who got invited to such things. Cara was the one who loved gatherings, and she'd never extended the invitation to me.

As if to punctuate my unspoken thought, Brock wrapped an arm around Cara and tucked her into his side. He used to complain I was too short and he felt like I was sniffing his armpit. Cara was taller. They could bang foreheads for all I cared.

"I thought you worked at the Bozeman location," Brock said.

Cara rubbed her hand across his chest. The two of them were sickly sweet, sweeter even than the huckleberry syrup I used for cocktails.

"I do. I took on some hours at the bar because it's fun." And so I could afford more books.

"Oh!" Cara stuffed a finger toward me. "You're the social media girl."

Brock had likely not been complimentary when describing my job. Had they had a good laugh at my expense?

"Yep." It was social media *management*, but I wouldn't elaborate. The only people I needed to justify my job to were the Baileys, and I respected them a hell of a lot more than these two. One Bailey in particular. His face had become the heroes in the stories I read. Especially the romances.

Especially the dirty romances.

"What can I get you two to drink?" I asked before I could blush. Wouldn't want them thinking it was because I was embarrassed about my job.

"Isn't this a tasting room?" Brock asked, his mouth turned down as he eyed the tables and the large windows that viewed the lobby.

"It functions as one yes, during the day. The Baileys have taken to calling it a cocktail bar so tourists know they can do more than sample in the evenings. But tasting room and bar are interchangeable for us." I snagged a laminated sheet from under the bar and plopped it in front of them, anxious to serve them and move on. "Here's a menu if you want some ideas."

Cara forgot the table she'd initially been interested in

and slid onto a stool. "Ruby." Her expert pout had only gotten shinier and puffier. "It's been forever. We used to be such good friends."

We had been. Then her family had gotten money, moved out of the apartment building I was raised in, and Cara had found herself some friends with clothing and hairstyles that matched hers. She no longer wanted to talk books, didn't care about Percy Jackson or Katniss, and definitely wasn't interested in discussing film adaptations and how they never lived up to the book.

"It's a busy night," I lied. Everyone was taken care of, and a brief scan showed all the drinks were at least half-full. Damn. "What would you like?"

"A mojito," she drawled. "It's the perfect summer drink." Her wide smile returned. "Don't you think? This place has mojitos, right? I know it's in the boondocks, but I'm optimistic."

My right eye twitched. It only did that when I'd been staring at a screen for too long, which was most days, but Cara stressed me just as much. "So FYI, mojitos tend to be rum-based drinks, but I can make you a Copper Summit version with our original line of bourbon."

She laughed, a sharp, cutting sound. "Isn't a mojito a mojito?"

"This is a *bourbon* distillery," I said.

Brock bristled, more defensive over Cara than he'd ever been for me. "She said she'd like a mojito."

"I'm just trying to highlight the difference, so there're no surprises." I attempted the same megawatt smile Cara had displayed. "Predictability is a good thing in a bar."

He flinched and looked away.

Cara's gaze sharpened as if she sensed the dig. "I guess I can't expect much excitement in a town as small as Bourbon Canyon." She put her chin in her hand. "Do you live here, Rubes?"

Some days, it felt like there was more for me in this little town than where I'd been born and raised. I pinched off the longing before it could ignite. "No. I'm still in Bozeman." I grabbed a bottle of Copper Summit Original and started on the mojito. "What can I make you to drink?" I asked Brock. The sooner I served them, the sooner they'd leave. I hoped.

"I'll just take a bourbon. Neat." He straightened like I was going to challenge him.

I didn't. He hated whiskey. If he thought he could gut through a glass of plain bourbon in front of his girl-friend, who was I to argue? It was a chance to squeeze some joy out of the night.

I slid the mojito in front of Cara and poured the drink for Brock.

She took a sip and frowned. Then she shrugged and smacked her lips. I was about to scoot out from around the bar when she asked, "What have you been up to since graduation?"

Why did she want to visit? For most of high school, she'd pretended I didn't exist. "School and then work. You?"

"Mm." She sucked more of the drink down. "Same. I'm working for my parents' real estate company now."

A thread of envy wound around my heart. Cara had walked into her family's company. And Brock probably still worked as a project manager for his dad's construction company.

My mom had toiled away at three jobs trying to keep

us afloat while I'd been growing up. Now, she worked as a remote bookkeeper and had spent her time since I'd graduated catching up on everything she'd missed after becoming a teen mom.

"What a wonderful opportunity." There. I'd been the bigger person. I saw my exit in the conversation and went for it. I was about to duck out from behind the bar when Cara put her left hand out.

A knot in my gut cinched so tight I almost doubled over. A giant square diamond sparkled under the bar lights. How had I missed that monster ring? Well, she had been pasted to Brock since they'd walked in.

Brock had never bought me jewelry. No guy had.

No guy had bought me anything.

"We're getting *married*." She sang the last word.

"Congratulations." The envy had returned. I didn't want Brock, but why did a superficial person who body-surfed on others' feelings get to be spoiled? "Excuse me. I need to check on the other customers."

I distracted myself from all the old feelings of inadequacy Brock and Cara exposed with orders and refills. While I was adding a splash of ginger beer to a bourbon mule, Brock took a sip of his drink and sputtered.

I gestured to my cheek. "Gotta shut off this part of your nose, remember?"

After I'd gotten the job with the Bozeman location of Copper Summit, I'd bought several bottles to try. I'd tackled them like I had a semester final. I had been filled with excitement and ideas to promote the product. Unlike Brock, I had been through a tasting session at the distillery. I could sip and enjoy the flavors playing over my taste buds. Brock had nearly swallowed his tongue and snorted bourbon out his nose.

Annoyance crossed his face. "A good bourbon wouldn't do that."

I refrained from rolling my eyes and brought the drink I'd prepared to Jason.

"Thanks, Ruby," he said. His gaze narrowed on me. "Everything okay?"

My face was hot. Embarrassment. Irritation. Frustration. The night had started out so well. My skin showed all my emotions. I didn't tan well and flushed easily. "I'm good. Just getting a little warm."

I grabbed some empty glasses on my way back to the bar and took a few more orders. When I returned, Cara and Brock had their foreheads tipped together. His bourbon remained untouched since his first attempt, but her glass was empty except for ice, mint leaves, and a lime wedge.

I took her glass. "Need a refill?"

"Yes, please, Ruby."

I tensed, waiting for some dig after that, but she actually sounded sincere.

She draped herself over Brock and kissed him. It was no quick kiss. The two were making out. I had to endure the smacking sounds while preparing another mojito. The metallic clang of the shaker didn't faze them. I was a helpless bystander.

Cara pulled away and licked her lips. "Mm." Her dreamy gaze slid toward me. "We're having our wedding in town."

Surprise flitted through me. Mental note: find out when they were getting married and make sure I wasn't in town. Another giant party I was not invited to. "Oh?"

"We're moving here." She kissed Brock's cheek and somehow had enough lipstick left to leave an imprint on his skin. "I'm opening a real estate office, and his family's decided to do the same."

"That'll make your life *exciting*." Petty, yes, but Brock's fleeting, irritated expression was so satisfying. "Congratulations again." I continued assembling the drink orders. A lemonade special, a blackberry bourbon, and another bourbon mojito. They were best-sellers during the summer. I needed to make some posts with them, but I'd refrain in front of the two lovebirds.

"I hope it all works out." Her pout returned and she spread her hands. "It was all falling into place for a whirlwind wedding, but then the country club called earlier and told me they're no longer offering wet bar options. The person who was supposed to work our wedding quit, and they're too short-staffed for the Fourth the week after."

"That stinks." I had no clue how country clubs worked, but Cara used to fantasize about being the happy bride, and she had her . . . well, Brock wasn't Prince Charming, but she had her groom. "I'm sorry."

She eyed the bottle of Original in my hand. "Does Copper Summit do wet bars?"

"I . . . don't know." I wasn't involved in the everyday workings and that was something my boss, Wynter, would want to keep separate. The distillery social media feeds didn't dig that deep into Copper Summit business.

Cara leaned over the bar. "The president of the club actually said that Copper Summit has provided wet bar service before. That's why we came tonight."

Brock grunted and looked away. "I suppose there's no one in charge around to talk to."

I wished I had more information, if only to make it

seem like the social media girl wasn't a lowly position in front of Brock. "I can leave a message for—"

Cara gasped. "You could work it. Oh, I'd feel so much better if you were in charge. You're so organized."

Was that a compliment? Without an insult? "I'm not . . ."

"Or would that be weird?" Cara looked from me to Brock. "With your history?"

Yes. "I mean, I'm not going to create drama. I'm too *boring* for that." I hadn't been able to resist, and apparently, I was no better than Cara, getting digs in when I could. "You two are clearly in love."

She beamed. Brock's lips formed a line, but he grasped Cara's hand. "I want you to have a stress-free day, baby," he said to her. "No need to worry over any single ladies in attendance. I only have eyes for you."

Maybe it was their affectionate display or having endured the sloppy make-out session, but Brock's assumption that I was single and would be pining for him rubbed me in all the wrong ways. It was like having sex with him all over again. "I'm not single."

Shit.

The lie was out, and I couldn't take it back. I swallowed the acid crawling up my throat. At least I shouldn't have to prove it.

"Then you should come as a guest. There are more people who can do the wet bar."

My laughter came out thready. "Uh, if they *do* wet bars."

"You have to come to the wedding," Cara said, a note of finality in her voice. Delight grew across her face. "I've lost touch with so many people from the good ol' days. It'd be great to have you."

Good ol' days? Other than how we dressed, that was the starkest difference between us. Graduation had been the happiest day of my life. It had meant I wouldn't have to see people who made me feel horrible about myself on a daily basis.

"And I'd get to meet your boyfriend," she said in a singsong voice. "It'll be just like when we dreamed about our weddings. We'll be together."

Was she for real? As if she hadn't come in here and low-key insulted me earlier?

Pleased, she hugged Brock. "Isn't that wonderful? We'll have people from the past and present there to show us how far we've come."

"Mm-hmm." How did I get out of this? I had to have something going on that weekend. She'd mentioned whirlwind planning. It had to be soon. Whatever excuse I gave, it had to sound natural. I could not be humiliated by getting caught in a lie about my single status. Not by my ex.

I hadn't cried for days just to let Brock get to me again. I hadn't relived every other breakup with an ex who'd said similar things only to repeat the cycle when I wasn't even dating anyone. All those typos Wynter had called me on after nights of terrible sleep could not happen again.

I hadn't even been able to get myself off. So much for proving that I wasn't the reason it had taken so long to orgasm. Their wedding would be the great libido robber. No, thank you.

I cleared my throat. "Excuse me. I have to get these out before all the ice melts."

I loaded a tray with drinks and scurried off. I strug-gled to get my breathing under control while I delivered the orders. At every single table, I asked if I could get them something else, practically begged, but since we were nearing closing time, they all passed. Damn the tasting room for not being open later on weekends.

What did I do? Find a date before the wedding? I'd only been single a year, but maybe I could use an app and just ask them to pretend with me. Was there a Tinder for fake dates?

My back was to the lobby entrance as the door opened, a waft of air crashing into me. A wave of heat followed.

It was *him*.

I turned, my gaze drawn to Tenor Bailey like there was no one else in the room. He stopped by Jason, probably talking about ranching. Jason's land bordered the Baileys' ranch. Tenor might run the finance department at Copper Summit, but he worked with Bailey Beef just as much.

The breathing I had tried to get under control quickened. He was so big. Tall and broad-shouldered, he was the tallest of all his brothers. Tenor had a way of slumping, of curling in on himself when he might otherwise loom over people. Was he aware?

Tenor Bailey occupied my mind far more often than he should.

He pushed up his solid-framed black glasses. Behind the lenses, his thick lashes were a few shades darker than his brown hair. He didn't have a beard, but scruff always graced his square jaw.

He was scratching at his cheek as he listened to Jason. Tenor did a lot of listening. He wasn't blustery or quick to add his two cents. Those qualities attracted me. I was a fluttery moth and he was a bright flame.

The guy could run numbers faster than should be humanly possible, but he never lorded over everyone how smart he was. The brainiac wore blue jeans and a simple rust-colored polo with a black Copper Summit logo on the breast. The cowboy boots that completed the look also consumed far more of my brain than they should.

One time, I'd seen him in a cowboy hat when he'd stopped in after helping with calving and I hadn't been able to speak around him. A nerdy cowboy was my kryptonite.

A customer scooted his chair out, bumping into me. I jumped and nearly dropped my empty tray. "Sorry," I squeaked.

Tenor glanced up. When his gaze landed on me, my pulse jumped. His pecan-hued irises were as unique as he was. He lifted a brow with an unspoken question—*Are you okay?*

I was never okay around him. He was older and confident and a lot more man than I'd ever associated with. I nodded and scurried back to the bar.

Cara's second mojito was already empty. She leaned over, her eyes taking on a fevered glaze. Was the alcohol hitting her that hard already? "You have to tell me. Who are you seeing? Do I know him? Is he from Bozeman too? Wouldn't it be funny if I'd dated him?" She guffawed and hugged herself to Brock. "I saved the best for last."

Brock's mouth curled into a smug smile as he slid his gaze off me and to his fiancée. "Me too."

Jackass.

"Aw." Cara had damn hearts in her eyes. "So? Who is he?"

I was back in the car, stuck on the train tracks with

Locomotive Cara bearing down on me. "Oh. Um . . . you wouldn't know him."

I ran some fresh water to clean the dirty glasses I'd picked up earlier. Tenor broke from Jason and chatted with another customer, leaning down instead of towering over the guy. Gah. He was so considerate.

Cara put her elbow on the bar top and rested her face in her hand. "Try me."

I scrubbed at an imaginary smudge on a glass. "He's not from Bozeman." I tried for an apologetic smile.

Brock's eyes narrowed on the way I was frantically washing the same clean glass. "It's a small world. Who is he?" His tone was cajoling. He thought he had me.

Dammit, he did have me.

This wasn't fair. He was the one who'd brought his fiancée into the place where he'd known there was a possibility of seeing me. He and his saturated kisses could fuck right off. I would not admit I was single. I would not give him the satisfaction of knowing he was right. I would not give him even an inkling that my social life had gotten even less thrilling than when we'd been together.

Tenor came around the bar. "Hey, Ruby. How's it going tonight?"

His deep voice washed over me, but it only fueled my determination. "Hi, Tenor."

Cara's gaze turned awestruck as she took him in. "Tenor?" She giggled. "What kind of name is that? It's so . . . *unique*."

The way her voice pitched up scraped against my patience, warning me what would come next. A hidden insult. A snide remark. My pulse pounded at my temples. I might lose my job for this, but it was either that or jump the counter, knock her to the floor, and slap my hands over her mouth.

"Isn't it a great name?" I slid an arm around Tenor's waist. He stiffened, a hard wall of muscle. "Also, meet my plus-one. Tenor's my boyfriend."

*Oh god, oh god, oh god.* What had I done?

Cara and Brock stared at me.

Tenor's brows knit together.

I was flat on the train tracks, smashed to bits, and had only myself to blame.

🔩

Tenor

I hadn't been anyone's boyfriend for a lot of damn years. I had to have misheard.

Ruby's arm was around me and she was close enough I could smell her limoncello scent. I inhaled deeply. In the past, I had caught a delectable whiff of her, but I'd never been this close.

I might have inappropriate thoughts about the petite marketing pro, but I always shoved my X-rated ideas out of my head as soon as they arrived. Not only was she much younger than me, she was an employee.

An employee who was smashed up next to me, inciting all those earlier ideas I'd had about her. "Ruby?"

The mouth of the woman across from us dropped open and a shrill squeal left her. "Ruby. Oh. My. God. He's a *snack*. Like a whole buffet."

I steeled myself, trying to figure out if this woman

meant it as a compliment or not. Did I want to be a buffet? The guy next to her scowled.

"He's the whole seven-course meal," Ruby said with knowing confidence. "Um, Tenor. This is an old friend of mine, Cara, and her fiancé, Brock."

I dipped my head, flailing to keep up with the turn of events.

"I hope you have a nice suit." Cara's grin was wide.

What the hell was going on?

Brock studied me with a slight frown. His date's delighted gaze danced between me and Ruby.

I immediately knew this woman's type. She was polished, her hair as sleek as her portfolio probably was. Something about her put me on guard. I stayed far away from women like that.

Brock was exactly like someone I'd expect to see with her. His gelled, dirty-blond hair crested in the middle like an ocean wave. His clothing was just like hers. Some brand name that cost more than it was worth. He was probably the only guy in the place not wearing jeans.

"Why do I need a suit?" Diligently, I tried to keep my mind off the lush body pressed next to me. Ruby's hips hit below mine and her breasts—

She was my *employee*. I would not notice how her tits were perfect handfuls.

"For our wedding. Ruby is invited, naturally. We're old friends." Cara gave me a coy look and Ruby stiffened next to me.

I nearly put an arm around Ruby. She was bothered by this Cara, but I didn't know why. Nor did I know why Ruby had claimed I was her boyfriend. I wasn't a guy who liked to act without all the information. "I need to steal Ruby for a minute."

Because I was a glutton for punishment, and that couple was watching, I slipped my hand over Ruby's and tugged her to the back office. Energy zinged up and down my arm. It was like my nerve endings had just been waiting for her touch to come alive.

I gritted my teeth and led her to the storeroom behind the bar.

"Wanna tell me what—"

"I'm so sorry," she whispered, dropping my hand and clapping her own over her crimson cheeks. "I can't believe I did that." She released her face and balled her hands into fists at her sides. Her ruby-red lips were set in a mutinous line. "I cannot stand him."

This was not a Ruby I'd seen before. She was usually quiet, not speaking to me unless I had to ask her a question. She was more animated with my sisters, but this flush on her face was new. How far down her neck did it go? Was a blush ghosting over her—

*Shut it down.*

I crossed my arms over my chest. She looked up, guilt scrawled over her face, and more than a little fear simmered in her eyes. I couldn't help towering over her, but I hunched more to keep from intimidating her. "I thought you said you were friends with her, not him."

She scrunched her nose. "He's my ex-boyfriend."

"The guy with the coif?" He didn't deserve her. I had no clue who he was, but it didn't matter. She'd been wasted on him.

"He dumped me last year."

Fucking idiot.

She hugged herself. "Cara and I went to school

together. We used to be close. Best friends. Then we *so* weren't. Apparently, they're getting married." Her smile was tight. "I'm invited. Oh! She talked about having a Copper Summit wet bar. I didn't have much info for them—"

"Ruby. Explain."

She snapped her mouth shut. Her lower lip was just a little puffier than her top. The perfect little shelf to nibble on.

She worked for me. How many times did I have to remind myself of that?

I could fire her.

*No*, I couldn't. I'd hate myself. My brothers would beat me, and my sisters would kill me and hide the body.

"I don't know how it happened. We were talking about the distillery and wet bars, then whether I'd work it, but how it might be inappropriate because I've seen the groom naked. And he assumed I was single. I told them I had a boyfriend. So Cara invited me as a guest, but she wanted to know about you. I mean, not *you*, but my 'boyfriend.' " She tossed up air quotes and huffed. She glared at a shelf of extra highball glasses. "He smirked like he just knew I was single. I couldn't let him be smug about it." She let out the cutest growl.

"*Are* you single?" I intentionally hadn't asked the question before—to myself or anyone else.

Her flush blazed back and she nodded.

The information was beginning to sift into place. "You don't want them to know you don't have a boyfriend?"

She shook her head.

"So you named me as your boyfriend?"

Her eyelids drifted shut. Dark eyelashes rested stark against her skin. "Sorry."

Okay. She was humiliated, and if I was to pick between Ruby and the happy couple out there, the choice was a no-brainer. "And we're supposed to be going to some wedding?"

"No. No, it's fine." She waved her hand so quickly I was offended. "I don't want to drag you into it. I'll clean up my mess."

I hadn't thought twice about the wedding, but disappointment welled inside me. "Is the wedding in Bozeman?" Wasn't there something about a wet bar?

She shook her head again. "In Bourbon Canyon. They're *moving* here." She screwed up her face. "They moved here? I don't know." She prodded at her forehead. "I'm going to tell them I can't make it. I have something that weekend."

"Do you know when it is?"

She blanched. "No."

I bit back a smile. Disgruntled, flustered Ruby was working her way under my skin farther than quiet, competent Ruby ever had.

I wanted to help her. She was under the Copper Summit umbrella and we protected our own.

And I couldn't stand assholes.

I took her hand in mine once more. "Let's go find out when the wedding is."

# CHAPTER TWO

Ruby

Stunned, I let Tenor lead me out of the storeroom. I'd been ready to save as much face as possible by telling them I actually had a busy summer. But Tenor's big hand had clamped around mine. Strength radiated through him and into me.

"Sorry, guys," he said to Brock and Cara and draped a heavy arm around me. Who needed a weighted blanket around this guy? "I had to make sure Ruby actually wanted to go to a wedding."

Cara blinked rapidly. Brock inhaled and straightened as tall as he could. He would never get close to Tenor's height, and sitting down, he looked like a toddler in a booster seat compared to Tenor. I probably looked like a posable doll, one with bright-red cheeks.

Still, I snuggled into Tenor's side. It was for show and maybe because I was an opportunist. When else would I get an up-close-and-personal feel of this man's body? The wall of muscle I pressed against did things to my hormones. Gave them ideas about what else I could be doing with Tenor. As if I hadn't imagined exactly what since I'd started working here a year and a half ago.

I'd been hired on when Brock had needed one of his "breaks." We'd reconnected during my bourbon sampling days. Brock had probably seen the lineup of bottles and thought I had infused excitement into my life.

Tonight was a little too thrilling. I couldn't look around the room. Could customers see Tenor's arm around me? Cara might not know this wasn't normal, but a lot of people here tonight would.

My mom always said one lie bled into another, and before you knew it, the cascade would drown you. As long as I perished out of Cara and Brock's sight.

Cara recovered from Tenor's faint insinuation that her wedding might not be the event of the season. "Oh, absolutely. Ours won't be stuffy. It's an outdoor wedding at the golf course. The house we're building—that Brock is building—overlooks the course."

"Hole nine," Brock boasted.

Adoration filled her face and Brock puffed his chest out. "T-minus four weeks," she lilted.

"The end of June?" I asked.

"The last Saturday." She smiled like a Cheshire cat. "I'll get you an invite. Where can I send it? Do you two live together? I keep telling Brock we'll have to, like, become outdoorsy people or something. What is there to even do in town?"

"It's downright boring," Brock said.

Bourbon Canyon wasn't my home, but I bristled in defense of it.

Tenor gave my shoulder a reassuring squeeze. "My dad always said boredom is the sign of either a dull mind or a dull life. Fill one or the other and you won't be bored."

Brock's jaw clenched and his eyes sparked.

"You can mail it here or just drop it off next time you're in town," Tenor continued, his easy tone belying any insult to Brock. "This is my second home."

"You work the bar too?" Brock asked with a hint of superiority.

"I work all over Copper Summit, though I'm not at the Bozeman facility as much as I used to be. I'm one of the owners." Tenor's direct gaze landed on him, and I nearly felt sorry for my ex.

Tenor could be intense when he didn't work against his innate presence. I'd watched him for too many hours in the distillation room. He was quiet and focused, always looking like he was hunting for the guys who'd killed his puppy. He stayed away from the crowds. Teller worked the tasting room with a tour, but Tenor always locked himself away in his office or at a computer.

Tenor held his hand out. "Tenor Bailey."

Brock cleared his throat and accepted the shake. "Brock Gibson." His voice pitched up at the end and he winced. Tenor didn't look like he'd even been trying to crush my ex's grip.

Cara rested her chin on her hand. "We were asking Ruby about having Copper Summit do the wet bar, but she's not in the know. She's just dating the boss." She winked at me. "You don't need the deets when you have him."

I funneled more energy into holding my smile. This conversation exhausted me.

Tenor nodded, but his expression said they could eat shit; he wouldn't care. "We're able to provide wet bar service. If you're interested in having Copper Summit help with your special day, either I or my brother Teller are the ones to talk to. But if you don't mind, I'm gonna help my girl get ready to close now."

"Oh yes." Cara slid off her stool, giving Tenor another once-over, then shooting me a *look at you!* grin. She squeezed Brock's biceps. "We should get going, babe. Let these two lovebirds close up."

"I'd rather have you to myself anyway." Brock drew his fiancée in for a kiss with flashes of tongue.

Ew. I used to be on the receiving end of that inept tongue. I shuddered.

Tenor put his mouth close to my ear. "Ignore them."

I nodded, and as he pulled away, cool air surrounded me. The man was a furnace, and I'd been toasty warm.

I grabbed a rag and followed him to a table. He cleared the empty glasses and I wiped. The tingle of curious gazes was on us, but I continued working. I stayed close to Tenor. If Brock and Cara ever quit sucking face, they should see us together.

We moved to another empty table. Finally, Cara pulled away and wiped her lips. I should get her a set of handkerchiefs for her wedding gift.

Brock swiveled his head around and disappointment filled his face when his gaze landed on me and Tenor doing our thing and not paying attention to them.

I swiped around the table until my back was to them. "You were right," I said quietly. "Ignoring them was best."

"She's insecure and he feeds off it," he murmured. "She might even be jealous of you."

With her looks, her job, and my ex, Cara was *not* jealous of me. She had a superiority complex.

Another couple got up at the table next to us. The guy smacked Tenor good-naturedly on the back, and they started chatting. I smiled at the woman. She ran the coffee shop. I usually stopped there when I came to town before my shift.

She glanced curiously between me and Tenor. Oh damn. People had noticed. How were we going to play this? How were we going to pretend to be a couple for a wedding in a small town that adored Bailey business? A lot of the guests would probably be from Bozeman and old classmates of mine—not that they'd remember me—but the happy couple was still moving to town. Would one wedding date be enough to sell the idea that Tenor and I were a thing? Could I count on Cara to be so self-absorbed that she didn't notice?

Yes, probably. Brock might be so into his new wife he wouldn't track the lack of me and Tenor after his wedding.

What incentive did Tenor have to keep the ruse going? He was a nice guy, but my crazy announcement had to be stretching the limits of his generosity.

I needed to freshen my cleaning rag. Tenor juggled several empty glasses. I took two from another cleared table. Relief was a breath of fresh air when Cara and Brock wound through the room for the door.

I smiled brightly. "Nice to see you again." Might as well finish the night with another lie.

Acid churned in my stomach as I rinsed my rag and washed the glasses. Tenor deposited more glassware, grabbed the cloth, and went back to clear up more tables.

Everyone was gone. It was nearing closing time, and there were a few other bars in town that people went to for darts league, bingo, or bands. Copper Summit knew what it was—a tasting room by day and a cocktail bar by night—and didn't try to compete with them. I appreciated the casual, quiet atmosphere. So many people from all around the world stopped in, and chatting with them had become one of my favorite things.

Tenor steadily cleaned the front while I stayed behind the bar. I got the dishes done, restocked, and cashed out the till. Using the tablet, I uploaded the numbers for the night and sent the reports to Tenor, surreptitiously peering at him from under my lashes.

He was crouched nearly to the floor, peering under a wobbly table. It'd be fixed by Monday. That's just how Tenor was. When he saw something needed to be done, he did it. He didn't expect fanfare or a pat on the back. He was humble. A trait that shouldn't be rare, but in my experience with guys, it was.

He rose, uncurling that powerful body. My stomach dipped and twirled.

When he turned, his longish hair fell over his forehead. He shoved it back and pushed up his glasses. The tingles spreading across my skin rerouted, shivering down my spine and curling through my belly.

He was like Clark Kent. If he slicked back his hair and lost the glasses, he'd be kryptonite to oodles of women. As it was, the shaggy, nerdy look did enough damage to interested parties. Me being one of them.

Tenor was safe to admire from afar. He wasn't abrasive, he listened, and he kept his distance. I didn't have to worry that a giggle would give him the wrong impression about me. He didn't field flirtation; I'd seen many a tourist try. Therefore, I knew there wasn't a chance and could fantasize away.

His attention was on me, and he wasn't slouching. He could be across the bar in three strides. He could pick me up and set me on the edge of the counter and—

Heat bloomed across my cheeks. That'd never happen.

Oh crap. I was staring. I jolted and looked around for my purse. "We're officially closed."

"We should talk," he said.

The tingles and swirls were gone. Anxiety filled their place. "Yes. I got you into a mess."

He waved my words away and came around the bar. Yep, three powerful strides. I'd need six. But he didn't take me in his arms and toss me on the counter because he couldn't stand one more second apart. That wasn't a surprise. His bending to dig in a cupboard was.

He withdrew two short tumblers and a bottle of Copper Summit Gold from a bottom cabinet. That was where the Baileys stored all their special bottles they didn't serve to the public. I'd never served a drink from there.

He poured a finger in each and scooted one over. He lifted his chin across the bar. "Have a seat."

A shiver traced over my skin. A subtle command. He wasn't bossy or pushy. He wasn't loud or brash. And I ate it up like the attention-starved woman I was.

"Thank you." I situated myself on the same stool Cara had sat on and crossed one leg over another.

His dark gaze lifted and met mine. Surely he hadn't been looking at my legs.

I took a small sip. Copper Summit Gold was one of the best. A top-shelf spirit, it had the most complex flavor profile in our line. Vanilla, oak, and spices mingled without one element taking over. It was robust, yet smooth. Rich, yet simple. Pure bourbon, the way it should be made.

I had pitched a post describing it as so established it had the full charisma and not just the "rizz," but Wynter had shut it down. I had thought that as the youngest sibling in the Bailey family, she'd be open to new ways to reach the just-turned-twenty-one crowd. So far, she was proving me wrong.

Cocktails were a way to capture younger consumers, and she knew that, but we'd never grab their attention with Copper Summit's uber-polished aesthetic. We were entering the world of short video, and *rizz* was the terminology I needed to be using.

The golden bourbon inside my glass almost glowed under the soft bar lights. I dug out my phone and snapped a few photos. I never forgot the older crowd who loved their bourbon neat and insisted that it was a sipping drink. The counter was the best place to capture images.

Tenor watched me without saying anything. His hands were propped on the counter and he stood like he was bracing himself.

I slid through the images and held my phone out for him to see. "That'd make a good post."

The tumbler was in focus, the amber liquid inside catching the light. But behind the drink was Tenor, strong arms braced on the bar top. He was slightly out of focus, thanks to the setting I'd used, but he captured as much attention as the drink.

He frowned. "Why would you use it?"

"It gives the drink a personal touch, and you would

get the attention of males and females alike." How many women would stare at it like me?

His brows drew together. "How?"

Was he oblivious? I fluttered my fingers around the screen. "Guys see that and think, 'Maybe I could look that strong drinking Copper Summit Gold.' Women look at it and wonder if you'd be the one serving it."

The furrow between his dark brows deepened. "You can't even see my face."

"That adds to the mystery. You can be anyone to them."

His lips thinned. "Junie's the face of Copper Summit."

"Junie doesn't speak to everyone." I clamped my teeth down on my lip. My inside thoughts had escaped through my mouth. I wasn't usually that forward. I made suggestions, and when I was shut down, I dropped it. Copper Summit wasn't my business to run. It was Tenor's, and maybe I didn't shut up around him because he'd already saved me once tonight. If we kept talking shop, he wouldn't have a chance to tell me what a tragically bad idea going to the wedding was.

He was still propped on his hands, his shoulders hitched up. "She speaks to our demographic. They know her. She's familiar. And now she's famous in her own right."

"I know. She's brought a lot of new customers to Copper Summit." I spun my glass in a circle. Junie also gave me more rein when it came to managing her personal social media. Working for her fueled so many ideas that I would love to use for Copper Summit, but my first attempts had not been successful.

"But you don't think that's enough?"

I shouldn't be having this conversation with him. "I don't want Wynter to think I'm going around her."

"You're off the clock. Speak freely."

Uh, no. Unlike what Cara and Brock thought, I was not dating the boss. He was helping me out. "It's nothing. I just think all of you Baileys are amazing and I think the public would agree."

"By seeing my headless body behind a glass?" he asked, his tone gently prodding.

I should quit talking, but I loved my job. I loved studying the market and following the campaigns other companies used, and not just other distilleries. Anything food and beverage would do. Most entertainment industries were worth monitoring. Even fashion influencer accounts told me a lot about how different age groups reacted.

"Actually, I'd prefer the head attached. You each would attract your own audience, and you could do it without sharing much personal information. Anything would be related to the distillery and your roles within it. Even the ranch would be cool. A faces-of-Copper-Summit type thing. More than the bland headshots in your brochures."

He cocked his head like he hadn't heard me correctly. "Bland headshots?"

Yep, I should've quit speaking. Could I answer without digging more of a hole? "Don't get me wrong, brochures work for an older crowd. Anyone older than me, at least."

His mouth formed an amused twist. "You're saying young people don't like us?"

"No, trust me. All ages like you." *Shit*. We'd been talking about the family and I'd singled out him. "They love the polished scraps you give them, but they'd go feral over the flannel. Every single one of you. The product needs to sell itself, but the key to growth is to build a community around the Copper Summit story, and not just the family origin, but the family as they are now. And it'd give me more content to work with."

Tenor and his brothers, Tate and Teller, worked around the distillery, hauling out used mash or unloading bags of grain. I'd caught the show more than once. Muscles and rugged country guys making bourbon sold unsurprisingly well to both a male and female audience. Tenor wore baggy shirts, but they couldn't hide how his body bunched and flexed when he moved, and the man moved like a melody. He'd sell some spirits.

I could take still shots, video, do interviews. Junie shouldn't be the only face of Copper Summit.

"You've talked to Wynter about all this?" he asked quietly.

I lifted a shoulder. "Yes."

He pressed against his hands. "Really talked and not just agreed with her because she's your boss?"

"Yeah?" My voice pitched up.

Quiet, he studied me like he did with the rest of the world. When his lips pressed together, I knew he thought the same as his youngest sister when it came to updating the distillery's brand. "I don't want to attract an audience." He took a drink. His mouth worked slightly as he rolled the bourbon over his tongue, then his Adam's apple bobbed when he swallowed.

"Fair enough." I understood, and I was relieved to drop the subject. I didn't want to create waves at my job. "I don't like to be on camera either."

"Why not?"

I looked like a knockoff Snow White. My curls usually frizzed and my clothing was too cutesy to be a woodland princess. But I liked my style. Mom had taught me how to be a master thrift shopper. I wasn't going to sell bourbon, and there was nothing wrong with being realistic. "I don't have the vibe," was all I said.

Ugh, but I knew who did.

"Maybe if Cara and Brock decide to book Copper Summit for their wedding, I can ask Wynter if we can make a deal with them. We could get some images from the event to show how young and versatile bourbon can be."

He took another drink, emptying half the glass. "About this wedding." He polished off the rest of his bourbon and washed the glass, his fingers deftly handling the cup and the cloth.

My pulse jumped. "About that. I think people saw you with your arm around me."

He was going to bail. He'd been willing to save face in the moment, but that was the extent of it. Cara wasn't his childhood frenemy. Instead of panicking, I should be helping him think of a way to untangle himself from the lies I'd told tonight.

I could always show up to the nuptials solo. Oh, sorry. Did I say boyfriend? I meant boyfriend material. Not my boyfriend.

It wouldn't be the most humiliated I'd ever been.

"Bourbon Canyon's too small," he said, sounding not at all surprised. He'd probably clocked everyone's reactions before me. "People are going to be asking Mama or my brothers about us. And then there's the wedding. We'll have to pretend to be together around town too."

"You mean, like fake dating? You'd do that?" Why?

He could just say no and be on his thick-thighed way. Why would one of the most-wanted bachelors in Montana let himself be tied up in a pretend relationship?

He lifted a shoulder like we were talking about which cocktail I should post next. "If we go back on it now, then Cara and your ex will most likely find out. She'll get away with making you feel bad, and I don't like the thought of that." He shook his head for emphasis. "Not at all."

"People are going to talk."

His right eye twitched and a cloud of tension rolled over him. "And this time, I'll be in control of the narrative."

What other times hadn't he been in control? He wasn't talking and it wasn't my business to ask. It wouldn't take much to convince people. The town's grapevine would take over and fill in the blanks. Fake dating Tenor Bailey. He wouldn't have to do much to be better than all my real dates.

I couldn't believe I was even entertaining the idea of a date, real or not, with a Bailey—

I gasped. "Your family." The embarrassment choked me. The coolest family I knew would find out I was a popularity charity case. They'd hear about how I had to pretend to have a boyfriend while I was a full adult. "Oh my god. I can't ask you to lie to them. That's not very most valuable employee of me." There were no parking spots for most pathetic employee either.

"Hey," he said soothingly, ducking his head to catch my eye. "It's fine. We don't have to tell them. You'd be doing me a favor."

I let out the most undignified snort, but unrefined was the theme of the night around Tenor. "How?"

He drummed his fingers on the countertop before answering. "It's been a while since I've had a girlfriend. They think I'm hung up on my ex, and this'll show them I'm not."

Working over his words in my head, I couldn't find a hole in them. Either that, or I was too relieved he was willing to go full ruse with me to look harder. "You're willing to break the hearts of all the women patiently waiting for a date with you?"

"I can put a pause on my life of serial dates." He smirked, but his eyes were shadowed. "You'll be doing me a favor."

I doubted that, but I wasn't in a position to argue. The only other option was to tell the entire family I admired that I'd cornered their loved one into going out with me. "Okay. So we know what we're doing."

The flood of adrenaline that had been fueling me all night suddenly drained. I smothered a yawn with my hand. I still had to drive back to Bozeman tonight. The trip only took about forty minutes to get to my actual apartment, but it'd be close to midnight before I got home. Past my bedtime, and my emotions had been through the wringer tonight.

A lot of women my age were at clubs or even married and expecting kids. I didn't even have a cat.

"Where do you stay when you close?" he asked.

"I commute. It's not a long drive."

"Every night?"

I nodded. "No big deal."

His mouth formed a troubled line. "Why didn't you say something? We could set you up somewhere."

I was touched by his concern, but I squirmed under

his attention. People weren't usually concerned about me. "You don't need to."

"You're my employee."

Didn't mean he had to worry about me. I shrugged and lifted my bourbon to my lips. He snatched the glass from my grip. "What—"

"Not if you're driving."

"I'm twenty-five, Tenor. I can handle one drink before I drive." I hadn't planned to finish all of it, but pride was pride. My stomach growled as if to announce that I also hadn't eaten.

"Twenty-five. Jesus," he muttered. He dumped the bourbon down the drain.

I gasped and leaned over the counter. "That's like thirty dollars!" And a pour was cheaper at the cocktail bar than anywhere else. I sat with a plop. "I'm not that young."

"I'm thirty-eight, Ruby." He pushed his hair off his face. "Thirteen years. Christ. People are going to think I'm robbing the cradle."

"It's not like I'm fresh out of high school. It's not a big deal."

"Normally, it's not, but I haven't . . ." The muscles in his jaw flexed and he looked away. Something bothered him. Something because of me.

I let out a sigh. None of this was his fault. He was allowed to have issues with it. "You shouldn't have been dragged into any of this. I didn't think, and I'm sorry."

His steady gaze landed on me, the yellow flecks glinting. What was going on in that brilliant mind of his? "You can stay at Mama's tonight, and we can get you something to eat."

"I do not need—"

"You're my fake girlfriend," he said, his tone challenging. "Isn't that what I'd do for you?"

I snapped my mouth shut. "How far are we going with this? Staying at your mom's seems pretty serious."

Translation: *Tell me everything so I don't foolishly mistake your consideration for actual interest.* I'd have to write it on my mirror at home. *You and Tenor are not a thing. He's pretending to save your ass.*

He narrowed his eyes while considering my question. "It says that we're getting more serious. Then it'll make more sense to my family when we go to the wedding together."

All that echoed in my head was ". . . go to the wedding together." Traitorous hope rose in my stomach. *This is not real.*

Regardless of my mental warnings, the one small sip I'd had lit in my belly, spreading warmth through my abdomen. "Just what does that mean?"

"We'll talk about it. After you eat and get a good night's sleep."

"Are you sure I can just drop in on your mom?"

"She'll be delighted." At my dubious look, he shrugged those big shoulders. "I grew up with foster kids arriving at all different hours. Now her house is almost empty. She'll love having another room filled."

"I thought your brothers-in-law . . ." I frowned. "Brother-in-law's brothers?" I shook my head. Wynter's husband had been a foster. His two brothers were much younger than him and now worked for Mae Bailey. "How do you keep everyone straight?"

"They're all family. Lane and Cruz are staying with

her for now, but they go to Denver a lot to learn about distilling and Foster House." He rinsed my glass. "You gotta remember there were seven of us after my parents adopted the girls, plus the foster kids who'd come and go. Mama can have five people staying over nowadays and it'd feel empty to her."

"Oh." That was sweet. I'd grown up with no siblings. My stepdad hadn't been around for long. It'd been just my mom and me, and since I'd graduated, we'd traded roles. She was off seeing the world and I had settled down. "I guess if she doesn't mind. Then we can discuss everything tomorrow."

"I'll be there in the morning helping with chores. I'll grab you for breakfast and then we can talk."

Butterflies took flight in my stomach. I hadn't ever been this excited for a real date. If just fake dating Tenor filled me with giddy anticipation, then I had to be careful. A whole month of pretending could go to my head, and I couldn't let it.

It was just after eleven at night and I was sitting in Mae Bailey's house, at her kitchen table. She was in long pajama pants and her salt-and-pepper hair was in a French braid.

"I can make decaf." She rummaged in a cupboard and looked over her shoulder. "Of course, we always have bourbon."

Tenor was standing at the door, his arms folded across his chest. "You can go to bed, Mama. I'll make sure Ruby gets something to eat and finds the guest room. And I'll text Lane and Cruz to make sure they're presentable in the morning." He ended the last part on a low growl.

Mae set a mug on the counter and quirked a brow at her son. "Good idea. Cruz seems to think every day is boxers-only day." She chuckled. "To be young and lack self-consciousness." She patted Tenor's arm. The top of her head barely reached his shoulder. She turned to me. "Don't worry about noise, Ruby. My room is upstairs. Lane and Cruz might be young, but they hit the hay fairly early and sleep like the dead. Though early for them might be midnight." Her fond smile showed how much she cherished them. "Good night."

"Good night, Mrs. Bailey," I said.

She stopped on her way to a large, open living area. "If you call me Mrs. Bailey again, I might have to revoke the welcome." Her eyes twinkled. "Mae or Mama are all I've responded to my whole life. Sometimes more colorful names, but never Mrs. Bailey."

"Thanks, Mae." When she left, I was alone in the kitchen with Tenor. "Your mom is amazing."

"She is." He opened the fridge and peered inside. "Looks like there's leftover pork chops, mashed potatoes, and . . ." He lifted the aluminum foil off a glass container. "Squash or sweet potatoes. I can't tell."

My stomach clenched. I was so damn hungry. Usually after a bar shift, I wolfed down toast when I got home, or waited until morning and woke up ravenous. "Does she make that big of a meal regularly?"

"She wouldn't consider this a big meal, and yes." He pulled out the dishes. I rose and crossed to a cupboard that I hoped had plates.

He glanced at me. "What are you doing?"

"Helping?"

"Sit. You're a guest."

"I'm your fake girlfriend." Saying it didn't make it more real. More fake? It was too late to decipher what was happening.

"You're not a fake guest." He turned toward me, not slouching at all. "Sit."

The low grumble rippled right over my skin. I went back to the table.

He prepared two plates. I felt moderately less like an intrusion if he hadn't eaten either. "That's a lot of food. Are you sure your mom wasn't saving it for someone?"

"Mama can throw a four-course dinner together as quickly as I can make a sandwich." He tossed one plate into the microwave and busied himself with making coffee. "She always makes more so anyone who stops in has food."

"She's unreal."

He leaned against the counter. "She is."

His answer lacked emotion. So did his expression.

Actually, he was like that a lot. He seemed like the most mellow brother. Teller would stomp around the distillery on occasion. He didn't take his irritation out on people, but we could tell when he was in a jovial mood or when he was pissy. The same with Tate, but he was quicker to smile. Because he was married with kids?

At first glance—and second and third—Tenor came off as the calmest. But no. That wasn't correct. He just hid what he was feeling. The little bit we saw was the tip of the iceberg.

The smell of coffee and savory pork chops filled the air. My mouth watered.

A shirtless man around my age sauntered into the kitchen. He was scratching his chiseled chest. His dark hair was longish, like Tenor's, and rumpled like he'd been lying down. "Damn. Something smells good."

Irritation flickered across Tenor's eyes. "Get a shirt on. We have company."

Surprise flitted across the guy's face and he frowned. "This late?" His gaze landed on me. "Oh shit. Sorry. Didn't know you had someone over." He ducked into a room off to the side and I heard a metal lid clang. A dryer.

"Sorry about that," Tenor said and swapped plates in the microwave. "That's Lane."

"I should've assumed since he has more than boxers on." The corner of Tenor's mouth lifted and I wanted to pump my fist in the air. I'd made him almost smile. "No worries. It's his home."

Tenor's face softened. "Yeah, it is."

While I never minded seeing a chest as defined as Lane's, there was only one man's torso I was interested in gawking at. But Tenor wore his shirts too big for me to do more than imagine the muscle underneath.

Lane came out in a Mountain Perks T-shirt that might've been Mae's from the way it was glued to his chest.

Tenor's mouth flattened. "Seriously? That's the best you could do?"

Lane pressed his fingers to his chest and adopted an astonished expression. "Perhaps it's my ankles on display that torment you."

I smothered a snicker.

Tenor shook his head. "I'll give you extra chores tomorrow just for that."

"Bring it on, old man. Mm. The pork chops. Mae made, like, fifteen of them. She has a sixth sense for when you're going to swing by for food." His long legs ate up the distance between me and him. He stuck a hand out. "Sorry. My manners are rusty because I usually hang out with my brother or this guy all day. I'm Lane."

"Ruby." I shook his hand. I'd seen Lane and his brother Cruz around but had never been introduced to them.

His shake was perfunctory, but Tenor straightened, his eyes narrowing like he was worried Lane would pick me up and haul me to his bedroom.

Lane snapped his fingers. "Social media girl," he said warmly, with a hint of admiration. So unlike Cara when she'd said it. "I follow the accounts. I've been studying them. You do a good job."

"Thank you." I might've beamed a little. It was one thing to get compliments from my employers, but Lane wasn't directly involved in Copper Summit, though he *was* familiar with the industry. From what Tenor had said, he'd been training with Myles at his whiskey distillery outside of Denver.

"Rough night at the bar?" Lane asked, leaning against the counter next to Tenor.

Tenor's face was impassive. "Don't you have an early morning?"

One of Lane's dark brows arched. He looked from Tenor to me, then back. "Oh. Yeah." He let out a theatrical yawn and stretched. His shirt rode up above his waistband. "It's past my bedtime. Got those chores in the morning. The goats don't like it when I'm late with their food."

I bit back a grin, but heat flooded my face. I wasn't

ready for everyone to think there was something between me and Tenor. What if they didn't think I was good enough for him? Would they have issues with my age? At least I couldn't help that. I'd tried to change for Brock but it had never been enough. Cara probably didn't go to bed by nine on Fridays just so she could read.

By the time Lane was gone, the food was done heating up. Tenor brought both plates to the table.

He poured some coffee, then retrieved a bottle from another cabinet and splashed some bourbon into each one.

"What line is that?" I asked when he set them on the table.

"Solemn Summit."

"The one named after you." All the Baileys had a special barrel named after them.

He sat next to me. Only the corner of the table was between us. "I shouldn't be surprised you know them all."

"You know, when I got the job, I went out and bought a bunch of bottles to try before I started." I'd used all my tip money from the serving job I'd had through college.

He was midslice of his pork chop. "You bought them all yourself?"

"I was excited." I still was. "It's a dream job, and I wanted to be good at it."

He cut a chunk of pork off. "We'll reimburse you."

"That was eighteen months ago."

"Doesn't matter." He swiped his meat through his potatoes and shoved the forkful in his mouth.

"Oh. Thank you." I took a bite and groaned. "So good."

Tenor paused, his fork in the air.

I patted my mouth with a napkin. "Sorry. My mom isn't a big cook. If it's not from a box, she can't make it."

"Mama's food is the best, but it's been basically her full-time job most of her life."

"My mom's sensitive about it. About her cooking." I loaded up on mashed potatoes. None of my family could cook this well. "I think it's because she had me so young. Then my stepdad, or my ex-stepdad—I never know what to call him. Bill. They've been divorced for several years. We don't talk much anymore." He'd met another woman who hadn't liked that his stepdaughter was still in his life. "Anyway, Bill used to tell her she could scorch water."

"Did he cook?"

"No."

"Then why was he complaining?"

"I asked him that once. He didn't have an answer, and Mom pointed out what a good question that was." Bill and my mom had divorced shortly after. I'd been sad to see him go, but the atmosphere at home had gotten lighter. Mom quit trying to be superwoman when he wasn't there and could just be Mom.

I finished my food about when Tenor did.

I took a sip of the coffee with bourbon. "Mm. I think this is the only way I can drink decaf from now on."

"It's the only way any of us can drink it."

I chuckled and caught a flash of a smile from him before he closed his lips around the rim of the mug.

My heart fluttered. I longed to push his hair off his

face and take those glasses off. Or leave them on, as long as I could see sharp cheekbones and intense brown eyes.

"Cara and Brock might be moving to Bourbon Canyon, but we won't let them bother you if they keep coming into Copper Summit on your shifts."

I scoffed. "You Baileys can do a lot, but you can't control other people."

His steady look said maybe they could.

I shivered. His attention warmed me faster than the hard coffee. "She shouldn't have power over me. She wasn't even that bad, but I felt like I was in middle school again, wondering why she was making me feel bad in front of her new friends. I had a weak moment and dragged you down with me."

"We'll make sure you're safe."

I let out a nervous laugh. "The only part of me that Cara's dangerous to is my pride."

He shook his head and rose, taking both of our plates. "People like her shouldn't get away with how they treat others."

I followed him with the mugs. "I'm sure she has her own issues." Tonight, she hadn't been nearly as hurtful as when we'd had classes together in high school. I'd sat with my other friends at lunch, the quiet, bookish ones who also liked Hollywood gossip. They'd been my refuge from wondering why I wasn't enough. That lunch table had been my oasis. I'd looked forward to it. In the tasting bar earlier tonight, I hadn't had a table of friends to look forward to. I'd had to be my own oasis.

He turned abruptly. I tipped my head back to meet his gaze. The yellow in his eyes sparked. Contained energy rolled off him. I was a short statue in front of a towering Tenor.

"She very well may," he said, "but she has no right to make others feel worse because of them."

He said it with so much vehemence I put a hand on his chest. His heart thudded under my palm. "It's okay. I know what she's like." I did know what she was like, which was why I hadn't been able to bear her doing it to Tenor. "It's just been a blissful seven years since graduation, and she took me off guard."

But now I was alone with Tenor, touching him. Hard to have regrets— Oh my god. I had my hand flat on his hard pec. I jerked my arm back. "Anyway, I didn't want to cost the distillery her business with the wet bar."

He gripped my wrist. The power in him was intoxicating. Did I look like a Chihuahua barking up at him? He'd be a Great Pyrenees. He looked fluffy, but there was a lean dog under that fur, and they were insanely protective.

Geez. Having a bunch of ranchers as regulars was getting to me.

He ran his thumb over my skin. His gaze was on my lips. The air between us charged, and my breath quickened. "I'd rather lose her business than let her affect you."

He released my hand, and just like that, I wasn't an oasis. I was an island. A deserted island.

"I'll show you where the room is." He scooted around me.

Stupid me. I'd made this situation even more uncomfortable for him. He probably worried he'd lead me on. I needed to do better.

I followed him through the house. The main area was three times the size of the first apartment Mom and I had lived in. With its open floor plan, the house's ceiling soared above me, wooden beams crossing from the walls to the peak. Despite all the wood, the space had a lived-in feel. Cozy throws covered the two couches and a love seat. Pillows were tucked in each corner by the armrests. A giant stone fireplace claimed its space as a showpiece, but the large-screen TV mounted above it made it more inviting.

Wow.

He led me down a short flight of stairs. I stopped by a row of photos. A framed family picture centered the grouping. A younger Mae and her late husband, Darin, grinned from the middle of a gaggle of kids. Tate and Teller stood taller than their dad. The sisters were so young, but I could still pick out who was who. Summer's solemn face was between the older brothers. A redheaded Autumn smiled next to a grinning Junie—that girl had known she'd be commanding a full stadium one day. Wynter's pale hair gave her away. And behind them was another boy. The shirt on the kid in the picture was tight around his stomach. He was shorter than his brothers, but he was bigger in other ways, and his face was rounded with full cheeks. Dark-framed glasses were perched on his face.

I met Tenor's gaze. The muscles in the corners of his jaw flexed and his expression had turned guarded. I suddenly felt like I was prying into his personal life just by looking at a family photo. "I can't believe you were once shorter than your brothers."

"I was never the littlest brother."

I shrugged. "You're always going to be their little brother."

His expression softened slightly. "Right." He disappeared around the corner like he couldn't get away from the photos fast enough.

I took another step and landed by his senior picture. He wasn't smiling in his like his brothers had. His arms were crossed and he was wearing clothes much like he wore when he didn't have his Copper Summit polo on—an oversized shirt, this one a white button-up, and black jeans. Same longish hair. Same dark-framed glasses. But he'd leaned out, and even seated, it was obvious he'd grown at least a foot since the earlier photo.

I skipped down the rest of the stairs before I could get caught spying. Another sprawling family room greeted me. The fireplace was smaller and less ornate, but the TV was not. A couple of couches lined the room with a few recliners. This house was set up to host, that was for sure.

Tenor was beside another hallway, waiting for me. A wall of doors lined the space behind him.

He pointed to two next to each other. "Cruz and Lane are in those rooms." He spoke low and gestured to another door in the middle of the hallway on the other side. "The bathroom. There'll be extra of anything you need. Mama's always ready to take people in, and she's got more supplies than a hotel."

"I wish my mom would've had a Mae in her life."

"Yeah?" he prompted.

I bit down on my lip. He wasn't interested in my past. One of my college dates had asked why I was such a downer when I'd told him Mom's story.

Tenor studied me, waiting for me to continue.

"You don't want to hear about my family drama."

An emotion I couldn't identify lit his eyes, then he was back to impassive Tenor. "I don't mind."

He was easy to talk to, and maybe after the glaring reminder I lacked friends in my life, I wanted to talk. "My mom had me just before she turned eighteen. Her parents cut her off, and my dad wasn't interested in a relationship, so she was left on her own. She went to school online and worked at a daycare since she had no one to help with me."

His face grew harder the longer I spoke. "She was left alone with a baby?"

"She's a strong woman. But she really can scorch water."

His lips twitched. "Where'd she get your name from?"

Caught off guard, I blinked. "Um, she said it was her favorite gemstone and that they're a symbol for love and commitment, which was how she felt about me."

"That's beautiful." His gaze dipped down to my lips.

My pulse kicked up. This wasn't real.

I wanted it to be real.

A door opened down the hall. A guy wandered out in red boxers, squinting down one side of the hallway. "Why's the light on, bruh?" He glanced over and did a double take when he saw me. "Oh, hey. We got company."

"Yeah, so put some pants on," Tenor said through gritted teeth but Cruz just shrugged.

I ground down on my cheek to keep from laughing. "Hi, I'm Ruby."

"Cruz." He scratched his bare chest. "I gotta use the bathroom, then it's all yours." He shuffled across the hall to the door Tenor had pointed out earlier.

"Sorry about that," Tenor mumbled. "I trust them with my life. Just not heavy equipment when they're bored. At least Lane fixes whatever they break." Concern scrawled over his face. "Do you feel okay here? Safe?"

"I always feel safe around the Baileys."

"You don't know Cruz and Lane."

"Oh." Tenor was so damn sweet. Should I have been worried? I trusted all the Baileys and I included the Foster brothers in that group. Call me naive, but I wasn't worried. Yet Tenor was concerned about me and for me. Huh. Why couldn't I have found a guy like him?

Because I *had* found him and he'd never been interested. I lusted from afar. I was near him, but in his mind, he was only helping me. "It's fine. Really."

"I'll sleep here too." He winced. "Unless that makes it worse for you. Three strange guys."

I laughed. "You're not strange, Tenor."

Cruz came out of the bathroom, looked at me, smirked at Tenor, then sauntered to his room.

"Put on pants next time you come out," Tenor called after him.

"Sure thing, old man." Laughter edged his voice. His bedroom door clicked shut.

Alone again with Tenor. Just how I liked it.

"I'll stay in the room next to yours," he said. "Anything you need, give me a holler. Knock on the wall or something."

"Is that your old room?" So far, I'd talked about me. Tenor knew the situation around my birth, my ex-friend, and that I hated to admit I was single in front of an ex. He'd revealed nothing about himself. The old family picture had given me more clues about him than the man himself.

"Yes. You can use the bathroom first. I might run

home in the morning before chores and change. Then I'll be back and we can talk in private."

Talk. About us. I'd get him to myself again.

I could get addicted to having his intense energy focused on me. He was like that with everyone though. I wasn't special to him. But at least I'd get to pretend I was.

# CHAPTER THREE

Tenor

I rubbed my temples while sitting in the lower level's family room. There was now a big-screen TV on one wall, thanks to Lane and Cruz. A pile of Coke cans heaped over the garbage. If I checked under the cans, I'd find a few bottles of bourbon and Foster House whiskey. The downstairs had become a bachelor pad, but the guys were respectful about having the basement mostly to themselves.

Mostly. Except for when I brought pretty little employees home.

I worked hard to ignore her appearance. Those short skirts that showed off her curvy legs. The way she sometimes tied shirts at the waist or wore cropped tops so I'd catch a glimpse of her stomach. She was good at her job and didn't need me leering at her. Staring at her would be easy to do. That round ass of hers. The way it wiggled when she walked—

Fuck me.

I had to pretend to date one of the youngest employees we had. It'd been hard enough to act like I wasn't attracted to her, to steer clear of her and the company's social media accounts. Now I also had to act as if a girl like her would be happy with a guy like me. Lane didn't call me *old man* just because of my age.

I was content with my life. When my empty house bothered me, I came here and traded shit with the guys.

And I'd dived in to help Ruby because I was so damn content with my single life.

I checked my watch. It was almost nine. Should I wake her up?

The door of the room she'd been in creaked open. She stumbled out, yawning and rubbing her face. Dark smudges rimmed under her eyes. Her dark hair swirled wild around her head and the white shirt she'd had on hung half unbuttoned. Her skirt hitched higher on her thighs than it had been last night, baring even more of her creamy legs. She was barefoot.

Fuck me.

When I had agreed to go all in, I'd become her distiller in shining armor. The way she had looked at me —damn. A stronger guy might've resisted and let her down gently, done damage control instead of making more, but I'd convinced myself that helping her was getting one over on someone who punched down in life. Someone had to teach those people a lesson in humility.

I'd told myself that getting closer to her had nothing to do with those curvy legs and that ripe ass.

She sighed and knocked on the bathroom door. Looking up, she saw me staring at her like a fucking perv.

Her cheeks flamed the color of her name and she tugged her skirt down. "I slept too long."

"Not at all." I should be a gentleman and drop my gaze. I didn't. I had to be comfortable looking at my *girlfriend*. "Take your time."

She smiled and ducked into the bathroom. The guys had already been up and were in the shop repairing the main bar on the sickle mower. I'd found a few extra things to do to keep them busy and out of the house. Ruby didn't need more bare chests or guys in nothing but underwear.

They were her age. I wasn't.

But it was my job to protect her, and I didn't know if she wanted to get hit on by Lane or Cruz. Admittedly, they'd be decent around her, if a little flirty.

The skin under my collar grew hot. I tugged at my T-shirt. I would not let her down. I was a man of my word. Besides, my deal with her might stop those looks from my brothers and sisters. The ones that worried I wasn't getting out enough. Like I was no longer properly socialized and would just stay in more and more rather than facing the world and the judgment it could offer.

I might have to wait for that benefit until after they berated me for dating an employee.

Several minutes went by and she stepped out. Her hair was secured in a band. A puffy ponytail blossomed behind her head. She'd buttoned her white top but had left it hanging over her skirt. "I have to grab my purse."

She scurried to her bedroom and a punch of lust hit my gut. The back of her skirt rode up higher, something I had noticed last night. When we'd been cleaning the front part of the bar, I had put myself between her ass and any pairs of eyes in the place.

She emerged. "Sorry."

"No problem," I said as if I hadn't ever thought how easy it'd be to bend her over in that skirt. To flip it up and run my hand— Christ. Where was my control this morning? I indicated the covered plate on the table in front of me. "Hungry?"

Her eyes flared wide. "You brought me food?"

"I heated up a breakfast sandwich." I'd made them— after she'd gone to bed—to heat up this morning. There'd been no way I could sleep after that evening. I'd had to think about this fake dating scenario, to tell myself it was nothing like before. I'd intentionally be a fake boyfriend.

She peeled the aluminum foil off the sandwich. Her pink lips parted. "That's huge."

"The egg is farm fresh." I took the thermos I'd set on the end table and put it by her plate. "Here's some OJ."

"Oh my god, you think of everything." She balanced the plate on her lap, her legs tightly closed, and took a bite. Her eyelids fluttered shut. And there was that goddamn moan.

I couldn't tear my gaze away. I leaned closer. Would she moan again? That noise was indecent in all the best ways. She made it over food, but when the sound reached my ears, the what-ifs circled in my head.

What if I could make her sound like that?

What if she did it while I was in her—

*Shit.* I could not think about her that way. She'd been vulnerable last night. She still was. I had her reputation in my hands, and I'd make sure to do right by her. She was too young, too innocent. I would not take advantage.

She peeled the top bun back. "Is this sausage from the farm?"

"Yeah, it's deer meat Teller and I got last year mixed with pork."

"I don't think I've ever had deer meat." She did a little wiggle, and I had to look away.

Gawking at her would be taking advantage.

I propped my elbows on my knees. "You eat and I'll tell you what I was thinking."

"Okay," she said around a mouthful.

"I don't want to lie to my family, but I know you don't want them to know." Ordinarily, I'd never mislead my mom and siblings, but when it came to my personal life, I wasn't the most transparent. This would make them talk. It'd make everyone talk.

The skin under my collar itched. It was for Ruby. It was to save face for Ruby, and we might get an event booked with the wedding. I'd deal with the rest as it came.

"No." She set her sandwich on the plate. "That's not fair to you. Your siblings and your mom won't hold what happened against me, and I'd be asking them to lie." She sighed. "I made a mess."

"You didn't." She had, but I absolutely understood why. If my tormentor in high school came back to taunt me, my first instinct would be to protect myself too. "They don't need to know. We'll date. We can say we've kept it to ourselves until we knew we were serious about each other."

"Will your brothers believe it? Lane and Cruz?"

I swallowed hard. Did she mean that they wouldn't believe a girl like her would go for someone like me?

"You're with them all the time, aren't you?" she asked.

If she meant I was working all the time, then yes. "I have a fair amount of free time." I had a lot of off time that my family wasn't a part of. My interests weren't always theirs and that had been part of my issue growing up.

"Between the distillery and the ranch, you work a lot though."

I waited for defensiveness to rise, but her tone lacked the judgment I usually heard. "Have you been watching me, Ruby?" I liked the idea too much.

"No!" She covered her mouth, her gaze horrified. "I sounded like a total stalker, didn't I?"

"No, you didn't." I chuckled, but pleasure rippled through me, along with shock. I could not flirt with this girl. I was not a guy who flirted. Long ago, I'd vowed to only be myself, and since no woman had been interested in that, then I wasn't interested in dating.

A guy could only put himself through so much suffering. "We'll tell everyone we started talking when you picked up shifts in the tasting room. Then we started talking on the phone after hours."

She nodded. "Because I wanted to hear your voice."

I pressed my fingertips together. She liked my voice? No, that was part of the ruse. "I don't think they'll ask, but sure. We can say we've been on a few dates but not in Bourbon Canyon."

"Right. Because it's too small a town."

"Wednesdays."

"Wednesdays what?"

"That's when we went out. I'm usually out of town Wednesday nights."

Doubt filled her expression. "That's the other shift I work."

Shit, it was. "After you get back to Bozeman, I meet you somewhere."

"Yeah. That works out really well and doesn't have to involve elaborate stories."

The next part was the hardest. I'd turned all the possibilities over in my head, but there was no getting around it. "Which means we'll have to do the very real things people do when they date."

Her eyes went wide as saucers.

Dammit. "No, not that." Wasn't that reaction what all guys wanted when a woman thought she'd have to sleep with them?

The flush in her cheeks darkened. "No— I didn't think— I mean—" She took a drink, tipping the thermos all the way back like it was the hard stuff. She swallowed and exhaled. "What exactly do you mean? You made it sound serious."

"Holding hands. Touching." My voice dropped on the last word.

"Kissing?" She giggled like it was an absurd joke.

The idea of kissing Ruby should be appalling. I'd worked at Copper Summit since I was sixteen. Unofficially for years before that. There had not been one employee I'd wanted to kiss. Ever.

But as soon as I'd agreed to fake dating, the door had been flung wide open. What exactly would we have to do to sell this relationship? How far did she want to go? How often could I feel that satiny skin?

Her poleaxed expression knocked each question out of my brain. I needed to fix this. "Of course I don't think we'll have to kiss. Much. I'm just saying—"

"I didn't like Brock's kisses," she blurted.

Good. "Okay."

"He was sloppy. I don't think kissing should be sloppy. I guess sometimes when things really get going, but—" She shook her head and blinked. "I haven't had a good kiss, come to think of it." Her expression changed to offended. "I don't date much, so I don't have a ton of experience. But between paper dry and careless drool . . ." She set her plate on the coffee table. Her sandwich was half eaten. "Wow. I'm the common denominator. It's me. No one wanted to go out with me, and when they did, it was me that was the problem. You must think—"

"It's not you." I would bet my job on it. Both of them. "And I can prove it. Besides, if we can kiss once or twice at the wedding, it'll look more real. Like we've done it before." Was I making a valid excuse or a selfish one? I wouldn't answer.

"Practice, you mean?" She sounded breathy.

"Sure."

She licked her lips. That tongue of hers was a few shades redder than her lips. Would it taste richer? "Now?"

She didn't need the practice. Still didn't stop me. I took my glasses off and shoved the coffee table across the carpet. I was on my knees in front of her before I knew it. "The first thing I'm going to show you is that you're not the problem."

She tipped her head back to meet my gaze. The chair was so low that I was still taller than her on my knees. "How do you know?"

I propped my hands on the armrests. "I saw your ex's messy kiss."

"Maybe it was me—"

I claimed her mouth. Ripe, plump lips parted in surprise but I didn't take the kiss further. Not yet.

I added pressure and she kissed back. No. Definitely not her. She was sweet from the orange juice, savory from the breakfast sandwich, and soft. So damn soft.

I pulled back only enough to murmur, "How's that?"

"It's the Goldilocks kiss." Her breath whispered over my mouth. "Not too dry. Not too wet. Just right."

"There are some circumstances when nothing is too wet." I tipped her chin up. "Open for me, Goldilocks."

As soon as her lips parted, I dove in. I licked into her warmth, and her flavor deepened. Sweet and savory. My growl resonated between us. I plundered and sucked, forgetting about the technique I had once studied so intently.

Something about Ruby made me throw all my good sense out the window.

I curled a hand around the back of her neck to bring her closer. She let me. Her head tipped back and she was clutching my shirt like she was afraid one of us would drift away.

A needy moan left her.

*Yes.* The sound was different than her delicious food moan, but it burrowed into my consciousness just the same.

There was nothing wrong with this woman. In fact, I'd make it my mission to fake date the hell out of her. After me, she'd know when any other man didn't measure up.

At the thought of another guy dating her, I deepened the kiss. She wrapped her arm around my neck before I flattened her into the back of the chair. When I licked, she met me stroke for stroke, that plump mouth working under mine.

Finally, I could nibble that pouty bottom lip of hers.

A whimper left her and she dug her hands in my hair. All my blood rerouted until a nearly painful erection started behind my zipper.

I had a hand around her waist. It'd be easy enough to sweep up her shirt, but this was just supposed to be a kiss. I didn't want it to quit being a kiss.

"Whoa!" Cruz's voice broke through my haze of arousal. "Mae! Tenor's making out in the basement!"

I ripped my mouth off Ruby, but I didn't rear back. I kept her covered in case her skirt had ridden up or her blouse unbuttoned during our make-out session. She drew her knees up, grazing my erection. Another reason I wasn't pulling away. "Jesus, Cruz."

He held his hands up like I had a gun trained on him. "Hey now. Don't shoot the messenger. Mae's outside anyway." His grin was unrepentant.

"What do you need?" I asked through clenched teeth.

Lane was behind him, shit-eating grin in place. "We just came back for a catnap. Cruz is throwing tantrums left and right."

Cruz shot a glare over his shoulder. "You know how I get when I don't get my beauty sleep."

"With your face, I can't tell." Lane snickered.

Cruz elbowed him, then they both settled down and grinned at us. Two grown men acting like goddamn boys. I usually didn't mind. They'd had a rough upbringing. But they were the reason I wasn't kissing Ruby right now.

"Go to your room," I growled.

Lane barked out a laugh. "Nice to see you again, Ruby. Can you make sure the old man doesn't take his crankiness out on us?"

Ruby's hands were no longer around my neck. She gripped the armrests. "I'll tell him to be nice."

In case I thought I couldn't get any harder, I did.

They finally moved, going to their rooms.

I tipped my forehead against hers. "Sorry about that."

"What part?"

"They're basically my obnoxious little brothers."

"They listen to you." She ran a finger down my cheek, bumping over the stubble I'd left on my jaw.

"Sometimes." I was still crowding her. I pulled back. "My study was thorough. The guys you kissed were frogs."

"And you're a prince?" Was that a note of hope in her voice?

"No, Goldilocks. I'm just a bear who'll show you how to know when the porridge is just right." I rose and adjusted my fly. My dick must have the outline of my zipper imprinted on it.

She tipped her head at my action, bewildered. Did she not think she could get me as hard as stone?

"It doesn't matter if this is real or not. I'll treat you right." I held my hand out. "Time to go talk to my mom."

Ruby

. . .

My lips were puffy from that kiss.

*Perfect.*

The Goldilocks kiss. I had wanted more. I hadn't wanted him to stop. I had been consumed.

From a kiss.

That kiss had been more than just right. And he'd been aroused. The bulge behind his jeans—huge. When my knee had brushed against it—hard. The way he'd hulked over me—hot.

My hand shook as I pushed stray strands of my curly hair out of my face. I was climbing the stairs in front of him, clutching my purse. He was behind me. A wall of heat.

How long would he have kept kissing me if Cruz hadn't interrupted?

I would've been fine for the whole weekend.

When we reached the top, Tenor took my dishes to the sink. At least one of us had our wits about us.

How was I going to face Mae when I'd just had her son's tongue in my mouth? We were both adults, but I had been a guest yesterday. Today, I'd been tonsil diving with Tenor and loving it.

Tenor braced himself on the counter. "I need a minute."

I snorted. "I need like an hour." I pressed my hands to my cheeks. "My face is burning hot."

"After following you up the stairs, I don't think an hour is enough."

"Ha. Right."

He pinned me with a hard gaze over his shoulder. "Christ, Ruby. You really don't know?"

Had I done something wrong? "Know what?"

"How sexy you are."

A nervous laugh escaped me. "You don't have to—"

He spun and strode across the room. I squeaked and backed up until my back smacked the wall.

He ran his thumb across my lower lip. "This mouth makes a guy think of nothing but long kisses." He dragged his forefinger down my neck to my chest. "Don't get me started about these." Farther down. He stopped at my waist, but his burning gaze was on my legs. "If I wasn't a better man, I'd ban tights from the dress code at work."

He noticed when I wore tights? I did on cooler nights, but the days were growing warmer.

His face was inches from mine. I had the strongest urge to rip off his glasses and smash my mouth against his.

He straightened and stepped back. Cool air flooded between us. "That'll be my goal for the next month. You worry about keeping Cara and your ex off your back, and I'll prove the problem in your relationships was never you."

No one had ever said anything so sweet to me.

He turned, giving me his broad back. Before I could recover from the abrupt withdrawal of his attention, he went for the door and opened it. "Ready?"

Time to face the kindest woman I'd ever met and lie to her face.

Timidly, I stepped out. Goose bumps that had more to do with the loss of his heat than cool air dotted my skin. The breeze carried a warm kiss that promised a nice day.

Mae was walking up the hill from a shed that had a bunch of red and white chickens darting around it. She beamed. "Good morning. I hope you slept well and that the boys didn't disturb you when they charged inside."

Tenor fell in step beside me. His jaw was tight. I almost felt bad for Cruz and Lane and the retaliation they'd face. *Almost.* I could've still been kissing Tenor.

"Thank you so much for letting me crash last night." I twined my fingers together. Just be casual.

I didn't do well getting introduced to parents. Brock's mom and dad had asked so many questions about my job in a way that had made me feel two inches tall. They had kept referring to me as an influencer. It hadn't been the term, it had been the tone. The judgment. The lack of interest. But Mae knew my job. Half the battle was done already.

"You're welcome anytime." She hitched a basket full of eggs on her arm.

"Hey, Mama. We're dating. Just so you know." Tenor put his hand on the small of my back. Some of my stress drained out of me as if he was absorbing it.

Mae's brows lifted, but she smiled. "That's good to hear."

He stroked his thumb along my spine. "We didn't, uh . . . I slept in my old room."

Mae chuckled. "Well, it wouldn't have been the first time you kids were up to shenanigans in the house." She turned her fond gaze toward me. "Darin used to live for catching Junie and Rhys getting up to something."

I smiled, her humor infectious. She'd lost her husband a few years ago. I'd never met him, but the things I'd heard only made me envious. My dad could be . . . a lot.

"Are you two heading to town?" she asked.

"I've gotta get back to Bozeman." Other than

needing a change of clothes and a shower, all I had waiting for me was my books, but I'd intruded enough. "But soon."

"The room's always open if you need a place to stay," Mae said.

"She might." The heat of his hand chased away the last bit of chill from the morning air. "She closes the bar Wednesday and Friday nights."

"Oh, it's fine." I'd been driving back and forth for months. "It's not open that late." Especially on Wednesdays.

She wandered past us with a pleasant smile that was almost a smirk. She shifted her gaze to Tenor. "Between your place and mine, she always has a bed."

Tenor stiffened and I sucked in a breath. *Tenor's place?*

He didn't drop his hand from my back. "Do you close next weekend?"

"Yes. I don't have an end date." My chest grew tight. An overnight at Mae's with Tenor next door had been bad enough. I'd been awake the whole night, my brain insisting that Tenor was close enough. I'd imagined him next to me, heating the bed as he slumbered. "Since Autumn and Wynter backed off on their hours for their babies and I have nothing going on . . ." Didn't that sound like he'd won the fake dating lottery? "But seriously. It's not a long drive at all."

He led me to my car. I'd go anywhere that strong hand steered me. I was lucky my legs worked after the kiss. We stopped at the driver's door.

"Can you stay the next weekend and we'll go out Saturday?" His gaze skated away. "I can't do Wednesday nights."

"Next Saturday is fine. I can stay here Friday if that's okay with your mom."

"You can stay with me."

*Oh*. My pulse started to climb as excitement rose to a record high tide, but his offer was only for show. Could I do that and still tell myself this was fake?

"I have a spare room," he clarified.

My nervous laugh carried away on the light breeze. Of course he did. "Right. Yes. That'll work. It'd probably look weirder if I stayed with your mom. Like I was saving myself for marriage." His brow furrowed, and I realized my error. "I'm not! I haven't . . . waited." I exhaled, but my chest was so tight it ended in a squeak. That was awkward.

The ghost of a smile played over his lips. "Was Brock sloppy at that too?"

"When you said that there are times when there's no such thing as being too wet, that'd be news to Brock."

He laughed, his head tipping back and his Adam's apple bobbing. My breath ceased and I was helpless to watch. His laughter also saved me from being embarrassed by what I had said.

He sobered, but the smile was still in place, wide and open in a way I'd never gotten to witness before. "We can get them an instruction manual for a wedding present."

I grinned. "If only I was brave and vengeful enough."

His smile faded. "My place is . . ." He swallowed and looked away again. "It's a bachelor pad."

From what I'd heard, he'd built a cabin in the hills like his brothers. I hadn't seen their places, but the log house behind me was impressive. What would his home look like? "If you don't want me—"

"It's not that." He pushed his glasses up and shoved a frustrated hand through his hair. "It'll be fine. You can stay with me. And I promise to keep my hands to myself when we're not trying to sell this to anyone."

He didn't have to. Not at all. But it'd muddy the waters more than my brain was already trying to do. I had to be comfortable with his touch, but that didn't mean he wanted to crawl into bed with me.

He was slouching again. What didn't he want me to see? Did he have an especially eclectic porn collection? Was he a hoarder? Just plain messy? A bachelor pad could look like a lot of things.

"Okay. It's a . . ." Date wasn't the right word. "Sleepover."

His smile returned. "I'll have movies and popcorn."

"Whoa. Don't get too wild," I joked and his expression went somber. I'd said something wrong, but I couldn't figure out what. My nerves were going to send that breakfast sandwich back up. I needed to leave. "See you then!"

I dove into the driver's seat.

He put his hands on the frame and leaned in. "Everything okay?"

I scrambled for a way to keep things from getting more uncomfortable. "Just wondering if you're a boxers guy too."

Astonishment lifted his brows. Mission accomplished?

His chuckle was soft. "I'll keep my shirt on. Don't worry."

"Then shirtless Fridays will be up to me."

His pupils dilated and he leaned in closer. "Jesus,

Goldilocks, don't tease me like that. I'm only a man," he said in a low voice and pressed a kiss to my lips.

Just as he was pulling back, an engine sounded behind us and tires crunched on gravel.

Alarm filled his eyes, but like before, he didn't jerk away. His jaw flexed when his gaze landed on Teller's pickup.

"Busted," I said, not at all guilty. Surprise kisses from Tenor were now my favorite thing. So was making him break that calm composure.

He took a step back, and I pulled away. He never stopped watching me as I wound down the long drive to the main gravel road that led to the highway.

# CHAPTER FOUR

Tenor

Teller was waiting in the Copper Summit conference room with his feet kicked up on the table. A smug look was on his face.

When I entered, I glared at him. "Didn't you ask enough questions yesterday?"

He'd grilled me after Ruby pulled away. *Was that Ruby? What was she doing here? Did I see you kiss her? What the fuck are you kissing her for? Do you know how old she is? Do you know how old you are?*

I'd finally walked away and started on the to-do list I'd given Cruz and Lane. I'd been changing oil on one of the tractors when those two shitheads had walked by making kissing noises.

I knew why I never dated. Now I had more reasons.

I sat at the end of the long table opposite Teller in my normal spot and opened my laptop.

Tate walked in, scratching his short beard and

looking like he'd been yanked from the middle of the pasture in his blue jeans, black T-shirt, and green plaid flannel. Our monthly meeting was today. All my siblings and I would meet and review the month, last quarter, and the year to date and plan Copper Summit's future.

Tate sat across from me. "How's it going?"

Teller's boots thumped down to the floor. "Maybe we need to ask Ruby."

My stomach dropped. When I'd committed to the ruse with Ruby, I'd known dealing with my family would be an issue. They would have opinions, and Ruby was considerably younger than me. Would they be afraid I was taking advantage of her? I wouldn't throw her under the bus for explanations. My family could deal.

Tate frowned, glancing between us. "Why Ruby?"

Teller folded his hands on the table. Like me, he was wearing a rust-colored polo with the company logo on the breast and blue jeans. Distilling was a science, but the work attire was casual. Teller and I had started wearing branded polos so tourists could tell us apart from the other employees, but even we didn't wear them all the time. No one wore slacks. Mostly jeans.

Except Ruby liked to wear skirts. Not long, flowing ones. She wore flirty skirts that made her hourglass figure more of a roller coaster.

"You'll want to ask Tenor why." Teller smirked, but his gaze was ruthless.

I inhaled a measured breath and closed my laptop. *Here it goes.* "We're seeing each other."

Tate's eyes flared wide. "You and *Ruby?*" He glanced at Teller. I didn't have to look at my other brother. His irritated gaze was burning into my skin.

"Yes," I said evenly. "We finally decided to make it

public. I anticipated your reactions." I shot Teller a glare. He was unrepentant.

"Of course we'd react." Tate sat straighter. "She's young."

Teller made a tsking noise. "He took so long to date again because he had to wait for Ruby to get out of high school."

"She's a goddamn adult," I snapped. Hadn't I had the same reservations? Ruby was young, but she was in her midtwenties. She was a full-on adult with a career. And she'd had awful boyfriends who hadn't shown her what a prize she was.

I could do that for her.

"She's an employee," Teller added as if we hadn't argued about that yesterday.

"We don't have no-fraternization rules at Copper Summit." I felt like a dick pointing that out.

Teller tapped his notes. "That's why it's on the agenda."

"Without being approved," I shot back.

Tate held a hand up. "It's something we'll discuss when the girls get here. You know they don't like it when we do business without them."

Teller glared at me.

"I'm not going to hurt her, all right?" My brothers were worried about Ruby in my care, and that gutted me. What about me made them think I'd hurt her? My reasons for steering clear of dating and women weren't because I was the bad guy.

"You'd never intend to hurt her," Teller conceded. "But she's not the only one I'm worried about."

I frowned. Were there more people I was pretending to date and didn't know about?

"*You*, dumbass," he answered. "How many years has it been? All of a sudden, you're kissing a young—younger— employee in our mom's driveway."

"You know why I don't date," I said.

"Does Ruby?" Teller asked.

"Does Ruby what?" Wynter breezed in. Her white-blond hair was back in a ponytail and she wore pajama bottoms and a loose yellow Foster House shirt that was probably her husband's. She was working from home today and had only come to Copper Summit for the meeting.

"We'll wait until you all get here," Tate said as soon as Teller opened his mouth. "We don't need to repeat this four more times."

"Junie's calling in." Wynter took the seat next to me and set her giant water bottle by my laptop. I moved my computer farther away. She claimed they didn't leak, but I didn't want to tempt forty ounces of ice water. "She's in . . . Where is she playing this week?"

"Wisconsin," Tate answered as Summer breezed in. She sat next to him.

My oldest sister wasn't dressed much differently than Wynter, only she'd tied her shirt. The braid of her straw-berry-blond hair flopped over her shoulder. "Are you talking about Junie? She's in Milwaukee today, then they're going to Detroit."

Autumn entered and glanced around. "Last one here. Dang."

"Technically, Junie hasn't called in yet," Wynter said.

Autumn sat on the other side of her and puffed a hunk of her auburn hair out of her face. She was wearing a loose summer dress at odds with the dark circles under her eyes.

Summer frowned at her. "Is Sawyer not sleeping well?"

Autumn sighed. "She's got a cold. All stuffy and can't sleep. Gideon had her on his chest in the recliner for half the night. I took the other half. He almost didn't let me, but I reminded him that I had a meeting and he'd have to take over sick care for part of the day. I might actually nap in the office before I go home."

Summer and Wynter nodded. The three of them had become moms fairly close together. Tate's oldest had been in elementary school when Tate had moved back to Bourbon Canyon to take over the ranch when Dad got sick. Then he'd married Scarlett. Between my four sisters and one sister-in-law, the niece and nephew count added up. And with each one, my chest grew tight, something that felt too much like envy sprouting between my ribs.

They were all settling down and growing their families.

But I'd quit looking for Miss Right. My Goldilocks. Some guys were just meant to be single.

The conference phone rang. Teller answered it and pushed a button. "Hi, Junie."

"He-ey. Everyone there?"

We all answered her.

Teller snapped a sheet of paper. "First, we're going to talk about a fraternization policy because Tenor's dating Ruby."

I closed my eyes against the surprised chorus of my sisters.

"Seriously?"

"Tenor!"

"Ruby? I never would've guessed."

"Oh my god. She's so nice."

I didn't track who said what. I peeled my eyes open. My brothers looked grumpier.

"It's nothing serious," I said weakly, but Tate's gaze darkened like that had been the worst thing to say.

"She stayed at Mom's last night," Teller said. "So did Tenor."

Wynter let out a delighted gasp, but Teller pursed his lips. My sisters weren't reacting the way he wanted. But then they hadn't been there when I had made my vow to quit dating.

"Because she closed and planned to drive back to Bozeman." My voice was full of accusation. I didn't make the bar schedule.

"It's a short drive," Summer said. "I make it all the time." She was in charge of the Bozeman facility Ruby worked out of.

"In the daylight," I insisted. "She's driving after dark."

"And before the other bars shut down," Wynter said. "I talked to her about it when she started. She said it was fine. She can make her own decisions."

"Tell that to Teller and Tate." I pointed at them. "They seem to think I yanked her right out of the cradle."

Wynter snickered, and Autumn covered her mouth with a hand, but her eyes were dancing.

"I see." Summer folded her arms. "My biggest worry is that the relationship might go south and we'd lose an amazing employee."

"Exactly why we need a policy," Teller said.

Tate cleared his throat. "Dad was always against it. He said the community was too small to have policies in place. We don't have an endless supply of employees."

"We're in charge now," Teller said tightly.

"What is your real concern?" Autumn asked softly. "Ruby's a great girl. Tenor's a good guy."

My sisters' more enthused reaction bolstered me. They'd been worried about me and thinking Ruby and I were growing more serious would soothe them.

Teller ground his teeth together and met my gaze. "Katrina."

My head snapped back like he'd hit me.

Autumn's green eyes flashed like a forest fire. "I really didn't like her."

I had. That had been the issue. I had fallen so hard for Katrina. After so many other failures, I'd doubled down with her. I'd been desperate to make us work. But she'd been just another in a short line of women who'd wanted me to be something else. Women who expected Tate or Teller and got me.

Unlike the other girls who'd broken things off and quietly moved on, Katrina had not been quiet. She'd let me know exactly how I had humiliated her in every way.

"Ruby's not Katrina." My mouth was dry. I had no intention of getting that close to Ruby. I'd treat her right like I'd learned to do, and I'd stick to our arrangement.

"She's a sweet girl," Summer agreed. "But it won't stop us from worrying about you. You two could be great for each other and decide to part ways regardless and we'd still be worried."

I appreciated her concern, but it was unnecessary. "I wasn't that bad after the breakup with Katrina."

They all blinked at me.

"What?" I asked, irritable.

"You turned into a hermit," Teller pointed out, not hesitant to say so like the others. "And you still are. It's been what, ten years?"

Autumn and Wynter nodded. They'd been the first to visit me. After Teller had told them I had imploded.

Were they keeping track? I did not isolate myself that badly. "I'm over her."

"We know," Tate said. "But she still did some damage."

"Maybe I was waiting for someone I felt wasn't like Katrina. Shouldn't you be grateful I'm back in the dating pool?" I didn't want to hear their answer, and I was done with this conversation. I was dating Ruby for a month and they didn't need to know why. "So we talked about a fraternization policy to keep me and Teller from dating any employees. I have a couple of things to add to the agenda too. First, I was approached about providing wet bar services for a wedding. Wynter, is there anything you'd like us to talk to them about as far as getting marketing content for you?"

"Oh." She thought for a moment. "I can keep it in mind."

"Just in case we want to remind the community of all the different capacities we can work in. Retail sales are down for the third quarter in a row, so are orders for the upcoming quarter." The conversation with Ruby had stuck in my brain, among other things when it came to her, but she'd clearly been afraid to ruffle any feathers. Marketing wasn't my area, but maybe Ruby was onto something. Maybe we needed a small refresh instead of relying on the holiday season to hit our goals. "And then we need to discuss how Scott Townsend is blaming

Copper Summit for almost costing him his liquor license."

Teller's face screwed up. "What's Scooter saying this time?"

Relieved that I had diverted everyone from the topic of me and Ruby, I reiterated what I'd heard from the city commissioner. Scott "Scooter" Townsend owned a bar on Main Street. He was my age and the guy I might've turned into after the breakup with Katrina if I had kept dating and getting rejected—mean and resentful. I'd had a close family, and my dad had yanked me out of my house for chores and fishing and hunting trips until I decided that I'd just never date. Problem solved.

Scooter's family wasn't close and his wife was Teller's ex. She hadn't been an ex when she'd started dating Scooter. Because of that, Scooter thought Teller—and Copper Summit by proxy—was after him. In reality, he was a paranoid narcissist.

I opened my laptop now that we were discussing company issues. What Ruby and I were doing would not affect our work. I wouldn't allow it. Just like I wouldn't fall for another woman again.

❦

Ruby

I kicked my feet on the island of Mom's kitchen in her condo and interrogated her. "Are you being safe? Is he really a decent guy? Have you met his parents?"

Mom rolled her eyes. "You're not my mom," she whined.

I grinned and took a bite of a nectarine. "I'm serious. You just met Dave."

"Daniel."

It was hard to keep track. Last year, she'd dated a Teddy, a William, and a Kennedy. Then there'd been the twins. She'd gone out with one, then the other.

My dad and stepdad had made Mom commitment phobic. We were opposites in that way. In a lot of ways. She was taller than me with light brown hair and hazel eyes. My dad had dark hair, blue eyes, and was under six feet. She was an adrenaline junkie and I was allergic to thrill.

Any other traits I may or may not have gotten from more distant family would stay a mystery. My memory of the grandparents who'd raised him was foggy. Mom had never trusted her parents with me after they'd kicked her out, and I hadn't been inclined to extend an olive branch as I had gotten older.

"Daniel loves the outdoors and he loves to travel. I think he's coming to Vegas with me." She dumped spaghetti in a pot. Simple pasta dishes were how we'd survived. "I'm leaving tomorrow. I'll be gone for two weeks."

I leaned over the side of the counter and tossed my pit into the garbage. "People think I'm an influencer, but they have nothing on you. You could post your travels and get sportswear sponsorships."

"You have a stable job, which is something to be proud of."

I wouldn't go on trips and pick up men like her. Mom had crap taste in men. I tried not to blame her for my luck with dating, but it'd been hard to stray from her example. Self-centered men with brash personalities. Catnip for someone like Veronica Casteel.

Mom's phone buzzed. She glanced at it and smiled. "Daniel?"

"No, your father. Another hiking meme." She failed to bite back her smile.

I always suspected Mom had never gotten over Dad. He hadn't been her first infatuation, he'd been her first *love*. One-sided love. Part of me had hoped he'd put her out of her misery once he hit forty and ask her out, but it'd been a year since then and he was still happily single in Helena, playing tennis and making money. At least they had stayed amicable, which was a challenge with someone like my dad.

I hadn't gotten any sophistication from him. I was more like Mom had been in high school before she'd discovered the excitement of the outdoors. She'd been quiet and studious, according to her. At least I'd learned from her example. No studlete like my dad had seduced me and used me when he'd been in town for a football camp. I'd waited until college before *my* crappy dates.

I had a studlete now. I could enjoy him for an entire month. "I've started seeing someone." A tiny thread of guilt wound around my conscience. I didn't want Mom to worry. She'd hated on Brock when he'd broken up with me. I couldn't let her know that he'd made me feel so bad I had made up a boyfriend.

Who'd turned out to be real. Sort of.

She turned from stirring the noodles. "You are?" Her curiosity was tinged with concern.

"He's from Bourbon Canyon."

She pulled a face. "Oh. That place."

It didn't matter that Dad hadn't lived in Bourbon

Canyon since he'd graduated, Mom would never like that town. "I know, but he's a nice guy."

"What's his name?"

"Tenor. He's, uh, one of the Baileys."

A brown brow ticked up. "Like the Copper Summit Baileys? Your boss?"

"One of them."

She put the spoon down and folded her arms. "Oh?"

"It's not like that, and it's nothing serious."

She snorted. "It rarely is for men. He gets to play, and you get to repair your heart when he's no longer interested."

"All I care about is bringing him to Cara Simonson's wedding."

Her lips pulled back in disgust. Mom carried more of a grudge against Cara than I did. She'd had to wipe too many tears. "Why would you want to go to *her* wedding?"

"Because she invited me when she came into Copper Summit for a drink. With her fiancé . . . Brock."

Mom's jaw dropped open. "*Brock* Brock?" When I nodded, she sucked in a scandalized gasp. "That's just— I can't believe—" She snapped her mouth shut. "You know what? They fit each other."

"A perfect pair." They could make the exciting life together they both seemed to crave. "So I need it to be serious enough for Tenor to go to the wedding with me."

"I can accept that. But keep your eyes open, baby girl."

"If he wears Patagonia and asks me to take a hike with him, I'll run the other direction."

Mom tried to glare at me, but she laughed. "He can't leave you if you leave him first." She didn't know the wedding would be our last date. She turned to stir the spaghetti. "Just, you know, maybe don't mention your dad. He was kind of a hellion in Bourbon Canyon. His grandma said he wasn't well liked, and small towns can have long memories. I'd hate for you to get a hard time because of how he acted."

I couldn't imagine how unhinged a teen Dad must have been. He was rough around the edges as an adult. "I haven't. Robert Morgan is never a topic of conversation."

"It's better that way."

When I first got the job, Mom had warned me that Dad had been a wild, unrefined kid. Selfish and self-absorbed. Loud, with typical alpha male behavior. Dad had been sent to live with his grandparents in the Bourbon Canyon area when he was in elementary school. She said he had more tact as an adult, but he was still opinionated and blunt. To me, and to his clients. Somehow, he still made a good living in sales.

His grandparents were gone now, and he'd moved to Helena as soon as he'd graduated, but that didn't mean no one remembered him. Since I hadn't wanted to risk my position, I had kept quiet. It wasn't exactly a conversation starter, talking about my dad who knocked up my mom in high school and didn't stick around to parent much more than a weekend a month.

If Tenor and I were dating for real, he might be someone I could talk to about my dad. Or he might think it was a sign I had daddy issues and that was why I was insanely attracted to an older man.

No, I wouldn't mention my dad.

Ruby

My stomach had been a ball of nerves all night. I was staying with Tenor tonight. I hadn't talked to him all week. Other than legitimate emails about advertising budgets and which influencers I could negotiate with, there'd been no contact all week.

It was half an hour before closing when Brock walked through the door.

Why was he here? I looked behind him. "Where's Cara?"

He sniffed as he looked around, his lips turned down. "I'm supposed to fill out papers for the wet bar at our wedding."

"Oh." I glanced around, but I already knew there'd been no contract left behind. Why didn't they have him do it online? "I can message Teller real quick and see where I can find them—"

"It's your boyfriend." Brock's frown deepened.

"Tenor?"

"Do you have more than one?"

He lashed out when he was irritated. In the time we had dated, I had often been the target. Why had I stayed with him after I had realized that?

Maybe I did have daddy issues. "Tenor's more than enough."

He made a disgusted noise, but his gaze stroked down my body. I wore a tighter shirt than normal, but the pale yellow paired nicely with my dark hair. Purely coincidental and not at all because I liked when Tenor's gaze roamed over my body. My black skirt hung looser and was twirlier than the one I'd worn last weekend. I'd buy more skirts if there was a chance to have Tenor's warm hands on my legs again.

The door from the lobby opened and Tenor entered. His hard gaze landed on Brock and his eyes narrowed.

His pickup had been in the lot the whole evening, then a couple of hours ago, he'd left. He'd returned an hour later but hadn't come into the bar. It wasn't like I'd been watching the door for my entire shift, hoping he'd hang out with me for a while. Thankfully, I'd had a couple of four-tops and a smattering of couples to take my mind off his absence.

Tenor stalked toward us, weaving around the tables as if he couldn't just stomp on one and crush it. "Brock. Thanks for coming." His tone was flat.

He came around the bar and stopped next to me, putting his hand on my back. I leaned into his touch. Funny how a week had felt longer when I'd been waiting for another moment just like this.

"I'm in the area, thanks to my *fiancée*." Brock brushed

a palm over his hair. "Surprised you're not with the times."

"We are." Tenor made circles with his thumb on my back. "Have a seat."

Brock cocked his head. "I could've signed electronically."

I might've just been wondering the same thing, but I wanted to growl at Brock for dissing Copper Summit and Tenor along with it.

"Yep. You could've."

Brock and I both waited, expecting Tenor to elaborate. He didn't, and I bit back a smile. Brock sat, annoyance scrawled over his fine features. He danced his fingers over the collar of his sharp pewter dress shirt, and the arrogance was back in place.

Tenor grabbed the bar's tablet and poked around, pulling up documents. He started rattling off cancellation policies and the types of drinks—bourbon only— we'd serve. I was about to leave when Tenor started covering media policy, outlining what the distillery would and wouldn't take pictures of, what the media release entailed, and how much of a discount the couple would get if they agreed.

Had Tenor asked Wynter about that? Wedding events didn't fit her usual themes of bold, original, and family. Excitement started taking hold. Would I be able to take some of the images? I looked forward to working the wedding rather than attending.

I lingered long enough for Brock to succumb to the generous discount and sign, then left them to clean up newly empty tables. I spied on them as best I could. Tenor didn't offer Brock a drink or wait on him in any other way. Tenor's low voice rumbled. He was professional but also disassociated. Brock could slam his fist on the table and tell him there was no way Copper Summit would serve one drop at his wedding and Tenor acted like he wouldn't care.

Brock fidgeted as if his annoyance would tear out of his skin, and while I was washing glassware and restocking, I got a front-row view. He was used to being treated like a VIP. In his father's company, he was almost the boss. In Bourbon Canyon, he was an outsider. Someone who had to prove himself. And if push came to shove, he'd likely fail.

My night massively improved.

Finally, Tenor closed the tablet and extended his hand. "Pleasure doing business with you."

"Of course." Brock tried to be smooth, but his voice was tight. He accepted the handshake and stalked out.

Tenor and I were alone at the bar.

"You were ruthless," I said, pride gushing from me. "You were completely professional and absolutely cold."

He leaned against the counter and folded his arms. He wasn't slouching again. Was he at ease around me? "Is that a bad thing?"

It was hot. Utterly smoldering. "When it comes to him? No. He needs to be knocked down a peg."

"I've found less is more with people like him. Plus now I have video proof he was here to go over the terms of the contract in case he and Cara want to retaliate for whatever reason. I've gotta protect the company."

"Not many others see through people like Cara and Brock. I didn't at first." Cara had been my best friend. I'd continued giving her a chance, believing her that I had been too sensitive or that she had just been kidding until I finally admitted that she didn't make me feel good about myself. And she was likely doing it on purpose.

Brock had been my boyfriend. I had handed him my heart and he'd left it on the curb. Three times.

"I'm holding out hope Cara, at least, has matured since then, but she's with Brock so . . ."

"Some are insidious with their insults." He pushed his glasses up. "Others are blatant. The insidious ones are just as hurtful."

I hugged myself. "They weren't exactly wrong. Neither of them ever lied to me." Their brutal honesty was what had hurt the most.

"If Brock didn't say 'it's not you, it's me,' he's an asshole. People don't have to be cruel when they break up with someone. Just like friends don't demean friends."

"Brock definitely gave me a long 'it's not me, it's you' speech."

"He's an idiot."

Apparently Tenor had his own history with people like Cara and Brock. Brara? Crock? I giggled. Tenor lifted a brow.

"I combined their names to make it easier to think of them," I explained. "Since they're a pair now—Crock."

The corner of his mouth lifted. "I can't even say it, or I might accidentally slip around them."

"And then we'd lose all that primo content!" My curiosity refused to abate. "Can I ask about the media release and discount?"

"I discussed your idea with Wynter." My alarm was soaring before he shook his head. "I left you out of it. But the night before our meeting, I ran the numbers.

We're down this quarter, the lowest retail sales numbers in the last five years. The retailers are putting in smaller orders, and that trend can't continue long before we're scrambling. We can blame a lot of things—the economy or the cool start to summer—but the fact is we're down, and we shouldn't just be counting on holiday sales to boost us."

Pleasure wrapped around my heart like a vine. He'd taken my suggestion to heart. "Who's going to get the images?"

"You. We're going anyway. Wynter said she'll cover all the dos and don'ts with you."

I wanted to grin from ear to ear, but I played it cool. "Pretty soon, I'm going to get an image of you and Teller in the feed and then Copper Summit's engagement metrics are going to explode. I can see the views racking up now. There'll be so many shares—exponential. All that free marketing!"

"Good try, but this face does not need to be on anyone's feed."

"You'd stop the scroll. Trust me."

He grabbed a rag. "I'll help you close down."

Teller wasn't against being featured, but putting him in any graphics went against Wynter's wishes. With Tenor, it was something else. He truly didn't think he was enough to get anyone to care.

Didn't he own a mirror?

I'd do the world a public service and stare at him as much as I could.

After we'd finished closing duties, he let me out of the bar and locked it behind us. Time to leave. With him. What I'd been waiting for all week. Tingles spread through my body. The fake sleepover. Only I really would be under his roof.

"The roads to my place get pretty dark," he said softly. "I'll drive slow."

I wandered toward my car, parked a few spots down from his blue pickup, and tipped my head back. Tall trees lined the lot, but the sky opened above them. The sounds of frogs filled the night. "It's always so quiet out here. So peaceful."

"Yeah." His voice drifted to me. "It's beautiful."

I didn't dare look at him. If his gaze was on his truck, I'd feel foolish. Like this, I could pretend he meant *I* was beautiful. This weekend was all about being fake.

I inhaled a deep breath. The scent of warm grain surrounded me. If I ever worked at another company, I'd miss this smell.

I got in my car and followed Tenor.

He drove by his mom's place and turned down a road I'd never been on. Wynter had told me once that her parents had divided off portions of their land for each kid. She'd built on hers and now lived there with Myles and their daughter. Same with Tate. Summer's land bordered the home she had with Jonah. Though Autumn didn't plan to develop hers. She lived on her husband's family land. Junie had a cabin somewhere close to Rhys's place. Teller and Tenor had each built homes, but they were the last ones single.

The road took a few more meandering turns before Tenor pulled into a gravel loop. Light cut through the darkness as a garage door opened. In the swath of my headlights, all I could make out was a smaller log home with large windows. A rectangular gray shop with black trim was positioned on the other side of the loop. The view must be fabulous during the day.

I'd get to see it.

So many perks to fake dating my boss.

He pulled into one side of the big garage. Tools neatly lined the shelves and a workbench was built into one wall.

I whistled, grateful he couldn't hear me. The garage alone was as big as the apartment I'd grown up in.

He hopped out and waved me into the spot next to him.

My stomach knotted up. When the garage door closed behind me, I inhaled a shuddering breath.

*This isn't real. I'm not his girlfriend. He's only being nice. In fact, at the wedding we'll be more like coworkers.*

I could so easily picture this scenario in my future though. Driving home after a day at the office and having Tenor greet me.

The image vanished. My imagination couldn't go that far out of bounds.

"Where's your bag?" he asked.

"In the back seat."

He retrieved my suitcase and ushered me to the door of the house.

Was this how it should be? Brock had never carried my bags. If I'd stayed at his place, he had barely looked up from his computer. His work had been more important than me. I'd get a head nod and a "What's for supper?"

"Just go on in," Tenor said from behind me.

My heart crawled into my throat. There was no way this could get more surreal. I'd walk in and find a mess. Beer bottles and takeout containers littering the floor and piled on the counter. It didn't matter that Bourbon Canyon didn't have much for takeout options. And he'd have a weight bench instead of a couch and a big-screen TV. Maybe an Xbox. Or a PlayStation. Or both.

I opened the door and he flipped on the light after me.

Log walls rose to beamed ceilings. The space wasn't large like Mae's house, but it had just as much character. Across from the kitchen, an impressive rock mantel framed the fireplace on one side of the house. The open floor plan was broken only by a wall that must border the bedrooms and bathroom.

"Nice." The smell of savory food wound through the air. My stomach clenched. I had forgotten to pack a meal for work. "Whatever you had for dinner smells amazing."

"I haven't eaten yet. I came home to throw one of Mom's meatball dishes in the oven. It should be warm for us."

I had thought he'd barely noticed it was my night to work. I'd thought he'd just hung around for the meeting with Brock. But Tenor had left to get dinner ready.

My throat grew thick. How low had my standards been?

Tenor was going to show me. And then he'd be gone.

Tenor

The meatballs tasted like sawdust. Having Ruby in my house messed with my head. This place was my safe haven. Anxiety clawed up my throat until I wanted to ask her to leave. Even worse, I wanted to show her that any poor sexual experiences hadn't been her fault either.

She chattered about her day and I struggled to hold on to my humanity. The way her shirt molded over her breasts derailed my best intentions. And that goddamn skirt. It twirled over her lush thighs, teasing me with each move.

She hadn't worn that skirt for me, but when she walked—and goddamn, when she bent over to wipe off tables—she became my own personal show. She performed just for me.

I had to be the responsible one here. I had power over her. Not just her job but with her reputation. I would never be like her ex—or like mine. Or like any of the other people in our past. Yet I was caught between wanting to toss her out in the dark and haul her off to my bedroom.

I stabbed a meatball. My appetite had fled as soon as she'd fluttered her eyelashes over her first bite. I was ravenous, but not for food.

This was what happened when I cut myself off for so long. No. I controlled my body. I could handle my urges.

"Your home really is beautiful." This was the second time she'd gushed about the house.

"Thank you." I shifted in my seat. My unruly dick kept trying to join the conversation.

"I can't shut up about it, I know. I tend to prattle on about the things I like." She crossed one leg over the other under the table and I bit back a groan. "Mom and I always lived in apartments. After I moved out and could support myself, she could finally buy a condo."

While I was interested in her life, the first part had caught me. "Who said you prattle on?"

"Oh, um . . ." Her gaze flicked away and she dug her teeth into her lower lip. "Mom always laughs about it, but I never got the sense she was annoyed."

"Brock?" I gritted out the name.

"Yes, him too. Other guys I dated. My dad. 'You talk a mile a minute, Rubes. You don't give a guy a chance to finish a thought.' " She gave me a tight smile before taking a drink and shifting her gaze away. "I only let Dad call me Rubes."

My brows lifted. I'd been ready to hunt Brock down and tear his limbs off one by one. Her dad? Did he know she didn't like being called Rubes? "I grew up in a house often filled with foster kids. Some would stay for days, some for months. My own sisters were fosters who my parents adopted. I shouldn't be so shocked to hear about how parents treat their kids."

She blinked. "He's not that bad." Her smile was self-deprecating. "But he has no patience. We get along better as adults." There was a note of longing in her voice. "When he comes to visit, we play tennis."

"I used to play." My rackets were stored in the garage. None of my family played, so it was something I rarely talked about, except with a few friends from school. "I still do sometimes, with my old coach and when a friend comes home to visit his parents. Sometimes I'll meet him in Billings to get a quick game in."

"Is that your Wednesday nights?"

"No."

Her expression was expectant like she was waiting for me to elaborate. I wouldn't.

"I enjoy it," she continued after a moment, toying with

her fork. "Dad's usually more relaxed when we're playing. He learned to play in order to get ahead at his job."

"They say tennis and golf are the best ways to network."

She grinned. "He doesn't have the patience for golf." She set her fork down. "Maybe we can play sometime."

I'd never played with a girl. I had joined tennis so I didn't feel like such a loser with football stars as siblings. The last thing I had wanted to do after school was get slammed around by other kids. I'd had enough fear of that during my school day. So I'd joined our small tennis team. "If you promise to take it easy on me."

"I'm not to be feared, don't worry." Her laugh curled around me. I'd never be able to rest within these walls now that I'd heard her laugh here. She finished her last couple of bites and stood, taking her plate with her. "You cooked; I can clean."

I rose, nearly knocking my chair over. She was a guest. Mama taught me better than this. "No, I got it. I can show you your room. It's the first door on the right."

She hovered by the sink, her plate in her hand.

My heart raced. I had cleaned the house and put away everything that could possibly cause her to think or act like I was nothing but an irresponsible man-child. My hobbies were my own. I'd share my enjoyment of tennis and be a gentleman.

"Sorry." I pushed a hand through my hair. I needed a trim. I usually did, but I hated the barbershop. Salons were worse. I wanted my hair trimmed with no chitchat. Between Gary, the barbershop owner who tried to get as much Bailey dirt as possible, and Riley at the salon trying to shampoo my hair with her tits shoved into my cheek, I just let the length go. "Mama made sure we're proper hosts even though I told her no one was ever visiting or living out here but me."

Surprise flitted over Ruby's features. "You don't want anyone out here with you?"

"Present company excluded." My lame attempt at a rescue didn't soften her shock. I doubled down so she'd know how serious I was. This was my line in the sand, and if she was worried I'd pursue her after the wedding, I'd put her mind at ease. "No plans to get married either."

Her eyes were round. "Oh."

That was that. "Go ahead and set the plate down. Get some rest. I'll be gone for a while in the morning to help with chores."

I usually spent most of my weekends helping around the ranch, but I couldn't have Ruby wandering aimlessly through my house. She didn't seem like an invasive person, but I also couldn't have her peeking into my bedroom.

I'd shoved everything from the spare room in there. A path around my bed was all the space that was left. I could've taken my stuff out to the shop, but I didn't want everything to get dusty. And I didn't want to store it in one of the ranch's outbuildings. My family had a way of butting in without meaning to.

She rubbed her hands together. "Okay. Well. Good night."

There had to be a way to diffuse the awkwardness. Unlike her dad, I liked when she prattled. "I'll try not to surprise you with any shirtless moments."

She laughed. "Don't threaten me with a good time."

Her cheeks bloomed red and she scurried down the hallway.

"First door on the right," I reminded her. I was smiling when I loaded my little-used dishwasher. Sometimes, Cruz and Lane or my brothers came over, but I didn't host otherwise. Nor did I feel the need to hide my hobbies from them.

Ruby was different. She made me wish for a lot of things I'd given up on. But she wasn't mine. Never would be.

# CHAPTER SIX

Ruby

*Don't threaten me with a good time.*

Embarrassment continued to flood my system even the next morning. I couldn't quit throwing myself at him. He'd practically held up a billboard last night that said he wasn't interested in anything long term. His stated disinterest in company or marriage had danced a little too close to my fantasies.

I had to be realistic. Tenor was just another guy. He was kind and considerate. He'd kissed me until I couldn't think straight. But he was a guy, and when it came to men, I was never their pick. In Tenor's case, no one was.

I tied my hair back and went out to the porch. It was after lunch and Tenor hadn't returned. He'd messaged that they'd had some cows get out, he'd be a while, and to help myself to anything in the fridge.

His fridge was pristine. Gleaming on the inside. It looked as staged as the rest of the house. If he said he rented this out to vacationers, I wouldn't be surprised. The cabin was gorgeous, but the longer I was here, the less lived in it appeared.

I compiled a ham sandwich, then ate at the table and studied the place. No bookshelves. There was a corner that was completely wide open. Had something been stored there at one time?

Tenor Bailey was a mystery I wanted to keep working on, but I shouldn't. I'd only get my hopes up again. It was bad enough that I was giddy for our date tonight. More excited than I'd ever been. Was it because I knew we weren't going anywhere? All the pressure was off?

My anticipation could also be from Tenor. He was town royalty. When I was younger, Dad would ask me about school and regale me with his glory days. The disappointment on his face when I confessed I hadn't joined the tennis team had stayed with me. Or when he'd ask about my friends or who I was dating.

*Your best days are passing you by, kiddo. You gotta live a little and get your nose out of those silly books. People are going to think you're desperate.*

I ate my sandwich and tried to forget Dad's words. When I was done, I went into the guest room that lacked all life with its beige comforter and white walls and dug my book out of my bag.

Tenor had a porch swing that was calling my name and a view I'd sell myself for. If only Tenor was taking bids.

The rolling hills were blanketed with pine trees. The same pine trees soared above the cabin. Tenor's land was tucked farther northwest of Mae's house, close to the forest, and the terrain was more rugged hills. The mountains were so close I could touch them.

I appreciated the view . . . and then dove into my phone. I pulled up other Montana distilleries and screenshotted any posts showcasing them out and about in the community. I had tentatively brought this up to Wynter, but when she approached me about the wedding, I wanted to be ready with data.

After opening a spreadsheet, I collated my observations along with screenshots and source distilleries, then branched out to Wyoming and Colorado. I'd do more states while at work. Then I pulled up some influencers I recalled were getting married and scrolled through their reception shots, zeroing in on the comments to glean what people liked and disliked.

I had a whole marketing plan formed by the time I put my phone down and picked up my book. I was in the mountains, not just looking at them out windows. It was relaxation time.

I had been reading for a couple of hours, enjoying the light breeze and listening to birds squawk and chirp and the swing squeak when Tenor pulled up in his pickup and parked in the garage tucked beside the house. His footsteps sounded heavy as he grew closer.

I closed my book and devoured his swagger. His easy gait was strong and sure. He wasn't wearing a cowboy hat, but his hair was crushed against his scalp like he'd had one on all morning. His loose shirt was untucked, but couldn't hide the width of his shoulders. He crested the four steps in one leap, his boots thumping on the floorboards.

"How's it going?" He leaned against the railing.

My hormones went haywire at the relaxed, long-legged cowboy. He ruffled his hair and some strands fell over his forehead, hiding him again.

"Good." I wouldn't mention that I had spent much of my time working. It'd been held against me in the past. *Put that goddamn phone down.* Half the time, I had expected Brock to finish with *and make me some dinner.* No, I wouldn't reveal everything. I spread a hand over my book, instantly protective.

He glanced down. *"Pride and Prejudice?"*

"Yes, it's a favorite. I read it all the time." My lie tasted sour, but I was used to hiding what I read.

"I read it once."

"Really?" I had too. Once was enough. "Did you like it?"

"Wasn't my thing."

"What is?" What did he do all day?

He shrugged and squinted over the hills. "If I'm not working at the distillery, I'm on the ranch. Not much time for reading."

If my lie tasted sour, his response was downright acrid. I couldn't put my finger on it. Perhaps like me, he'd gotten shit for his taste in books. Hurt skimmed over the surface of my skin and it was laughable. If I wasn't willing to be transparent with him, how did I expect him to be honest with me? He had no reason to be. Couldn't we be at least friends while we churned through the fake dating pool?

I took the fake book jacket cover off. "I'm not actually reading Jane Austen."

His brow creased, and he leaned forward to look at the real cover of my book. The shirtless man with a smoldering stare gazed right back at him.

"I read a lot of different genres," I explained. "Thrillers. I love psychological thrillers because there's less gore on the page. Fewer gruesome scenes. Some women's fiction. I used to be into fantasy . . ." I ran my lower lip between my teeth. Dad's laughter when I had shown him what I was reading rang through my head. The curl of disgust on Brock's lips when I spent money on books with a guy on the cover or a dragon. Or both.

"You like genre fiction?"

Genre fiction was a good description but not entirely accurate. I enjoyed most genre fiction. I devoured one genre in particular. "Mostly romance, really."

He returned to his relaxed stance, folding his arms over his chest.

Whoa. The way that position anchored the fabric of his shirt to his chest started a throb between my thighs that was just wrong. We were talking about books. I was a guest in his house, and last night he'd admitted to not wanting visitors.

But he hadn't made fun of my taste.

"Tell me about your favorite book," he asked.

His question surprised me. I didn't sense a taunt or an underlying purpose to explain why romance books shouldn't have a place in my life like one of my exes had tried to do. That was likely because he had thought orgasms were mythical and had been afraid one of my books would reveal they weren't.

I rearranged the fake book cover over my novel just to have a place for it. And because the chest made me wonder what Tenor looked like without a shirt. "I have a lot of favorites."

He remained quiet.

Discussing this with him pumped my cheeks and my belly full of heat. "One of my favorites is actually fan fiction," I finally answered. Why had I thought honesty was the best policy?

"Cool." If he was shocked I'd admitted to loving fan fiction, he didn't show it. Maybe he didn't know what it was. Did a lot of distillery-owning cowboys read fanfic? "What makes you like it more than others?"

I swallowed hard. Brock had brayed like a donkey when I'd told him. "It is unique. Something different."

His sharp gaze narrowed. "Has someone made you feel like shit about it before?"

I nodded, my gaze skating away. "I've been accused of working too much and hiding in fantasy worlds." As if my boyfriend couldn't get off his computer when I walked through the door and give me a kiss.

"That sucks." Something weighed heavy in his tone like he knew how it felt to have a personal passion get laughed at. Had he ducked out of a book club because his girlfriend had said it was the biggest waste of time he'd ever heard of?

"It does," I agreed.

"I like to work a lot too." He crossed to me, his shadow falling over my lap. He gently pried my hands off my book, then he removed the cover and set it beside me on the swing. "This is a no-judgment zone."

"You're judging me about hiding my books," I teased to keep from passing out from how close he was and the way he was bent over me.

The corner of his mouth tipped up and he stepped away.

I didn't want him to leave me alone. Words piled on my tongue. I could explain my favorite fan fiction one more time. "It's a dark story, but the thing that drew me in and held me hostage was that the hero did everything for her. Everything he did was for her—you'd have to read the story." Because I was not explaining a dark romance to Tenor. My heart would not survive. "But once she was in his life, it was her. And I just loved that. His entire motivation became her. That all hooked me, but I loved the way it ended. The war was over and it was just them. Living life. Being normal and happy together." I wiggled my fingers in the air. "Wizards and witches living happily ever after. It's not realistic, I know."

"Neither are superhero movies and no one gives guys shit about those." When I snapped my mouth shut, he continued, "It's the principle behind them. Heroes would do anything for justice. Heroes would do anything to protect what's right. Heroes dedicate their lives to what's important and people celebrate them for it. But in the end, they do it so others—and themselves—can live a normal, quiet life."

I blinked. Whoa. I'd never heard movies explained like that. I enjoyed them, but they were nothing more than entertainment with attractive leads. More than that, Tenor had understood exactly what I had been saying. I didn't need a man in tights with a cape to keep my car from falling off a bridge. I needed a guy who asked about my day because he really wanted to know.

He pushed a hand through his hair. "I've gotta get cleaned up and then we'll go out."

"Oh, I need to get dressed." While thinking long and hard about why I'd taken Brock back twice.

His gaze raked down my body. I wore blue shorts that I often used as pajama bottoms and an orange Zoo Boise T-shirt. "You look fine."

I most certainly did not, but I appreciated his effort. His goal was to show me how much more I deserved in a relationship, and he'd already made his point. I fanned myself. "Tenor. Stop. You're going to ruin me for other men."

His eyes darkened. "Anything you wear looks good, and it's just Curly's."

One thing I knew about Tenor was that he didn't waste words. I'd take that response and bottle it up to use the rest of my life.

He pushed off the railing. "But if you want to wear that skirt again from last night, I won't complain." Then he disappeared into the house.

The skirt from last night I had worn hoping he'd like it. I bit back a grin and kicked the swing back, gazing across the trees. My heartbeat spiked when he got that hot look in his eye. Tenor spun me one way and then the other. How was I going to get through this date without tripping over myself and falling for him?

Tenor

Ruby walked out of the guest room. Her hair spilled onto her shoulders and was pinned up at the sides. Her curls flared out around the clips. She was wearing the skirt. She smoothed her hands over it, her smile timid.

I could gobble her up. I stuffed the urge into the recesses of my mind. I had years of discipline to call on, but Ruby's presence could obliterate it all.

She wasn't wearing a yellow shirt like yesterday. Today's shirt was a tucked-in, fitted red top. The short heels on her feet with a strap over the top of her foot were innocent but sexy, which fit her perfectly.

Lust punched me hard and low. I envisioned crowding her right back into that room and stripping each item of clothing off of her soft curves. "You look good." I turned and opened the garage door, holding it for her.

"Oh, uh. You too."

I'd put on my nicer jeans, the ones I wore when I ran to Billings on Wednesdays, and my shirt was a navy-blue polo, my only one that didn't have a Copper Summit logo on it.

She passed me to get into the garage, her limoncello scent lingering in the air.

Goddamn. As if I needed to test my resistance more.

I followed her to the passenger door of my pickup and held it open, ignoring the pleasure of seeing her car in the garage parked next to mine.

I might've been able to ignore the way her skirt rode up her legs in the dimness of the garage, but when I backed out and sunlight flooded the cab of the pickup, her creamy thighs drew my eye. Everything about her did.

I had made a big mistake. I should've just agreed to be her date. I shouldn't have kissed her.

Then what would I torment myself with at night when I was alone in bed?

I gripped the steering wheel until my knuckles turned white. The drive to town was quiet. She was pressed to the window, murmuring about the gorgeous view.

My hold on the wheel loosened slightly. I admired my surroundings every day. I never took them for granted, but I'd also never had anyone to share them with.

The cabin was higher up in the foothills where the trees thickened and the pitch of the land increased. This wasn't a sprawling valley like the places my sisters had. The portion of land I'd been gifted was rugged. Perfect for solitude, which was exactly what I'd been looking for when I'd built out here.

I turned onto the highway into town and the acid in my stomach started a low simmer.

"You've been to Curly's before?" I asked more to distract myself from the date.

"A couple of times for lunch when I came here to meet Wynter. I can't imagine how busy that place gets on a Saturday night."

Shit. My knuckles were white again.

Ruby smoothed her skirt under her legs. Her excitement filled the cab and only cranked up my guilt. I did not want to do this.

By the time I parked in the lot, I wanted to crawl out of my skin. I'd purposely come early in the evening when there'd be fewer customers, but small groups walked into the double wooden doors. More cars flowed into the lot behind us.

I didn't kill the engine, just glowered at the restaurant. In my periphery, I could see Ruby's hand on the door handle.

Kill the engine and walk in with her. That was all I had to do.

That was it.

A warm hand landed on my arm. "Tenor? Is everything okay?"

I closed my eyes and exhaled. "I don't—" She deserved some sort of explanation, but I couldn't delve into my previous humiliation. But when I looked at her wide, worried blue eyes, I couldn't allow her to think any of this had to do with her. "I don't like attention on me." The idea of getting stared at scratched under my skin.

Confusion glimmered in her eyes a moment before understanding sank in. "And people will see you on a date."

"That's what we want them to see."

"True. But a date can mean many things. It doesn't have to be diners staring at us while we eat. I get gawked at when I'm here with Wynter. A Saturday night? We'll be their dinner show just eating the buns."

The burn in my stomach cranked higher. "I owe you a supper."

"Hmm." She rested her elbow on the console and put her chin in her hand. "Where else would you go on a date in town?"

"I haven't been out in a . . . long time . . . with someone."

Her smile was encouraging. "You've been single for a minute?"

I shook my head. "I don't date anymore."

She was quiet a moment and I let her read into my statement however she wanted. "Just like you don't have people over to your house?"

"Like you with your work and your books, I don't like to be judged based on how I live my life."

"And you have been before? Judged by how you live?"

"Yes." How I lived, what I did in my free time, what I wore, and what my priorities were. The urge to share more with her was strong, but I tucked it away. Not today. Not ever. It was easier being alone than facing that.

She dug her phone out of her purse. "What would you have eaten if we'd ordered?"

"The beef tips are my go-to at Curly's."

She nodded and poked at her screen. Bewildered, I watched as she pulled up Curly's menu and hit the contact info. When they answered, she rattled off my order and one for her—the chicken primavera. After she hung up, she shot me a satisfied smile. "Twenty minutes. Then we can find a place for a picnic."

Acute relief cooled the sting of humiliation. I should be able to take her out to a goddamn restaurant. "This was supposed to be a date."

"It is. I'm sure people will see us together just driving around. Should we take the food back to your place?"

I tapped my fingers on the steering wheel. I didn't want her to feel like I was squirreling her away or, worse, embarrassed to be seen with her. "There's a park by the river."

"Perfect." She crossed her ankles, drawing my eyes to her bare legs.

"You really do look good tonight."

She tugged her skirt down. "Thank you."

I put my fingers on the hem, her warm, bare flesh just under the fabric. I hitched it back to where it had been. "You never have to hide from me." The last thing I wanted to do was make her self-conscious. "You shouldn't have to hide from anyone."

If I thought she'd melt under my reassurance, I was wrong.

She searched my face. "You don't have to either."

Startled, I drew my hand back. My defenses slammed into place. "I'm not hiding. I just like my privacy."

Her expression said *you sure about that?* "Of course. Sorry." She looked out the passenger window.

Dammit. None of this was her fault, and I missed her attention on me. "Ruby." I rubbed the spot between my eyes. "You know why I helped you?"

She finally turned back to me and the pressure inside me eased. "Because you're a nice guy?"

"I want to be a nice guy because I don't ever want anyone to feel the way I did. The way others made me feel." First, it was the jackass in school. Then, Katrina and her father. "You've seen my childhood pictures. You can imagine some things I might've experienced growing up." And beyond, when I had thought I'd left those feelings of wanting to be anyone else but myself behind. "I'm sure you can connect it to why I don't like being the center of attention."

"That's awful."

I only lifted a shoulder. "It is what it is."

She put her hand back on my arm. I'd spill my entire history if it meant she touched me more. "People can be horrible. Let's make tonight about us." Her eyes widened. "I don't mean us, like us, but—"

"I know." I traced a finger over the back of her hand. "Fuck them. Let's have a quiet picnic and enjoy the nice evening." I lifted my touch from her and grabbed the door handle. "I'll go get the food. Wait here."

## CHAPTER SEVEN

Ruby

The evening was gorgeous. A light breeze ruffled the leaves in the trees, and behind them, pine trees reached into the air. The park was quiet, with a family at the far end on the playground. Every so often, joggers and bicyclists would cut down the walking path on the far side of the trees.

Tenor had some lantern-looking contraption that was supposed to keep the bugs away. It sat on the end of the picnic table. The spicy citrus smell of citronella emanated from it.

My hair ruffled in the breeze. He had a cowboy hat on and I was doing everything I could not to gawk at him. The hat kept his hair from falling against his face, making the hard cut of his cheekbones more visible. When he chewed, the muscles in his jaw flexed. The way he sat, his arms were bent and there was nothing but biceps. Could I just squeeze one and see if it was real?

"You have really big muscles," I blurted. Wow. What a stupid thing to say. I couldn't snatch the words back, so I kept my expression interested as if I hadn't uttered the world's worst pickup line.

He poked at his beef tips. "The summer after my junior year, I had a growth spurt. And then another. I'd always been on the tall side, but not this." He waved at himself.

"I wish puberty had done that for me. All I got was a shiny forehead that photobombs every picture and Cara's comments that abs are made in the kitchen and not on my couch."

He stalled with his fork punched into a hunk of beef. "She said that?"

Among other things. My brain scrambled for a way to make me sound less cringey. "You're very powerful. I'd love some of your muscles."

"Don't lose those curves, Ruby."

A dart of desire went right to my heart and morphed into something warmer. Cozier.

His gaze was direct. "You're just right, Goldilocks."

If we were standing, I'd fling myself right into his arms like a spider monkey, arms and legs wrapped around him. I had needed to hear that, even if he didn't mean it. He was only on a date with me because he felt sorry for me.

"I know this is hard to believe." I couldn't keep the faint sarcasm out of my voice. "But guys aren't racing to get into my drawers."

"They are. You just don't see it." He shoveled the rest of his food into his mouth and picked up his to-go containers. He dumped them back into the paper bag they'd come from.

My food was gone, so I did the same as him.

He took the bag and went to the bear-proofed-as-could-be trash bins and tossed everything inside. "Come on."

Disappointment registered like a boulder sitting on top of my delicious chicken primavera.

A sneaky part of my brain insisted that Tenor just didn't want to be seen with me. He'd told me his reasoning and it was awful. But really, I couldn't shake the conviction that he just didn't want to be saddled with a fake date. Regardless, I followed him like a good little girl.

When he turned the truck toward town instead of out of it, I frowned at him. "Where are you going?"

"To prove a point." His eyes were narrowed behind those thick frames, and the rest of his profile was strong under his hat. He parked downtown. The coffee shop was across from us, closed for the night. The only places open downtown were the bars and I hadn't been to any of them. The closest was Flatlanders Prohibited, two blocks away.

I tugged the hem of my skirt down. I wasn't used to sitting right next to a guy while I wore it. The damn thing really did ride up. "I hate to say it, Tenor, but there's no point getting proved." Only that he could drive me anywhere and I'd go without question. Maybe one question, but seriously, I didn't care about his answer.

"You're going to go in first," he said, pointing to Flatlanders.

"In the bar?" Pickups lined the curb in front, but the bar wasn't as busy as Curly's. Didn't mean people wouldn't stare and talk.

"Sit at the bar and order whatever you want," he continued. "Then see if you even have to pay for that first drink, or any of the ones after."

"I'm sorry, what?"

"You think I'm lying about the male attention you get. I think you're oblivious."

I wasn't oblivious. I was practical. "Brock told me that 'adorkable' wasn't sexy."

"We've already established that Brock knows two things, and that's jack and shit."

I sputtered out a laugh. "Oh my god. No, we haven't explicitly said that, but now that you have, I agree. Still . . . Cara's beautiful and sophisticated. I'd date her if I didn't know how toxic she was."

"You're hands down prettier than her."

I drew back. "No, I'm not." I looked like a rabid poodle on my best days. After college, I'd been terrified I wouldn't land a marketing job because I didn't market myself well. I wore clothing I liked, not what was in fashion. I knew what was in fashion. I could identify trends and then mimic them. But others would see me and wonder how in the world I could be together enough to run a social media page. The Baileys had taken a chance on me because I could identify patterns, what was working, and understand the algorithm. I'd been observing the world my whole life. Social media was turning those observations into posts.

Tenor clenched his jaw and tipped his hat toward the bar. "Go in first. Pretend you don't notice me when I go in. I'll sit in the corner."

Uh, no. I would not be going into a bar to get ignored in front of the man I wished I could tempt the most. "I thought Scott Townsend hated the Baileys."

Wynter had filled me in when she'd given me the tour through town my first time in Bourbon Canyon.

"I heard he's out of town this week, and this place attracts more single guys than couples, but I don't think that'll be an issue. You'll probably get at least one drink from a guy with a wedding ring."

Add that to the list of things I didn't want to experience tonight. "Why are you so confident? I'm the one with history in this exact subject."

"You've hung out at a lot of bars?" A gotcha glint lit the yellow in his eyes when he saw the answer on my face. "So when you went out, you were usually on a date?"

I knew what he was getting at, and I was ready to concede. Since I was digging my own humiliation hole, I'd add to it. "I read on my nights off, doesn't matter if it's a weekend or not. I'm thinking about getting a cat."

The corner of his mouth tipped up. "Let me know when you're ready for one. We always have barn cats that are cuddle monsters."

Figured he was a cat guy. Since he was so damn perfect already. "You can see I'm well on my way to cat-lady status. I'm not getting hit on in bars."

"Prove it."

Something inside me woke to the challenge. "Fine. But you're going to have to, like . . . fake date me even harder to make up for this."

His pupils dilated. My cheeks were on fire. What—the hell—had I just said?

He leaned over the console. "If I'm right, you're going to have to wear a skirt every night you're at my house and I'm not even going to hide how much I like checking out your legs."

He sounded serious, as if he couldn't wait for the next skirt I wore.

I had a closet full of them.

If I did this, I'd either get more unofficial dates with Tenor, or I'd get him admiring my body? "It's a deal."

"I don't take bets I'm going to lose," he warned. "Get your sweet ass in there, Ruby, and show them whatcha got."

Shivers zinged down my spine. I got out and added a little sway to my ass, the hem of my skirt kicking at my legs. The sun was sinking in the horizon, but the night was still young.

Free drinks. As if. The only time I'd gotten a free drink was when a barista had given me the wrong order in a drive-through and I'd already taken a sip.

Once I stepped inside the dim bar, my bravery faltered. The place was half-full and people turned to look at me. Lots of men. Tenor had been right about that.

I lifted my chin. That was all he was right about.

As I made my way to the counter, the irony came into clear view. Why did I want the guy who was dating me out of pity to be wrong about how desirable I was?

I climbed onto a round stool. The top squeaked as I swiveled. A faint scent of mustiness lingered under the damp smell of hops and old wood. This establishment had to be decades old and it had definitely seen better days.

The bartender looked to be a few years older than me. He was several inches shorter than Tenor, but he was good-looking enough. A little too similar to Brock for my taste.

He propped a hand on the top of the bar and his gaze dipped down to my boobs. "What can I get you?"

"Bourbon and—"

"We don't carry Copper Summit," he said to my chest. "If that's what you're wanting."

I was nothing if not loyal. "I don't want lower-quality bourbon." One blond brow ticked up, and I smiled sweetly. "How 'bout a Malibu and Coke?"

He patted the countertop and walked away. Behind the bar, bottles of spirits were lined up. I was used to serving only bourbon, but my content-creation brain wouldn't shut off. I could do some smoky bar shots. Could I talk one of the Bailey brothers into being the fuzzy image in the mirror? The hint of handsomeness that was behind the bourbon. I could easily picture it with any of the brothers, but I'd rather see Tenor. My own personal post.

The door opened and a spear of fading light stabbed across the floor. A big shadow darkened the room again. Tenor. It took all my restraint not to look. From the way my body flushed, I knew I was right.

His heavy footfalls faded into the corner of the bar. I wanted to look so badly, but I couldn't without smiling and waving.

My drink slid in front of me. "That'll be six dollars," the bartender said to my chest.

Six dollars. A small part of me died inside. I was showing Tenor he was wrong and the shame burned hot. I didn't intend to be a sexpot in life. I was happy with where I was and how I looked. I just hated how others could affect that.

I opened the top of my purse.

Someone slid onto a stool next to me. "I got it."

Shocked, I gaped at the new arrival. He was probably in his thirties, wearing a white T-shirt with a flying pig on it. I couldn't make out the words, or I'd be as bad as the bartender. The man's ball cap was grungy and not in a faux-worn sort of way. From his glassy eyes, he was likely a few drinks into the night.

I almost told him it was fine, but I had made a bet. I also might lose my feminist card, but it felt good to have my drink paid for. "Thank you."

I took a sip. My Coke was the lightest brown I'd ever seen. Didn't the bar owners realize soda was cheaper than rum?

The new arrival stuck his hand out. "Travis."

"Ru—" Did I want to give my real name? People might not know me, but I also didn't want them to remember me. I wasn't sure how this night would end. "Just Rue." I took a big gulp to fortify my nerves.

I was so out of my element.

Travis's brown eyes twinkled. "Well, just Rue. You from here?"

I snorted. "You must not be if you have to ask."

"You got me." The corners of his eyes crinkled and a slow grin spread across his face.

Oh god. He thought I was flirting. I'd been serious. If he was from Bourbon Canyon, he'd likely know he hadn't seen me at the grocery store or in church or grabbing a coffee, no matter our age difference.

"I'm not from here either," he admitted.

I sucked down half my glass. Tenor's attention bored into me, all smoky heat, igniting a spark in my belly and traveling lower. The feeling wasn't Malibu fueled, though that wasn't helping.

"Whatcha doing in town?" He leaned closer.

I inched away. "Uh . . . work."

The bartender slid another pale-brown drink in front of me. "Malibu Coke from the gentleman at the end of the bar." He lifted his chin toward the side closest to where Tenor was sitting.

I looked, but my gaze skipped over the guy a little closer to my age than Travis. Behind him, Tenor was tucked into a booth, glowering into his phone. He appeared oblivious to everything around him, but I knew better.

The second guy who'd bought my drink smiled.

"Th-thank you." Two drinks in less than ten minutes? Were there no other women in town?

Tenor had been right. The only other ladies in the bar were playing pool with a couple of guys. A group of three men older than my dad sat behind me in a booth, and the rest were pairs of men and a few singles, in addition to those who'd forked over cash for my Malibu Cokes.

I was prime rib at a hot dog stand. I giggled like a middle school boy. Hot dog was the worst analogy. The second guy must've thought I was smiling at him. He grinned wider.

"You know him?" Travis's whiskey-scented breath wafted across the shell of my ear.

I leaned a little farther away. Tenor hadn't looked up. I dragged my gaze off him. "No, I don't." When I twisted to face forward, I nudged him hard with my shoulder. He didn't back off very far.

Suddenly, I didn't feel like prime rib. I was a lame zebra on the Serengeti.

I was a slow duckling with eagles flying overhead.

A sick deer surrounded by coyotes.

Should I be astonished or insulted? Tenor had been right. But then I was almost the only game in the place.

A couple of women stumbled into the bar, laughing. Each one wore tiny jean shorts and cropped tees. Their long hair covered more than their shirt. One of the girls smiled and waved at the guys in the booth. They took the table in front of Tenor, surreptitiously checking him out, but he never glanced up.

Instead of tracking the new arrivals, the guy who'd bought the second drink picked up his bottle of beer and moved to the stool on the other side of me. "Have we met before?"

Was he seriously asking, or was that a pickup line? Would I have wondered before Tenor had made me try this stupid experiment?

Still, it was just two guys, and there were the new arrivals with their booty shorts that would surely get all the men's attention. I might still prove Tenor wrong.

# CHAPTER EIGHT

Tenor

Four fucking men surrounded Ruby. Their laughter, mingled with hers, filled the bar. It had been three hours and she was on her fifth Malibu Coke—not having to turn over a single dime to pay for any.

Allen, the jackass bartender who wouldn't quit ogling her tits, was known to pour the drinks strong. Not only did too much of a good thing ruin a good drink, but it was expensive as hell. No wonder Scooter couldn't turn a profit and fix up this place.

Ruby held her phone out and all the idiots crowded around her. She'd been taking pictures of her drinks, of them, of Allen, and gushing about how good they'd look on a Flatlanders Prohibited poster.

Allen, the fucker, got her to send him the images— and her phone number in the process. Slick bastard.

I was scowling at the group when a pair of jean-clad

hips blocked my view. The hem of those shorts didn't cover much leg.

Cassie Horner and her sister, Andi, had arrived shortly after me. I'd thought they'd leave me alone, but I wasn't so lucky tonight. I wrapped my hands around my beer bottle. It was the only way I knew I'd get a measured amount of alcohol. I was lucky to get served at all. Pure nosy confusion was the only reason Allen had come to my booth.

"Hey, Tenor," she purred.

Cassie had always let me know she'd be interested in something. It hadn't mattered if she was seeing someone or not, she hit on me and Teller whenever our paths crossed.

"Evening, Cassie."

She slid into the other side of the booth.

Alarmed, I looked around for Andi. Surely she wouldn't ditch her sister. I had to keep an eye on Ruby.

Ruby was fine. More than fine. Which was my problem.

Andi was headed toward the hallway the bathroom was in, but then she stopped to talk to the table of guys who ran the implement store. Shit. She could be a while. I'd been hung up once for an hour when I'd encountered one of them at the gas station.

Ruby laughed and kicked her feet at something the guy on her right said. He'd been several years behind me in school. Still older than her.

Cocksucker.

"Whatcha doing later?" Cassie asked.

I shrugged, my gaze on the group at the bar, and she leaned closer.

A whoop went up and Ruby cheered with each of the

men. Allen set another glass in front of her. Was this drink six?

She was laughing and taking a pull when she turned and saw me. Her gaze narrowed on Cassie and she knocked back half the glass. I'd been trying to act like I wasn't spying on her, but this time I waited for her gaze to clash with mine.

She arched a brow. I kept my gaze steady, promising. What I promised was yet to be determined.

Ruby ran her tongue along her teeth and flipped her hair as she turned back to the first man who'd bought her a drink.

Cassie glanced over her shoulder. "You know her?"

"She's an employee."

Cassie looked again, then back at me. "Is she why you're here?"

Yes. "I'm just watching out for her."

"Uh-huh." She braced her elbows on the top of the table. "You watch all your employees that closely?"

If I told Cassie we were dating, this little setup would look weird as hell, like some sort of torture kink I didn't have. But then if she heard Ruby and I were dating later, it'd look messed up. The only thing seeing Ruby surrounded by horny men did to me was flip the switch on my caveman brain. I wanted to toss her over my shoulder and haul her away. Then gouge out every man's eyes who saw her ripe, round ass in the air.

I forced my stare off Ruby. Cassie waited for an answer.

The only thing Cassie was guilty of was being optimistically forward. I would give her an answer of sorts. "We were on a date, and I got tired of her thinking she's not desirable. So I told her to sit at the bar and see how many guys approached her."

Cassie ruefully shook her head. "You brought her to the right place. Andi and I weren't even going to come here because we wanted to talk and have a drink and be left alone. But the price is right, and I get a little pick-me-up from Allen staring at my boobs."

A low growl rumbled out of me. Allen stared at Ruby's tits like he could see through her top.

Cassie reclined in her seat and folded her arms, grin in place. "You're really dating her?"

I nodded, hating the lie but knowing this was exactly what we needed—word to get around without becoming a spectacle. "It's a new thing."

She barked out a laugh. "I'll say. Here I was thinking Katrina was right about you."

I bristled. Who knew what *she* had said. I gripped my beer bottle. "She probably was, but Ruby's not like her."

"Definitely not." Cassie sighed wistfully and ran her hand over her pale tresses. "I also assumed tall blonds were your thing. I even thought maybe you and Katrina were getting back together."

That got my attention off Ruby. "What?" Why the hell would she think that? Hadn't my ex spewed enough dirt about me to turn everyone off? *You're nothing but an overgrown man-child, Tenor! You catfished me.*

The beer bottle I gripped held firm against my ever-tightening grip.

"She was in town at Christmas. I ran across her at Broken Oar, and she asked if I'd seen you lately."

My stomach dropped. Broken Oar was another downtown bar. Katrina was asking about me? A good way to ruin my day was to see her. To know I hadn't changed, and she was still right about me. All of them had been right—every woman I had dated and that dickwad from school. "Her grandparents still live in town. She's not here for me."

The grandparents, I didn't mind. They still called me a nice boy when I ran across them in the grocery store. Even Katrina's mom had been nice enough. Her dad though . . . It was a toss-up who sucked the most. Bobby from school, Katrina, or her dad.

"She still wants you," Cassie said.

I grunted. "Doubt it." My gaze strayed to Ruby. Her face didn't just turn red from embarrassment. The spirits had given her a solid blush. How far down did it go? A question that had repeated in my brain far too many times tonight.

Cassie followed my gaze. "Katrina's out of luck," she muttered. She leaned over the table again. "I'm confused. You were obviously right about men tripping over themselves for a taste of Little Miss Snow White. Why are you still sitting here, letting her get hit on?"

Why was I?

Because she could have anyone. Not some workaholic who had lived with his mother until he was almost thirty and spent all his time helping his family. And when he wasn't, he had "hobbies to be ashamed of," according to Katrina. Hobbies that had made her embarrassed of and for me.

"She gets to choose who she's with," I said.

Cassie's eyes flared. "You'd let her go home with one of them?"

Ruby was a bundle of energy. She swayed in her seat and laughed, but she was also beyond tipsy. "No. She's drunk. But she's having fun."

Cassie tipped her head. "That girl might be enjoying herself, but she's also a ninja. She's not having the fun you think."

I eyed Ruby again. She spun one way, took a selfie, then another.

"Every time someone gets handsy, she moves," Cassie clarified.

Frowning, I kept studying the Ruby show. She had told me how much she loved her job, so I assumed the photo shoots were a part of it. She had free rein to take pics and pose with people who didn't mind being in the shot. Hell, maybe she had personal accounts to post on. I would be the last to know. I used my phone for communication, checking the weather, and tracking market prices for the ranch.

A guy with a wedding ring would crowd too close from behind and she'd jerk around to laugh loudly at another guy's joke. Then when fingertips touched her leg, she was twisting the other way.

Shit. "I've gotta go."

Cassie's laugh followed me out of the booth. I stormed across the bar and pushed through the two men crowding behind her. "Time to go."

A chorus of male dismay rang out.

Ruby clutched at me. "Tenor. Oh my god—I think . . . I think you might be right."

I helped her off the stool and she wobbled. "Of course I'm right."

Allen was pouring what might have been her seventh drink and ogled her ass. I wedged myself between Ruby and all the guys.

Someone tapped me on the shoulder. "Dude, the lady doesn't want to—"

I glared at the first man to approach her. "You really want to tell me what the lady wants, Travis? Or do you want me to tell your fiancée how you spent your night?"

Ruby's scandalized gasp rang behind me. "You're engaged?"

All the guys went silent.

"How 'bout you, Kenny?" I asked one of the men trying to paw her from behind. "You didn't even bother to take your ring off?" The anger inside me was rising to alarming levels, pushing against my temples. The other guys were single as far as I knew. Allen was a good target. I'd been so determined to let Ruby have what she wanted I'd been willfully ignorant of what had been going on. "So help me, Allen, if you keep leering at women, they're not going to find your body." Allen paled. I had the right type of land to lose a whole-ass person in and he knew it. "I might just dump you off the nearest overpass for pouring her drinks so strong tonight."

Fucker had done it on purpose.

I prompted Ruby to head toward the door, but she wobbled again. I picked her up, slipping my arm behind her back and my other under her knees.

Her breath hitched. "You're so strong." Rum-scented breath wafted across my nose. "Just like the drinks," she hissed before dissolving into giggles.

A slow clap preceded me out the door. More applause broke in.

Ruby tried to crane her neck to look over her shoulder and the move only made her breasts rub against my chest. "Who was that?"

"Probably Cassie and her sister."

"Oh." That plump lower lip was out with a pout. "The one you were talking to?"

"She's just a friend."

"Friend *with benefits*?"

"No. She hits on both me and Teller and neither of us is interested. She wouldn't be either if I actually dated her."

She tipped her head back. A groan left her. "The stars are beautiful, but I'm dizzy. You can put me down, you know. I can walk." She kicked a leg up to show her short heels. "I've just been sitting for so long."

"I know." She was also drunk.

"I think those guys were flirting with me," she whispered. "I didn't know Travis was *engaged*. Asshole."

"Yep." I was close to the pickup and wishing I'd parked another half mile away to keep holding her. Carefully I set her on her feet and opened the passenger door.

I hovered while she climbed in, albeit a little unsteadily.

Before I shut the door, I leaned in. "Why the hell do you doubt they were flirting with you?" I'd known exactly what had been in each one of those guys' heads. I wanted to do the same things to her.

She blinked those big, innocent eyes. "I was the only choice."

"No, you weren't."

She wrinkled her nose. "Does Allen know where a woman's eyes are?"

A small laugh gusted out of me. "No. I don't think so, Goldilocks."

I closed the door and got in behind the wheel.

She sank into the seat and gazed out the window.

"The stars really are beautiful tonight. The only chance I really get to see them is from the parking lot at Copper Summit." She twisted in her seat until she was facing me. "Thanks for rescuing me."

"I should've done it earlier."

A sigh left her. "I enjoyed the attention, but it was also stressful. Are men usually so handsy?"

"Yes."

"Not you."

Around her I was.

She curled her legs under her and was quiet the rest of the way home. In the dash lights, I made out her closed eyes. Dark lashes rested on her cheeks and her mouth puffed slightly open.

I parked in the garage, hoping she'd stay asleep. She did.

I loaded her in my arms again and carried her into the house.

"You're so strong," she repeated against my chest and wrapped an arm around my neck.

Good thing I was close to the guest room, or I'd be doing this with a hard-on.

I entered the room and was instantly surrounded by the limoncello smell of her. There was no way I could move all my shit back into this room and spend any time in it without thinking of her.

I placed her on the bed. She whimpered and reached for me. I grasped her hands in mine. They were warm and soft. I kissed her fingertips and released her. "Get some rest, Ruby."

"Mmm." She rolled over. The back of her skirt hitched up. I ripped my eyes off her and stumbled for the door.

I was not going to leer at her like Allen when she was sleeping. Instead, I went to my room, shut the door, and toed off my boots. Then I turned my bedside lamp on, yanked my shirt over my head and tossed it in the laundry basket by my closet.

The bathroom door squeaked open. I paused, making sure she wasn't retching or didn't need help.

After a few moments, the sink turned on. Good. I took off my belt and shoved my pants down. I folded them neatly and draped them over a pile of cases that I had stacked by the closet until I could put them back into the guest room.

I ripped my blankets back just as my bedroom door opened. I froze as Ruby entered, yawning and rubbing her eyes.

Panic coalesced in my chest. Shit, shit, shit. "Ruby."

She blinked, her eyes going wide. Her gaze touched on my chest, and she drew her fingers across her collarbone. Her attention traveled lower and she mouthed *wow*.

I scrambled for a shirt, but I had none near me. The closet was behind her.

She cocked her head, studying me. Then she closed the distance between us.

I backed up until the backs of my legs hit the end table. "Ruby . . ."

She traced the faint silvery lines at my shoulders. I had hoped my old stretch marks would go away as I got older, but no such luck. They'd faded but were still visible. I jerked like her fingertips were pure voltage.

I gulped. I wanted her touch, but I also wanted her to forget seeing a thing. Not many people had ever seen me shirtless.

"You have such a nice body," she murmured and danced her fingers over my pecs.

My dick had taken note of her presence in my bedroom. The oxygen being supplied to my brain was getting dangerously low. Soon all I'd have was that caveman that wanted to throw her on the bed and flip her skirt up. "You need to go back to your bed."

Those ripe lips puffed out. She snatched her hand back. "I knew you were only taking pity on me."

I grabbed her hand and held it. "I'd be between your legs right now if you weren't drunk."

That was supposed to have been a threat, but it came out as a confession.

"I am not dru—" A giggle left her. "I might be a little. Those drinks were really strong." She hitched my hand closer and inspected it. "You're big everywhere." She gave my crotch a pointed look. "Like, really big. Am I dreaming?"

She sucked in a breath and looked to the stacks of bins around me. Interest filled her eyes and a smile lit her face.

Fuck. She wasn't dreaming, but this was my nightmare. The taunting was coming.

"What's all this?" She bent over to peer inside the display case. "Are those figurines?"

"They're models."

"Of what?"

*Here we go.* "It's, uh . . . Warhammer."

She squinted harder. "Warhammer?"

"Tabletop gaming," I mumbled.

She turned to peer at me. "Come again?" She bent over the stacked black bins to look at a clear display case behind them. "Are they, like, orcs?"

"Yeah, actually, those are actually Orks." I scratched behind my neck, put my hands on my hips, then shoved my fingers through my hair. How much of this would she remember when she was sober?

"What do you do with them?"

Her curious tone helped unknot some anxiety. "I buy the models, then I paint them—"

She rose with a gasp and swayed. I caught her elbow.

"You painted these?" She held on to me as she bent back over. She traced the plexiglass, leaving a smudge behind. "So many small parts."

"That's part of the appeal."

She rose again and used the same finger to follow my old stretch marks. "You're a real artist. What else do you do with them?"

My mind fogged with lust. What had she asked?

Right. Exactly what I had never wanted to explain to another woman again. "I get together with others—mostly guys—and we . . . play."

She blinked. "Oh. That sounds fun."

I blew out a gusty breath, surprised. "Really?"

"I mean, you could have a giant blow-up doll collection. Porn. Guns."

"I have guns, but I don't paint those."

She giggled and spun around. When she bent over to look at another case, I bit back a groan and aimed my gaze at the ceiling. Too late. My heartbeat slammed through my dick.

"I bet you give really good orgasms," she said.

Desire rammed into me. The war I'd been losing over my erection was done. I had to have heard wrong. "What'd you say?"

She straightened, then bypassed me and crawled between my sheets.

Dear god, she was in my bed. Her limoncello scent would be on my sheets. "Ruby—"

"All that patience?" She scooted to the other end. Then she curled onto her side facing me and pulled the covers to her chin. "All those tiny details? The reverent way you have everything stored? A guy that pays that much attention to models can probably find a woman's clit." She snorted. "I don't think Brock knew what a clit's function was."

How did I respond? Why was she in my bed? "It's been a long time, but yeah. I know exactly what a clit is for."

"So you don't date and you don't fuck?"

"I can control myself." Tonight suggested perhaps not.

She rolled her eyes back and moaned. "Control and patience. Tenor, you're like the hero in my fanfic. So tightly wound that when he blows . . ." She turned her sultry smile on me, her gaze traveling down my body.

"I'm not a hero in anyone's story."

"You saved my pride." She patted the other side of the bed. "Come on. Get in. Can you shut the light off?"

I almost did as she asked without question. "You should go to your room."

"You're warmer. And you won't touch me." Her eyelids drifted shut. "I'll have to make myself come again thinking about how you kissed me."

"Jesus, Ruby."

She cracked an eye open. "I said your name when I did too."

A drunk Ruby was a painfully honest Ruby. My erection was growing painful. "Christ."

"Nope. *Your* name." The blankets shifted. "I remembered what it was like to have you towering over me with that big body of yours," she groaned. "So nice."

The covers jostled again. She was moving her legs apart. "Ruby." Her name came out alarmed. Terrified. Excited.

If she got herself off in my bed, I'd never get another peaceful night's sleep. I'd have blue balls and memories and nothing else.

"God, Tenor. Your muscles are so hard." She rolled to her back, her knees creating little mounds under the covers.

"You can't do this. You're drunk."

"Just a little." She smiled at me, all sleepy and sexy. "I've built up a decent tolerance, trying all the Copper Summit lines." Another moan. "That tongue of yours . . ."

If I kept standing here, I'd dive right under the sheets and bury my head between her legs. "I'll sleep in your bed."

"Don't leave," she whimpered. "I've liked you for so long."

I froze. "How long?"

"When Brock dumped me, I didn't feel guilty anymore noticing you. Then I got obsessed," she hissed and arched up. The blankets pressed against her hand and I could see it move. She was working herself like I wanted to.

She might be under the influence, but she also wasn't stopping and she was exploding soon. If I left and she remembered this in the morning, would she blame herself? If I stayed, she could blame me instead of being humiliated. I couldn't let Ruby feel bad about herself.

I flipped the light off and climbed between the sheets. I stretched out next to her. I wouldn't participate, but I'd be right here with her. "How wet are you?"

"So wet," she whispered.

The room was bathed in darkness, but I drank in as much of her profile as I could. "Put a finger inside."

She paused. In the dark, the weight of her gaze rested on me. Then the covers rustled as she did what I asked.

"In and out, Goldilocks. I want it to be just right for you."

"It'd be better if it was you."

I could imagine her little pout. "I know."

I'd told her I'd show her what she was missing, and from the sound of it, her ex had missed her clit a lot.

"What would you do to me if it was you?" She was talking in a whisper, but pure, unadulterated desire laced her tone.

I'd face any regret later. Right now, I'd indulge her because when it came down to it, that was all I really wanted to do. "I'd spread those pretty thighs of yours wide open." I was rewarded with a groan. "Then I'd look my fill. I bet your pussy matches your name. Ruby red and just right."

"Tenor," she gasped.

"That ignored clit of yours would get lots of attention."

"Yes."

"From my tongue. From my fingers."

"Tenor." The bed rocked as she ground against her hand.

"Is that finger still in your tight pussy, Ruby?"

"Yes."

My dick throbbed like she was fisting it. "Add another." Her breathing stuttered again, but her hips quit pumping as she did it. "I bet you're nice and full now."

Her hair rustled against the pillow when she nodded.

"Now ride your hand and pretend your thumb is my tongue, licking your clit in tight circles."

Her moan dragged out. "I don't want to come yet."

"You're going to." I could only suffer for so long. I didn't want to jack off next to her and miss anything.

"I love it when you're bossy." She arched high. "Oh god."

"Say my name."

"Tenor." She let out a cry. "*Tenor.*"

The bed shook with her orgasm. "That's it, Ruby. Let it go. I'm right here."

Another cry. "I wish it was you." Then she went lax, panting next to me. "That was the strongest orgasm I've ever had, and you didn't even touch me."

I couldn't move. If the blankets brushed against me, I'd come as fast and hard as a rocket. Then I'd have a mess to clean up and I didn't want to leave this little cove we'd made.

"Goodnight, Tenor," she said in a soft, sated voice.

"Night, Goldilocks."

Her breathing evened out. I listened to her until my erection got less excruciating and I could finally rest. In the morning, I'd find out if she hated me for this.

Ruby

.  .  .

I woke to a dull thud behind my temples. I cracked my eyes open. Rows of books faced me.

I squinted at the spines. My headache sharpened. The spines all had different names, but one of the books was propped up and faced out. *Warhammer 40,000*.

Warhammer.

When did I get all these books?

Clarity snapped into place. With a gasp, I sat up. I was in Tenor's bed.

Heat flooded my cheeks. I'd walked into the wrong room and I'd stayed.

He'd been shirtless.

He'd been pantless.

He'd been so hot. A column of muscle with fine silver lines at his shoulders and just above the waistband of his underwear around his hips. Tenor was a boxer briefs man.

The other side of the bed was empty, but I was surrounded by his scent, soap with a hint of pine.

Memories cascaded in. His hot words in my ear. My climax. I was still in his bed.

Oh. My. God. I'd gotten myself off right next to him. I'd started before he was even in bed!

I pressed my hands against my sweltering cheeks.

But he hadn't left. I hadn't scared him away.

I couldn't believe I'd done that.

I smacked my tongue against the top of my dry mouth. A water bottle was on the nightstand, along with a bottle of pain reliever.

My hangover wasn't awful, but I needed the water, or it'd get worse.

Why had I drunk so much?

Right. The nerves from having so much attention from men. The heavy-on-the-Malibu and Cokes. My boobs felt dirty from Allen's attention.

But I'd had fun taking selfies and photos of the drinks. My creator brain didn't often get to run wild with people, but those fellas had been up for a lot. Amazing what guys would do to get into a girl's pants.

Except for Tenor.

He'd stalked right in and literally picked me up.

My stomach fluttered. A lurch followed.

Water. Then food.

I chugged the bottle. Before I went searching for food, I swung into the guest room and gathered fresh clothing. I took a quick shower and towel-dried my hair. Dressed in navy linen shorts and a gray shirt that said nothing but *Bookish*, I trudged to the kitchen. A pan covered with aluminum foil in the fridge had a note on it with heating instructions.

I lifted the foil and my stomach rumbled. Breakfast burritos. Had he made them?

I heated up two. I didn't overindulge with alcohol often, but I got ravenous when I did.

When I was halfway done with the second one, Tenor walked in.

He drew himself up and stuck close to the door when he saw me.

My mouth was full but I gave him a lopsided smile that was probably more like a grimace. Time to face the reckoning.

I swallowed. "So last night . . ."

He slouched against the door. "Yeah . . . about that—"

"I'm really sorry if I made you uncomfortable," I rushed on.

He cocked his head like he hadn't heard me. "Made *me* uncomfortable?"

"I don't usually act like that. I invaded your space and then I . . ." My words caught in my throat. How embarrassing. "I was just inappropriate."

He crossed the distance between us in seconds, planted his hands on the table, and leaned in close, his face inches from mine. "If you think having a beautiful woman get herself off to the thought of me in my bed makes me uncomfortable, you didn't see or feel the erection I've had ever since." He tilted my chin up with his rough fingertips. His brown eyes were bright behind his lenses. "That was the hottest night of my life."

I scoffed. What he said refused to register. He'd been out of my league even before I'd seen him with his shirt off.

He didn't take his fingers off my face. "Do you know how badly I wanted to taste you?"

But he hadn't.

He took my hand and prompted me to stand. "You're sober now."

I was. "The water was really thoughtful. Thank you."

He gripped my hips and lifted me. My ass was planted on the top of the table and he wedged himself between my legs. "You're welcome." He took his glasses off and set them beside me. Then he planted his mouth on mine.

I curled my arms around his neck and greedily returned the kiss. He hadn't kissed me last night, but he hadn't let me make a spectacle of myself alone.

*If you think having a beautiful woman get herself off to the thought of me in my bed makes me uncomfortable, you didn't see or feel the erection I've had ever since.*

He'd been into it?

He pulled back, keeping his forehead against mine. "I wasn't going to take advantage of you, Ruby. But don't think that means I wasn't interested."

I hated that I needed constant reassurance. He was hot and cold, sometimes flashing back and forth in an instant. The man was so carefully restrained.

Memories from last night crystallized. The shock on his face when I walked in had morphed into self-consciousness. The rigid way he'd stood when I gave his body attention. It was the same when I had spotted all the belongings haphazardly stashed around his bed and dresser.

"I'm just a man, Goldilocks. Just because I've sworn off relationships doesn't mean I don't react to having a sexy woman in my house."

Well. That was a splash of cold reality on the heat his words had caused. He wanted to fuck me, but he didn't want to be with me otherwise.

I wasn't completely let down. He was affected by me, and I'd soak that up while I could.

His eyes were a warm brown, always putting me at ease, but in their depths, the intensity simmered. Was I the only one to see it? Why did he hide the real him? "Were those bookshelves in your bedroom originally in the dining room?"

He worked his jaw, but he didn't pull out of my reach. "Yes."

"Why did you move them?"

He propped his hands on the tabletop on either side of me.

I traced my fingers along his forehead and down the sides of his face. So many facets to this man and I found each one fascinating.

"After high school, I didn't go to college. I didn't need to. I had a job waiting for me, so I just took classes that would help me with my position at the distillery. I didn't even build or move out right away."

"There's nothing wrong with that."

His laugh was cynical. "Women don't really find that attractive." He nodded toward my empty plate. "Mama made those."

"They were really good."

"And she gave me the meatball dish. If you check the freezer, you'll find a lot more meals. Ready to heat."

"I wish my freezer was full of your mama's food."

He shook his head. "I hardly have to cook, Ruby. I got my job—both of them—because of my last name. I don't have a degree, and my mom still cooks for me. If a woman gets beyond that, it's my gaming. My *toys*."

"They're not toys." At his militant look, I shrugged. "I guess they are. But, Tenor, you work hard. You work all the time. Your mom loves to spoil you. If she didn't give you food, would you stomp around and complain?"

"I know how to feed myself."

I poked him in the shoulder. "That's the difference." I flung my hand toward the bedroom. "Those figures are pure art. I don't know much about tabletop gaming, but does it hurt anyone? Is it inherently selfish when you play? No. I bet it's not. My stepdad used to leave Mom for weeks at a time to go on snowmobile trips. He did it one winter when she broke her ankle and was hobbling around on crutches. He went gambling in Vegas when I was home with mono and

Mom couldn't find a sitter. Context is everything, Warhammer."

His forehead crinkled. "Did you just call me—"

"Yes, and I'm going to keep doing it. You work hard. Everyone knows it. So you have a hobby some people don't understand? Fuck 'em." I ran a finger down his chest. "Next week, when I stay here, we're going on a day date when it won't be some big reveal. Then you're going to show me how you paint those Orks."

"Space marines." His gaze skated away. "I have a new unit to paint."

"I know of books with naughty space marines. I'll buy one to read while you paint them."

His eyes lifted to mine. Disbelief lit their depths. "You're really something, you know that?"

He made me feel like it. "When we go to Crock's wedding, we're going to show up as a united front. They're going to be so jealous about how comfortable we are with each other." The idea was more appealing as I thought about it. I hadn't noticed how anxious I'd been around Brock, just waiting for a comment about something he didn't find attractive. One weekend at a time, Tenor was wiping away that toxic residue.

He was stroking my lower lip again. Then he withdrew his hand and dropped it to his side. He took a deliberate step back and cool air flooded between us. It was a good thing my body wasn't steaming. "Next weekend, we'll do what we enjoy together. No judgment."

So he wasn't going to kiss me again, but a weekend of hanging out wasn't a bad consolation prize. "That sounds just right."

"I'm glad you think so, Goldilocks. But remember . . . you'd better be wearing another skirt Saturday night."

ber . . . you'd better be wearing another skirt Saturday night."

# CHAPTER NINE

Tenor

"I made extra." Mama gestured to the two trays stacked on her countertop while she rinsed dishes at the sink. "Wynter said Ruby likes pasta dishes, so there's a taco spaghetti bake and chicken linguini. That one was Cruz's favorite."

"Thanks." I gathered the containers, feeling moderately better after Ruby had made this seem like such a normal thing last weekend. Even more, she'd sounded almost envious.

Yeah, I could cook for myself. I could cook for Mama too. But she missed taking care of a brood of kids. She hated making small dishes. Preparing a feast and portioning it out for various kids delighted her.

Since I lived alone, I didn't chow through her gifts as quickly. I had a nice stash. Something Katrina had thrown in my face. *You're pathetic, Tenor. You thought you could hide that from me?*

My throat burned. Ruby had acted fascinated by my collection. Had she just been placating me? She still needed me to show her ex up.

Mama hung a dish towel up. "Ruby at your place?"

I nodded. I'd followed her home from the distillery last night. I'd appreciated her bare legs in a maroon skirt. The one she'd worn before had been longer. The ballet flats she'd paired with it had given her a sexy librarian look.

She'd been tired, and I had fed her some of Mama's enchiladas and ensured she got to bed. In the guest room.

One night in my bed and I'd become a man obsessed, hankering for another hit. I'd gone to sleep alone, looking forward to spending a day with her. Anxious as hell about doing what I normally do any other night, only with Ruby as a witness.

"How are things going?" Mama asked quietly.

"Good," I said, full of sincerity. "She's unexpected."

"I'll say." Mama's smile was fond. "She's good for you. I was in the grocery store yesterday and Wilna asked me if it was true."

Wilna worked at one of the churches and she ran the annual bachelor auction fundraiser. She'd suspended it last year due to diminishing returns, but she continued to hound me and Teller, insisting our participation would bring back the bids. "Did you send her my sympathies that I can't be one of her bachelors?"

"I did, in fact." Mama chuckled. "Poor Teller."

"You don't sound that sad for him."

A mischievous glint shone in her doe-brown eyes. "Might be good for him."

"Depends who buys him."

"He can donate a weekend of work."

"You know that's not why anyone will bid. He'd probably make it a month to really drive up bids." Women wouldn't be bidding on his handyman skills.

Her smile said she knew exactly that. Mama wasn't pushy about her kids settling down, but she wanted us to. She would be sad when Ruby and I parted ways after the wedding.

*It didn't have to be like that . . .*

No.

*But what if . . .*

I didn't work with what-ifs. Distilling and ranching were well-researched sciences. Financials were exact. Ruby had been nothing but unpredictable since the night I kissed her.

For now, she needed me. There was no reason to wait around after and find out what about me repelled her.

Teller entered the house. He spotted the pans I was holding and looked around.

"They're in the freezer," Mama said.

Teller grinned. "Thanks, Mama." He nudged my shoulder. "Want to invite your girlfriend to a barbecue tomorrow? Tate's got some brisket smoking."

My family had been having barbecues my entire life, and I always looked forward to them. Lately, our gatherings had a hint of bitter with the sweet. My sisters had all found the love of their lives. Tate and Scarlett still acted like newlyweds.

"I'll ask her." With Cruz and Lane, Teller and I didn't stand out as the bachelors of the group. Now, they didn't think I was single. Pretending for a month was one thing, but being around them together for a family gathering—that was different. That was too close to real.

I didn't look forward to seeing firsthand what I would be missing when Ruby and I fake broke up.

Ruby

Tenor had insisted on cooking—roast and fried potatoes —likely to prove he could after he had shared that he'd been criticized for subsisting on his mom's food. Growing up eating plain pasta meals and heat-n-serve food, I gave zero fucks if he subsisted solely on Mae's meals. I would too if I could.

After we finished eating, I didn't let him ban me from the kitchen to help clean up. We worked alongside each other, casually chatting about what he'd done that day. Tenor and his brothers had worked cattle, some-thing to do with vaccinations for the calves.

"How 'bout you?" he asked, hanging a dish towel up.

I wiped off the island. He'd revealed that he ate at the island instead of the table most of the time, so I'd insisted we sit there. "I sent myself some post ideas for the fall." Waking up in a cabin by the mountains filled me with all sorts of inspiration. "Junie sent me some images. I made some edits for her." I pushed a lock of hair behind my ear. "I'm brainstorming what to do when she's done with her tour."

"Fewer pictures?"

I nodded. "It'll be more important than ever to keep her connected with her audience. We'll work on making her seem like she's around when she's not around, you know."

"I'm actually glad I don't know."

I chuckled. "Exactly. I would not want her life. Then I called my mom."

"She doing okay?"

"Better than okay." I folded my arms and leaned against the counter opposite him. I'd much rather be chatting Tenor up in his house than trying to get free drinks at the bar. "She finished her hiking trip with Dave—Daniel. This one's Daniel."

"This one?"

I pursed my lips. "Mom's a player."

His brows shot up. "Not how I expected you to describe her."

"I think she's always been hung up on my dad, but one of the good things he did when he was younger was not lead her on." I fiddled with the end of a lock of hair that had slipped free. "He said he wasn't ready to settle down, but he'd work to give her child support and take me for a weekend a month."

"You're not close with him?"

"Yes and no. We have a decent relationship, but I made the mistake of crying to him when I got dumped for the first time." I held in my wince. *First time.* Tenor would wish he could take back that smoldering kiss last weekend. "He said I should quit feeling sorry for myself. 'Suck it up and move on, kiddo.' " I mimicked Dad's rough voice.

"Ouch."

"Yeah, it didn't feel so good at the time. I think he thought the guy probably had a point when he said that I should broaden my horizons so we had more interests in common."

"No, the guy was an idiot."

"Some people just don't work out." I didn't want to defend the men who'd shattered my hopes and insulted me a little in the process, but we just hadn't been compatible. That was what it came down to. I just wished they'd have told me right away. That particular ex had sulked for two months before he'd finally broken up with me.

I should've dumped him after a month.

"My dad told me to suck it up once." Tenor got a faraway look in his eye. "After . . . After my last breakup felt like a long line of failures with me as the common denominator," he finished, using my description.

"Ouch."

"Nah, it wasn't quite like that. He mostly meant that I had to come to terms with the reason for the breakup, which was that she didn't like me for who I really was. He told me to own it. Own everything about me, and that's what I did."

"Your dad was a smart man." I'd never known Darin Bailey, but someone like Mae wouldn't put up with a douche.

"He was." Tenor gripped the edge of the island. "He encouraged me to wait before I built this place. To make it something I wanted versus a knee-jerk reaction to Katrina's words."

"Katrina?"

His jaw turned to stone. "My last ex. She moved away shortly after we broke up."

His tone said it all. It was her who'd convinced him he wasn't what women wanted. It was her who'd made him take himself off the market. What a damn tragedy. I hated her.

"I say it's time to spite our exes and do our totally uncool hobbies."

The corner of his mouth curled up. "No judgment."

"No judgment, Warhammer."

I ducked into the guest room and grabbed my book. I slipped the fake cover off before I left the room. I'd stopped at a bookstore and bought a sci-fi romance with something close enough to space marines. It hadn't been easy to find. I had ordered two online just in case.

By the time I returned to the main area, he was laying out a measuring mat I'd seen my dad's grandma use for sewing. He paused when he saw me, his gaze flitting over his items.

I brandished my book with the abs on the cover with one hand and waved my phone with the other. "Should I admit to how badly I want to scroll through all the cocktail recipes ever served at Copper Summit and see if we can come up with some signature specials just for the wedding?" The more I thought about the idea, the higher my excitement crept. "If Wynter goes for it. Anyway, that's my wild Saturday night. Cocktails and Orks. I'm actually stoked about it."

He let out a soft, relieved chuckle. "Talk to Wynter. I think it's a good idea, and if word spreads, I think we'd pick up more events."

Finally, he resumed what he was doing. On top of the mat, he placed a cup of water and two pieces of paper. One of the standing lamps from his room loomed at his side.

A tiny but hulking figure of a space marine sat in front of him. More were off to his side in another black plastic container. He dug out small paint bottles of black, white, and gold from the container he'd set on the chair next to him. He shook each bottle as he laid them out.

I tucked my phone in my pocket and hugged my book to my chest. "Mind if I watch for a while?"

"It'll be boring."

"Right now, it looks fascinating." I dropped into a chair at the end of the table.

"Tell you what, I'll explain my process, and after you read for a while, we'll talk about that."

"That might get awkward. My space marines have sex."

He chuckled, deep and pleasing. "Then I'm definitely holding tight to my terms."

Since I liked when he was playful and open with me, I set my book on the table. "Deal."

"All right." He adjusted the light to shine above his shoulder and onto the miniature. I picked up a paint-brush with short, narrow bristles. "There are a lot of details. I've already washed these, and I'm going to paint on a base layer. But since I thin the paint a little, it'll be about two or three coats. Then I'll paint the details. The platform is last and it has a textured paint."

"You do all the models one at a time?"

"It takes some time. I have to wait for all the layers to dry, but I enjoy the process. I'll have a video playing or an audiobook."

"What do you listen to?"

That earned me another sidelong look. "Warhammer."

I laughed. "That's cool though. You can consume it in different forms. Books, games, art."

He paused dabbing blue paint on the paper. "A lot of people would think it's a triple waste of time."

"How many of them would spend an entire Sunday watching football? Or is it Monday? Both?"

"You're asking the wrong guy." He swiped his brush across the base.

I spectated through the painting of one figurine. By the time he was done, the marine's uniform had gold embellishments and the weapons it carried were black.

I ducked down to squint at the finished product. "So much definition. Do you 3D print these?"

"Some people do. But a lot of places that host games prefer that sets are purchased through them instead of bringing homemade ones. I like to support the game shops anyway." He dug out another figure.

The longer I was around Tenor, the clearer it was how much terrible behavior I'd tolerated in my dating life. Not just in the treatment I'd accepted from my partners but with them as *people*. Tenor was thoughtful and generous.

If I watched him much longer, I'd crawl onto his lap and tell him to paint me. But he hadn't made a move on me. "I'm going to read."

He caught my hand and stroked his thumb along my skin, then let it go. Tingles spread from where he'd touched me, up my arm and down my spine.

"Remember to take notes," he said in a low voice.

The banter. Those moments he touched me like he couldn't make himself stop. I'd take all this with me after the wedding. Grinning, I sank into the corner of his couch and tackled the cocktail menus from the tasting bar I had emailed to myself. I started a new email to myself with thoughts and ideas to send to Wynter. Once I was tired of typing, I picked up my paperback. Most of my job was on a screen, and I treasured getting lost in a paperback.

Shortly after I started reading, Tenor went into the kitchen. He brought me a rocks glass with a finger of bourbon.

I smiled my thanks. "Bourbon and romance novels?"

He held up his glass. "Bourbon and Warhammer."

I grinned and took a drink. Mm. Copper Summit Gold. He was spoiling me with the best. I would not settle for less again.

I'd read through a good chunk of the book when he took my phone off the end table. Surprised but intrigued, I didn't stop him as he stood back and snapped a picture. Then he kneeled next to me and showed me the image. I looked relaxed. Happy. He gently took the book out of my hands.

"Time to live up to your end of the bargain."

"Well, there's this human woman—" My smile caught. Oh no. The story was super steamy. The love interests had gotten physical within three chapters. It hadn't even been intimacy. That was still developing. They'd just been down and dirty. How much had Tenor been joking about wanting to swap stories? "And she meets this space marine," I continued weakly. "He rescues her actually, um, by buying her from an intergalactic sex auction. Only he has to, like, actually use her as his sex slave to get them both out safely."

He arched a brow. "Naturally. And what does that entail?"

How far was he going to take this? And why was it so easy for me to push at his limits? I had to hold back. "It's not like your painting. I can't show you."

"I highly doubt that." He gently lifted the book from

my hands and paged through it. His gaze darkened and a muscle in his jaw jumped.

I knew what he was reading. I wanted to sink through the couch.

" 'Sit on my face,' " he began. " 'Put that pussy where I want it the most.' "

My heart thudded. Those words in his deep voice were so much more than what had run through my head when I read them. I was going to burn through the couch. From embarrassment or desire? Yet I didn't grab the book from him. *More, please.*

He wasn't scoffing, but I'd heard all the arguments. I could head them off before he brought up the first one. "I know, I know. It's not realistic."

He frowned at me. "How do you mean?"

"Sit on his face? He'd get smothered in real life."

"That's the point."

I opened my mouth. Shut it again. He sounded so certain. "How would you breathe?"

He held my gaze for a moment, then dropped his attention back to the page. "I believe the characters make it through. 'That's right. Come hard for me, like a good little wench.' "

"It's a pet name. Just between the two of them." I managed to sound normal. My brain was flashing back to last weekend. *Now ride your hand and pretend your thumb is my tongue, licking your clit in tight circles.*

I squashed a whimper. I was warm and achy. Needy. He was kneeling close to me and reading a sex scene. Out loud.

"That doesn't explain why you think sitting on his face is unrealistic," he said.

"Come on," I scoffed. "He'd suffocate."

"Guys are willing to take the risk."

"No, they're not." I didn't have much experience in this area, but what I did have conflicted with the book. "Guys get impatient enough when the girl's on top and taking too much time. If she's sitting on him?" I gave him a flat look. I was dying inside, but my certainty was strong. "He'd shove her off before she's even close."

Tenor's gaze narrowed. Then he deliberately slipped my bookmark off the end table and saved the spot I was at. He put the book to the side. "That most certainly should not be the case. Ever."

A nervous laugh left me and I shrank into the corner of the couch. "Sure."

"Ruby." My name gusted out of him. "If only I could show you how wrong you are."

"It'd be a bad idea." I had no clue why. It sounded like a fabulous option. He was supposed to show me what I'd been missing. Didn't that include orgasms that weren't an inconvenience?

"Yeah," he said quietly, his gaze dropping from my face to my bare legs curled under me. "A bad idea. Messing around more would muddle things."

More. Last weekend, we'd messed around. Because of me. He hadn't wanted me to feel bad, but he also wasn't looking to end his dry spell with me.

My pride wanted a little something. A tiny sign that said he might be going to bed as full of want and longing as I did, and it wasn't from the scene he'd been reading. That it was from my presence. It was from the memory of last weekend and how nice it'd been to be kissed with heat and passion. That he couldn't get over how easy it was to talk me through the fastest, hardest orgasm of my life. A sign that maybe a guy like him would seriously want to be with someone like me, and not just for sex.

I chided myself. Foolish delusions from the boring girl. He'd been more than tolerant after I'd crawled into his bed. He'd also been clear that he wasn't looking for a real girlfriend or even a fling. Not with me.

"Exactly. Can't get things confused." I stretched my legs out on the couch and my hemline rode so far up my thighs my skirt might as well be off.

I wished Tenor was the one taking it off.

Fire simmered in the yellow of his irises, and he raked his gaze down my legs all the way to my toes. Then dipped his head and seemed to gather himself before handing me the book without looking at me.

"Thank you," I said, taking it from him. The charged air between us was pulsating, but it had an undeniable awkwardness I didn't like.

He nodded, and without touching his gaze to my body, he rose. An impressive bulge pushed at his zipper. He turned and adjusted his crotch like he couldn't take one single step otherwise.

I opened my book, unable to resist prodding at the odd tension between us. "I'll continue taking notes."

All I got was a grunt and he went back to the table. I continued reading, pleased I wasn't the only one uncomfortable.

# CHAPTER TEN

Ruby

Horses grazed in the pasture by the barn closest to the house. Red and white chickens darted around on the other side by a cute shed. The shop doors were thrown open and camp chairs dotted the cement slab in front.

I was accustomed to being around the Baileys. Each one of them was essentially my boss, and after the first few months of employment, the worst of my timidity had worn off.

Today, it had roared back in full force.

Wynter pushed her pale, loose braid off her shoulder. "I'm glad you're here. I always wanted to get to know you outside of work, but I don't get to the Bozeman office like I used to. Now that I'm split between home and my office here, I don't see you much at all."

"It is nice here," I agreed. I liked my coworkers, but the Bozeman facility didn't have the hominess of the

Bourbon Canyon location. It made sense. Copper Summit was a family company, and it had all started here.

"Are you sure you don't mind working the wedding? You're a guest. I told Tenor I didn't want to dominate your time off."

"Not a problem at all." Even if Cara and I were close, I wouldn't mind. "I look forward to it, and I even have some ideas. My email is ready to send tomorrow." I didn't want to dominate her off time either.

She tapped a finger on her can of root beer, her expression curious. "Was turning the wet bar into content your idea?"

"No?" Damn. I couldn't sound more guilty. The last thing I wanted to do was overstep my place or make my boss feel like I'd outmaneuvered her. "I might've mentioned it, but it was in conversation only, when I was just rattling off ideas."

She cocked her head. "You don't do that with me."

"I . . ." I swallowed. "I want to do what I'm told."

She patted my shoulder. "I promise I'm not scary. I need to hear you rattle, and I want you to be comfortable saying, 'Wynter, listen.' " She sighed. "In fact, when Tenor pulled up the numbers, I realized I'd been remiss. Our family is tighter than ever, and it's coinciding with our numbers dropping. We're coasting and we can't afford to do that forever. So please, don't just email. Give me a call. Tell me all your ideas."

"I will, but you might regret it," I said lightly, but inside I was squealing.

"I might regret it if I don't listen."

She didn't hold my talk with Tenor against me, and

she wanted to hear more. This weekend had somehow gotten even better.

Summer approached us, a loose dress swirling around the tops of her boots. Jonah had their son in his arms and was talking to Teller by the two grills.

More than one grill. Mom had tried a small electric grill once. She'd started a fire and dumped a potted plant on it to extinguish the flames. We'd tossed the grill after that.

Summer smiled. "You get something to drink?"

I lifted the same kind of root beer Wynter was drinking. "Yes, thank you."

Tenor's presence had been requested by Lane and Cruz inside the shop and I hadn't wanted to follow like some little girl who couldn't be alone. At least with the two younger Foster brothers, I wasn't the youngest adult.

"How's it been?" she asked, care lacing her voice. "With Tenor?"

Autumn saw us and started for us. She tugged on Scarlett's arm as she passed where she stood with Tate. I didn't know Tate's wife well. She was a quiet school teacher who worked with Autumn. But being married to the eldest Bailey was close enough to having a say over my job. Nerves lit up in my stomach. I took a small sip of root beer. Too much and I'd belch in front of everyone. It'd be like burping in a job interview. I'd already gotten the social media manager job. Now I needed to sell myself as Tenor's significant other.

"Don't start with the good stuff before I can hear," Autumn said as she drew near.

"I ditched Sawyer with Gideon when I saw you all

gathering." She grinned at me, unashamed. "I won't call Junie so she can eavesdrop. We have *some* decorum."

Wynter giggled. "I was trying not to pry." She elbowed Summer. "So I'm glad you asked."

"There's nothing to say." Other than the time I got myself off in his bed. Or last night when he'd read part of a sex scene. My cheeks grew hot.

Summer snickered. "Oh, this is really going to be good." She held up a hand, looking green around the gills. "Not too graphic, please. He's our brother, and I don't want to lose my appetite."

I smiled. What would it have been like growing up in such a big family? Having so much support that everyone was in your business? I was grown and Mom stayed out of my personal life. She was there if I needed her, but she wasn't *there*.

Next week, she was going camping again with Daniel.

"We're still learning each other." That was true without giving them details, or worse, lying about how there was nothing but unwanted chemistry between me and their brother. "He's an incredibly private man."

Autumn nodded. "I couldn't believe he ventured back out into the dating world. I was so happy to see it was with you. I trust you with his heart."

Her words touched me while adding a heavy amount of longing. His heart was untouchable, and he'd set a boundary last night. The least I could do was respect it. So, yes, they could trust me with him, but also, they didn't have to worry. Tenor could enforce his own limits.

"I'll do right by him." I smiled. "I promise."

Wynter gave me an appreciative grin. "That's the thing, Ruby. We're not worried and you can't imagine how relieved that makes us. He's been so guarded since —" She pressed her lips together.

"Katrina?" I asked.

The sisters nodded.

"The fallout was devastating," Summer answered. "He took the breakup really hard."

"I don't think it was the breakup," Wynter clarified. "Not by itself. I think she said worse things about him than that asshole from high school ever did."

The other sisters' nods were solemn.

My heart went out to a young Tenor. "I've heard a little," I admitted, "and it's just awful. Both with his bully and his ex. Tenor's been the best . . . everything . . . ever. I've never felt so special." Nothing about my claim was a lie.

"When you find the right guy," Summer said, "you'll be his center."

"Yeah." The word gusted out of Autumn. Her dreamy smile dug its way into my brain.

*When you find the right guy, you'll be his center.*

Didn't that sound amazing? To be someone's first thought and priority? Someone that I could be myself with? Someone who would get over himself to have me?

Too bad my life wasn't a book.

◦◦

Tenor

"I'll be honest," Teller said, moving hot dogs to the higher rack on the grill, "I thought you would've scared yourself off from Ruby by now."

I handed him the plate of hamburger patties to put on next and checked on Ruby. She was standing with Wynter and Autumn. Were they talking about Copper Summit stuff, or about me?

"Why would you think that?" I asked more to stall him than to talk about the dark-haired woman I wanted to sidle up behind and wrap my arms around. I'd press a kiss at the nape of her neck and—

"She might actually get to know you. Can't have that," he finished sarcastically.

I hated that I knew what he meant. "She doesn't care about Warhammer."

Teller gave me a *duh* look. "No one should."

I lifted a shoulder. I should've mingled with Gideon and Myles. Or helped Tate chase after his kids with Scarlett. To be fair, Tate was probably trying to watch Scarlett's ass as much as their kids.

Jonah took a drink of his cherry lemonade. "What about Warhammer? What's wrong with it?"

"Nothing." Teller gave me a pointed look. "But his ex thought it was childish."

Jonah's forehead creased. "You could be into creepy dolls. Who cares about a game?"

"It's that it wasn't just a game," I said. "It's that I read the books, I collect the models and paint them, and I go to weekly game nights. With my units packed in nice cases. All while still living with my parents, at the time."

Jonah had known me when I was more open about my hobby. By the time I had dated Katrina, he'd become a reclusive mountain man. He didn't know any of the story.

"You sound like you're defending her," Teller said, his lip curling with disgust.

"I'm not." I appreciated his support but pretending she'd solely been in the wrong didn't help me. I had intentionally hidden that part of myself from her. She'd felt duped. "Most women aren't going to want their partner to be that invested in something else on top of the relationship and their full-time job."

"How are you balancing it now?" Teller asked.

"I paint and she reads." It had been one night and I spoke as if we'd had our routine down for years. A little spear of want went through my chest.

"Still doing the game nights?" Jonah asked.

I nodded. "Wednesday nights. That's when she works at the bar." I didn't mention that it was pure coincidence.

Jonah shrugged. "So it's that easy."

"We're only dating; we're not married." That had been Katrina's argument. *What will it be like when we're married? You sold me a lie.* You're *a lie.*

I was a lie. Then and now.

"Or . . ." Teller tossed the burgers on the grill. "Ruby's not a superficial prick who only thinks of herself and her image and she doesn't see you as another accessory."

"Katrina was a superficial prick." Didn't mean she'd been wrong. Besides, it hadn't just been her telling me I was a dud. My family had stood up for me against the asshole from school and his friends, but he'd said the same thing. I was a loser without my family backing me up. Then there'd been the girlfriends before Katrina, telling me they wanted more, they expected me to be different, and why wasn't I more like Teller or Tate.

Thoughts of all of them made me itch to be closer to my pretend girlfriend. "I'm gonna check on Ruby."

She was chatting with Wynter when I walked up. I looped my arms around her waist, glad to have an excuse to touch her. Had to make this look legit. If only it wouldn't be indecent to slide my hands down those bare legs of hers. Her flimsy skirt went past her knees, but the way it swayed with her hips was hypnotic.

She cast a surprised look over her shoulder but smiled. "Hi."

"Hi yourself," I said as if I hadn't talked to her a half hour ago.

Wynter smirked. "Is this how sappy Myles and I were?"

"You still are," I shot back.

Myles came up behind his wife and tucked her into his side. He had a lemonade in his other hand. Mama must have their little girl, Elsa. She was always in grandma heaven during these gatherings.

Myles handed the lemonade to Wynter. She took a big drink and wiped her mouth with the back of her hand. His eyes crinkled at the corners as warmth infused them. He swiped at her lower lip with his thumb.

"Exactly," I said.

Ruby giggled and hooked her hands on mine. "It's so sweet. I always wanted that."

Wynter winked. "I think you have it."

Ruby stiffened under my hands, and I commiserated. Our goal was to look legit, but moments like this felt too fucking real.

Mama came out the back door of the house with a giant bowl in one hand while holding Elsa on her hip with the other. Both Myles and I jumped to help her.

He waved me off. "I got it."

"Ten bucks says she'll give him the bowl, not the toddler," Wynter said as she watched her husband jog across the gravel stretch between the house and the shop.

"I'm not taking bets I'm going to lose," I said.

"Hey, Wynter," Ruby said, "there's one more thing on Monday I wanted to talk to you about. I'm just mentioning it so I don't forget. I don't want to bombard you with work stuff on a weekend."

Wynter waved off her words. "Technically, I brought it up first. Bombard away."

Ruby's grip on my hands tightened. "So, um, last weekend I was at Flatlanders Prohibited." She glanced back at me. "For research purposes only."

"I wanted to prove that she'd get hit on," I said because Wynter would dig for the story.

"So you took her to Flatlanders?" Wynter screwed her face up. "You could've taken her to Broken Oar. What a waste of potential Flatlanders is."

"It's not terrible." Ruby's answer was light and sweet, much like her. Flatlanders was run-down and poorly managed. "But I took some pictures, and I sent them to the bartender, Allen . . . since he gave me his number."

A low growl left me, and Wynter snickered.

"They must've made it back to the owner. She wants to pick my brain, but I want to clear it with you. I only planned to give her general tips for increasing social media engagement and help her brainstorm."

Wynter's expression turned doubtful. "She? Madison?" Her gaze lifted to mine. "You think Allen sent her the images instead of going to Scooter?"

Ruby pulled away to study each of us. "Did I do something wrong?"

"Madison is the owner's sister," I explained. "She doesn't live in town, but she's moving here. Allen might've bypassed Scooter because he wants a job and Scooter is running Flatlanders into the ground."

"Does Madison know you work for Copper Summit?" Wynter asked hesitantly.

Worry infused Ruby's eyes. "I don't know. I forgot that they don't know me." She grimaced. "They think my name is Rue."

I placed my hand on her lower back and stroked her with my thumb.

"You're free to meet with her," Wynter reassured Ruby. "But she might not want to talk with you once she learns you're on Team Bailey." Wynter winced. "That's how she'll see it."

"I can go with you," I offered. "Just in case she gets mean."

Wynter shook her head. "Madison's not mean. She's . . . defensive. Her mama and daddy hated the Baileys. Now Scooter owns the bar and hates the Baileys. Madison was a year ahead of me in school and she had nothing to do with me or my sisters."

"Maybe I do need reinforcements." Ruby leaned into me. "I'll tell her who I am first and see how she reacts. If she wants to meet, I'll be back next weekend." She glanced back at me as if asking for permission.

The idea she might skip a weekend unsettled me. "Yeah, you will," I growled.

Wynter groaned. "Yep. I can see it. Myles and I really were incorrigible."

"You still are," I replied. "*All* of you."

"Well, now you're included." Wynter squinted at the grill where Teller chatted with Lane and Cruz. "Now we just have to find someone for Teller."

"Teller doesn't want to be found." Teller could be married tomorrow if he wanted to be. There were plenty of willing tributes in town.

Wynter didn't take her eyes off our brother. "Wilna's hunting for him. I bet she'll convince him to be a bachelor."

I laughed. "No."

Ruby looked between us. "Wilna?"

"She runs the bachelor auction." Wynter propped her hands on her hips. "The fate you saved Tenor from. But I don't think Teller's going to be so lucky. I'd bet a hundred on it."

"I'm going to take that bet." I dug out my wallet and flashed Wynter a hundred.

Her face turned smug. "You're on. I'm going to ask the others if they want in."

"You guys are betting on Teller?" Ruby asked.

"I'm betting on Wilna," Wynter said. A kid called out and she twisted her head to find Myles and Elsa. "I'd better see if she's hungry." She started walking away. "Let me know how it goes with Madison," she called over her shoulder.

Ruby turned into me. "I'm glad you weren't in the bachelor auction. I never could've outbid anyone."

"I would've paid someone to bid on me for me. I'd have cashed in my retirement." I shuddered. "The deal between us benefits me too."

"Glad I could help. So how are we fake dating next weekend?"

"Let's go to Curly's."

Her smile fell. "You don't have to."

I took her hand. "I want to. Others are going to talk, and I'm not that insecure kid anymore. I have to quit acting like it."

"If you want to back out before then, I won't take it personally."

"I won't back out."

Her lips curved up. "It's a date, then." She touched the tip of her nose and winked.

# CHAPTER ELEVEN

Ruby

I spent my Friday shift at the bar waiting for Tenor to walk in and help me close. Closing time was fast approaching and he was nowhere to be seen. Teller's pickup was still in the lot, but where Tenor usually parked next to him was empty.

Two guys were at a corner table. I'd served them before. They usually talked quietly together before leaving ten minutes before close.

I washed some glassware and stocked behind the bar. Before long, everything was tidied and ready for the next day. The scrape of chairs announced the customers' departure. Just as they were walking out, the door connecting the tasting room to the lobby swung open.

Teller entered and he nodded when he saw me. "Hey. Just gonna make sure you get everything locked up okay. Tenor's helping Lane fix some hydraulics." He scratched his beard. "We're haying soon."

"Oh. Okay." Acute disappointment hung heavy on my shoulders. Tenor was busy fixing a tractor on a Friday night when his girlfriend was supposed to be arriving at his place?

I wasn't his girlfriend. Tenor wasn't Brock ignoring my arrival. But the new handkerchief dress I had bought with my tips from the last month was wasted on regulars who were all either married or not interested. Nor was I interested in them.

"Thank you," I said, regaining my composure. Even if I were Tenor's girlfriend, I wouldn't pout because he hadn't helped me close. I'd get on with what I was doing. He wasn't avoiding me. It's that we weren't really a thing. "I just need to cash out and clean that last table, then I'll be done."

"No rush. I got the table."

He grabbed the rag while I counted the small amount of cash that had come in tonight. When we were done, I sent the shift reports to Tenor and tucked the tablet away under the bar.

Would he be at his place when I got there?

As if reading my mind, Teller leaned a hand against the bar and propped his other on his hip. "Tenor said he left his door unlocked." He tapped his fingers on the countertop. "Everything okay between you two?"

Alarm flooded into my veins. Why would Teller be worried? "Did he say something?"

"He's been in his head more than usual."

I ran through the events of last weekend. The barbecue at Mae's had been fun. We'd eaten next to each other, I'd chatted more with his sisters and Mae, and then I had headed home. Like most weeks, we hadn't messaged each other. I spent Monday through Friday a single gal. Perhaps a little melancholy. I might've missed Tenor. I might also have interpreted his weekday radio silence as proof he wasn't into me.

Overall, things between us were normal for a couple who was fake dating. "I can't think of what might be bothering him. The wedding maybe? We haven't made a big splash in public yet and he hates attention."

The wedding or our nondate tomorrow night. If either was the case, we didn't have to go. That'd be the end of us, but as much as I wanted Tenor—a lot—I wanted a man who couldn't get enough of me.

"He does hate it." Teller's gaze went icy. "That jackass in school really did a number on him." He gave me a sharp look. "Did he tell you about Bobby?"

I shook my head. "No details. But he spoke a bit about what it was like for him."

"Tate and I tried to interfere. The asshole was in my grade even though he was older than me, but he was good at getting to Tenor when he was alone. Nasty kid."

"Poor Tenor," I murmured. "I'm sure he didn't fight back."

"Tenor always makes sure he's the bigger guy. It's why the breakup with Katrina was so hard on him." Teller swiped a hand down his beard. "He tried to be the best guy she could dream of. He was everything but himself."

"I doubt that." Distaste for the conversation danced on my tongue, leaving a sour tang. "Tenor is always himself. She just didn't look very hard."

Teller barked out a laugh. "It's nice to see he's gotten better taste since then. Just don't let him scare himself off. You're good for him. We can all see it."

"He's been good for me too." There'd be no scaring him off. I hadn't gotten him in the first place.

Teller didn't go for the door. "Wynter also asked some probing questions. About how Junie shouldn't be the only face of Copper Summit anymore. Asking if I'd like my picture taken."

"Oh." I couldn't decipher his tone. Was he unhappy with the idea? "Yes. I can crop out your face. Blur it or get angles that preserve your anonymity."

"No one wants to see my face."

I rolled my eyes. "I had this same talk with Tenor. People very much do want to see your face." I made a frame with my hands and he was at the center. "The whole plaid-and-bearded thing? Catnip. People who never thought to sample bourbon will be thinking about it after seeing you with a glass." I dropped my arms.

He tugged at his polo. "I'm not wearing plaid."

"You wear it enough."

His brows drew together. "I still don't see it."

"I'd *get* them to see it." Just a picture of him the way he was now would make a good post. "But like I said, I'd work in your comfort zone."

"I don't need to be targeted as the last single guy in a bourbon empire."

Some guys would be on board. Snagging women who came for tours with hearts in their eyes? Not Teller, apparently. I respected him for it. "I'd keep that in mind."

He considered me for a moment. "If you can talk the others into it, then I'll think about it."

"Are you saying that because you're sure Tenor won't agree?"

His smirk told me I had busted him. "How long have you been going out?"

"A few—" I almost said weeks, but we'd told them . . .

what again? "Months. A couple of months." I managed not to make it sound like a question.

"And I haven't seen him pop up anywhere in a photo. If he's on board, then I'll do it. How'd the meeting with Madison go?" My surprise must have been obvious because he winced. "Sorry. We're a family company, so that means we're in everyone's business."

"You should run that by Wynter for a marketing slogan."

He grinned. "Somehow, I don't think that will sell."

My brain was already in post mode, thinking of fun sayings and images I could get for it.

*A family company means we're in everyone's business.*

*We're in everyone's business and in everyone's glass.*

*Want this family in* your *business?* That could go with an image of any of them.

None of that would happen of course, and neither would helping Flatlanders Prohibited. "I texted Madison to let her know where I worked"—that my name was Ruby and not Rue—"but that I would love to help her with the general stuff. There'd be no conflict of interest. She said thanks, but no, thanks."

Teller shook his head. "She's as bad as her brother."

"She was professional about it."

"The Townsends shun Baileys and good opportunities."

The conflict seemed to go back farther than when Teller's ex had run off with Scooter. Either way, it wasn't my business.

We walked out of the bar and locked up. Teller waited for me to get into my car and drive away before he left.

The trip to Tenor's was dark, but I'd traveled the roads enough that I was comfortable.

The light in the living room was on. Excitement rose in my belly. Was he home?

Just as I parked in the empty garage, my phone dinged.

**Tenor: There's food in the fridge. Help yourself. I'm going to be late.**

I stared at the message before stuffing my disappointment down and sending back **Ok**.

I gathered my things and went inside. His place was quiet. Peaceful. Still beautiful, and with his bookshelves and his painting supplies spread across the table, it was homier than the first time I'd stayed.

My phone buzzed again. A thrill twirled in my stomach as I dumped my suitcase in the guest room and dug my phone out of my purse.

**Dad: Hey, Rubes. You around?**

**Me: Are you in Bozeman?**

**Dad: Will be. Want to meet for a match?**

I grimaced. He picked up tennis when he needed to network beyond glossing over his glory days of football, but he was still an obnoxious jock at heart. He made a casual game of tennis into a cutthroat competition. He'd taught me to play on my weekends with him, and he'd urged me to join the high school team. Torture sounded a lot like practicing after school for hours, not to mention how Dad would scream at the sidelines. I hadn't wanted to experience him getting removed from a tennis game. We still had father-daughter matches, but at least I could limit his shit talk to just us.

**Me: Sorry, I'm out of town this weekend and next. Another time?**

**Dad: Soon. I've got another meeting lined up.**
**Me: Can't wait.**

I looked around the empty cabin. On the plus side, by the time I met up with Dad, I wouldn't have to hide from him that I was seeing someone from his old hometown. This arrangement would be over by then.

Tenor

I had missed Ruby all damn week. I'd missed her last night. I was missing her this morning.

I finished at the ranch. I could hang out all day, but the other guys had everything covered. Mama had made muffins and here I was, rushing home with them.

After parking outside, I jogged to the door. The sun was bright and the birds were happy. Unlike last night when I'd entered a quiet cabin. Ruby had been asleep in the guest room.

She hadn't helped herself to my bed while I wasn't there. I'd stood in the hallway like a fucking stalker, watching her door, listening for any movement, desperate to see her after a long week of coming home to an empty house.

Fuck, I was in a bad way.

I entered the house. The place was quiet.

"Ruby?" I went to the kitchen and deposited the huckleberry muffins on the counter. Mom had also sent another dozen eggs. My stomach clenched. The breakfast sandwich I'd brought with me to do chores had long since burned off.

No answer came. I checked the garage. Her car was gone.

Dammit. I closed the door and peeked into the guest room. Her suitcase was open on the bed.

I pinched between my eyes. *Get it together.* We had a date tonight. Not a date, dammit. We were going out to eat. For show.

I could wait until she returned to see her. Was she wearing a dress or a skirt?

I'd know in a short time. All I had to do was be patient. I could paint a couple of models while waiting. Mow my lawn. Pull some weeds. Dust. There was plenty to do while waiting for her.

I reached for my phone before I could deliberate further. I typed out **Where are you?** and sent it.

I waited, rooted in place in my hallway.

**Ruby: Mountain Perks.**

I was outside and in my pickup within seconds. I flew to town, only obeying the speed limit when I hit city limits. Downtown bustled with activity on a Saturday morning. Cars lined the block around the coffee shop and the boutiques next to it. I took the first spot I could find a few blocks down.

In the coffee shop, I spotted Ruby right away. She sat at a back table, facing away from the entrance, book in hand. Her coffee mug was pushed to the side and an empty plate was at the edge of her table.

The couple who owned the hardware store passed me.

"Hey," Buddy Kenwood greeted, sticking a hand out. "How's it go—"

"Good to see you." I gave him the quickest handshake ever and continued past him.

I probably knew everyone in the place, but I didn't stop to look. My strides ate up the distance between me and Ruby until I leaned down, tipped her face up, and pressed a kiss to those lips that continued to haunt my dreams. It was for show. That was the only reason I was kissing her.

A small, surprised squeak left her, but she brought a hand to my face and ran her thumb over the scruff on my cheek.

I pulled away enough to say, "Hey."

Her lips curved up. "Hey yourself." Bewilderment filled her gaze. She closed her book and set it down. The *Pride and Prejudice* cover was firmly in place. "Is everything okay?"

The conversation around us had dwindled. Attention was likely planted right on us, but I didn't care. "Yes." Now it was.

I swiveled around and sat on the small, round metal chair across from Ruby. I glanced at the other customers. Some curious looks were cast our way. My high school tennis coach gave me a nod, his smile wide. I dipped my head in return.

I folded my hands on the tabletop. "I missed you."

She lifted her brows and looked around. Comprehension filled her eyes, along with acceptance. Damn. She thought I was doing this all for show.

I was. I had to be. I could not miss Ruby this bad when next weekend was our last time together. "You're not wearing a skirt."

She was wearing goddamn blue jeans and those fuckers might undo me worse than a dress.

"I wore a dress last night." She shrugged with the sassiest attitude I'd ever seen.

Another thing I'd missed. "What do I gotta do to get you to wear it to dinner tonight?" I leaned to the side just a little and checked out what I could see of her lower half. "Those jeans though, Goldilocks. Damn."

Her cheeks pinked. "Are they just right, Warhammer?"

A few weeks ago, I would've died in public if anyone had called me that out loud. I'd be transported back to school when I'd gotten teased for joining the board game club. Then to ten years ago at the gas station, answering questions about my secret nights away from Bourbon Canyon. Katrina had worked hard to make me sound like some creep who catfished women.

"Anything you wear is just right," I said.

Her smile turned shy and she looked down.

I reached across the table and grabbed her hand. "I mean it. It's not for"—I lifted my chin toward the main seating area—"this." I drew my hand away. I wasn't doing everything for show, but touching her was getting harder to resist.

How many times had I pictured her in the same positions I'd read about in that damn book of hers?

Every night. Multiple times.

She flicked the edges of her book and that damn fake cover. I didn't care if she wanted to conceal it in public. Just never around me. "Did you get what you needed done in town?"

"What do you mean?"

She laughed. "You surely didn't drive in for coffee with me." She pointed to the empty spot in front of me.

I hadn't made the trip for coffee. I had made it for her. When I'd come back to an empty home, I'd fled to town and right to her. That wasn't very fake boyfriend-like. "No, I gotta stop at the hardware store." Which was closed, or Buddy wouldn't be here right now since he worked most Saturdays. Hopefully she hadn't seen him. Even better if she didn't know who he was.

"I was just going to return to the house and wait for you," she said. She licked her lips like she was hesitant to say something.

"Ruby?"

She shook her head. "It's about work."

"You know I don't mind."

"You might about this. I talked to Teller last night."

Ah hell. I knew what she meant. Teller and I had read the email and pushed off the topic until the next meeting. I should've known I couldn't escape it when my weekend guest was the brainchild behind the idea. "Updating our brand?"

She grimaced. "You talked to Wynter?"

"She said we should discuss it at our next meeting, but that including more of us informally might help growth, so whoever wants to help you out should talk to you."

She nibbled her lower lip. "And you didn't talk to me." I opened my mouth to apologize, but she shook her head. "It's okay. I don't want to make anyone uncomfortable. Teller isn't hyped about it either. I just wish I could show the real heart of Copper Summit, which is all of you."

"We put our heart out there."

"You put out a polished version. People want to feel like they're getting backstage access."

I tapped her book, hidden under what she hoped was a more socially approved cover. "You wanna show off those abs?"

She looked taken aback for a moment, then she gave me a sheepish grin. "Touché." She put her hand on mine. "The thing is . . . I wouldn't press so much if I didn't think that you guys are just used to the way it is here in Bourbon Canyon, where everyone knows who you are. The town loves your legacy. Out there?" She fluttered her other hand toward the window. "Copper Summit is just some bourbon with June Bee's face on the ads, and the spirits market it getting more crowded. Being a family distillery isn't the selling point it used to be. It's pretty much the standard."

A vise squeezed tighter around my ribs. She was right. More and more niche distilleries were popping up, each with its own unique story. I wanted to help her, but I also wanted to make bourbon. I wanted to run the numbers. I didn't want to deal with the people. "Sometimes it's bad enough getting recognized in my hometown."

She tried to hide her disappointment but failed. "I'll figure something out. You do enough. So does Teller. Maybe Wynter and Autumn will let me get some content while they're creating recipes. Wynter liked my idea of letting customers name some cocktails." She patted my hand. "I'll head back now and you can finish your errands."

The subject might be dropped, but I couldn't escape the notion I'd let her down. She had a point. I just couldn't put myself out there, and I'd rather not revisit why. "Let me walk you to your car." I took her empty coffee mug and plate to the bin by the trash and followed her out.

She went to the driver's door and I propped my hand

on it. I was playing with fire, but I also couldn't pass up a valid reason to kiss her.

She tilted her face up and I leaned down. I kept the touch to a mere brush of our lips. Any more and I'd end up pinning her to the door and plundering her mouth. All in the name of putting on a show.

"See you in a bit," I said as I stepped back.

She bit her lower lip. "See you."

I stood on the sidewalk and watched her go. Now I'd have to drive around town for half an hour because I had no damn errands to run.

# CHAPTER TWELVE

Ruby

Diners packed Curly's. Every table was full. Tenor and I had been seated in the middle, close to the front. Everyone who entered would turn from the hostess booth and see us. I'd heard about Curly's seating preferences from the Baileys, but this was the first I'd witnessed it.

The mayor was sitting at the table next to us. Bourbon Canyon royalty, front and center.

The gaze of other customers burned into me. In the coffee shop, I had felt the weight of others' curiosity. Here, the load was amplified, and I didn't miss a few of the envious glances from various women.

I had gotten one of the most coveted bachelors.

As much as I wanted to gloat, I couldn't. Tenor tried to appear at ease, but his shoulders were rigid and he'd pushed his glasses up three times in the last two minutes.

This was the same man who'd given me two sweet kisses at Mountain Perks, though there'd been fewer witnesses.

"We did not have to come here tonight," I said quietly and snagged a bun. If he wanted to go, I had to get them while they were warm.

"It's just taking some getting used to." He pushed the menu to the side. He'd never cracked it open. "I get to show off the prettiest woman in here."

I laughed, but warmth packed in the places around the soft bun and maple bourbon butter in my belly. I'd put on the red handkerchief dress I'd worked in last night and paired it with ballet flats. I was extra short compared to Tenor, but his hot look had said he could gobble me in one bite.

Again, he could, but he wouldn't.

A woman walked by who was probably between my age and Tenor's. She had long dark hair hanging down her back in a braid and shrewd eyes. Her gaze caught on Tenor, then she glanced at me and did a double take.

She stopped next to me. "Are you Ruby?"

Surprised, I nodded.

She didn't smile. "Madison Townsend."

"Oh. Nice to meet you!" I held out a hand.

A line formed between her brows, but she eventually shook my hand. Her grip was firm, no-nonsense.

"I'm really sorry about any miscommunication," I said. "I'm happy to talk to you if you change your mind."

"It's not my mind that would have to change." Her gaze softened only slightly. "You might want to steer clear of Flatlanders though. Scott thinks you're a spy."

A spy? Shock heated the back of my neck. "I'm sorry."

She waved me off. "I just don't want trouble, and you're clearly with the Baileys."

"Just one Bailey," Tenor said evenly.

"Of course." Madison's smile was saccharine sweet. "We all know Teller doesn't stick with one woman for long."

"Maybe it's because Scooter will try to marry her," he said without missing a beat.

Red infused Madison's cheeks. "Both of them lost with that one." She whisked herself away, heading to the back of the restaurant.

"I hate to say she's right," Tenor said.

"What was that about?"

"Scooter married Teller's ex, but they weren't exes when Scooter started sleeping with her. Madison was the one who told Teller, and from the way he tells it, she enjoyed breaking the news."

Ouch. "That doesn't help the bad blood." I thought more about what Madison had said. "Is Teller a player?" I shook my head. "Sorry. It's none of my business."

I hadn't seen that side of Teller. There were other single women who worked at Copper Summit, but Teller and Tenor—until me—were nothing but professional around them.

"No. He's decisive about what he does and doesn't want, and he won't make any promises. He also doesn't date much." Tenor shrugged. "It's hard to date a lot in a small town. Not many options."

Or in Tenor's case, he didn't want to risk getting shamed for his interests again. I would not be doing that. Everything about Tenor was interesting. "Do you have other games you play? I don't think I could get into

Warhammer, but is there anything else? Cards? Board games?"

His expression tightened. "I joined the board game club in middle school."

"That's cool. What was your favorite?"

He stared at me.

Suddenly nervous, I took a drink of my water. Had I said something wrong?

"I got a lot of shit for being in the board game club," he admitted.

I wrinkled my nose. "People find anything to step on to make themselves feel better."

He relaxed. "Trivia games were my favorite. And Jenga. Now I have a closetful."

I smiled. "Only a closet?" His Warhammer collection spilled beyond an entire room.

He chuckled. "I might have to add on just for them. Tate's oldest, Chance, comes to play. He'll hang out with me, Lane, and Cruz sometimes, so he's not always lumped in with the younger kids."

"Let's play some tonight."

He pushed his glasses up. "You want our date to be Curly's and a board game?"

"Sounds fun."

His expression turned calculating. "I think we should add some stakes."

•  •  •

Tenor

I placed a green chip on the Sequence board. "That's five in a row. Take your shirt off."

Ruby blinked and pursed her red lips. "You did not—" My diagonal line of green chips couldn't be denied. A scandalized gasp left her. "Another joker? You are too damn lucky!" She'd already lost her pants in the last game—after having dressed in her pajama top and bottoms when I'd suggested the stakes.

She closed her eyes and sucked in a breath. Still squeezing her eyelids shut, she ripped her shirt off. I drank her in. A pale-yellow lace bra cupped her creamy tits. She peeled her eyes open.

"Now that's incentive to win a game." I discreetly adjusted myself. How easy would it be to haul her to the back bedroom? If I asked, would she get herself off again? Would she let me watch?

I shouldn't have tossed down the wager, but a small part of me feared she'd be bored by a dinner-and-board-game date night. Another part of me was just a selfish guy with a sexy woman under his roof.

Her full tits jiggled with a shiver.

"Cold?" I asked. I'd bundle her in one of my sweaters if need be.

"*Exposed*." She scowled at me, but her lips twitched into a smile. "I'm fine, but we should try another game." She got up, her hips swaying in matching underwear. She tugged at the hem. "I can't believe you talked me into this, but it'll definitely make us seem more familiar with each other next weekend."

That goddamn wedding.

The date was bearing down on me. Did Ruby feel the same sense of impending loss?

Perhaps she wanted to return to weekends in her

own home. She probably missed her friends. She might even want to get a real boyfriend.

The idea made me feral. I nearly rose to haul her to my bedroom.

She went to the door that would've been the pantry for someone whose mama didn't supply him with meals. I had a few staples tucked in the corner if I ever got stranded, but the rest of the shelves were filled with games.

I had to get a hold of myself, or a flirtatious game of strip board games would derail all my honorable intentions.

"Oh my god, I haven't played Battleship in forever." She withdrew the box and turned. Her bottom lip was pinched between her teeth and delight danced in her eyes. "That was the thing about being an only kid. I didn't have enough friends to play games with."

She sat and did a little wiggle when she opened the box. Her smile never left her face as she took out the game units. She was really enjoying this. Pleased, I placed my ships.

When I'd dated in my early twenties, I'd felt like I had to do backflips to entertain the women I went out with, and Bobby's taunts had rung through my head the entire time. Didn't help that he'd been proved right. No one but my family would like me. I was too sloppy, too big, too clumsy, too slow, too whatever.

"Losers go first." She grinned wickedly. "B-seven."

Grateful to get yanked out of the past, I shoved my hair off my forehead and put a red peg in my destroyer. "Hit."

She clapped and giggled, her delight a show just for me. We continued to play.

Ruby Casteel was amazing. As she took down my destroyer, my admiration grew. I was into her. That sweet smile. Her body. The way she blushed.

I flipped my unit around. "You sank my battleship. Shirt or pants?"

"Hmm . . ." She rubbed her chin and eyed me. "I'll never pass up you without your shirt."

I used to hate taking my shirt off in public. Still did. Until that growth spurt, I had avoided it. My tennis teammates had wanted to practice on weekends. All of them would go shirtless but me. Girls I'd dated had made me self-conscious with the comparison to my brothers. Katrina had sent me information on gym memberships, claiming my morning runs weren't enough and we could work out together.

I stripped off my shirt. I didn't run anymore. Nor had I ever enjoyed the gym. Without a partner's opinion to worry about, I hadn't questioned my decision. But the look in Ruby's eyes was nothing but appreciation.

She did that little wiggle in her chair that almost had me surging over the table to drag her onto it for my own personal dessert. "Do I try my luck at more Battleship or . . ." She rose and went to the game closet. "Exploding Kittens? What's that?"

"It's a card game. Chance loves it, but it's better with more players."

She continued to stand in the opening. I continued to eye her ass. "I feel like you'd decimate me at Scrabble."

"Especially when you can't use the slang you young'uns are used to."

She laughed, tossing her hair back. "No wonder Lane calls you old man."

A dark cloud passed over my good mood. "It's exactly why. This whole night is why." She turned and I waved my hand over the table. "I don't go out unless it's with my family, and I love game nights. I'm not exciting. It's not because of my age."

"You're my kind of excitement. What does that make me?"

"Special." Her eyes took on a shimmer, and I dropped my gaze. "Don't ever doubt that."

She abandoned the board games and took the chair next to me. "You know why I love my job?"

"Because you're good at it."

Her expression remained solemn. "It's because I never fit in. I can follow the trends, but they just don't look right on me. I can speak the lingo, but it's always just a little off. Online, though? It's like when people claim they can't read tone. I can do the trends, I can talk the talk, but *I'm* not the product. My posts land like they should. My content resonates with people, whereas I never did." She folded her hands on her bare legs. "And when something doesn't hit like it should or people leave mean comments, I don't take it personally. Not like when Brock broke up with me because I was *boring* and *predictable*."

I twisted toward her and took her hands in mine. Our skin was touching. Her legs were under my grip. "If he was bored with you, then I think he fell into the uneventful mind category."

Some of the sadness left her face. "Bet he never played strip board games."

"Bet he'd lose. Just like you're going to."

Her eyes went wide. "I will not lose." She squeezed my hands and winced. "How far down are we stripping?"

I raked my gaze over her half-nude body. "I have to win two more games."

She laughed and pushed at my hands. "I'm done. I can't. You're too lucky, and I'll be naked. I don't think I can keep pretending to be nonchalant. I have no shirt and no pants on around you. I'm very much chalant."

I tucked a wild curl behind her ear. "Go to bed, Ruby, before I decide to quit being a good guy."

"You could never be the bad guy." She didn't move for a beat, then turned and left.

I didn't have to be a prick to let her down. If there was ever a woman I didn't want to disappoint, it was her. Good thing the wedding was next weekend, or I'd keep figuring out ways to get her naked. The lines were blurring and I'd learned that on the other side was failure and heartbreak. I didn't want that for either of us.

So next weekend, once we put on a good show at the reception, I'd make sure Ruby got in her car and drove off. And it wouldn't be in the direction of my home.

# CHAPTER THIRTEEN

Ruby

People milled on the lawn of the Bourbon Canyon nine-hole golf course. Women in colorful dresses dotted the crowd, along with men in slacks and sport coats, all acceptable attire for the garden wedding.

I tugged on the bodice of my pale-blue dress. The bottom of the skirt brushed my ankles, and large white lilies decorated the fabric. I would've gone with a solid color, but with my luck, I would've shown up in a dress too similar to the bridesmaids'. Cara was likely the type of bride to kick me out for the grievance. As much as I didn't care for her, I wasn't interested in ruining her wedding. I hadn't needed to worry.

The four bridesmaids, two of them from high school who continued to act like I was invisible, wore tasteful, soft-yellow gowns, and the groomsmen, most of whom I had met while dating Brock, were in trendy blue suits.

As far as classiness went, the wedding hit all the right notes. The ceremony had been short and sweet. Cara had grinned at Brock, and she'd had to wipe her mouth after their first kiss as man and wife.

I took a sip of my blackberry bourbon. Jenna, the girl working the wet bar, was fairly new at Bourbon Canyon. She took a few shifts at the bar each week. Tenor and I had stopped to chat with her as soon as we'd arrived. I'd taken several pictures of the setup and her preparing drinks. Then I'd done a ton of snapshots of my cocktail.

The only subject I really wanted to photograph was Tenor. He was checking on Jenna again. Teller was running stock in the background, and he'd been so stealthy I'd almost missed him. I took at least ten photos of each of them.

Tenor nodded and started for me. I inhaled a shaky breath. The nerves in my stomach took flight. The real him was much more potent without a camera lens between us. He wore a pair of black cowboy boots with his charcoal-gray slacks. Once again, he wore a shirt a size too big, but it worked for him. The top button was undone to keep the look casual enough for a golf course wedding and his gray sport coat kept his shirt from gathering around his waist. He'd gotten his hair trimmed and he kept it combed off his head.

He adjusted his glasses as he reached me. He wasn't fading into the background today, not like he ever could. He cut a path toward me and heads turned. Most—but not all—the guests were from out of town. I recognized a few other classmates and they chose to pretend I didn't exist, but they couldn't miss the tall, handsome man who was *fine* in a casual suit.

"I got you another drink," he said, handing me a highball glass. "But there's a kicker."

"Oh?"

"I want to get a picture of you with it."

I almost laughed him off, but he was holding his phone like he was ready to shoot. "The contract said wet bar and employees only."

"Exactly." He took a few pics.

"Wait!" Had my mouth been hanging open? Did I look like Snow White had gotten into the evil queen's liquor stash?

"Payback. I saw you taking your opening." He pocketed the phone.

"I promise I won't post anything with you two." But on the off chance he and Teller would change their mind, I was ready. "How's Jenna?"

He tipped his head down. "Hanging in there. Apparently to keep from being a bridezilla, Cara assigned the job to her mom. Jenna got interrogated before the reception started about why there were no other options than bourbon."

The wet bar was a hit and Cara's mom could suck a lemon wedge. Teller had stocked plenty. "Good thing we told Jenna where to find a copy of the contract the new son-in-law signed. In person."

A satisfied glint entered his eye. "Came in handy. Mom of the bride turned beet red, but Jenna made sure to gush about how thoughtful it was Teller and I had included different signature mocktails to be served too. Then she said she couldn't wait to serve the drink Cara named."

"Jenna's a good one."

His gaze stroked over my face. "We hire amazing people."

"I have to admit, I like the name Cara came up with for the blackberry fizz." Instead of simple syrup, Wynter had used maple syrup. It was like a pancake in a glass, which was what Cara had named it.

"That was a good idea." Tenor put his hand on the small of my back, a move that never failed to anchor me and make me feel treasured. "Letting brides name a mocktail."

"And those brides feel like they got a backstage pass." I nudged him. "I promised you I'd keep you out of it."

"So then what are the pictures for?"

"My spank bank."

He sputtered and coughed. I handed him my glass for a drink. His expression promised retribution when he took a sip, but he was smiling when he set the glass down on the closest table.

A guitar plucking came over the speakers as the band got everyone's attention. With his hand still on me, Tenor and I faced the stage set up on the patio behind the clubhouse.

Fairy lights and yellow tulle decorated the pergola. Cara's laugh rang over the crowd. Brock was standing with his groomsmen, his gaze on me and Tenor. I grinned and lifted my drink in congratulations. His returning smile was tight.

I took my attention off him, feeling nothing but relief that I wasn't the one in the wedding dress saying yes to him.

Cara marched up to him, hooked her arm through his, and dragged him to the three-tier cake.

Tenor slipped his hand in mine and we gathered to watch the happy couple cut their slice of cake. As Cara adjusted Brock's hold on the knife, her "silly goose" rose over the notes from the band queuing up. Lines of tension ran along his jaw as his new wife corrected him in front of the crowd.

I almost—almost—felt sorry for him. He hadn't shown me what a good boyfriend was like, but I had been a good girlfriend. Was I the most exciting? No. The sexiest? Well, Tenor made me feel that way, but to Brock, I hadn't been. Yet I'd been a considerate, caring partner. I had asked about his day. I had brought him meals when he was sick, and I had never demeaned him in front of his friends or family. I had cared for him.

*Have your cake and eat it too, Brock.*

He'd wanted more, and he'd made me feel like less when it hadn't been my fault.

My time with Tenor had shown me that. Tenor had said he'd show me I wasn't the problem in my relationships. He had, and we weren't even dating for real.

Brock and Cara each balanced a small square of white cake with raspberry swirls in their hands. Cara lifted her piece to his mouth—but he smashed his chunk into hers. I wasn't the only one to gasp. Tenor gave his head a small shake and squeezed my hand.

A scandalized squeal shot from the bride and she smudged her cake across the groom's face. The couple might be laughing now, but their eyes shot fire.

"I've never been so glad to have been dumped," I murmured.

"I was thinking the same," Tenor replied quietly. "She reminds me of my ex."

"You wouldn't have rammed your piece of cake into your new wife's face."

"Not even if I was begged to." He leaned down to whisper in my ear. "I would, however, feed her each bite so slowly, so carefully, so sensually the crowd would have to look away."

My breath caught and intense jealousy fired in my stomach. Who was the lucky bride and what lake could I throw her in? "I'm not sure I'd want to see Crock do that either."

His chuckle was low, and I grinned. I leaned into him, letting the warmth of the bourbon fill me as the evening cooled off a few degrees.

After the sweet mess was cleaned up and the couple returned to mingle, the band started. Cara, with a freshly washed face and damp stains on her dress, dragged Brock to the middle of the dance floor.

I had to give it to her. Other than the cake fiasco, she could put on a good party. Too bad she and Brock would be permanent residents of Bourbon Canyon once their honeymoon was over. The bones of their new house overlooked the ninth hole. How often would I have to see them? I wasn't pining over my ex, and I was no longer intimidated by her, but I'd rather have this little town be my sanctuary.

When the bride and groom's first dance was over, all the guests were welcome to join them on the dance floor. Tenor twined his fingers through mine and lifted the glass from my other hand. He set it on a nearby table, then led me toward the dancing couples.

"I—I don't dance." My wedge shoes made it easier to navigate the grass until we hit the hard platform of the dance floor, but they wouldn't help me find some rhythm. I had two left feet. In wedge heels.

"You don't have to." He twirled me into him. "Just follow me."

I draped an arm around his big shoulder and hung on while he coaxed me through some steps. Eventually, I caught the pattern and hugged closer to him. "You're good at everything."

"Don't ask me to line dance. I'll be on my ass in seconds."

I giggled just as a couple bumped into us.

Cara's crystal blue eyes pinned me. "Ohmigod, you made it." She peeled away from Brock and yanked me away from Tenor. A cloud of perfume smothered me as she tossed her arms around my neck. "So glad you could join us. But then you had to since you're also working, right?" The insecurity was a surprise. She was the bride. This was her day. Why worry about my reasons for attending? She'd made it clear I wasn't important in her life.

"Uh, congrats again." I pried myself away from her.

She caught my wrist. "You and I should catch up after Brockie and I get back from Jamaica. I don't know anyone in town."

"Sure." She most likely wanted to use me to get clients. We had nothing else in common and no other reason to hang out. "I'll be around Wednesday and Friday nights at Copper Summit."

Tenor curled an arm around me and pulled me back toward him. "Then I tend to dominate her weekends."

Oh. Yes. I had a boyfriend I was in Bourbon Canyon for. That was, until people figured out Tenor and I were no longer dating.

How would that go?

Did we make an announcement? Tell people one by one? Or did we just do our own thing and let others wonder?

I preferred the latter option. Others could privately wonder what I'd done to scare Tenor Bailey away.

"We'd better let you keep dancing," Tenor said. "Don't want to take away from your first night as a husband and wife. Congratulations. Beautiful wedding." He spun me away.

I didn't bother to look at Cara or Brock. I rested my head on his chest as he swayed me to a slow song. "That was the smoothest exit I've ever witnessed."

"You don't owe her a second of your time."

"She hasn't been *bad*."

"But she doesn't make you feel good."

True. Cara wanted to rekindle a friendship that she'd killed off. She would no doubt agree with Brock about my work and my romance novels. I was dull. Except with Tenor, when that was okay.

I smiled and soaked up his heat as he led me around the dance floor. Over the next two hours, we danced, checked in with Jenna, tracked down Teller, and laughed when some single women from town spotted Teller and tried to drag him onto the dance floor. Tenor didn't leave my side.

Once the crowd started thinning, my happiness dimmed. This was it. The end of my month with Tenor Bailey. It was over. I was back to being fully single. For real.

He led me along the sidewalk around the clubhouse to the parking lot.

"I can't believe that's over," I said to distract myself.

No more weekends with Tenor. No more hanging out casually with his wonderful family. No more quiet nights in his cabin in the middle of nowhere.

When Cara had first invited me and I'd roped Tenor into my lie, I'd thought I'd wither away from embarrassment each day until the reception, which would be the final nail in the sarcophagus of my personal life. Instead, I'd had a wonderful time with my fake boyfriend.

The stars overhead twinkled brightly behind wisps of clouds. I tipped my head back to admire them and sighed. Tenor would be gone in the morning when I woke up and drove out of his personal life. He'd return to being one of my bosses. Only I'd know how firm his lips were when he kissed me. How coaxing his tongue could be. What he looked like in nothing but boxer briefs.

He'd know what I sounded like when I came next to him in his bed.

Totally normal working situation.

"What if it wasn't quite over yet?" he asked.

My hopes surged. *This is it!* screamed somewhere in my brain. He wanted to date me for real. The month with me had only shown him that he was ready to see someone again, and I was that someone.

I really liked him.

I wanted to find out where kisses like his could lead. I clutched my hands in front of myself. "What are you thinking?"

Tenor yanked the passenger door open. "Since you aren't driving home tonight, I have a stop planned."

That didn't sound like *I can't live without you, Ruby. You're my Goldilocks. Just the right woman for me.* But I'd go wherever Tenor took me.

"Okay. Show me what you've got, Warhammer."

## Tenor

I drove toward my place but turned off on a rutted path between the trees. They were thinner on this side of the road as the foothills rose and dipped across the land. The trail didn't quite extend to a creek that was mostly dry after the spring runoff.

When I reached a small clearing, I swung the pickup around. The box of the truck faced the best part of the view. During the day, it was breathtaking in a simple way. A slice of Montana that didn't make it onto the post-cards but was stunning all the same with its simplicity. Trees and rolling hills led to the mountains. Farther to the north was the back side of a popular ski resort, but here it was quiet. Peaceful.

Perfect for my last few moments alone with Ruby. When we returned to the cabin, she'd retreat to her room. I'd go to mine with nothing but memories of how that dress of hers swirled around her hips. How good she felt in my arms. The way she clung to me.

Ruby Casteel was a vixen who had no idea of her sex appeal. Had her douchebag ex been too wrapped up in himself to see it?

At least it hadn't been Ruby getting her face plas-tered with cake after her vows. It hadn't been her eyes filled with disappointment and betrayal. Cara must've told that dick she didn't want a cakey mess on her big day and he'd ignored her.

The highlight of the night was that it hadn't been Ruby in that fitted wedding dress, promising herself to someone forever. The relief cooling me all night was startling. Ruby wasn't off the market.

In the morning, she'd be fully on the market. Back in the dating pool. She would return to Bozeman and our paths would only intertwine when it was about work.

Fuck.

"I've never been this far out of town," she said, peering out the window at the darkness beyond. "The sky is so vivid."

"The light pollution from the ranch doesn't reach this far, and the clouds are clearing off."

Her eyes shone in the dash lights. "Are we stargazing?"

The genuine excitement in her voice amplified my own. "Yeah. You said you never get a chance to."

"No." A line pinched in her forehead. "You remembered."

I remembered everything about her. She liked fruity bourbon cocktails, no bitters—she frowned ever so slightly whenever she had to use bitters to make a drink. She preferred her books smutty and her reading private. She didn't think she could dance, but she trusted the right man to lead her. When it came to food, she loved anything homemade, but not by her. And when she slept, fully relaxed after a climax, the world could disintegrate around her and she wouldn't wake up.

I liked to study, and Ruby was my favorite subject.

She opened the door and hopped out, breaking my reflection.

Ruby was special, but I wasn't the guy for her.

Except she seemed to like me. Appreciation filled

her eyes when she checked me out. Her grin and excitement were real when we were together. And she got along with my family.

Why couldn't it work?

Right, every breakup ever. In the beginning, I'd set out to prove to her that she hadn't been the issue. When she attracted men who would trip over themselves to be with her, she'd see I wasn't a catch. An older bachelor with board games in his pantry and a cabin built for one wasn't a catch. The orgasms wouldn't be worth it.

I climbed out in the dark, cool air.

"The Milky Way just opens up above you." Awe filled her voice.

I had put it there.

From the back seat, I dug out a pad and some blankets, along with a small bin I'd stashed before we'd left for the wedding.

I juggled everything in one arm and dropped the tailgate. The moon was almost full, giving me enough light now to see a shadowed Ruby and her curious expression.

"You came prepared," she said.

I spread out the foam pad I used for camping. Teller and I used to go more often. Then I flipped a blanket over it. "I didn't think we would stay at the wedding that long and I didn't want you to be let down by a boring night."

"I'm certain no night with you could be boring."

"Exhibit *A*: painting tiny models."

She laughed. "You underestimate how much I love to read for hours on a comfy couch."

I almost believed her.

"I'm glad I went to the wedding. That feels weird to say." She leaned against the edge of the tailgate as I finished arranging the pad and blanket. "I got some closure I didn't know I was looking for—from Crock as a whole. I don't want anything to do with either of them and I have nothing to prove. Whatever they made me feel, it's about them. Therefore, it means nothing. Yet, at the same time, it is because of Crock that I'm able to reach beyond the standard brand of Copper Summit. And because of you."

"It wasn't me. I just nudged the ball, so it was easier for you to get it rolling." Would I feel the same if I went to Katrina's wedding? Maybe. The urge to prove myself was still strong, and I'd sworn to leave it all behind. And if I had to see my childhood nightmare celebrate the beginnings of a happy life? If I had to cater to him in any way? No fucking chance. That guy had been a menace as a kid and as an adult. The only closure I could imagine was hearing he'd gone to jail for being an insufferable asshole.

Ruby was a better human than me.

"Want some wine?" I pulled the bottle out of the small cooler.

She hopped up on the tailgate to sit with her legs dangling down. "You brought wine?"

"Rhubarb wine. It's from a winery in Miles City."

"You go out of your way to buy Montana-made products, don't you?"

"The people and businesses in the state have been good to us. I want to give back." I used the corkscrew I had packed and opened the bottle. "The glasses are plastic," I said as I poured and handed her a cup. "Didn't want broken glass ruining our date. Our last fake date," I amended before I could fool myself.

"Last fake date," she echoed and held up her cup. We

clicked them together for a dull cheers and exchanged smiles.

Fuck, I wanted this to be real. If it was, I'd down this wine and wait until she finished hers. Then I'd tip her backward and crawl on top of her, spreading those lush thighs of hers wide. I'd keep the dress on but slide it up her body until she was bared to me.

Lust kindled hot in my gut. I gulped half my wine.

The appreciative noise she made when she took a drink didn't help my dirty thoughts. "You think of everything."

It was one of my greatest faults. *Too much thought, not enough sincerity.* Wasn't that what I'd been told before? I'd lost track of which woman had said that.

I climbed next to Ruby and we sat side by side, our heads tipped back to look at the stars.

"I was wondering how we do this," she said quietly. "How are we going to fake break up?"

Goddamn fake breakup. "You can tell everyone whatever you want."

She let out a delicate snort. "Why yes, we're no longer seeing each other. He was a perfect gentleman, a fabulous kisser, and he could dance like a dream. But!" She clicked her tongue. "He can't line dance, so I kicked him to the curb."

I chuckled. "That'll work."

"I'm not throwing you under the bus," she said in a serious tone. "You've been nothing but amazing."

That hadn't mattered before. "We just grew apart. You can blame the age difference or the fact that I'm your boss. You can let people assume whatever they want to." Anyone in Bourbon Canyon who'd been around during that time with Katrina would realize I was the problem.

"Okay," she almost whispered.

"You can still stay at Mama's on Friday nights."

She bumped my arm. "I promise I'll be all right."

She would be, but that also meant she wouldn't be at my place. "If the weather gets bad, keep her in mind."

"Sure."

I recognized her stubborn tone. "I'll pick you up and dump you on Mama's doorstep if you think you're driving in stormy weather."

Her laughter rang through the night. "Okay, okay. I promise." She gently kicked her legs. "I don't work at the bar for a week and a half."

Dismay filled me. Shit. The Fourth of July was this week. We only kept the bar open as a tasting room for the tourists who flowed through the area and came for tours and gift shop purchases during the holiday. The cocktail bar would be closed at night, then reopen the week after the Fourth to give the temporary employees plenty of time off.

"What are you going to do for the Fourth?" I asked.

"Ummm . . . soak up the AC and read. You?"

"I help with the parade. Tate does a float every year for Bailey Beef, and Teller and I arrange one for Copper Summit. Cruz and Lane are coming back and they ride horses behind the ranch float."

"That sounds fun."

"You should come down." What was I doing? This was our last night. A clean break. "We can pretend a few more days. Unless you're going to hang out with your mom."

She blinked at me in the dark. "Even when my mom

is in town and not off frolicking in some national park somewhere, we don't do Fourth of July holidays. She always worked for holiday pay and either got a sitter or sent me to my dad. He never took me to the parade. Dad doesn't have the patience for crowds of people."

"Then come down. Hang out. You can get some pictures and we can pretend for another day."

She smiled and I swear the goddamn stars twinkled brighter.

# CHAPTER FOURTEEN

Ruby

I perched on a camp chair beside Tenor. His frame was folded into a red chair, and he had his elbows on his knees. Next to him was Summer's husband, Jonah. On my other side was Mae. Gideon and Myles were beside her. Like Tenor, the guys all wore boots, jeans, and a simple T-shirt. It was like I'd gotten plunked in the middle of a hot-country-boy photo shoot.

I wore another skirt. I wasn't working the bar, but I couldn't help myself. I got a few more days to pretend Tenor was my boyfriend. This was more of a fun day with a friend. Tenor had felt bad when he'd learned I was alone for the holiday. That was all.

Tate's two younger kids were riding on the Bailey Beef float with his wife. Gideon had a ball cap pulled down low and he held Sawyer, their baby girl. Autumn rushed down the sidewalk and took the chair he'd packed for her and set up beside him. She beamed at her husband and kid. My heart wrenched. She looked so happy, so content. And the sizzling burn in Gideon's eyes when he looked at his wife was straight out of one of my romance novels.

Then there was Myles. He was as smitten with his daughter and baby boy as he was with his wife. Wynter had been behind Autumn, but she didn't sit in the empty chair next to Myles. She perched on his lap next to her daughter while holding a swaddled Devon. Myles wrapped a possessive arm around her hip while still clutching Elsa.

Tenor clapped his hands at Elliot. The boy reached across Jonah for his uncle. Tenor snapped him up and set him on his thigh. Elliot played with his hat, his round face full of concentration.

I was toast.

Wanting Tenor when he was a single man who was dedicated to his family was one thing. Starting to wonder what it'd be like to do more with him—like get married and have a family—was a dangerous road to go down.

He'd built his house to accommodate a bachelor. Not a family.

I wanted Tenor, but wanting everything with him, when he'd shown no signs of desiring any of that in return, only proved I wasn't fit to keep pretending. I'd have fun today. Then I'd have to let reality bitch-slap me in the face tomorrow.

My phone started buzzing. I checked the screen. Mom.

There was the reality I needed. I was my own worst enemy at getting strung along. Even my parents had other people they wanted to hang out with.

The parade was set to begin in ten minutes. "Excuse me." I rose. Tenor gave me a look that asked if everything was okay. I waved my phone. "Mom's calling."

He nodded as his nephew pried his ball cap sideways.

"Hi, Mom," I answered as I scurried to the mouth of an alley that went behind the coffee shop. All the floats and emergency vehicles were lined up and waiting for the go-ahead a little over a block away.

"Hey, Ruby. How's it going?"

"Good. I'm in Bourbon Canyon."

"Oh." She sounded surprised. "Is it getting serious with this guy?"

"No, but he knew I was alone for the holiday." I hadn't intended to point that out to Mom. She'd lived her life tethered to me, and I was an adult now.

"You need friends. And *not* Cara."

I chuckled. "She's on her honeymoon and I doubt she'll be inviting me to house parties anytime soon." Leave it to Mom to hit on the crux of my issues. I was lonely. I'd never had a big network. I needed friends.

I peeked out at the line of Baileys waiting for the parade to start. The other members of the family would wave to us as they coasted by in their trucks with the floats or from horseback. My empty chair waited between Tenor and Mae.

For once, I wasn't so alone.

"Are you home?" I could get together with her tomorrow since I was leaving after the parade.

Unless Tenor asked me to stay longer.

"Actually, no. Daniel and I want to tackle the Pacific Crest Trail."

"Oh, wow. Isn't that the one from that movie?"

"Yes." Mom's voice pitched up. "It's going to be epic.

Just me and Daniel. If we come out of this still talking, it's going to be amazing."

Since Mom usually went on long trips just to shake a partner, it would be amazing. I wouldn't worry about rushing home, then. "Well, be safe."

"Did your dad get ahold of you?"

"Yeah. He wants to meet for some tennis."

"He called me too, and I told him you're seeing someone."

I grimaced. "How'd he take it?"

"A little upset, but I didn't give him any details. Told him it was new and you weren't talking about much. I didn't even tell him you're spending a lot of time in Bourbon Canyon."

"Thank you." Dad was hard on the guys I dated. He said he knew what he'd been like and didn't trust them with his daughter.

When I'd started dating my first boyfriend in college, Dad had somehow known about the guy's juvenile record. He acted like I'd been writing the guy in prison and jumped him as soon as he got released. Before he'd met Brock, Dad had told me Brock's parents were in financial trouble with their company and I'd better not marry him. The first time I'd gone out with Brock after a "break," Dad had asked if I wanted him to slash Brock's tires.

Sometimes, he could be a really good dad. Sometimes.

"He's trying to recruit me for a doubles game," Mom said. "Wants to meet your new man."

Crap. Mom tempered Dad. He was on his best behavior around her. But there was no new man. "He wants to smear my new man's face all over the tennis court." I let out a long breath. How did I work around this? I needed to start laying the groundwork. If all else failed, I'd tell Mom the real story and she could help me fend off Dad. "If you're going to be along, then I'll ask Tenor if he's up for it, but he's pretty busy."

So busy, and then it'd be too late. We'd have broken up. I'd make sure to sound regretful when I broke the news to my parents.

"Daniel and I won't be back until the end of the month. Any time after that."

I'd have plenty of time to come up with an innocuous reason why we hadn't worked out. Dad might still demand to know who my guy had been, but I'd deal with that later. "Okay."

"Sounds good, peanut. Happy Fourth!"

I slipped out of the alley. The beginning of the parade was approaching my group.

My group.

I loved hearing from Mom, but today, her call was a reminder that while she loved me, I wasn't who she wanted to hang out with. Not unless I got a pair of hiking shoes and could keep up with her. I had tried once. I'd sworn I had developed asthma and couldn't finish without an inhaler. Then I'd been convinced I'd had altitude sickness. It was why I was never invited now.

I tucked my phone away, glad not to be home alone while Mom and her boyfriend of the month ran off. Drums from the high school's band filled the air. I stayed standing with everyone else until the flag passed, then I sat.

"How's your mom?" Tenor asked. Elliot was back on Jonah's lap and snoozing through the band.

"Planning an even bigger hiking trip."

His mouth quirked. "Living the dream, huh?"

"Now that she's able to." I waved to Summer from where she was perched on the Copper Summit float by a set of mini silver stills. Copper-colored fringe lined the trailer bed. Jenna tossed out special gummy candies that looked like tiny bottles of bourbon. Teller drove the pickup, lifting his hand every few feet to wave.

I snapped photos of the float, the candy, and the people. I caught Teller in a wave, Jenna midthrow, and Summer among the stills. With the movement, I was grateful I had a phone. Wynter and I had discussed always using a phone instead of calling on my rudimentary photography skills. Polished authenticity. I hoped I could use some of these to show how amazing the brand was, even with some of the shine.

In fact, I preferred it without the gloss. The Bailey family and their employees were pretty damn spectacular all on their own. They were the reason for the high-quality product.

The Bailey Beef float rolled past us. The trailer had a giant brown cow on the back. Square straw bales lined the edges. Tate's kids, Brinley and Darin, waved from a bale cove and Scarlett tossed candy. Tate gave his mom a little salute from the driver's seat.

As I took more pictures, a wave of wistfulness crashed over me. The Baileys were such a big family, yet they spent so much time together. They weren't just related, they were friends.

Once, after Mom had married Bill, I'd asked her when she was having more kids. She'd guffawed. *I already gave up my life once. I'm not doing it again when I'm so close to the finish line.*

That had stung.

Mae waved one of the little American flags that the grocery store employees were handing out as they walked by the float with a giant paper bag of groceries. A handful of candy was tossed at us, and she laughed.

"You know they're my favorite, Alma," she called to the woman tossing goodies.

Mae glanced at the ground between us, then at me. "The apple flavor is my favorite. Go ahead—before the kids find it."

I found the little wrapped candies that had landed by her water bottle. I tried to hand it to her, but she waved it away. "I'll sneak some from the kids." She winked. "The grandma tax."

I grinned and unwrapped the apple taffy. "It's been forever since I've had one."

"We'll get you more." She threw up an arm. "Hey, Macy. Buddy," she called to the couple walking behind the hardware store float.

Another handful of candy was tossed our way. It clattered onto the sidewalk at my feet. A mix of mints and fruit taffies. Mae gestured to the candy and I picked it up. I offered her some first.

She took an apple-flavored piece and winked. "Since there's extra."

I turned to Tenor and held out a handful of treats. "Your mom's peddling sugar."

"She'll make sure you leave loaded if you want." He jutted his chin toward the small group of kids holding a local dance group banner. The parents were cruising around with pails of candy, tossing handfuls. "She's already hitting them up." He leaned over the arm of his camp chair. "It's so she can take some without looking like she's really the one who wants it."

Grinning, I tucked the candy in the cupholder in the armrest and took out one of the mints. I unwrapped it and popped it into my mouth.

More floats rolled by. More candy was thrown and collected, and I had more fun. Mae would tell me little tidbits. The dance group was run by a family who'd moved here a few years ago. The bank president drove the pickup hauling the bank's float, and he reserved the tasting room at Copper Summit every year for the Christmas party. She even introduced me to the mayor as she cruised by with small fliers that had beef sticks taped to them.

The end of the parade was in sight. I had no idea it'd be this long for such a small town. My happiness diminished little by little. It'd be time to go. There was no big gathering at Mae's place, at least not one I was invited to. Everyone would go their separate ways to hang out with family and friends. I'd return to my empty apartment. Me and a romance novel.

Maybe I should try hiking again.

My feet already felt the blisters.

"There's a street dance tonight," Tenor said. "If you want to stay."

I blinked at him. Was he asking me out?

He shrugged, his gaze drifting to the classic Cadillac convertible driving by with a poster for the senior center hanging off the side. On my right, Autumn yelled out, "Hank!" and the driver waved.

Tenor's attention landed back on me. "Unless you have plans."

I jolted. "No. No plans. I'd love to stay. I still can't dance though."

"You did just fine at the wedding."

When I'd been in his strong arms, letting him lead me around. That had been mere days ago and I had the chance to do it again. Unless . . . Tenor was some in-demand dance partner and I'd be left on the sidelines.

We were still pretending to date. So I'd get a few dances with him. That was better than being burrowed in my couch, reading a book, and wondering if Tenor was deciding to date anyone for real. "I'd love to."

His answering grin almost made it feel like a real date.

Tenor

The bass of the band thumped around us. Sunlight was slowly fading and the streetlights were taking over. People twirled on the dance floor around us. Unlike the wedding, this music was pure country. Nothing but two-step and line dancing all night long.

Ruby tripped over her feet, but I held her until she got back in step. "I don't think I could do this without you," she muttered.

I wouldn't want her to. I wanted all her dances. "You're doing well. Don't worry about it. I have big feet to trip over."

She playfully swatted my shoulder. "You do not. I mean, you do, but they're not the reason for my lack of coordination."

"As long as you're having fun, that's all I care about."

She yanked her concentration off the ground and what our feet were doing to look at me. "I really believe that."

"Why wouldn't you?"

She lifted a shoulder, moving easily with me now that she wasn't concentrating so hard. "You're the first guy I've met where it's not all about you."

I didn't have enough going on for it to be all about me. "This is your night out."

"It's yours too." She studied me as I spun us around Tate and Scarlett. How could they move when he had her plastered so close to his body? I took notes and held Ruby a little tighter. "Tonight can be about you too."

If tonight was about me, she'd be in my bed and naked. No, I wasn't going to be selfish. Nor did I want her to feel used. "I'm having fun too, Ruby. Don't doubt that."

She gave me a dubious look.

The song wound down and the first strings of the next thrummed. A whoop went up in the crowd.

"If you want me to make it about me," I said, leading us out of the section of the street portioned off for the dance, "then it'll be me sitting out a line dance."

She laughed, the light sound so damn perfect. "You really were serious. Well, I can't line dance either, but it's nice to see that you have one weakness."

I had a lot more, she just chose to ignore them. It wouldn't last long before any novelty she saw in me wore off. It always did. Even before Katrina, my relationships had died before takeoff. We'd go out a few times, mess around, and then the plainness of my life would hit them, and they'd drift off. Nothing had lasted longer than a couple of months.

I sat at one of the picnic tables that my family had claimed. Ruby slid in on the end, a broad grin on her face. A flush stained her cheeks from dancing and she bumped her heel against the pavement to the beat. The top button of her shirt was undone and it gaped open. My gaze was drawn to it as I kept hoping to catch a glimpse of those plump mounds I'd seen during our board game night.

Cruz danced toward us, his black T-shirt shrink-wrapped to his chest. Like me, he was wearing his good blue jeans, only his were worn at the bottom from his boots. His good jeans got a lot more use than mine.

He held his hand out to Ruby. "A little Tush Push for the lady?"

Her eyes flared wide. "A what?"

"It's a dance," I nearly growled. What the hell was Cruz asking her for? He practically had a line of ladies following him around.

Lane popped up behind him. "Come on, Ruby. We'll teach you the steps."

She glanced at me. "Oh, no. That's fine." Her curious gaze turned toward the three lines of people doing a hip bump.

"Go ahead," I said. I couldn't give her this experience. The idea of line dancing crawled under my skin like a thousand different bugs. Mama had taught us to dance, but line dancing in public and becoming a spectacle had to be one of the circles of hell. Yet Ruby was having fun and it wasn't fair to hold her back from something fun. A skill that she could take on future dates. She deserved someone who wouldn't duck her phone's camera, someone who could keep up with her all night.

I ground my teeth together. Fuck those guys. At least I'd get to witness her sway those hips first.

"No. Really, it's fine." Her smile was reassuring. "I like hanging out with you."

Now I felt shittier for holding her back. "And I like watching you shake your ass."

Cruz held his hands up like he was innocent. "I'll be teaching, not ogling. Can't have the old man mad at us." He shot me a shit-eating grin as Ruby rose.

She leaned over to whisper in my ear. "I'll give you a few extra shakes."

I groaned. Lane shook his head and followed his brother and the girl who left me wondering why the hell I couldn't skip to the good part and leave the fake behind.

# CHAPTER FIFTEEN

Ruby

My laughter mixed in with the music. I kicked my heel out, then my other one and spun, adding a little more ass wiggle than I normally would. The burn of Tenor's gaze branded my ass. My hips would be sore tomorrow. Muscles I hadn't used in years, if ever, were getting called on tonight.

Cruz and Lane had been both patient and enthusiastic when teaching me the steps of each line dance. In between, Tenor stalked out to the dance area and swooped me into his arms for two-stepping until another song with a popular line dance came on. Then he'd leave again, relegating himself to the picnic table while more and more of his family surrounded me.

Wynter whooped next to me, and beside her, Autumn grinned.

At the picnic table, Myles and Gideon hungrily watched their wives across from Tenor. Jonah lifted his chin to

Summer. She grinned and scurried out. Tate and Scarlett were in the line behind me and Teller was next to them.

The song was winding down.

Wynter grabbed my arm, still giggling. "I'm going to be sore in the morning."

I nodded. "I was just thinking the same thing."

I started for the picnic table just as a slow ballad started.

A woman with skintight blue jeans and a shirt that barely went past her bustline sauntered up to Tenor. She cocked her head toward the dance area.

I slowed. Tenor adjusted his glasses, gave the woman a faint smile, and shook his head. She pouted and kicked a hip out, but he cocked his head to meet my gaze.

The relief hit me like a tidal wave. He'd passed her up. Then his smile broadened. He rose, that powerful body uncoiling like a cobra, and stalked toward me.

"Care to dance?" he asked in that deep voice, the other woman forgotten.

"Have I ever turned you down?" Giddiness swept through my veins, flushed out by hot desire. There wasn't much I'd deny him.

Tenor made me feel wanted. How was that look he gave me fake? The way he held me while we danced? We weren't at arm's length like some other couples. I tripped over his feet because we were so close. My head was less than an inch away from his hard chest.

We enjoyed each other's company. Yet he hadn't asked me out.

I couldn't look at it too hard. The agreement was clear.

Only the wedding had come and gone and now we

were on this fake date, pretending among his family and thoroughly enjoying ourselves.

Maybe he wasn't sure about me. I wasn't sure about me either. If I couldn't keep someone as shallow as Brock interested, how would I attract a guy with as much depth as Tenor?

*Just enjoy tonight, Ruby.* This weekend, when I would be alone in my apartment for the first time in over a month, I could ask that question.

I didn't keep track of time, but soon enough the band was shutting down.

Tenor led me toward the picnic tables where his family was gathering, bidding everyone goodnight. Mae had all her grandkids for the night. Only Junie and Rhys were missing from the group.

"Your mom is brave to take all the kids at once," I said.

"She loves it." Tenor looped a relaxed arm around my shoulders. I sank into his hold, so strong, so secure.

As I walked with Tenor to his pickup, I continued to root myself in the present. I couldn't dwell on the future. Tenor's goal had been to make sure I knew what I should expect from a guy, but he'd proved how high I should set my standards. He was like a gold standard, except . . .

He wasn't tripping over himself to be with me.

We had chemistry for days, and some hot nights, but he never pursued it. He'd had plenty of chances. He'd been hurt before and I wasn't enough to tempt him into the real dating world.

It wasn't me; it was him.

No matter what realization I had come to, I wouldn't

let it take away from tonight. "That was such a fun night," I gushed after we loaded up.

"Best Fourth I've had in a while."

Not the best Fourth ever? I shook off the thought. Today might've been an encore of a facade, but I'd use it as a very real example of how good being with a guy could be.

He wove through town to the darker outskirts of Bourbon Canyon. Soon, we lumbered down roads lit only by headlights and the partially obscured moon above us.

The faint yard light outside his cabin came into view. Shadows of trees behind the house and shop gave the view dimension. The peak of the house blended with the piney tops of the trees.

"Your place is even gorgeous at night," I said, grateful I got one more night here. Pleased I had another sleepover with Tenor and his closed-off heart. So pleased and so grateful—for one more night.

"Yeah. It's my own retreat." The corners of his eyes crinkled when he smiled. "For those nights when I don't have a date to the street dance."

"Well, anytime. I'm your girl." I rolled my lips in. I hadn't meant to sound like I was throwing myself at his feet.

He wasn't replying. Or making light of it. His profile was hard in the glare of the dash lights. Was there something I could say to cut through the discomfort growing between us?

"I learned how to line dance," I prattled on. "Didn't think that would ever happen. Now I can cruise all over Bozeman and jump in line at all the bars."

His eyes narrowed and he adjusted his glasses, his jaw clenching and unclenching. "Yeah. A good skill to have."

"I mean, you can make bourbon and sell it for enough profit to keep how many employees afloat? And I can do the Boot Scootin' Boogie."

He chuckled. "You never know when it'll come in handy."

"I might surprise myself."

He parked in the garage. Longing hit me at the sight of my car beside his blue pickup.

*Don't succumb to wishful thinking, Ruby.*

Inside, he toed out of his boots. I slipped out of my shoes and groaned. "I think my toes are going to hate me in the morning." I bent to rub a foot. "Is that the real reason you all wear cowboy boots? A bigger toe box for dancing?"

"That might be a selling point."

I grinned. "I can't shut my marketing brain off."

He scratched behind his neck and wandered through the kitchen. Usually when I came over after my shift on Friday nights, we ate together. Cleaned up his kitchen while chatting. Then we moseyed off to bed. Except for that one night I'd gotten drunk and dove between his sheets.

Yeah, I'd like to relive that. His deep voice whispering naughty things to me in the dark . . .

Heat flushed through my vessels and coalesced between my legs. I hadn't drunk much more than two beers tonight. The warmth was arousal. Desire. I wanted Tenor in a very real way. Nothing was fake about how my body reacted around him.

"Sit," he said, gesturing to the couch. "I'll give you a foot rub."

I was caught between wanting to swan dive onto the cushions and being frozen with mortification. "You want to rub my sweaty feet?"

Despite the possibility of my stinky dogs, hope started to rise. What if he wasn't tripping over himself, but tiptoeing? He was cautious, and Tenor wasn't a guy who'd make the same mistake twice.

"If it makes you feel better," he said, "I put my face close to abscessed hooves all the time."

"Ew. Is that as gross as it sounds?"

"Can be. Now sit."

My body reacted before my mind could. I padded across the floor and dropped in the corner of the couch. He sat in the middle and lifted my legs onto his lap.

A guy who wasn't interested wouldn't rub my feet. Guys who *had* been interested hadn't given me a massage of any sort.

He traced a finger over the tips of my summery-red-painted toes. "The color matches your name."

"It's my favorite."

He dug into the balls of my feet with his thumbs, dragging a long groan from me. His thighs clenched under my calves, but he continued.

"God, that feels good." My eyes rolled back in my head. I had been missing out. Put this on the list of things I'd demand from a guy from now on. Could a girl come from a foot rub?

"You act like you've never had a foot rub before." His voice was thick.

I kept my eyes closed or I'd be throwing orgasm faces nonstop. "I haven't."

He paused. "Never?"

I cracked an eyelid open. His aghast expression

almost made me laugh. "I think my bar was in the basement for expectations."

He grunted and continued with the massage, working his way down to my heels and back up to my toes. I tried to hold back my moans, but the man was a wizard with his fingers.

He continued to knead up to my ankles. Then he made it to my calves. I melted into the cushions, nothing but a pool of divine relaxation. "You are doing a good job of making sure no one lives up to you."

He stopped massaging. His mouth was tight and a crease slashed across his brow.

Damn. I'd made things awkward again. Just what I got for getting my hopes up. I scooted upright. His hands were loose around my lower legs. I gingerly lowered my feet to the floor. The crease on his brow deepened.

"I should get to bed." I rose but he stayed where he was.

"I want to kiss you again."

It was my turn to freeze. Had I fallen asleep and entered the most wonderful dream? No, if I was dreaming, his mouth would be on mine and I would be under him already. "Why don't you?"

Pain highlighted the lines on his face. His whole body was rigid. "I don't want to cross the line. I might not come back."

Brock and my other exes might have strung me along, but I had never begged. They had asked me for another chance. Tenor wasn't requesting a first one. He didn't want a relationship, and he didn't want to mess around. He wasn't tiptoeing, he was backtracking. As hard as it was to respect his wishes, I wouldn't pressure him.

So all I said was "I might not have minded."

I forced one foot in front of the other until I was closed in the guest bedroom. I exhaled and sagged against the bedroom door. Would he decide the line was worth crossing after all? Would he show me that what sizzled between us was worth the risk? Would he realize I wasn't like Katrina?

I had never been drawn to a man like I was to him. I wanted him. I could picture it. I could envision us together. Something that I had thought was a girlish fantasy and that he had shown me could be real. But both parties had to be on board and he was pushing my ship away.

Soft movement came from the living room. Muffled footsteps grew closer and ceased outside of my door. My chest rose and fell. Was this it? Would he finally cave to the promise of how good it could be between us?

My lungs stalled the longer time stretched on.

Then movement again. Away from my door and down the hall. His bedroom door clicked shut.

I squeezed my eyes shut and swallowed. A wave of grief washed over me. For what could've been, even just for tonight. But mostly for me, for that girl who just wanted someone to want and keep wanting her. Was that too much to ask?

# CHAPTER SIXTEEN

Tenor

On Sunday night, Mama had invited me over. Cruz and Lane were leaving on Monday. She missed them when they were gone, and every time before they left, she made a big meal as if to remind them they always had a home in Bourbon Canyon.

I scraped the leftover mashed potatoes out of the pot and into a plastic container. Cruz was humming while loading the dishwasher. Lane was helping Mama clear the table.

"Where's Rubes this weekend?" Lane asked as he carried in a pile of plates to hand off to Cruz.

"She doesn't like being called that."

"No kidding?" He sounded surprised. "Dang. Thanks for telling me."

Lane was a good kid.

He was almost Ruby's age. Pressure pushed against my temples. A feeling that had plagued me since

Thursday morning when I returned home and Ruby had been gone.

What had I expected? I had told her I wanted to kiss her. And then I hadn't. Nor had I confessed to what I really wanted to do—strip every bit of fabric off her curves, spread her out on my bed, and devour her.

Yeah. I wanted to do a fuck ton more than kiss her. Wasn't that the whole issue?

I finished with the potatoes and moved on to the gravy. When I was done pouring that into a container for the fridge, I turned. Cruz had his arms crossed and was leaning against the counter, staring at me. Lane had his eyes narrowed on me while rubbing his chin.

"What?" I asked, suddenly cranky.

"We're just waiting for your answer," Lane said casually, but worry darkened his blue eyes. "Where's Ruby?"

"She's been spending every weekend here." I searched the kitchen for something to do, but anything I'd need to do it with was blocked by the guys. Damn. "She wants to be home for once."

"Did she say that?" Cruz asked.

No. I could just tell them now. Rip the bandage off. Ruby and I were over.

What reason would I give them? I bored her? She'd found someone else? We didn't click? None of those options sat well with me, nor would they buy that we didn't click after the street dance, when I'd barely let her out of my embrace.

"She's got family," I said. Although she'd mentioned her mom was on a workation. And her dad was in Helena. The guys didn't need details. "She has a life."

"You haven't been introduced to her family?" Lane asked. "Does she have siblings?"

I shook my head. The last time I'd met the parents, I had gotten grilled and I'd failed. Then I'd been humiliated in my own hometown. "She's an only child, and we haven't been dating long. No need for me to meet them."

Neither of them nodded.

"Is it a thing?" Lane asked. "That you're so much older than her?"

"I don't know," I answered honestly. We'd never discussed meeting her parents, and now it wasn't necessary to meet the parents of someone I wasn't dating. "She said her parents were teens when she was born, so yeah, it might be an issue. I'd be close in age to them."

Cruz let out a low whistle. "That can up the pucker factor, but it'll be all right. Someone would have to be a real jackass not to like you."

It had not been all right once upon a time. "Not if they're expecting some CEO like Myles or Gideon."

Lane scoffed. "You're no different than them. So you don't wear a suit. You still help run Copper Summit."

I helped. At least now I had my own place—on land given to me by my dad. I had nothing of my own other than my games. "Not everyone sees it like that."

"Fuck 'em." Lane clapped me on the shoulder. "You're a solid dude, old man."

"I'm a boring dude, or you wouldn't call me old man."

Cruz and Lane exchanged a look that was a whole conversation.

My irritation leaked out. "What?"

"We joke about your mellow life," Cruz said, "but that's not why we call you old man."

Lane nodded. "We started calling you old man

because you've taught us more than our old man ever did."

My chest grew tight.

I'd shown these guys the ropes like I'd done with every foster kid who'd stayed with us long enough to learn a little ranching. Cruz and Lane had been young adults when Myles had learned about them, but Mama had welcomed them in and they'd agreed to work for Bailey Beef. They'd never been just employees though.

Cruz crossed his arms. "To be fair, it's hard to teach us anything from jail."

"I have that going for me," I said gruffly.

"Thanks to the Baileys, so do we," Lane said, his expression sober.

"He's talking about me," Cruz added. "I'd have definitely seen the inside of a jail if you hadn't made me shovel cow shit."

I smirked. "We used a loader."

Mama swept into the kitchen. Her lips tipped into a wry grin when she noticed how far we hadn't gotten with cleanup. "Lane, do you mind taking over for Tenor?" She looked at me. "Get us a couple of glasses. I'll be on the porch."

Mama wanted to talk. I ignored the chasm forming in my stomach and did as she asked. With two fingers of Solemn Summit in each rocks glass, I found Mama outside. She slowly rocked in one of the chairs. Another was empty on the other side of a little stand.

I handed off the glass and sat. "What's on your mind?"

"I was going to ask you the same thing."

I swirled the amber fluid in my glass. Had I acted differently over dinner? "Nothing."

"I thought Ruby was going to be with you."

"She has her own life."

Mama rocked and took a sip. "Things okay between you two?"

One weekend apart and everyone thought we were over? We were, and that didn't help my rising frustration. I really should be honest. I was lying to Mama. I had already lied to her. This was my moment to make things right, but I couldn't. I told Ruby I'd keep her confidence. "It's not healthy to be together all the time."

"It's not," she agreed. The gentle scrape of her chair mixed with the crickets and frogs. "Teller said you were having fun with her at the dance."

"Yeah."

"It's okay, you know."

I gripped the armrest of the chair. I wasn't rocking. Mama was in that mode where she could see right through me. She could open the lid of a mental box I had padlocked for a reason. "What is?"

"To trust her."

My mental box snapped shut. "I do trust her." Ruby had put all her confidence in me to treat her right, so that was what I'd set out to do. And I'd let her in. Not intentionally, but she'd catered to me, strip board games and all.

"Mm." Mama took another drink.

"I do."

Mama rotated her glass like I had done. "I think you want to. It's been a long time since you put yourself out there."

I pried my fingers off the armrest. "It's not easy." I'd give Mama that much truth.

"I can't imagine it is, but it'll get easier. If she's the right one, you'll want to try."

I started rocking. Our movements were out of sync. I took a drink and gazed into the darkness beyond the circle made by the yard light. Nothing but dark pastures greeted me.

*If* Ruby was the right one. I'd made a pact with myself. I wouldn't go through another Katrina. No one would make me feel like I wasn't good enough again. No one would mock me to my face again. I wasn't enduring more pitying looks because I was a pathetic bastard. I'd had enough as a kid, and then, because I must not have gotten the message, I had endured more as an adult.

But I was even older, and that came with perks. I could choose who I surrounded myself with. Ruby had been one of those choices—as an employee. As a girl-friend, she'd leave. They always did.

*If she's the right one . . .*

I didn't tell Mama it wasn't about who was right for me.

But who I was wrong for.

✧

Ruby

I wiped down two newly emptied tables and brought the glasses behind the bar to clean. Only a few customers remained. Tenor's truck was in the parking lot, but I had yet to see him. I hadn't heard from him since the night of the street dance.

What did it mean?

The question ricocheted all around my head, leaving dots of fear behind. I knew what it meant. Which was even worse. What I needed was a little acceptance.

For a week, I'd watched my phone, hoping he'd text something as simple as asking me how I was doing. A little *can we talk*. Or even a *what's up*?

My phone had stayed silent.

Wednesday night, I'd foolishly held out hope that I'd see him even though he was never around Wednesday nights.

The two guys remaining rose and pushed in their chairs. Jason gave me a wave. "See ya later, Ruby."

"Have a good night," I called at their backs.

I flipped the open sign to off. Tenor had helped me close all but one weekend for the last month, but there was still no sign of him.

I swallowed my disappointment and continued closing duties. Alone. I punched through cashing out the till and sending the reports to Tenor. My heart twisted as I hit send. Just another mundane email to one of my many bosses. A man I was nothing but an employee to.

I shoved my hair off my face. I'd worn a damn skirt today too. I tugged at the blue material. It was a longer skirt with a dress shirt tied at the waist in a country chic style. I thought it made my hips look wide, but after the way Tenor had watched me shake my booty at the dance, I'd been bold.

"Sweet summer child," I muttered and stacked the clean glasses back on the shelf beside the bar.

Good thing I'd given myself plenty of mental pep talks or I'd be in tears by now. I'd be reliving every breakup speech ever. Instead I heard *I want to kiss you again* over and over in his deep voice. Not sure that was better.

I took stock of the bottles behind the bar and tapped my chin. "Two bottles of Original." Talking out loud made me feel less alone.

I replaced those and stood, staring at the rows of bottles. Various pints, fifths, and liters decorated three levels. The most popular lines. Holiday special batches from years past that were only served at this location. The most expensive top-shelf Copper Summit special barrels that were also only sold here. I'd taken so many pictures of this setup for background graphics and stand-alone images.

Seconds ticked by. I gave myself a shake. I was stalling. It was time to go. Tenor wasn't coming. He was probably waiting for me to leave before he locked up. Avoiding the awkwardness—and me.

I grabbed my purse and rounded the bar.

The door from the lobby opened. I stopped short and my heart crawled into my chest.

Tenor turned into the bar and his gaze found me immediately. He crossed to me, his powerful thighs knocking a table out of the way. Intensity rode across his face and along his hard jaw.

Alarm fired in my veins the closer he got without saying a word.

"Is everything okay?" I tipped my head back as he approached and I inspected his face.

"No." He wrapped an arm around my waist and yanked me flush with him. His gaze bored into mine. "I'm tired of pretending I don't think about flipping those flirty skirts up and plunging into you whenever I want."

I drew in a breath, shock rebounding in my chest, making my heartbeat stutter. He hadn't tiptoed into the bar! "Then why don't you?"

A low growl rumbled in his chest. "I don't have any condoms. I thought I could—" He grimaced and jerked his gaze away, his jaw grinding. "I thought I could stay strong, or that not buying them would be enough to make me behave. You deserve better than me."

"Good thing I'm on birth control." I fisted my hands in his chest and rose to my tiptoes. I ghosted my lips along his jawline. "I happen to find your control very sexy." Frustrating. But hot. And only because he was right here, right now, admitting he couldn't stay away. "Shouldn't I get to choose who I deserve? Shouldn't I get a chance to prove that it's you?"

A growl emanated from him again. "Ruby." His eyes searched mine. "Tell me no and I'll fucking leave and never bother you again. Because you can do better. I swear you can."

He'd already been the best. I wasn't interested in searching for what he was already giving me—care, dedication, loyalty, and steamy kisses. Anything more than that was already like winning a lifetime of free books. "I'm telling you yes, Warhammer."

The desire in his eyes blazed, blowing the pupils until I could fall into him and lose myself. He took my purse from my arms and dumped it on the bar top. Then he lifted me to a stool and took his glasses off. He braced his arms on either side of me. His gaze stroked over my face and he lowered his head.

His lips touched mine, a slow, searching press that had me leaning back until my spine hit the edge of the counter. Even more pressure and I was opening for him. I kept my hands on his shoulders. His restraint was a tangible thing. Energy pulsated under my fingers, his muscles vibrating.

He plundered my mouth, twining his tongue with mine, and put a hand around the back of my neck. His thumb stroked along the edge of my jaw. All I could do was hang on. A little whimper left me. I wanted more, but I also worried I'd combust from the lust burning through my veins. My skin felt tight and much too hot. I squirmed under him, seeking some relief for the needy thrum between my legs.

Another deep sound rumbled from him. He kissed down my jaw and dragged his hand over my collarbone, between my breasts, to the base of the white shirt knotted at my waist.

We both watched him trail his fingers over the knot.

"I'm going to enjoy unwrapping you," he murmured.

"Here?" I asked, breathless. Did I care?

No. I did not.

"I shut the cameras off."

"You planned this?" I'd closed down thinking he would always be risk averse, that I would never be enough of a prize, and he'd planned to scramble my brains and my body.

"I was just going to ask you out. On a real date." He tugged the hem of my shirt free. It fell loose. He deftly worked on the lowest button. "Either way, I wanted a private conversation between us, and to not get your rejection on camera."

I could've laughed. Me? Telling him no? Tenor could

ask me to plan a bank heist and I would if it meant getting his mouth on me again.

"So . . ." He flicked open two more buttons. A strip of my stomach was exposed. "You can relax and let me unwrap you like my very own birthday gift."

The final button came free and the ends of the shirt fell to the side. He looked at my plain white bra like it was the sexiest strip of lace he'd ever seen.

He hooked a finger over the top of the cup of one and tugged it down. My nipple popped free. Appreciation darkened his eyes. He brushed a thumb over the tip and a shiver whispered over my skin.

"I knew they'd be fucking perfect." He did the same on the other side. My nipples were puckered, begging for attention, but I couldn't move. He gripped my hips and bent to draw one nipple into his mouth.

It was my turn to brace myself on the bar. I held on as he licked and palmed my breasts. The pressure inside me grew with no outlet. I squirmed again, seeking to find some relief.

He lifted his gaze and my pearled bud popped out of his mouth. "You're a needy girl, aren't you?"

"It's not enough."

His expression changed, the heat in his eyes consuming me. He dropped to his knees. His face was at my crotch and I almost sat up, but he still had me in his grip. "Don't move." His voice was low. Commanding. "I want you just like this. Open to me. Nowhere to go."

The bar was empty, the whole distillery was, but I only had the small round seat I was sitting on.

He lifted my leg from the stool's footrest and draped it over his shoulder. My hold on the edge of the bar tightened. My legs were spread and his face was right there. "Tenor."

"I like when you say my name." He kissed the inside of my thigh, working his way closer to the juncture. Need quivered inside of me.

"Tenor," I said again. I was on edge, ready to combust. If he didn't release the pressure humming between my legs, I might just implode, and then I'd miss out on everything.

Still, he took his damn time. My underwear was still on. A pink pair that didn't show seams. Nothing fancy. But the way Tenor looked at them, it didn't matter. His unyielding expression, the heat in his eyes—he wanted what was underneath.

"You're wet for me." He placed a kiss on the fabric, right over my covered clit.

A shudder made my boobs jiggle. "Yes."

He tucked a finger under the seam and dragged it through my folds. "So hot. So soft."

Nothing but a whimper left me. I was close to a release but so far away.

The corner of his mouth kicked up before he turned serious again. He tugged the underwear to the side. "It's been a long time since I've done this, Goldilocks."

"I have a feeling you're going to do it just right." Tremors ran up and down my spine. I was balanced on a precipice. If he backed away, deciding to wait or that he didn't want to break his dry streak for me, I'd be left empty. Unfulfilled. Bereft. On the other side was a whole new world of pleasure. A place I'd only dreamed about with him.

He held my gaze as he closed the distance between his mouth and my pussy, then he licked through me.

"Oh god." I arched toward him. Just like his kiss, he deepened the pressure, lengthened the strokes of his tongue, until he was centered on my clit. I let out a ragged moan.

Both of my feet were on his shoulders. I was still in my skirt. Only my breasts spilled over my bra, but otherwise I was concealed. Yet Tenor had stripped me down to nothing but raw nerves that were starved for pleasure.

"You taste as sweet as I imagined." His hot breath gusted over my sex. He licked again, moving his hands to keep the underwear out of the way and hold me open to him.

He dove in. If he hadn't had a good hold on me, I would've slid right off the seat. I dropped my head back and rolled my hips into his mouth as much as I could.

Tenor really was showing me everything I'd been missing. Even with my underwear still on, this was the most amazing sexual experience of my life. And Tenor was fully clothed.

All my focus was on my sex, nothing but energy coursing through me, centering on where he stroked my clit with his talented tongue. Any hold I had on my pleasure fractured into a million pieces.

"Oh my god, Tenor," I gasped. All my muscles constricted as unfiltered pleasure exploded from my core outward. "Tenor!"

My release went on and on, sweeping over me in waves. I shook against him but he held me tightly and kept stoking me higher and higher. The next second, he was rising. I kept my hold on the counter, the pleasure in my body still pitching me from side to side.

He dragged my underwear off and yanked his zipper down. I was trying to catch my breath when my gaze landed on his erection. It strained toward me, taut and veiny. Big and strong, just like him.

"It's massive." I widened my legs, the heels of my shoes pressed into his ass.

"And you're nice and ready for me." He notched himself at my entrance.

A quiver racked my body. Anticipation. An orgasm that was finished but also not completely done, another one climbing toward a peak, ready to go.

A slow push inside had me groaning. The sense of fullness was so right, yet he was barely inside. He drew back and shoved in a little deeper this time. I watched him push in, slide back out, and thrust in again.

I fisted my hands in his polo, drawing the fabric up to stay out of my way. I never thought a sight like this would get me off, but I was catapulting toward another peak. Maybe it was because I'd never come down, but I didn't think so. The way Tenor's body was rigid. How he was being so careful. That it was his cock stretching me open. Everything about him could get me off again and again.

I rocked against him, urging him to fill me completely.

"You're a greedy girl." His voice was gruff, thick.

"It feels so good." There was no wondering if this was it. Thinking that I'd built sex up again and my expectations were unrealistic. No. Inch by inch, Tenor rebuilt each and every expectation. I'd already had an orgasm that showed me I had most definitely been missing a lot.

He punched his hips forward, and I gasped, my eyes rolling back. "So good," I groaned.

"Fuck, Ruby." He propped a hand on the counter behind me, a tremor traveling through him.

I kept undulating my hips, the need inside of me growing more and more demanding. There was another precipice and I had to get there.

He clamped a giant hand on my thigh. "Christ, you've gotta quit moving or I'm going to blow."

"I can't stop. You make me so—" I moaned. He filled me so completely that any small twitch hit all the right spots. "I'm going to come again."

He pinned me with slitted eyes, his teeth gritted, like he was making a decision. Then he started moving, an erratic but strong rhythm. "So fucking wet and tight."

My ass scraped across the stool, but he clamped my hips in both hands and held me still as he plunged into me. "Yes," I hissed. I was so close.

"Fuck." He ground against me, the sound of our skin slapping together filled the room. "Fuck, Ruby. You take it so well."

I slammed to the top of my ecstasy and cartwheeled over the edge. "Tenor!"

I broke apart, splintering into a zillion pieces, but he held me together as he thrust in one last time. He clenched his teeth, throwing his head back. Hot release filled me and his big body shook.

When he quit shuddering and jerking, my legs started slipping down his hips. He gripped my calves, but I sank back, the hard line of the counter jabbing into my back. "Wow. That was . . . Wow."

Hair hung over his forehead and he was breathing hard, but his lust-filled gaze was on me. "I'll help you down. Then you're coming home with me. I'm not done yet."

Tenor

When I had woken up this morning, I'd anticipated a day full of self-torture, thinking about Ruby all day and how long it'd been since I'd seen her. Right before her shift started, I'd been glued to the goddamn window, watching the sway of her hips as she rushed toward the entrance. Her little skirt had swished around her thighs and then I couldn't leave my fucking office until my dick had calmed down.

I'd only meant to talk to her. Then I'd seen her. Kissed her.

Now we were in my bed, our clothing strewn from the garage door to my room. She was on top of me, her legs draped over each side, her knees grinding into the mattress. Fucking heaven.

"Ride me," I said through gritted teeth. "Just like that."

Her tits bounced as she rocked on top of me. "I can't believe I'm going to come again." Her eyes went hazy and she spread her hands out on my chest.

"It won't be the last time." I planted my hands on her hips. It took everything in me not to flip us over and fuck her into oblivion. But twice wouldn't be enough. My restraint was shot. Blown. She was mine for the whole night.

It wasn't just that I was having sex again. Nothing had ever been this good. I couldn't remember my previous times, but I'd never forget this.

Her walls fluttered over my dick and the rest of her

body shook. When her breath hitched, I knew I had her. She dropped her head back, her dark hair waving behind her. "Tenor," she gasped like she was scared of her own reaction.

"Come for me, Ruby."

Another shudder racked her body. "Oh god." The walls of her pussy gripped me so tight I couldn't believe she could keep riding me. First, long, hard strokes, and then fast.

"Tenor!"

Heat rushed between us. I was barely able to keep from coming while she rode out her orgasm. Then, as soon as she slowed, I rolled us and pinned her hands above her head. She hitched her knees up and to the sides.

I plowed into her until my climax hit me square in the balls. I had to grit my teeth against the onslaught of pleasure. Energy raced down my spine and out of me with my release.

I'd never skipped protection, but as soon as she'd said she was on birth control, I hadn't questioned the rest. Maybe I should've, but now that I'd come inside of her twice, I was a man consumed.

Sagging over her, I kept the bulk of my weight off her.

She let out a contented sigh. Her heels hit the mattress and she ran her hands up and down my back. "I did not think this was going to happen tonight," she murmured.

"Me either." I dropped a kiss on her neck and she shivered under me. I arranged us until we were under the covers.

She cuddled into my chest, tracing her fingers along

the old silvery scars around my armpits. "I don't want to ruin the mood, but what does tonight mean?"

It meant I'd done the worst thing possible. I'd proven that she was irresistible. That I could never get enough of her.

This was my chance to tell her that tonight was a one-off. A two-off. A three-fer before I was done with her. All I had to do was tell her that I still wasn't interested in dating. She was gorgeous. Sexy. I couldn't keep my hands off her, but if she wanted a relationship, she needed to look somewhere else. It had been hard, when all the others had left. Ruby could destroy me.

She went still. "If you don't want to—"

I closed my hand around hers. The disappointment in her voice was too much. I couldn't do it. Not tonight. Yet I wouldn't make promises I couldn't keep. "Do we have to give this a definition right now?"

"Oh. Okay. No." She tucked her head into my chest. "Of course not."

I winced. Fuck. "I like you. A lot. But I'm not ready—"

"No, I know." She leaned back to look at me. "It's all right. We'll just enjoy each other."

"You gonna still have sleepovers with me?"

She chewed on her lower lip. "Are you going to keep giving me multiple orgasms?"

I rolled her over to her back and slid down her body, pressing her legs open as I went. "Absolutely."

I rounded the barn, checking my watch. I'd only done it a million times today. I hadn't complained about getting up to help with chores since I was a kid and Dad had turned the light on in my room before the crack of dawn.

But after taking Ruby three different times last night and getting only a few hours of sleep, I'd gotten cranky having to drag myself from her warm, supple body.

Now, it was finally time for me to go. Tate and Teller could take care of the rest. Chance was baling hay in the flattest pasture we had while Tate was stacking the round bales at our storage point.

I found Teller hopping the fence by the horse pasture.

"I think I'm going to head out—" Blood dripped down our roan gelding's face. "What happened to Tenpin?"

"Not sure." Teller tried to get close but Tenpin tossed his head. "Whatever it is, it hurts."

Shit. "I'll call Dr. Sanders." The semiretired vet now only worked weekends, when he could charge emergency rates.

"Yeah, I don't think we'll be able to take care of this ourselves."

Dr. Sanders would have the good stuff.

I called him. Teller and I managed to coax the horse into the barn. We had a stall where we could treat him without outside disruption, and since the horse was in pain and anxious, we needed all the advantages we could get.

The next two hours went by in a whirlwind. Tate had dropped by to see what was going on. Then Chance had to take a look. It was good experience for the kid since this would be all his one day.

Unless I had kids.

No. I wasn't getting ahead of myself, and I wasn't going *there*. I'd only just started dating after swearing I wouldn't.

*You're going to hold my daughter back.* I shook the words out of my head.

I folded my arms across my chest and watched Dr. Sanders as he rattled off instructions to Tate. I should have been listening, but my brain was stuck on a pretty little social media manager.

I stayed where I was as Dr. Sanders drove away in his early-aughts Chevy pickup.

Mama was standing next to me, her arms crossed like mine. "He was probably playing with Nugget and caught his face on a fence post."

"I'll see if I can find where he hurt himself," Teller said. "Remove the hazard."

Mama chuffed. "Horses will create a hazard if there isn't one."

We all nodded.

I started backing away. The siren song of Ruby in my house called to me. "I'm gonna head out."

"I can always tell it's a Ruby weekend," Teller said.

Tate smirked. "Every weekend's been a Ruby weekend."

I wanted every day to be a Ruby day.

I ignored them and walked out.

"Hey," Teller called and I turned. "I checked my email this morning. Tell her we got two inquiries for next summer. Weddings, and both brides wanted to know if they could name a mocktail or a cocktail."

My grin spread wide. It'd only been two weeks since the Crock wedding, but Ruby had rolled out a dozen posts. Wynter had commented that they were getting more engagement than our normal content. I wouldn't be able to tell if it translated into sales for a while, but the possibility of booking more events was promising. "She's a natural."

"We also had to add more tours for the rest of summer," Teller said. "Her shit works fast." He exhaled a frustrated sigh. "I might have to get in front of the camera."

"We don't want to scare the tours away," I joked.

He glowered at me. "I'm gonna get you in a shot one day. We can compete to see who gets the most likes."

I didn't need to be compared to my brothers more than I already was. I didn't need more proof that I didn't measure up in the public eye. "Sure."

"She's good for you," Tate said.

I shrugged as panic clawed at my chest. I gave them a salute and continued walking away before they could sense something bothered me.

The last month had been amazing. It'd been pretend. Ruby had rolled with every facet of myself I had exposed, but that didn't mean it'd last. It only meant it'd hurt more if things didn't work between us.

Good thing nothing was defined, then.

What the hell was I thinking?

I wasn't. I couldn't stay away from her. Weeks of trying, of striving to be the type of guy she should date, had sapped my restraint. Ruby had dismantled my guards. Now I was flying through space without my armor, waiting to get blasted through the chest by an Ork.

Mama fell into step beside me. She moved like the bad guy in a horror movie. I could run from her, but she'd only walk calmly and somehow still catch up with me before I made it to an exit.

"Hey, Mama."

"Tenor."

When I got to my pickup, she patted me on the back. "Just a minute. I have some cookies to send with you."

"You don't need to give me treats to tell me something."

She smiled. The sun broke through some clouds, and her gray strands glinted in the light. "I was giving you the cookies anyway, but I wanted to ask how you're doing."

"I'm good."

"Ruby's a special girl."

"She is."

Mama tipped her head. "You're a special guy too."

I nodded. "Thanks."

"She's as lucky to have you as you are her."

I bit back a grimace. Mama was the only one to think that, but she was my mother. It was her job. "I know, Mama. I heard your message the other night."

Her eyes narrowed. "Mm." Her expression said *Did you?* "She treats you well."

She apparently wanted to make a point and didn't think it'd stuck the first time. "She didn't run screaming when she saw I played with toys."

Mama harrumphed. "All adults have toys, whether it's games or fishing or engines."

Sure. I did hunt and fish, and that had caused resentment with my ex too. Just another way I had ignored her needs.

"It's been, what? A couple of months since you two started dating?"

To them? Yes. But officially dating? Zero weeks. "Yeah."

The scrutiny intensified. "Mm-hmm. Have you met her parents yet?"

"It's not that serious." When her brows popped up, I backtracked. "We're taking it slow. No rush. She already knew you and every other Bailey."

"Have you been to Bozeman?"

"I don't have business in Bozeman." Dammit. Now she'd really suspect something. Not only was the other location of Copper Summit in Bozeman, but Ruby lived there. "I haven't needed to travel. She's in town every weekend."

"You don't have anything to worry about. You never have."

The berating I had gotten from Katrina's dad suggested otherwise. "Thanks, Mama."

She set her mouth in a line. She knew I was brushing off her pep talk. I wasn't meeting Ruby's parents anytime soon. We weren't serious.

Acid crawled up my esophagus. *Fake dating* should not be that much different from *not that serious*, but my stomach clenched at the idea and threatened to toss it back up.

I did not want to date. But I wanted Ruby.

My taste for her was stronger than my sense of self-preservation. I kissed Mama's temple. "Don't worry. I'm just happy being with her right now." And that was the truth, or I'd have left my grubby hands off her last night.

With a plate of cookies in the passenger seat, I arrived home. The house was quiet when I entered. Out front, she was sitting in the porch swing, rocking gently back and forth while buried in a book.

A punch of longing hit me between the eyes. I had been excited to come home to her. I'd been anticipating this moment since I'd rolled out of bed. And here she was. In my house.

Mine.

I rubbed my chest and went out the front door.

She looked up at me and smiled her lovely, serene smile. The sun broke out from between two clouds to shine on us at that moment. If I were a more whimsical guy, I'd see it as a sign. But I had more sense than that.

I dropped to my knees in front of her. "Hey."

"Hey yourself. How was your morning?"

"One of the horses nearly gouged his eye out." Her eyes widened and I shook my head. "Sorry. Probably not what you want to talk about." Katrina's words snaked through my head. *Ew, Tenor. Why would I want to hear that?*

Ruby waved like she was banishing my apology. "How is he? She?"

"Tenpin's a gelding. He didn't lose his eye. So far, there seems to be no nerve damage." I tugged her to the edge of the seat and held her so she didn't swing away. "How was your morning?"

"Quiet. I thought of running to town for coffee, but I walked outside and was struck with inspiration." She gestured to her phone on the porch boards. "I took a ton of pictures. I'd like to sprinkle in some Copper Summit history." She smiled. "Model-free, of course. I'd do a post each week for a few months or something."

"Teller told me he's getting inquiries for booking events next year."

Her face lit up. "Really?"

"Thanks to you."

"People loved the wedding content." She sat straighter, her hips wiggling. "Jenna was a natural. Locals have commented about how excited they were to see her pop up in their feed and then that triggered the algorithm to show more. And then when Junie commented, fans went wild."

A simple change we wouldn't have made without Ruby. "We're damn lucky to have you."

Her grin was radiant but almost shy. "You know just one small reason why Brock and I didn't work?" She draped her arms around my neck. "He was jealous of my job. He worked for his family, and he didn't get as nice a benefits package as I'm getting."

The asshole probably thought her position wasn't real work when she helped keep a family company afloat and thriving with her posts. "It was only the beginning of showing you what you deserve."

"Yeah?" A sexy smile played over her lips. "Anything else I deserve that you can show me?"

The world. I couldn't give her that. All I had to offer was a quiet slice of Bourbon Canyon. Nights at home painting models. Weekends where I was at the distillery or the ranch.

Katrina's voice beat in my skull like a drum. *It's like that damn ranch is your mistress. Is this because of that kid who was mean to you in school? You're too afraid of making something of yourself?*

I could give her pleasure. I'd studied hard in that subject and none of the material had been forgotten. "I think you deserve Mama's cookies. And orgasms."

She laughed, the sound a balm to the nerves that refused to die down. "Sugar and spice. I like it."

"I like you." I kissed her before I had to confront how much I liked her. Ruby was a dream girl. Any guy who wasn't an idiot knew it and some days I was too smart for my own good. It robbed me of self-preservation. Ruby was the sun and I wanted to soak up her rays just a little longer. "What are you doing next weekend?"

"Mm. Hopefully you," she said against my lips.

Fuck yes.

# CHAPTER SEVENTEEN

Ruby

"There's a band playing at the park," Tenor said over the steak wraps he'd made for dinner. He'd insisted I see that he could cook. I really didn't care. Good food was good food.

My weekends with him had spoiled me so much that when I was home, I subsisted on sandwiches and take-out. I couldn't face cooking my own mediocre meal and then eating it alone.

"Do you like them?" I asked.

He lifted a shoulder. "I'm sure they're fine. You wanna dance?"

I mimicked his casual shrug. "Only if you want to."

He set his wrap down. "Would you rather stay in and watch me paint again?"

He made it sound like the bottom-shelf selection, but it actually sounded really nice. It was the middle of July and the area was gorgeous. Still green, not yet too dry, the picture outside Tenor's window was paradise. If that was the backdrop to my evening? "Sounds like a fine date to me."

He wiped his fingers off. "You had a lot of fun at the street dance."

I smiled. "It was fun, but you don't need to recreate it every time we're together. I like quiet nights in too." Most of the time. I pointed to my empty plate. "Especially when it comes with good food. But there is one thing that is missing."

He lifted his brows. "What?"

"A glass of bourbon."

The corner of his mouth tipped up. "Bourbon's best enjoyed with family and friends."

"And what am I?" When his expression froze, panic rose in my blood. What must he think of me? He'd said casual. No definitions, and here I was, a week later, asking him to define me. I picked up my plate to take to the sink. "I want to study some accounts, and I have a new book. I can pour us some drinks. You don't even have to tip."

"Ruby."

His soft tone got me to stop. "It's okay, Tenor. Which bourbon do you want?"

"Your pick," he said quietly.

I took two rocks glasses out of the cupboard and bent to select a bottle that I hadn't tried yet. He had a bottle from the Copper Summit seventy-five-year anniversary special barrel five years ago.

When I rose, he was standing in front of me. He was working his jaw back and forth like he didn't know what to say.

I set the small, squat bottle on the counter and put a

hand on his chest. "I didn't mean to make anything awkward."

"You want more."

I did. And he wasn't promising more. It was me. I moved too fast, got too serious, and read too much into the men I dated. But Tenor and I weren't exactly dating. We were sleeping together.

Yet he'd asked me if I wanted to go to the park. That was date-like.

Confusion swirled in my brain. He wasn't hot and cold, but he was . . . stop and go. I couldn't force him to see me as a green light. He'd crashed and burned before, and for whatever reason, he saw me as a potential head-on collision. Meanwhile, I was stuck in a traffic circle, going round and round. Maybe in twenty-five years, he'd be sending me memes about romance novels. And I'd be my mom, giggling at them, knowing damn well I had never gotten over him.

I'd stay on my circular path until Tenor took a turn. Because I liked him, and there was a chance. I just needed to give him time and not ruin this. "I want to enjoy being with you and doing things that friends don't do with each other."

He clasped his hand over mine, holding it to his chest. A divot formed between his brows. Gradually, it went away and his gaze darkened. "What—exactly—is it that friends don't do with each other?"

The air between us thickened. He gave me an out and I took it. "They don't think about you naked when you're painting your models."

A brow arched. "Is that all?"

I licked my bottom lip and his gaze tracked my tongue. "They don't get off in each other's beds."

His pupils dilated and he crowded closer. "It was only you in my bed."

My heart started pounding and heat flooded my body. Thank goodness we were beyond the awkwardness. This was a much better place to be. "We can fix that."

"We can. You know what else friends don't do?"

Excitement blossomed in my belly, spreading that delicious heat that only Tenor could create. "What?"

"Show you how possible those impossible intimate scenes really are from your books."

A strangled sound left me. "I'm not sitting on your face."

He stroked his thumb up and down the side of my wrist. A shiver traced from his touch to right between my legs. A direct path. "Aren't you just a little curious?"

A lot curious. And a lot mortified. "No." My voice pitched up.

"Who knew you were a little liar." A slow smile spread across his face. "I promise you, Ruby, I would very much like that." He dropped his grip on my hand. "But it's your choice."

"It can't be a good look for a girl."

His gaze intensified. "It's the best view." He trailed his fingers over my collarbone, down the simple crop top I wore to the long, flowing skirt that was more comfortable for hanging out at home. "Those pretty pink folds, open and glistening, begging for my tongue." He flattened his hand on my hip. "Those legs clamped around my head, and those sweet little moans vibrating through your whole body and right onto my tongue."

My breathing quickened. Oh god. Was I going to do this?

Why not? Why not try it with a guy who made me feel treasured? This thing between us wasn't supposed to be serious, and wasn't that what two people having a fling did?

My heart raced. I was a vanilla girl. I didn't have much experience outside of vanilla sex. Smothering him with my pussy didn't feel vanilla.

Was I going to do this?

More importantly—was I going to miss out on the chance?

I lifted my chin. "Okay. Show me that's not far-fetched."

Tenor

Her shyness got to me. Dug into my chest real deep.

Was I a bastard for doing this?

I could give her this experience. I could show her how good it could be. How much I really liked it. We hadn't even started and I knew it'd blow my damn mind.

I should back away. Have perfectly spectacular sex in the bedroom. But she truly didn't believe a guy would like to have her on his face, all his for the taking. And that was just wrong. I led her to the couch and flipped the red-plaid throw blanket over the cushions.

Ruby glanced toward the window at the sun sinking toward the tops of the trees. "Right here?"

I'd take her anywhere, but I went back to that night when she'd been tucked into the corner of my couch and reading that romance novel with those scenes she didn't believe. "That night you told me you didn't believe it was possible? I very much wanted to show you then and there just how feasible it was."

Her eyes flared the way they always did when I showed real interest. Good thing she couldn't tell how much I really wanted her. It'd scare both of us away.

I lay on the couch, letting my feet dangle over the armrest, and tossed my glasses onto the end table behind my head. "Come here."

She stood like a scared little deer and I was the truck bearing down on her.

That was my error. I tapped my chest. "Just stretch out with me first."

She ran her hands down her skirt. The long fabric was just as sexy on her as the shorter skirts. More important, she felt comfortable in them.

Finally, she did as I asked. I tucked her toward the back of the couch and kept an arm banded around her. "I'm not going to ask you to strip and just crawl on top."

She chuckled, her muscles relaxing under my hold. "I was kind of scared."

"No, Ruby. All this is to make you more comfortable about how damn sexy you are."

She tilted her face up to me, a question in her eyes. Then she smiled. "You're always so thoughtful."

There was something else she'd wanted to say. I ran back what I had said.

Right. I'd made it sound like we were back to playing pretend. There was no such thing as fake sex, but I'd made it sound like there was no emotion involved. I couldn't take that back. Emotions were messy and they did me no good.

I used my fingers to tip her face back up. "I might be

thoughtful, but I'm being really fucking selfish right now." I rocked my hips up so my erection prodded her hip.

A sultry smile graced her face and she turned until our torsos were pressed together. She ground against me. Another groan slipped out of my throat.

"Fuck, Ruby. Keep doing that and I'll make a mess in my pants."

She did it again and I stuffed my hand into her hair and brought her lips to mine. She moaned against my lips. When she opened for me, I licked inside and stroked my tongue against hers. The kiss was a promise. That she'd be comfortable with what we were going to do. And that she'd fucking love it.

With my other hand, I bunched up her shirt. I wouldn't strip her down, but she had to know there was nothing to hide. She pushed up so I could drag the garment over her head. The bra she wore today was light-pink lace.

"I'm going to start here and work my way down." I tugged the straps down her shoulders, then pulled the lace cups down until her tits popped free.

Her hair swirled around her head, shadowing her face when it hung down. She was biting her bottom lip. The epitome of temptation.

I cupped each breast and rolled her nipple gently between my thumb and forefinger. A tremble went through her and her eyes slid shut. Perfect. She was getting out of her head. I slid my hands around her back and nudged her up so I could suck a pearly nipple into my mouth. Her moan resonated through her chest. Fuck, yes. I had her.

I gave each side equal attention. She was rocking

over my stomach. I hadn't been exaggerating earlier. If she had been doing this over my cock, I'd have blown. That wouldn't have stopped me, but I wanted this experience to be about her. It's what I could give her.

As she rocked, I bunched her skirt up and hooked my fingers around her underwear. For only a brief moment, she stiffened before she moved her legs so I could drag the panties off.

I released her tight bud with a pop. Lust hazed her eyes when she looked down at me. The flush on her cheeks was from me and I'd never get tired of putting it there. I could do it for an eternity.

I shoved the thought away and kneaded her ass cheeks before feathering my hand around her hip and down the inside of her thigh until I hit her wet heat. "I really want to taste you now."

I teased her, slipping a finger through her seam, touching on her clit and then reversing direction. She wiggled her hips, seeking more, trying to demand release. I wouldn't give it to her. Not yet.

"Do you want that?" I asked.

She swiveled her hips. "Yes."

I pushed a finger inside her tight pussy and withdrew it. She let out a whine.

*Yes.*

My erection pounded against my zipper. Soon.

I pushed into her again and a shudder rippled down her body.

"Ride it, Ruby."

She did. Greedily. Her tits were still spilled out of her bra. The show would haunt my dreams and rob me of sleep. Likewise, it'd get me through the next ten years of abstinence when it was time to let her go.

And she would want to go. It was inevitable.

Until then . . .

I took my finger out, loving how she sagged with disappointment, and urged her to crawl up. "Get on."

She scrambled up, and I helped her. At the very peak of her ascent, when her skirt was smothering me instead of her wet heat, she paused.

"You're going to fucking kill me if you don't get that pussy on my tongue," I growled.

That was enough to coax her the rest of the way.

*Finally*.

Her skirt draped over my head like a tent, but I didn't care. Her legs quivered as I sought out her clit, licking and nibbling. I had an ass cheek in each hand and I devoured her, stopping only to say, "So fucking good."

She was shaking, her climax only moments away. "I can't believe—" she moaned. "Tenor. Don't stop."

From disbelieving to begging. I grinned as much as I could with my tongue busy. Using the same finger as before, I pumped in and out of her. She cried out after the first wave of her orgasm crashed into her.

She gripped and squeezed my finger as she bucked. I held her to me.

"God, Tenor! Yes!" She rode me, milking every last drop of pleasure I could give her.

She pitched forward and I caught her.

"Stay right where you are," I said against her thigh. "I'm going to take you from behind."

Carefully, I slid out from under her. She had one leg propped on the floor and the other stuffed into the cushions. Without my hair to hold on to, she was clutching the back of the couch and the armrest.

The sultry, satisfied way she looked over her shoulder

at me was another image I'd never forget. A thoroughly sexed Ruby, on my couch, waiting for me to fuck her.

I yanked my zipper down and freed my dick. I hissed. The harsh movements were nearly painful and she was the only relief.

"Tenor?" Her eyes dropped down to my erection. "Take me hard and fast. Okay? It's what you need."

I couldn't respond. I did need it.

I hitched her skirt up, appreciating the creamy round ass presented before me, and placed myself at her entrance.

I slipped my hand around her hip. She stopped my progression with hers and shook her head. "Hard and fast, Tenor. Fuck me hard and fast."

I thrust into her. She was so damn soaked and I slid home like we were meant to fit together like this for eternity.

"Ruby." My body shook as I held myself still. It was a plea. All the sex I'd ever had hadn't been about me. I had studied it as diligently as I attacked everything else. I made it good for my partner. If it was good for her, it was good for me. I'd already gotten Ruby off, but this would be all about me. All about my pleasure. All of it.

"Fuck me, Tenor."

My hips kicked of their own accord, and I kept going. Fingers digging into her waist, I pounded into her, grunting like a fucking animal. Her moans mingled with mine. The slapping of our flesh filled the room, and when my climax hit me with the force of a freight train, I roared her name.

My breathing was heavy as I caught myself from collapsing onto her and spilling both of us onto the end table.

"Goddamn, Ruby." Her body still pulsed around me.

She let out a satisfied giggle. "That was nice. Very believable, Warhammer."

I ran my hands up and down her body. Her tits still hung out and I was getting hard again just thinking about it.

The build of my arousal was a nice distraction from how Ruby let me be myself. From how her complete acceptance of me made me think there could really be something substantial between us. "Tell me. Is there anything else you've read that you don't think could really happen?"

She turned her face into mine. "I'm not sure even you could replicate zero gravity."

"That may be out of my realm of possibility." I kissed her bare shoulder. "How about you research while I paint?"

"You're not talking about social media posts, are you?"

"Nope." I skimmed my hand up her thigh. "Come up with a few things to try out so we can do them next weekend too."

"Is that another invite?"

I'd invite her every weekend if I could. Move her in and—

Fuck, I couldn't get too far ahead of myself. I should push it off. Skip a weekend. But in this case, I was the anti-Goldilocks. Every weekend was too much, but at the same time, it was not enough. Damn.

Buried balls deep in her wasn't the place to think rationally. "Next weekend, Goldilocks."

# CHAPTER EIGHTEEN

Ruby

Every time I looked at the stool on the edge of the bar, my face burned. I scurried past to deliver two blackberry bourbons to Jason and his daughter.

"Thanks, Ruby," he said. "How's Tenor?"

Questions about Tenor caught me off guard. People still thought we were steadily dating, while in reality, things were new. Whatever those things were.

Were they new—or just slow? Plodding? Tentative? I'd like to think new, but Tenor set the pace and he made bourbon, a spirit that had to age for years to be called a bourbon. I functioned at the speed of a viral post, and he worked with aging barrels.

I smiled and went for a general answer. "I'm trying to keep him out of trouble."

Jason barked out a laugh. "It's a tough job with that kid."

I took their empties and went back behind the

counter. My phone buzzed. I squinted at the screen. At least five tennis emojis were next to Dad's message.

**Dad: Ready to take me on?**

I scanned the tables. Everyone had refreshed or half-full drinks.

**Me: When?**

**Dad: When can your new man join? What's his name again?**

**Me: Taking it slow. Don't know that we're at meet-the-parents level yet.**

**Dad: Have you met his?**

I chewed on my lower lip. If I said yes, he'd get pushy. If I said no, well, I hated lying.

**Me: I'll talk to him. Mom's not back yet anyway.**

**Dad: Did you hear she ditched Dave?**

**Me: Daniel?**

I had actually thought Mom would try to make it work with Daniel. The only guy who was a constant in her life was Dad. How hard was that for her?

**Dad: Whatever his name is, he's gone. Tell your guy we'll take it easy on him.**

**Me: No you won't.**

He replied with a bunch of laughing emojis.

Smiling, I looked up when the entrance door whooshed open. I caught myself before I could grimace.

"Oh, Crock— Uh, Cara. Brock. Hi." I snatched the rag from the sink and swiped at the already pristine counter. "How was the honeymoon?"

"Ugh." Cara rolled her eyes and took a seat on a stool. "Hot. Who goes to Jamaica in the summer?"

"But we barely left the room," Brock added, his voice low and suggestive.

I choked when he sat on the stool Tenor had taken me on. Turning my head, I coughed into my shoulder. "Sorry. Excuse me." My cheeks were hot, and I couldn't look at him. "What can I get the newlyweds?"

"Ooh, a mojito. That was yummy." She hugged Brock's arm.

Brock didn't return his wife's affection. "I'll have what that guy was having when I walked in."

Blackberry bourbon. He wasn't going to try neat in front of me again.

Cara leaned over the counter, her gaze tracking me as I mixed the drinks. "Why didn't we cross paths after high school? We both stayed in Bozeman."

Hadn't we been over this the last time we were here? "Our lives went in different directions." Mine had blissfully been away from hers until now.

"Is your mom still in that tiny apartment?"

The one she had paid for by herself while she raised a kid almost entirely alone? "No. She has a condo, but she's selling and getting an RV since her job is mobile and she's all about the outdoor life." That had been the news during her last call. The hike had been wonderful. She wanted to do it forever.

Brock snorted.

Cara's face screwed up. "Ew. Living in an RV is so—"

"Exciting," I finished brightly. "For a woman who worked three jobs while going to school and raising me, it's an adventure."

Mom might be flaunting her empty nest in front of her little birdie, but I'd defend her choice until the end of time, especially to Crock.

Cara stiffened. "Right. Of course." Her smile turned

sweet. "Does she need an agent? I still work out of Bozeman."

Oh. Shit. "Um, she has a guy."

"Who? I probably know him."

"I'll have to ask. I can't remember his name." Not a total lie. Mom probably had someone in mind. It wouldn't be Cara.

"You and Tenor going to build a house?" Brock asked. He used his straw to stir his drink. If he got half of it down, I'd be surprised. He reached into his back pocket and slapped a business card onto the countertop. "I have some availability."

I didn't pick it up. "Tenor has a house in the mountains."

Brock left his card and shrugged. "Some couples have an issue consolidating places. He might have a history in his house that's just a reminder for you."

He had no history in his house. Except for me. Well, I was the present. One day, I might be the past. A sharp pain stabbed between my ribs. "Excuse me."

I rushed to the stockroom. Waving my hand at my hot face, I paced where they couldn't see me.

What was my problem? I'd made a commitment not to rush him.

But I was getting impatient. I wanted to be important to him. I wanted to be wanted by him. Physically, I was, but the more we were together intimately, the more I longed to expand on the undeniable emotional connection we had. I wanted more moments like that first time in front of Curly's when he'd told me why being seen on a date bothered him. He'd confided in me and that had made me feel special. So terribly important to him. Yet not critical enough that Tenor declared he couldn't live without me.

Or . . . I could just be scared of indecisive guys who came and went from my life without committing until they told me I was too predictable. Brock was getting in my head again. The ass. I couldn't let anything he said get to me.

I sucked in a deep breath and scanned the shelves. What could be my excuse for darting away?

Glasses. I selected two and breezed back out. Cara had her head tipped toward Brock. She was drinking out of Brock's straw.

She slid his glass in front of her. "You should come out with me tomorrow night."

I blinked at her. "And do what?"

She giggled. "Girl things. We can come here. That is, unless you're working."

The idea of hanging with Cara in my safe space grated on me more than serving her. "I have plans. With Tenor."

She pouted and whipped the little purple straw around her drink. "You shouldn't make a guy your whole identity."

Whoa. A slow burn of indignation started in my gut. "I've been told it's my work I make my identity," I said coolly.

"I'll say." She snickered. "Since the boss is your boyfriend."

"We can do it another time." I should've shut her down, but this was the second—third?—time she'd asked. Was she lonely? I knew about that. But also, what about her new husband? Didn't she want to get lost in him?

Brock's eye twitched. Was he wondering the same thing? Maybe he didn't want his wife going out with me. Or was Cara his identity? Without her around, who would make him feel all powerful and manly?

Maybe I would meet Cara for a drink. We could go to Flatlanders Prohibited. That way, I could have a night out to show them I wasn't waiting around on Tenor, and she'd never want to go out with me again after a night of Allen staring at her boobs.

"I'll call you." She pushed her empty glass toward the edge and tapped the counter with her finger.

Brock's brow furrowed and he put a hand on her lower back. "Hey, hon. Let's get home. I have plans for you," he growled.

I held in a shudder, but Cara giggled. She slipped off her stool and draped herself over Brock. "By-ee, Rubes."

She was on her way out the door when she turned and snapped her fingers. "What's your number?" she called from the exit.

I was tempted to tell her to ask her husband, but I wouldn't go that low. None of us wanted the reminder of me trailing after Brock like a lost puppy. Waiting for him at my apartment when he was two hours late—because he took a nap. In the coffee shop when he'd stood me up because he got so busy with work and "forgot" to call me.

The second time, he'd said he needed space to reevaluate what he wanted in life.

I'd been a doormat.

Was I still being a doormat? Tenor treated me remarkably better, yet I was waiting for him.

Crock was watching me and so were the customers.

Oh. "Just stop in some Friday night," I said. "I'll see if I'm free after."

Perhaps Tenor would let me bunk with him if I was out late with Cara.

I did not want to go out with her.

As if I had summoned him, he entered from the lobby door. His brow crinkled when he saw Crock in the parking lot walking back to their car. He pinned me with his gaze, and concern fired in his eyes.

He nodded to Jason but swept past him, clearly on a mission. Jason opened his mouth and shut it.

"Everything okay?" Tenor asked.

The tension in my shoulders unknotted. "Cara asked me out."

He arched a brow. "Are you going?"

"I dunno. Maybe?"

"Why?"

"I . . . don't know. We used to be friends."

His gaze darkened and his jaw was rock hard. "You used to date Brock. Would you go out with him again?"

"No," I huffed.

"The guy I hated in school—he was abrasive at best. Mean at his worst. He was awful to me, and he'd corner me when no one was watching or when my brothers weren't around. He never got physical, surprisingly, but his verbal assault always hit its target."

"That's awful."

He shrugged it off like he didn't want to dwell on it, and I couldn't blame him. "It sucked, but I could count on him to be one thing—an asshole. Everyone could. He had a reputation. I think the worst thing that came from my interactions with him was that I thought every bully would be blatant. Then I started dating and all of Katri-

na's red flags were invisible. Her comments were insidious. Little digs here and there to highlight I wasn't like
my brothers, but I didn't notice them at first. Then,
after the blowup, I thought back, and yep, it was all
there. It's okay to give someone a second chance, but
you're already questioning if she's genuine. Cara already
showed you who she is. Don't waste your time on her."

How did I know anymore whether I was wasting my
time or not?

Cara might've been nicer than normal tonight, but
there was a strong chance she'd devolve back into her
normal style. She'd make friends in Bourbon Canyon.
They'd be other entrepreneurs like her. Business profes-
sionals. Not someone who tried to look and sound
trendy online all day while getting lost in smut all night.
I would no longer suit her. I would become boring. And
I'd be left wondering if she was really trying to use me to
feel superior or if she was oblivious to how she sounded.

I knew the real answer. It was always the same. With
Brock. With my other exes. Even with my parents. Just
once, I wanted the answer to be different. For someone
to choose me because I was me. And Tenor was. Kind
of. I could wait a little longer for him, but not for Cara.
"Okay. You're right."

He leaned close, his mouth to my ear. "I know."

Flutters erupted in my belly. Damn Brock and those
worries he'd planted. Tenor made me feel good about
myself. He was a guy I could bring home. Not even Dad
could find anything wrong with him. Except that he was
part owner of the company I worked for. Dad probably
also wouldn't be thrilled about the age difference.

Was there a chance Tenor would ever meet my
parents? We weren't serious, but would he play one inno-

cent tennis match just to appease my father? With Dad, the game wouldn't be so innocent. I never thought a game of tennis would be cutthroat, but Dad turned everything that way.

I could at least get Tenor on the courts. Ease into the topic. Just in case the day came. And maybe because I wanted to see my cowboy turn into a studlete. "Think you can get away tomorrow or Sunday to hit some balls around?"

"I don't golf."

I smiled. "That'd be interesting with rackets."

His right eye twitched. "I hope you're not talking about pickleball."

A laugh burst out of me. "You sound like my dad. What is the thing between tennis players and pickleball players? They're often the same people."

He drew himself to his full height. "Except when they're not and tennis players can't get any court time because of fucking pickleball."

My laughter grew and his expression got more disgruntled. He'd have that in common with Dad. "Any time those pickleball players aren't dominating the courts, then."

He ground his teeth together and glanced away, but his lips twitched. "There is always an open court." He caught my gaze and a devious grin spread across his face. "On the Bailey Memorial Courts." He winked. "To further encourage the growth of Bourbon Canyon High School's tennis team. No pickleball allowed."

"Of course. You're devious."

"I believe the term you're looking for is philanthropic." The corner of his eyes crinkled. "And I'm free whenever you want, Goldilocks."

Tenor

Turned out, Ruby wanted to hit the court as soon as she returned to Bourbon Canyon. This weekend, we'd scrimmaged for an hour. Yesterday, it had rained. Today, it couldn't have been more perfect for a match. Sunny with a light breeze, it wasn't too hot.

"You're really good at this." Ruby packed up her racket.

"Thanks. You're not bad yourself."

"I have some skills. My dad taught me, so I was learning when he was. He really wanted me to play in school." She shrugged.

There was something else she wasn't saying. "You didn't want to?"

"I didn't care, but Dad can be . . . It would've been like a football dad yelling from the bleachers."

"That doesn't pair well with tennis."

She flashed a quick smile. "Neither does Dad but that doesn't stop him from bringing his football energy to the courts."

I didn't elaborate on my experience. I had played from seventh grade until graduation. Tennis had kept me sane. It was a sport that tended to attract more mathletes than alpha-male athletes. I could expend my frustration on the court after a shit day. Nobody cared that I liked spreadsheets and Warhammer, and I won some matches.

My games hadn't been as anticipated as Tate's and Teller's football games, but I hadn't cared. With a gaggle of younger siblings and foster kids, my parents hadn't wanted to risk the noise level and distract any players. The fewer the spectators, the better as far as I had been concerned. Tennis had been it for me. I'd been teased moderately less for it than I had with Warhammer.

I tucked my racket into my bag with my spare. I always carried two. Old habits died hard.

She walked to her car. Her flirty little white skirt swung around her thighs. "That was a nice treat. I got to see you in shorts, and it was a mellow game."

It hadn't felt mellow when I'd wanted to toss the racket and haul her to my pickup. Playing while turned on was an inconvenient experience.

Missing her all damn week was another one. I'd nearly stayed home on Wednesday just to see her. There was no reason I couldn't miss a week, other than the sense I was being a traitor to myself. To the promises I'd made myself all those years ago when the person who was supposed to have my back stabbed it instead.

I was falling for Ruby.

Pressure squeezed my lungs together. The same sensation I'd gotten when I'd been cornered by that jackass in middle school and the first two years of high school. He'd seen the real me. He'd seen how different I was from my brothers. And he'd prodded every single insecurity until it was raw and exposed.

I pushed my glasses up. This wasn't high school. I was a goddamn adult, and Ruby was a good person. She wasn't superficial or fake. She wasn't Katrina. She was special, and I couldn't quit seeing her if I tried.

"See you Friday night?" I pulled her close, pressing her into her car door.

"Friday night."

I claimed her mouth. Her lips were hot from the sun, her minty flavor branding itself onto my taste buds. I could've kept her pushed against the door for another two hours, playing a game of a different sort.

Slowly, I pulled back and released her.

"Drive safe."

She nibbled her lower lip and shifted her weight. "Hey, um . . ."

The band around my chest returned. This was it. She was done with me. I couldn't pinpoint why, but I *knew*. I just wasn't enough for her.

"Would you ever consider a doubles game?"

Surprise eased the tightness around my shoulders. "Doubles?"

She nodded and squinted against the sun, uncertainty scrawled over her features. "Dad asked, and well, my mom would be his partner. She takes the edge off him. So . . . what do you think?"

My mind whirred, stalled, then circled again. "You want me to meet your parents?" The squeeze returned. I could barely draw a breath.

She flailed her hands around. "You don't have to, I swear. Meeting them would make this more serious than it is. I'll figure out something to tell them."

*If you think I'm going to let my daughter get engaged to some man-child still suckling from his mama's teat, you're dumber than you look.* I swallowed hard. "No, it's . . ."

I frowned, hating her declaration of how casual we were. But wasn't that the way I wanted it? Her blush was furious, and it wasn't from passion or the game. She was embarrassed.

The acid in my stomach crawled farther up my

throat. Would she leave thinking she'd overstepped? "I met Katrina's parents."

She drew back but didn't say anything. I appreciated the small downturn of her lips. A hint of distaste at my ex's name. I knew how she felt, because I felt the same every time I saw fucking Brock.

"It didn't go well," I continued. "They grilled me about what I did, what my future aspirations were, and what I did in my free time."

"And that's when it all blew up?"

I sucked my teeth against my lips. "It started with some bullshit from her dad and just snowballed into a large explosion and a few public tantrums from Katrina."

"She sounds delightful."

"Her dad was too. He had political aspirations. My last name made him excited. But he was expecting a Tate and he got me."

"No offense to your brother, but that's just stupid. He should've been delighted that his daughter had such good taste in men."

I smiled unexpectedly. "You would've been the only one with that opinion."

"I wouldn't have been. You just picked the wrong women."

They'd all bemoaned picking the wrong guy. The wrong Bailey brother. "Thanks for the vote of confidence."

Her pink lips turned down. "It's more than that. And don't worry. Dad can be pushy, but he usually only asks because it's the first test a guy can fail with him. I can make it clear we're not playing that game." She grinned. "Pun intended."

I shoved a hand through my hair. "No." A tennis

game with her father should be no big deal. I was an adult, and it wasn't like her dad was Katrina's father. "It was just a surprise." I wasn't expecting to relive the experience like it'd happened last week.

That cultured fuck's voice rang through my head. *You're a guy who lacks ambition of his own. You can't make my daughter happy. You can't even make your own money without your mommy and daddy's help.*

I blinked. The last part had morphed into Bobby's voice. I prodded at my temples. Dammit. I wasn't a goddamn kid anymore, standing quiet while someone trashed me. Nor was I some guy who'd gotten dumped. *Years* had passed. "I'll do it."

"Seriously, Tenor. It's okay. I'll talk to Dad—"

"No. Next weekend." I tipped her chin up so she could see how fucking serious I was.

"Mom's not back from her trip until the end of the month."

The cool beat of relief inside my chest couldn't be denied. I'd suck it up and meet her parents, but I'd take the extra time before then. "Whenever your mom's ready."

She put her warm hands on either side of my face. "Thank you. I promise to keep Dad reined in."

That was ominous. I gave her a quick kiss. "Drive safe."

Her saucy smile as she got behind the wheel would've been my undoing if she hadn't been driving away.

I waved, then tossed my tennis bag into my pickup. I checked my phone.

**Teller: You in town?**

I punched in my response. **Yeah. Ruby just left.**

**Teller: Meet me at Mountain Perks.**

I arrived at the coffee shop before he did. It closed in an hour. I lingered in my pickup until he parked behind me. Downtown was quiet for a Sunday. Only a few people drifted along the sidewalks outside of the shops. Only Mountain Perks and Lilly's Pad, the flower shop, were open. A small eatery at the end of the block had already closed for the day.

I got out and Teller lifted a brow. His gaze dipped down to my athletic shoes and touched on my basketball shorts. "Been a while since I've seen you outside of jeans."

"I wore a suit last weekend."

He whistled. "Never did tell me how that wedding was. The bride just put up a billboard outside of town if you're looking to buy."

"Not from her."

He flashed a grin. "She ain't making friends here, that's for sure. And her new husband is pissing off as many contractors as possible building that monstrosity of theirs."

"Good."

He laughed and we went into the coffee shop. The rich scent of roasted coffee beans surrounded us. I ordered a coffee with cream. Teller ordered something with caramel.

"Your drinks are getting fancier," I said after we got our order.

"Makes up for my life getting simpler."

"That's not a bad thing."

He scowled. "Not for you, old man. You found someone. I have nothing when I get home except for the cold foam residue around my glass."

"I hope you're happy for a long time with it."

"Not as happy as you and Ruby." He grunted. "I'm glad you took a chance on her. You're different."

The cream in my coffee curdled in my stomach. I wasn't different. I was the same. That was the issue. I hadn't changed for anyone, and that had always been the issue. "Did you invite me here to ask about Ruby?"

"In a way." He rolled his shoulders. "Wynter caught me, asked if I'd be willing to have pictures of me taken when I'm doing a tasting. I was against it, but after booking *three* weddings and now a reunion too next summer, I figured I'd see if my face could sell some bourbon. Ruby might be onto something."

As long as Wynter didn't ask me. "Not that I mind, but why couldn't this wait until we're both in the office tomorrow?" I didn't mind talking about Copper Summit business anytime or anywhere, but I'd never want to test whether my mug could sell a thing.

"We haven't talked much lately."

"You miss me," I teased.

His scowl was supposed to be playful, but I caught the flash of loneliness. "You buzz away as soon as you're not needed every weekend."

For Ruby, I did. Cruz and Lane had also returned to Colorado to help with Foster House. Was Teller feeling like the lone bachelor among a ton of happy couples? The whole family was pairing off, Cruz and Lane were slowly decreasing their time with Bailey Beef, and that left Teller on his own.

Did that mean I wasn't a bachelor anymore? Was I off the market? It wasn't like I had wanted to be on the market after my last foray. My emotions had taken a few hits in the last couple of hours. My feelings for Ruby were getting inconveniently deeper, and then I would be meeting her parents soon. Something that had never been pleasant. Also something that wasn't insignificant.

I hadn't wanted to name what Ruby and I were. That'd make it real. A word could be undone. A relationship could be ended. A girlfriend could become an ex. Love could turn to heartbreak. I'd been at this hopeful point before, wondering what amazing things lay ahead, only to be kicked to the curb and left behind.

All this was supposed to have been just a date to a wedding, and somehow, feelings had grown, blossomed, dug roots around my heart. Those tendrils would become permanent soon, but I had no control over whether they stayed or got ripped out. That power was in Ruby's delicate hands. And I'd had no one to talk to about any of it.

I massaged the bridge of my nose. "The whole thing with Ruby. It's not how you think."

Was I really going to do this? Now that the wedding was over, I felt less like I'd be shoving all the blame onto Ruby. I'd dug the hole I was standing in.

So I did it. I told him about how Ruby and I had *really* ended up dating. His eyes widened as the story progressed. Though I kept it G-rated.

"Damn." He shook his head, disbelief crossing his face. His astonishment spoke volumes even if he'd only listened. "You really think you were faking?"

"That's all it was." Her moans when she got herself off in my bed rose in my head. Maybe faking hadn't been all. "That was all it was supposed to be."

He pondered me for a moment. "Being alone was safe. Telling yourself it was fake was safe. So, now what?"

"What do you mean?"

"You're not in safe territory anymore. You care about her."

"Of course I care about her." And didn't that feel like the most dangerous thing I could do?

"You're not letting her in."

"I have." I'd opened so many doors to her that I'd thought would always remain closed to a woman. "She's seen me paint my figures."

"No, I mean—" He shook his head. "You're not ready to hear it."

Anger blazed a trail across the back of my neck. I'd opened up to him and he was chiding me? People had been telling me what I wasn't my entire goddamn life and I was sick of it. "What the hell is that supposed to mean?"

Teller dragged in a long inhale, tapping his fingers against his mug. "Relationships aren't about how fun you can make them. Katrina only cared about how it looked to the outside world. She didn't care about quality."

"Don't you think I know that? Katrina's not in my life anymore. I don't want her to be."

"I saw her last weekend."

The jolt of shock was unwelcome. "Okay?" I gave zero fucks about Katrina or that she was in town, even though she kept coming up lately. The only reason I hated running into her was that it made me feel like that pathetic guy from ten years ago who'd put up with her in the first place.

"She was going into Flatlanders."

That I hadn't seen coming. "Doesn't seem her style."

"I think she avoids you."

I snorted. "Yeah, right." It was lucky I hadn't moved after her little shit-talking tour. All of her former coworkers at the bank either gave me those knowing, sympathetic looks or avoided my gaze altogether. I had moved all of Copper Summit's financials online after that.

"People know you, Tenor. No one bought any of her shit."

"She wasn't lying."

"She's more fake than you and Ruby were pretending to be. She's trash and that's why she's going to Flatlanders. It's a shithole."

A woman walked by, stopped, and pinned Teller with a glare. My stomach dropped. Madison Townsend. Shit.

She folded her arms over a cream-and-maroon flannel. Her jeans were as worn as Teller's. "How exactly would you know? Been sneaking in undercover?" Her shrewd gaze shifted to me. "I expected better of you than spreading lies about my brother's place."

I didn't care to get dragged into the Scooter-and-Teller drama. I kept my mouth shut.

Surprise passed through Teller's eyes, but he quashed it quick enough with the calmness he used to really piss people off. "He doesn't have to, Mad Maddy."

Her left cheek twitched at the nickname. She ground her teeth together and fury flashed in her eyes. Teller's expression was aloof, almost teasing.

My brother could be infuriating with little effort. I almost felt sorry for her. But she could've kept walking and left the conversation with my brother between me and him like it had been meant to be.

Teller scratched his chin. "Did you move back because Scooter wasn't causing enough trouble?"

Her eyes sparked. "Do you only wag your tongue

about Townsends when you need to feel superior, Bailey?"

"Nah." His smile was slow. "I only let my tongue taste quality."

She jerked, visibly stung. "Someday, you Baileys will realize that not everyone has it as easy as you." She stomped away and slammed her way out the door, the bell tinkling for dear life.

I exhaled. "Jesus, Teller."

He frowned at me. "What? She started it."

" 'I only let my tongue taste quality,' " I mocked.

"You've heard how bad the drinks served there are."

He couldn't be that clueless. People thought I was the naive one of the Bailey crew. "You made it sound like *she* was cheap."

"What part of saying I only let my tongue—" He blanched. "She did not take it sexually," he hissed, but his expression was fraught, like he truly had only meant to insult the crappy bar pours and not the woman herself. I believed him, but I wasn't Madison.

"She did." I might've been indignant about her interruption as well if I hadn't seen her be sort of considerate with Ruby.

"She didn't have to start shit. If she's that loyal to her asshole of a brother, then she's probably just as much trouble." He waved it off and took a long pull of his coffee.

"Let's hope we never have to find out."

# CHAPTER NINETEEN

Ruby

Tenor's pickup was still in the lot when I pulled into Copper Summit. It was Wednesday night, but he usually left shortly after my shift started. He also stopped in to say hi, and I was already looking forward to it.

As I closed in on the entrance, I spotted lots of bustling inside. People around the counter. Wynter was coming toward the door. She smiled when she saw me, but it had the tension of *I hate to tell you this . . .*

She opened the door and held up a sheet of paper that read **Closed. Sorry for any inconvenience.** "I'm so sorry. I was hoping to catch you before you left Bozeman. I forgot you were meeting me earlier." She shook her head, her blond hair flying. "I got distracted in the flurry. I'm so sorry. We'll reimburse your mileage, of course."

Wynter and Autumn were behind the various cocktails in the bar, and today, I had planned to join them on their brainstorming sessions to create content. Wynter would be busy mixing and tasting, and I'd catch it all. I knew before I'd even started that these posts would be dynamite.

I wasn't worried about the drive, but I had looked forward to hanging out with Wynter and Autumn. "Oh no, what happened?"

I scooted around her and entered. Tate and Teller were behind the bar. Teller tugged at the collar of his black Copper Summit polo. Tate wore a green flannel with the sleeves rolled up like he'd come straight from the ranch, which he likely had. Each had a grim expression, and both of them were looking at something at their feet. A toolbox was open on the counter and various tools were scattered around it.

Wynter taped the sign to the door. "I found water on the floor when I came in here earlier." She grimaced. "One of the sink pipes was leaking and it got under the flooring."

I went to the edge of the bar and peeked around. A guy was sprawled on his back, most likely a plumber, his head tucked under the sink cabinet. A light glowed from the vicinity of his head.

"Sorry about your shift tonight," Teller said to me. "Hopefully, we can be up and running by Friday."

"No worries." I wasn't working for the money. The shifts were my social life.

Ouch. I knew that was the case, but also . . . if I didn't have my bosses, I wouldn't have friends.

I was about to dig my phone out, but I paused. Wynter had told me that Teller had finally permitted us to use him for content, but I didn't want to surprise him. My work wasn't supposed to be a jump scare for individuals. "Supporters love a behind-the-scenes peek. Mind if I grab a few shots right now? It'd just be profile shots."

Teller's jaw tightened for a moment. "As long as you don't use hashtags like #toowettowork or #amanandhisleaks."

Next to me, Wynter snorted, and Autumn giggled.

"I'm going to use 'a man and his leaks' for my new tagline," the plumber said.

"I promise, no embarrassing hashtags," I said. "I'll protect your honor."

He lifted his chin, gesturing for me to do what I needed to. For the next few minutes, Wynter and I tossed ideas back and forth and circled Teller. She got some images and so did I.

The whole moment was more humbling than it should've been. I was the social media girl, but now my ideas were getting put into play. I was flexing more of my marketing degree, and today I felt like one of the team more than I ever had. For a girl with no family connections anywhere, I was honored to be connected to this family.

"I'll send mine to you, along with the ones I get at the next tasting we can host." Wynter squeezed my arm. "Tenor might be in his office if you want to catch him before he leaves."

I'd already made the trip worthwhile. The cherry on top would be seeing Tenor before I went home to my empty apartment. "Sure."

"I'll help you find him."

She followed me out of the tasting room and into the lobby. A tour must've just finished. Several people milled around the souvenir stands and another three were in line to check out.

"Ah, there he is," Wynter said, nodding toward the large windows that overlooked the distillation room. "You can just go right in."

My gaze was immediately drawn to Tenor's broad back as he stood at the half ring of computer monitors the distillers used to log temperatures, batch numbers, and inventory. He propped an arm on the standing computer desk and scrolled through something I couldn't make out. "Let me know if you want to reschedule," I said to Wynter, my gaze still on Tenor.

"I called Autumn, and we decided to meet at Curly's and make an evening of it anyway. Myles was already planning to stay home all night with the kids. You should join us."

Pleased, I smiled. "That sounds fun." A whole lot more fun than driving straight back home while everyone else had plans.

"Great. Just head there after you're done talking to my brother." She rushed off and I ducked into the distillery room.

The door shut behind me, blocking out the chatter of the guests. The machinery in the production room on the opposite side of the stills was quiet, resting for the night. No glass clinking or forklifts beeping as they backed up.

The place was quiet. Just the mash in the short, wide tanks bubbling, a warm, grainy smell filling the room. Still riding my content-creation high, I grabbed a couple pictures of Tenor from behind. The shot exuded quiet power and contemplation. Competence.

God, he'd be catnip to the introverted bourbon lovers.

I wove around the tank to Tenor's side.

He clicked a button and the monitor went dark. He turned, his lips tipping up. "Hey."

"How did you know it was me?"

"I knew."

My belly warmed and I fought an *aw-shucks* grin. His gaze dipped down my soft yellow camisole top to my cargo capris. I wasn't wearing a skirt, but there was no less heat in his gaze.

I showed him my screen. "I'm not using these, but should you ever decide to put yourself in front of the camera, you should use them." I smirked. "For now, they're for my personal use. I may send them to Wynter only to show her the authentic aesthetic I had in mind. Unless you want me to delete them."

His gaze heated. "Not if you tell me exactly how you use them."

I'd show him. But later. I tucked my phone away. We were secluded but not private. Instead, I changed the subject. "I hear I'm out of a job tonight."

He nodded. "It's a mess, but a small one." His brow furrowed as he crossed to me. "They didn't get ahold of you in time?"

"Wynter forgot I was coming early. It was going to be a brainstorming night."

"But I still get to see you." He kissed me, nice and slow, but also tame if any of the tourists peeked inside. When he pulled back, the crease was still in his brow. "I was just going to leave. You can join me."

Surprise washed through me. "To your game night?"

His jaw was set, like he couldn't believe he had invited me, but he nodded.

"You really want me to come?"

A shadow flitted over his expression. The offer

hadn't been easy for him. He'd protected that part of himself for so long. He cupped my cheek. "Leaving every Wednesday night when I could hang out with you instead hasn't been the easiest."

A small gasp left me. This man made me feel so treasured. I put my hands on his shoulders. "Having our own interests is healthy. Wynter and Autumn invited me out." I smiled. "I'd have fun with you, but Warhammer is your thing, not mine. You go. Have fun. And we'll *connect* on Friday."

"For the weekend?"

I bit the inside of my cheek or I wouldn't be able to speak around my grin. "If I'm invited for the whole weekend."

"You're welcome anytime. My place is y—" He clamped his mouth shut. "My place is always open to you."

*My place is yours.* Was that what he'd been about to say? But he hadn't. Yet what he had said was still sweet. "It's like I'm your girlfriend or something."

"Yeah, or something," he said softly.

Tenor

I was finishing in my office when Teller entered. He closed the door. The interior walls of the office were tempered glass facing the hallway on the upper level of Copper Summit. Each room was dark, including Teller's.

He plopped in the chair across from my desk. He

reclined and locked his hands behind his head. "Must be a Friday night."

"Get a calendar and you'd know." I'd been working late each Friday night Ruby was in the bar.

"Did you see what Ruby posted of yours truly?"

I hadn't. I took out my phone and pulled up Copper Summit on each app. A filtered photo of Teller scratching his beard and pondering the leak had hundreds of comments.

**If I start drinking bourbon, will he show up?**

**I need to get to Bourbon Canyon ASAP**

**This picture makes me think about *cock*tails differently.**

The comments were . . . thirsty, and some were downright inappropriate, but Ruby had replied conversationally, yet professionally to many of them, stoking enthusiasm and spreading information about our products. "Damn. She did some good work."

"I was just thinking . . ." He rubbed his chin. "People really do want to get to know us. We can give them a little more."

The pictures of me from the distillation room rose in my mind. To me, the image was boring, and that was likely what others would think. Ruby knew me, so she liked it. "I'm good sitting this out."

His lips pressed together. "It's not that I don't respect your decision to keep offline. It's just, it bugs the shit out of me. Before Katrina, you'd have done it."

No. "Not everything stems from her." Before Katrina, there had been Bobby. Keeping attention off me had always been the goal.

"Sure." He gave me that narrow-eyed stare, like he was seeing right through me. "You ever go to Bozeman?"

I saved the financial report I was compiling and closed out of my computer. I took my damn time too. Teller wasn't here to shoot the breeze. "Get to your point."

He remained unfazed. "Relationships go both ways." I didn't respond. "Seems like only Ruby's going in both directions."

Irritation clawed along my skin. "I also work the weekends." I folded my arms. "Cruz and Lane are gone a lot more. You might be single, but I'm sure Tate wants to see his family." Ranching wasn't just a full-time job. It was a way of life, and it'd take over with no help.

"We can always hire someone."

"But you haven't."

He assessed me. "If we do, would you change? Suddenly stay home or go see Ruby and find out what she's interested in?"

"She likes to read."

"That it?"

I wasn't about to tell him what else she liked. "She likes to be here."

"Have you asked her?"

I pushed my glasses up and rubbed the bridge of my nose. "For fuck's sake, Teller. You gonna charge by the hour to shrink my head?"

"Nah. You know I'm not an expert or my ex wouldn't have run off with someone like Scooter fucking Townsend."

"Wendi divorced him, so her taste isn't completely terrible."

He grunted. "All I'm saying is that . . . Fuck, I don't know. You still seem to be holding back."

"What the hell do you expect?" He was looking out

for me, but he was also making me seem like a selfish jerk.

"Nothing. Just remembering what Dad told us once."

A lump of molten lead formed in my gut. My parents' marriage was something I had aspired to. They'd loved each other so completely. So honestly. Dad had doted on Mama, and she'd done the same. I had tried to follow suit only to be called duplicitous. A liar. "And what was that? 'Early is on time and on time is late'?"

He gave me a *don't be a dumbass* look. "After Katrina, and after Wendi, he told us not to let those experiences scare us from giving ourselves fully to the women we fall in love with. He told us not to let our exes stop us from finding real love."

"How's that going for you?"

"Terrible. You?"

I wasn't sure yet. Looking back, I hadn't been in love with Katrina. I'd been an infatuated puppy. She'd been beautiful and smart and sexy. I hadn't been comfortable being myself around her.

Ruby was beautiful and smart and sexy. She was fun and kind and genuine. Her laughter was infectious. I had switched where I painted at my table so I could watch her. When she was studying other social accounts, she'd bite her lower lip and crinkle her brow. When she read, a faint blush would dust her cheeks and I'd know she'd gotten to a naughty scene. Then she'd catch my eye and smile. Sometimes, we returned to our hobby. Sometimes, we got naked.

I could be myself with her.

I'd also stayed in my environment. She slept over. I was out of my comfort zone, but I also wasn't. Did that mean we were one-sided? Ruby hadn't told me what more she wanted.

I never asked.

"I don't know yet," I answered. "We're taking it slow and she knows it."

"Are you taking it slow or looking for a reason it wasn't meant to work?"

"No, Teller, fuck. Do you think I have to have an engagement ring already? That we're planning the guest list for the wedding? Picking baby names?"

He kicked up a brow.

An inferno started at the base of my sternum. I cleared my throat. "I'm older than her and I'm still her boss. I'm not rushing her."

He tipped his head, eyeballing me like he'd caught me in a lie. "You actually thinking of getting married and having kids? That might take a little remodeling."

His tone was just shy of taunting. He and Tate had given me shit for building a place a fraction of the size of theirs. Dad had sat me down to see how I was doing. I'd told him I was just fine. More certain of anything than ever.

Now I was only certain that I wanted to keep seeing Ruby.

"I'm not engaged. Ruby's not pregnant." The image of her with a rounded belly flashed in my head. Would she wear a maternity dress so the skirt would still swish around her thighs? I would be able to press the fabric tight against the bump—

Fuck. I was *not* thinking of getting married, and I sure as fuck wasn't planning kids.

Was I more open to the possibility? Maybe. But taking it slow meant not planning a fucking wedding before our first month of official dating was in the books.

Were we officially dating?

Teller was still studying me.

I had to give him something to get him off my back. "I asked her to come to Billings with me earlier this week. Happy with that?" She had turned me down, and I'd been . . . disappointed. I'd wanted to see her face when she entered the quaint little game shop. Her shy smile when she met the guys I played with. Her questions about our process and how we played. She wouldn't have been rude or embarrassed, and that realization had made me glad I had asked. I trusted her.

A thoughtful expression played over his face. "Actually, yes. That does make me feel better. It's definitely out of your comfort zone." He frowned. "Didn't she go out with Wynter and Autumn last Wednesday?"

"Yes. Because she knows we don't have to be glued at the hip."

He smirked. "Is that how you guys do it?"

"I don't need glue."

He put his palm toward me. "Treading too close to TMI."

"I'm also meeting her parents. Soon." Dread filled my gut. What would they think of me? How could I show them that I respected their daughter, that I wanted the best for her, even if that wasn't me?

His brows lifted. "Both of them?"

I nodded. "Her mom and dad want to play doubles."

He let out a low whistle. "Tennis even. Do they know who they're going up against?"

"That was a long time ago. And to answer your next

question, no, I don't know when." Hopefully it'd be a while. Next summer. The summer after.

He pushed himself to his feet. "Maybe you are making progress."

"Thanks for the vote of confidence."

"Anytime." He sauntered out.

I scowled at my desktop for several moments.

What the hell? I wasn't letting what Teller said get to me. Ruby and I were doing just fine.

I checked the time. The bar closed in a couple of hours, but I'd shut my computer down. I tapped my fingers on the armrests.

I wanted to see Ruby.

I wanted to talk to my girlfriend.

She was working and I'd either pitch in or be the customer who hit on her all night.

I was heading down the stairs when my phone vibrated. I waited until I hit the bottom before I checked. My boots thumped to a stop. First one. Then the other.

**Unknown: Hey, it's Katrina. Can we talk?**

I stared at the message. What . . . the fuck?

I had deleted everything about her, but she apparently hadn't trashed my number.

Fuck no. I didn't want to talk. I swiped to delete the message and continued to the bar.

Inside, most of the tables were full after a couple of nights of being closed. Ruby was laughing with a couple of guys by the front windows. She glanced over and the smile that graced her face was all for me.

There had never been a time after the way Katrina had broken up with me when I had wished she'd call or text. I had trusted her and she'd tossed it all back in my face. She'd purposely humiliated me. All this message had done was make me glad that I wasn't home alone painting my figures.

I had moved on. I hadn't stayed in one place. And I liked where I was at. Maybe I even more than liked who I was with.

My chest constricted and I struggled to draw in a breath.

Taking it slow. Just like I'd told Teller. I wasn't rushing Ruby. Most of all, I wasn't rushing myself.

## Ruby

Tenor drank me in like he was seeing me for the first time in months. It almost shredded my nerves. I had to talk with him about my parents.

"Let me know if I can get you anything else," I said to the couple I'd been talking to.

I met Tenor in the middle of the bar by one of the few empty tables.

He stroked his gaze over my face, only this time, his eyes weren't just full of heat. Tenderness lit the yellow flecks in his soft brown eyes. "Hey."

"Hey yourself."

"Busy night. Need a hand?"

"I've got it all under control."

"Well then." A slow grin spread across his face. "I'm going to sit at the bar and see if the pretty bartender will go home with me tonight."

Pleasure filled me. "Don't get your hopes up. I heard she has a thing for nerds."

He leaned close. "I have a thing for romance readers who like to act out scenes from their book."

My cheeks grew hot and I glanced around. People were watching us, but they couldn't hear. At least, I hoped they couldn't. "Like the car scene?"

His gaze sharpened. "What car scene?"

"You'll find out." I bit my bottom lip and scurried away. When I peeked behind me, he was watching me through slitted eyes.

One of the delivery drivers walked in with his wife. He spotted Tenor. "Tenor! How's it going?"

While Tenor was occupied, I busied myself behind the bar, mixing refills and new orders.

Tenor broke away from the new arrival and rounded the bar. He gestured to the four cocktails I was ready to deliver. "Want me to take these out or make a spiced old-fashioned and a huckleberry spritz?"

"I'll get to mixing." The locals loved talking to Tenor. I knew the feeling.

The couple I'd been talking to was in the latter crowd. They smiled and chatted with Tenor. He stuffed his hands in his pockets and slouched, as ever, trying to make the other party feel less intimidated. Instead of wanting to lord over others thanks to his size and authority, Tenor tried to diminish himself so others could shine.

He caught me looking at him and shot me a promising stare before returning his attention to the guests. Having him around made my already enjoyable shift better. For the next hour and a half, we worked together until the last customer left. Then we closed down the place.

"Whew," I said, hanging the rag up. "That was a busy night."

"Helps make up for the last two nights we were closed." Tenor closed the tablet. He'd done all the books for me. It wasn't my least favorite job, but I wouldn't be applying for his position anytime soon.

"Did you cash out your tips?" When he gave me a *hell no* look, I grinned. "Some of those guys were tipping you, not me."

"Owners don't take tips. It's the rules."

It was not, but I had noticed that if any of the Baileys helped me, they gave me all the tips for the night.

He folded his arms and leaned against the counter. A muscle popped in his jaw and he got a faraway look in his eyes. He was no longer thinking about cashing out for the night.

"You have something on your mind?" I asked.

"Maybe."

I waggled my fingers toward myself. "Hit me."

"I'd rather spank you."

Immediate heartbeat between my legs. "I don't read those types of books." Hmm . . . being turned over his knee? I'd already sat on his face. "Yet."

"Christ, Ruby. I'll have to wipe tonight's tapes too if you keep that up."

"Wouldn't be the first time."

"Or the second."

I grinned, but the heat in my belly swirled, lowered. Working was definitely more enjoyable with him. "So? What's up?"

He paused for a second, then he tugged me to him. "Nothing. My mind was on work and not you. I need to fix that."

I sank into his hold and leaned my head against his chest. He wasn't being honest. Maybe whatever had been on his mind wasn't my business.

It might not be, but couples talked.

I waited another moment. His strong heartbeat thumped under my cheek. I couldn't worry about something small like this. I was reverting to the days when Brock would be moody. Usually, that type of moodiness preceded a dumping.

Tenor wasn't Brock. Otherwise, I wouldn't be dating him.

I leaned back and pressed a kiss against his hard jaw. "I hate to break the silence, but my mom is back in town."

He turned into a two-by-four against me. "Oh yeah?"

"Dad's hitting me up for a date to play."

"Right."

I pushed away, but he didn't release me. I hadn't upset him badly enough to let me go, but he hadn't relaxed either. "You don't have to—"

"I said I would," he said gently. "Two weeks?"

"You need time to practice?" I teased. He was good at everything he did. If anything, he might let my parents win.

"I might need a refresher. I don't want to be a bad partner."

"You could never be." I raised on my tiptoes and placed a kiss on his mouth.

His arms tightened around me, cinching me closer to him. "Two weeks. Saturday or Sunday, your choice. I'll be there." He kissed me again, lingering longer this time. "Now, what were you saying about a car scene from one of your books?"

# CHAPTER TWENTY

Ruby

The weekend both crawled by and flew. Nothing had been out of the ordinary, but the entire time had felt different. Last weekend had been the same as the weekend before, only Tenor had returned after chores and taken me to town for a coffee and a stroll by the river. We'd chatted and he'd asked about any other hobbies and fun things I liked to do. At the risk of being underwhelming, I'd been truthful. I liked my job, and reading, and maybe I'd join a book club.

It'd been pleasant. But starting last Friday, the air had been thick. Full of unspoken thoughts. Not so much on my end. And now it was Sunday afternoon and we were nearing what I suspected was the reason for the odd vibe. We were meeting my parents in twenty minutes.

Tenor had taken his pickup and I was in my car. I'd be leaving for Bozeman from the court when the game was over. This time I found the courts on my own. Hard to get lost in such a small town. The football field and track sprawled beyond the small two-court enclosure. A row of tall bushes blocked the wind on one side of the chain-link fence. Sure enough, the brown sign attached to the fencing read *Bailey Tennis Courts*.

Tenor pulled in behind me and we both parked.

I stepped into the empty lot. "I'm surprised it doesn't have 'no pickleball allowed' engraved along the bottom of the sign."

"Tate convinced me that was going too far." Despite his joking tone, Tenor's shoulders were rigid as he dug his bag out and walked through the opening in the fence.

I tied my hair back with the band I kept on my wrist as Tenor dug out his tennis racket. He bounced a ball on the ground, then on his racket and back to the ground.

I sucked in a breath and willed the trembling in my stomach to stop. Today would go fine. My parents would love Tenor. Everyone did. Likewise, Tenor was so easy-going, he'd be cool with my dad's abrasive nature. My mom would make sure Dad stayed in line.

"Want to warm up?" he asked when I retrieved my racket.

"Yes." Anything to vent the nervous energy coursing through me.

We lobbed the ball back and forth, the dull thunk of our rackets mingling with the sounds of cars around us and kids playing at the playground across the street. Tenor was all fluid strokes and lean muscle. He could cross the court in a few steps while I sprinted and still missed the ball. When he ran, his T-shirt plastered to his chest while hanging baggy at his waist. Just as I was about to return one of Tenor's slices, I caught a glint of a red pickup. My shot went high and wide, landing over the fence and in the bushes.

"Sorry!" I checked again. Yep. That was them. "They're here."

"I'll get the ball. You greet them." He jogged toward the other opening in the fence and went around to the bushes.

I exited through the one closest to me to meet my parents. Dad had parked. His smile was snide, a determined glint in his eyes.

I sighed mentally. *Not today, Dad.*

Mom hopped out, dressed in capri athletic leggings and a blue athletic top. Her chestnut hair was drawn back in a braid. "Hey, kiddo. Sorry we're late."

Dad got out, his eyes narrowed on Tenor and his mouth twisted up. Unlike Tenor's long shorts and baggy shirt, Dad looked like he could swing a club or a racket in his green athletic polo and khaki shorts that hit midquad. "You know how your mother is. Bill didn't leave her because of her nagging; it was because she's always late."

"You left the first time I was *late.*" Mom's gaze filled with challenge. Dad had always given her shit about Bill.

There was a beat of regret in his eyes, but it was gone so fast I was probably deluding myself. Instead, Dad snickered and reached into the back seat just as Tenor trotted up. Glad he hadn't gotten this quick of an introduction to Dad's obnoxiousness.

Tenor politely smiled at Mom, his features guarded, and stretched his hand out. "Nice to meet you. Tenor Bailey."

Dad jerked back from the open door of his pickup and slammed it. "Tenor Bailey? Veronica, is that what you were hiding?" Dad's brows crashed together. "What the hell were you doing, Bailey? Trolling playgrounds to get with my daughter?"

"Dad!" Humiliation swamped me as my gaze jumped to Tenor.

Color leeched from Tenor's face and his nostrils flared. "Robert Morgan?" he gritted out. His horrified gaze slid to me. "*He's* your dad?"

Dread fought against shock. "You two know each other?"

"Shit yeah," Dad said, his tone hard. "Tenor and I go way back."

Tenor's jaw was granite. "I knew him as Bobby."

Tenor

Bobby Morgan was Ruby's dad. *Fuck.*

The last set was stretching on too long, but I would put a stop to it now. All I had to do was restrain myself from smacking this damn ball into Bobby's tanned face.

Rage vibrated up and down my spine. I took a long inhale, bounced the ball, exhaled.

Ruby had declared that we wouldn't play. Her mom had seconded that motion. Even Bobby had looked ready to pack it in, if only to get me away from his daughter. But there was no way I was letting Bobby fucking Morgan think he'd scared me off again.

I had hoped to never see him again. How was I dating his daughter?

It'd been big news when he'd gotten some girl in

Bozeman pregnant, and I'd heard he didn't have much to do with the mom. After graduation, he'd lit a path out of Bourbon Canyon and hadn't returned. The last two years of school after he'd moved were the best two years I'd had since he'd first moved to town. I'd thought I was finally free of him.

Until today.

Ruby's goddamn dad.

"Any day," Bobby taunted. "Unless you're waiting for my daughter to get older."

I cringed and bounced the ball. Inhale. Bounce. Exhale.

"Dad, stop it." Ruby's voice was filled with disappointment and exasperation.

"Robert, knock it off." Veronica's tone matched her daughter's.

Inhale, bounce, exhale. Ignore him. Like I had always done. I'd proved I wasn't the weaker one. I'd been able to endure his teasing. Yet it hadn't mattered. I just got those sympathetic stares. Those pitying looks. No one had seen me. They had just felt sorry for me.

Then Katrina had happened. She'd seen me. And I'd gotten those *so sorry* stares again.

I served. The thunk on the racket rang loud in my ear and the serve went wide. Fuck.

Bobby stuffed an index finger into the air. Even his signal for out was obnoxious.

Veronica retrieved the ball and tapped it back to me with her racket.

I caught it. Ruby cast a worried look my way. Did she want me to throw the game?

Or was that sympathy darkening the blue of her irises?

Everything I'd eaten for the last month curdled in my gut.

Memories scraped over my skin. The old feelings of being a spectacle. I was a grown goddamn man, but my childhood tormentor was right in front of me, targeting my weaknesses like he always had. Only this time my weak spot was Ruby.

The crawling sensation from being watched prickled over my skin. We had no spectators. It was just memories fucking with me.

I counted to five on my exhale. Relaxed. I called on the distance I used to find when Bobby confronted me. My fingers tightened around the yellow ball. If I didn't ease up, I'd crush it.

He scuttled side to side, waiting for me. "Hate to break it to you, but you're still old enough to be her dad."

The ball hit my finger on a bounce and almost got away. I fumbled but caught it.

"Dad," Ruby snapped, "we're leaving if you keep doing that."

Bobby held his arms out. "What? Am I wrong?"

It was a thirteen-year age difference. Wynter and Myles had almost the same gap.

But Wynter had been a little older when she reconnected with Myles, and—

Dammit! He was getting in my head.

"It's not right, Robert." Veronica's mouth was tight. "And you know it."

Bobby dipped his chin down, his jaw sawing back and forth. Miracle of all miracles, he kept his mouth shut.

I ground my molars again and pictured the most

perfect serve right to the corner and bouncing to the side. A nearly impossible hit to return. "Three–two," I called and served again.

The execution happened as I had planned, only I played dirty and sent it to Veronica's side. She was the less experienced player. Robert had been doing the same damn thing to Ruby. Veronica didn't have the speed to return my serve.

Bobby threw his racket down. "Veronica! My grandma could've gotten that."

"And she would've told you to shut your mouth or be polite," Veronica shot back.

Chagrin flashed in Robert's gaze. "She would've. Sorry," he muttered, keeping his profile to me like I wasn't supposed to see him apologize.

"Good game, guys," Ruby said, coming to my side. She reached for my hand, but I pretended not to see, holding my racket, my knuckles white. I took the extra ball out of my pocket and crossed to my bag.

Robert prowled toward his bag on the other bench facing their side of the net. "Who knew Tenor here could play some tennis," he muttered.

"He went to state," Veronica said. When we all looked at her in surprise, she shrugged. "Robert's not the only one who spies on your dates."

"He took first at state," Ruby said quietly, giving me a shy smile. But in the depths of her blue eyes was the pity I dreaded so much.

After all these years, people were giving me that look again. The *I'm so sorry you're a loser* look. Only this time, it was coming from my goddamn girlfriend.

"No kidding?" Bobby sniffed and rimmed his hands

  WALKER ROSE

around the waistband of his shorts. "I was gone by then."

He was four years older than me, but he'd only been ahead two in school. His parents had started him in kindergarten when he was six and then he'd gotten held back in second grade. Sending him to live with his grandparents in Bourbon Canyon had been a last-ditch effort to keep him from getting held back again.

Too bad it had worked out for him. He'd stayed until he'd graduated at twenty, and he'd been fucking mean about it.

I loaded up my racket and grabbed my water bottle. Ruby straightened with her bag over her shoulder.

"I've gotta get going," I said.

Surprise filled her eyes. "Oh. Okay."

I felt like shit, but I couldn't stick around Bobby Morgan.

"Why you rushing off?" Bobby bypassed his pickup to stand in front of mine.

The guy hadn't changed as much as he probably thought he had. I was mildly impressed Ruby and her mother could get him to be less of a cocksucker.

Ruby squeezed my free hand. "Thanks for coming."

I returned the squeeze, then let go.

Bobby folded his arms. His back was ramrod straight. "You have one conversation with us and suddenly you're busy?"

I bit back a *fuck off.* Heat wicked up the back of my neck. That's exactly what I'd been doing, but this wasn't a typical meet-the-parents scenario. "It's not like that."

"I don't get it. How do you have that much in common with a twenty-five-year-old?" Robert's snide tone made me bristle.

Ruby clutched her tennis bag. "It's not like that, and you can't blame him for not wanting to hang out with you."

Bobby's right eye twitched, but his expression didn't otherwise soften. "I'm afraid I know *exactly* what it's like, Rubes."

Veronica crossed her arms and smiled at me, her face strained with the effort. "Thank you for taking time to play with us, Tenor. Good game."

I dipped my head. "Anytime." But not with Bobby. I gave him a look that said as much.

Taunting blue eyes stared back at me. So much like his daughter's.

"Still live at home?" he asked, a clear jibe.

"His place is really nice," Ruby gushed. "A cabin in the mountains."

"On Mommy and Daddy's land?"

"It's not your business, Dad," Ruby warned.

"I'm worried about my daughter." Bobby lifted his chin, undaunted. "I worked up to vice president of the company I work for. I learned the insurance game just to get in my boss's good graces. I got nothing given to me."

Veronica shook her head. Frustration flashed in her eyes. "Nothing except time. Since *you* weren't the one hunting down babysitters. Come on. Let's go."

Robert at least had the grace to look abashed. He'd taken what he wanted as a teen. As an adult, he'd found out he couldn't do that and get ahead, so he'd learned to play the game. It was more than I had done.

Katrina's voice echoed in my head again. *If your family hadn't handed you everything, would you have made anything of yourself?*

Then Bobby's words from so long ago. *Did you send your sisters after me? Little girls doing your job.*

If I hung around longer, Ruby and her mother would keep defending me. They'd keep shooting me that goddamn look.

"Bye, guys," Ruby said. Her tone held a note of finality.

I nodded my head toward Veronica. "It was nice to meet you."

Bobby got behind the wheel, but not before shooting me a disgruntled glare. Veronica clambered in after giving Ruby a quick hug.

I needed to leave, but I didn't move. My mind whirled, morphing old memories with new. *Nepo baby. Man-child. Loser.*

Ruby waved weakly as her parents backed up and drove away.

"Tenor?" she started timidly. "I honestly had no idea."

"That your dad is my grade school nemesis?"

"I never would've guessed."

He was worried about her dating me. A guy almost her dad's age who was her boss. "Why didn't you tell me that your dad grew up in Bourbon Canyon?"

"I wasn't sure if you'd know him, and I'd heard he was a bullheaded kid." She got the same sheepish look as her dad. Another reminder. Bobby Morgan. Her mom hadn't married him. Ruby had her mom's last name, and she'd called her dad Robert. I never thought of him as anything but Bobby. "I didn't want to be judged for him —or by you when I was applying for the job."

I barked out a laugh. "Bobby Morgan." I shook my head. "Bullheaded is a tame word."

"I had no idea, Tenor. I'm sorry."

Just another goddamn *I'm sorry* because I'd been humiliated by someone who thought they knew me. I took my glasses off and pinched the bridge of my nose. "This isn't going to work."

The words were out of my mouth. I couldn't grab them back. I rubbed the back of my neck. *Shit.*

Why had I said it?

I had to. She couldn't stay with me after this. She couldn't witness this, then watch me paint models and eat my mama's cooking. She'd realize her dad was right. What did I have in common with a twenty-five-year-old?

I'd known this would happen, and I'd taken the risk anyway. I should've learned the first time.

Ruby's wide gaze turned watery. "What isn't going to work?" she asked quietly.

"Us." A vise cinched around my heart. My lungs struggled to inflate. This wouldn't work. It couldn't work.

"Because of my dad?"

No.

Yes.

"He's important to you, and I can't stand him," I finally said.

"He lives in Helena. You're not dating him."

"But he's right."

She drew back. "About what?"

"Your age." My nepotism. What we had in common. I was her boss. Other than fucking, what was there? I was proving her dick weasel of a dad right.

Her eyes misted over. "You're just not going to get over that? You're not going to try?"

I stuffed a hand through my hair. My glasses hung

limp in my other hand. Perhaps it was best not to see the fallout clearly. "This wasn't meant to be. We should've stuck with the fake dating."

"*You* kissed *me*." Her voice shook. "I like you, but I was prepared to walk away. I knew you wouldn't be interested. And then you shared yourself with me . . . and—and the book scene . . ." Red crept up her face. "*You* led *me* on. I kept thinking it was a dream, a fantasy, but I trusted you."

I flinched. She was right. About it all. I couldn't stay away from her. The weakness was me. "You deserve better."

She stomped her foot. "That's not for you to decide." She fisted her hands at her sides. "I'm very much an adult. You showed me what you thought I deserved, and I thought it was you. Now you'll let an old bully who talks shit for his hobby ruin this?"

"He's your dad."

"I can't change that."

"I went *to school* with him." Forget about him being my tormentor. We'd had some of the same classes. It was how he'd managed to find me and make fun of whatever I was doing, saying, or wearing.

She clenched her teeth and looked away, her eyes shining. Several moments of heavy silence passed between us. Guilt hung heavy on my shoulders. I should've never kissed her. I should have kept my dirty hands to myself. If I had, I wouldn't be left knowing exactly what I was missing.

"You're right," she finally said and sniffled. "You set out to show me what a good boyfriend should be like." She waggled her finger between us. "And this isn't it. I do deserve better. I deserve a guy who adores me. A guy who would fight for me and not just . . . give up. A guy who will at least travel outside city limits for me."

I flinched like she'd slapped me. Her words hit dead center of my chest.

"I knew you were holding back. That you didn't want to want me, and that's just . . . that's just *rude*. You said I should have a guy who's tripping over himself to be with me. Yet you're clotheslining yourself to stay away." She shook her head and her ponytail flung around. "I deserve so much better. I kept telling myself you're not Brock."

"I'm not like him."

"And I'm not Katrina. Or my dad! But you're acting like I am." Her laughter was full of scorn. "And you're using it as an excuse to string me along. I. Deserve. Better." Tears spilled over her eyes and down her cheeks. "Goodbye, Tenor."

Panic filled my chest, pressing into my ribs. It couldn't be over.

Hadn't I just declared it was? "Ruby—"

She made a disgusted noise and slammed into her car. She started the engine and whipped out of the parking lot, leaving me alone.

# CHAPTER TWENTY-ONE

Tenor

I set my laptop on the conference room desk and slumped into my chair.

Teller was at the head of the table, watching me. "Who pissed in your Wheaties?"

I grunted and flipped the computer open.

Teller steepled his fingers, his attention on me, but I ignored him.

For two nights, I'd barely slept. Yesterday, I hadn't talked to anyone. I was grateful Cruz and Lane were still out of town. I could do chores in the morning by myself. The horses and goats didn't ask why I was in a shitty mood when I threw their flakes of hay over the fence. The chickens liked being spoiled by me, but otherwise ignored me, and that was just fine.

Tate and Summer entered. I didn't have to look up. The tension in the air was palpable. I could practically hear them glancing back and forth, communicating with their expressions, but I didn't care.

The numbers on my screen got blurry. I took my glasses off and scrubbed my hand down my face. I was such a creature of habit that the lack of sleep was making me loopy. I'd been at work for hours and caught myself staring at my startup screen for the first hour I'd been in the office.

I didn't look up when Wynter and Autumn entered.

The room was quiet, but the weight of their gazes crushed me.

Teller's chair squeaked as he sat forward. "Wanna dial Junie in, Wynter?"

I sat back and folded my arms. My reports were at the beginning of the meeting. Nothing had changed and we were only in the beginning of the third quarter. Everything was on track and my updates would be short.

"He-ey," a groggy Junie said from the phone in the middle of the table. "How's it going?"

"Wild night?" Tate asked.

"Yes and no. We're nearing the end of the tour and I'm about to drop. I'll get a second wind and finish it out." Her yawn came over the line. "The jet lag is brutal though. So what's up with everyone?"

"We're good," Teller replied. "Except for Tenor."

"Oh no." The fatigue washed out of her voice. "What happened?"

My family was worried about me. I was ready to avoid their interference. I massaged my temples. "Bobby Morgan is Ruby's dad."

The immediate silence made me feel both better and worse. Also justified. Out of everyone, they knew what I'd been through because of that asshole. How it had affected future relationships. Their shock meant I was right to be disturbed.

So disturbed I had trashed everything with Ruby. "And I broke up with her."

A variety of responses peppered the air. I caught some *oh no*s and some *shit*s.

"You broke up with Ruby because Bobby Morgan is her dad?" Tate asked, genuine confusion in his voice.

"Yeah," I answered like it was fucking obvious why.

"But Ruby's nothing like him," Summer said. "*Nothing*."

I shrugged. "She's his kid."

Their uncomprehending stares rested on me.

"I get some of the worst behavior in my class," Autumn said cautiously. "And sometimes when I meet their parents, they're complete jackasses. But some are gentle souls who are struggling to parent a troubled child."

"And?" My crankiness was ratcheting impossibly higher.

"Sometimes," she continued, "I'll have the sweetest kid and one of their parents is a nightmare. I just hope the kid has enough good influences in their life to stay sweet. Ruby is that kid who stayed sweet."

"That's not exactly my situation," I said tightly.

"Then what 'exactly' is the problem?" Teller asked with a flippancy that made me want to run him down with the riding lawn mower.

Tate rested his arms on the top of the table. "Didn't Bobby ditch her mom almost immediately?"

"Sort of," I said.

"So Bobby didn't raise Ruby?" Tate pressed.

"He had visitation from the way Ruby talked. He's still an asshole too. We played tennis yesterday."

"Bobby Morgan plays tennis?" Summer asked like she was scandalized.

Thankfully, he hadn't played in high school, or I would've been out the one place I could escape him other than home. "Now he does."

Tate grunted. "I can see why it's a shock to you. Are they close?"

I lifted a shoulder. "She knows what he's like. She loves him. He's her dad."

"So she doesn't condone his behavior?" Wynter asked.

"I don't need my twenty-five-year-old girlfriend standing up for me to her dad," I snapped. I ground my molars together. Goddammit. I'd thought I was done with this humiliation.

Teller tapped his fingertips together. "Is it the twenty-five-years-old part that bothers you or the standing-up-to-her-dad-for-you part?"

"Both, I wager," Tate said.

My teeth ached as I clenched. All of it. It wasn't the age gap but the difference it represented. I was almost her dad's age, still working for my family, still getting food from my mama, still painting my figures at my kitchen table. "It's an issue for her dad, and as much as I fucking hate it, he's important to her."

Summer frowned. "Wasn't he older than you?"

"Yes." It was all semantics. "He's technically older."

"Like four years," Tate added.

"That's not scandalous," Autumn said. "She can deal with Bobby, and she can probably deal with him better than anyone. You like her, Tenor. *Really* like her."

I liked her a whole fucking lot. "She only thought she liked me."

"Ruby has always struck me as a person who knows her own mind," Wynter said. "So is it the age, or is that an easy excuse?"

I shifted in my chair, trying to find a more comfortable position. There wasn't one. "No."

"Are you sure?" she asked softly.

Yes. No? "Her dad—"

"Is a prick," Teller said. "A giant asshat. But you're giving him a whole lot of power over your life—again."

"It's not that," I argued.

"Then what is it?" Summer asked gently. "Because you really liked her."

"It was fake." There. I'd confessed.

They stared at me. Teller rolled his goddamn eyes.

"What was fake?" Junie asked.

I had forgotten she was there, or there'd be more attention directly on me. I pulled at my collar. "When we first started dating, it wasn't real. The woman who used to make Ruby feel like crap in school came into the bar. She happened to be with Ruby's dick of an ex. They were the wedding we went to a couple of weeks ago."

"But it wasn't fake after the wedding." Teller tapped his fingertips together.

He might think he was making a point, but he wasn't. "We started out as a lie."

"Sounds to me like you grabbed on to an excuse to date her," Summer said.

Tate drew in a sharp breath. "And now he's doing the same thing to end it."

Summer nodded.

"What the hell?" Did any of my siblings have my

back? I wasn't happy about the breakup. My sleep had been shit, and all I'd thought about was that disbelieving and devastated look on Ruby's face when I'd said we were done.

"We don't blame you," Wynter said, her tone full of sympathy. "You want to protect yourself."

"It's not that," I snapped.

They all stared at me.

I slapped the lid of my laptop down. "I don't need my girlfriend's pity." I stuffed my glasses back on my face. "I don't need my twenty-five-year-old girlfriend and her mother to stand up for me. I don't need them to fight for my right to paint fucking game pieces or get home-cooked food from Mama like I'm seventeen. I don't need Ruby to defend her boyfriend who never went anywhere and got by in life thanks to his family name."

The silence could've choked me.

"I see." Summer was the first to speak. She had one leg crossed over the other under the table, bobbing her foot, a line of concentration bisecting her forehead. "It's not Ruby or her dad. It's how the whole situation made you feel."

That damn pity I hated pulled at Autumn's features. "You went back to being that kid who just stood and took it from Bobby. And the man who stayed on the high road after Katrina claimed you were an overgrown mama's boy who lived in the basement."

No one talked about how the high road was full of losers. The respect I'd thought I'd get being the bigger guy hadn't been there. There were no awards for turning the other cheek. Sometimes you just got dick punched again.

"Well, if that's what you think about yourself, I guess I'm the same." Teller stretched back and slapped his stomach. "I've been eating Mama's fried chicken and rice all damn week."

"Scarlett made her breakfast burritos this morning," Tate added. "Hell, we all live on land given to us by our parents. Is that what you think of us?"

"Before you say I don't play games," Teller said, "I have to admit to losing an hour every night on that new word game Jenna mentioned last week."

"Oh!" Wynter poked her finger in the air. "That one —yes. I caught Myles playing that the other day. He played too long and didn't get the lawn mowed before it rained."

"Fine, I get the point," I said through gritted teeth, hating to admit that what they said did make me feel better. We were a close family, but I couldn't see behind their closed doors to what habits they spent their time on. But we all worked for the family's companies and greedily accepted Mama's food. "None of that changes how Bobby Morgan is a self-made man who sort of turned his life around on his own. He's going to use that to undermine me to Ruby."

"Is she worth it?" Junie asked. Ruby was worth everything. I didn't answer, just glowered at the phone's speaker. "Is she worth standing up to Bobby until death do you part?"

"We weren't getting married," I said.

"That's not answering the question," Teller retorted. He swept an arm in my direction. "Are you happier like this?"

I bit my tongue and glanced away.

"Is it really worth going home alone every night to never have to see Bobby again?" Summer asked.

They weren't going to let up if I didn't answer. "She loves her dad. I'm not going to ruin that relationship."

"He would be the one doing that if he alienates her," Autumn pointed out.

Tate shook his head. "Maybe it's not that. Maybe it's the possibility that she might listen to her dad and behave like Katrina. The worst of both worlds."

Acid in my stomach churned. The breakfast sandwich I'd had hours ago was like gravel in my gut. "She'd never behave like Katrina."

Ruby would never do that.

What if she realized how much better she could do? I'd rather make a break before it destroyed me completely.

The crack in my chest was enough of a death blow.

"Ah," Teller said on an exhale. "But she could leave like Katrina. That's the real fear. And with Bobby as her dad, that makes it all the more likely in that big brain of yours. You ran the risk calculation through some spreadsheet formula you designed and it wasn't absolutely zero. So you bailed."

His claim was a metal hoop around my chest, cutting off my breathing as if I was the barrel getting ready to be shelved for years. Had I done exactly what Teller claimed? "I don't know," I said woodenly.

"I bet she's worth knowing for sure," Autumn said, her voice gentle, like I was one of her distraught students.

"She's worth everything," I said without thinking first. Because *of course* Ruby would never hurt me on purpose. She wasn't like her dad. Nor was she like any ex

I'd ever had—except that she was an ex now. "I fucked up."

The truth was choking me. I had epically jacked up any chance I had with her.

"It's not too late," Teller said. "All you have to do is talk to her—"

"She claimed I was stringing her along. I destroyed her trust in me."

"Seriously, Tenor," Junie said, her tone chiding. "It's not too late. Rhys ghosted me *on purpose*. Then he planned to just let me go. *Again*. And now I'm June Bee Kerrigan Kinkade."

Wynter snorted. "Talk about ghosting. Myles ditched me a few times. Then I ditched him. He had to earn his way back."

"Jonah wasn't going to try." Summer gave me a pointed look. "He thought he knew better for me."

"Gideon left me," Autumn added. "Though he never sent the divorce papers, so there was that."

"I don't have a breakup story," Tate said, "but you guys had to buy me for Scarlett and I'd had plenty of opportunity to ask her out."

Teller leaned back in his chair, his hands behind his head. "You're going to have to work for it. Contrary to what you might think, you haven't had to do that before."

He had no idea what he was talking about. "I've been dumped by every girl I dated."

"They came to you," Tate said, "and when they left, you let them go without a fight. You never had to work that hard." I opened my mouth and he snapped his fingers. I pressed my lips together. "*Those* were the pretend relationships. Those were not the real Tenor trying to woo a girl."

"The real Tenor wooed Ruby," Junie said. "Just like the real Tenor had better make sure she doesn't leave Copper Summit over this. If I have to find another social media manager, I'm going to burn your house down with those paints you use."

The rest of my sisters nodded along.

*They came to you.*

Ruby had practically cornered me. And when our term was up, she'd walked. I'd gone after her. Then I'd gotten complacent. One road bump, albeit a fucking significant one, and I'd bailed. She'd been willing to talk it out. She hadn't stormed off, embarrassed that I was the kid her dad had teased for years. Before that, she hadn't left even after I had alluded to everything my exes had found wrong with me.

From the way Ruby acted, my work ethic, my love for my family, and my tame, useless hobbies were positive qualities. She liked me *more* because of them. She was the best damn thing to ever have happened to me and I'd tossed her away like a blown tennis ball.

"The next move is yours," Teller said lightly, but his gaze was level on me. "You gonna win your girl back?"

***

Ruby

I poked at my cold pasta. To be fair, only the marinara was cold. The pasta was lukewarm. My mom crunched on her lettuce salad next to me. She kept peeking at me out of the corner of her eye.

I put my fork down with a sigh. "You can say it."

When she swallowed, she reclined in her chair. "Your dad is worried about you."

"About me or about how I feel over the way he treated Tenor as a kid?"

"Mostly you, but I think he's seeing more of the lasting repercussions his behavior had. He's never been proud of how he acted when he was younger."

At least she didn't try to downplay what a wrench Dad and Tenor's shared past had thrown into everything. As for Dad, I wasn't answering his calls. I hadn't expected him to care, but he'd been trying to call once a day. When I didn't answer, he'd send a text telling me he wanted to talk.

I wasn't interested in hearing what he thought about Tenor, and I was even less interested in listening to him justify himself. Dad likely wasn't going to wax poetic about how he was a changed man.

"Tell him I'm fine." I picked up my plate and took it to the sink.

Boxes lined the floor by the dishwasher. More were stacked in the hallway and the bedrooms. This weekend, I'd help Mom haul them to storage. Next week, she'd close on the house. Then it'd be just me in Bozeman. Me and my job. Dad would still be in Helena, but I wasn't sure when I'd want to talk to him again.

"He'd rather hear that from you."

"Yep."

"I'm not defending him, honey. But he's your dad, and you're one of the few people who has gotten him to be honest with himself."

"You mean when he declared he couldn't be a dad full-time?" My irritation reached a breaking point. "How in the world did you fall for him anyway?"

I was lashing out, but I couldn't stop. The release valve on my emotions would burst, and I couldn't wait until tonight when I cried myself to sleep.

A weary exhale sounded behind me. I also couldn't bring myself to turn around.

"He can read people so well," Mom said. "That's likely what made him such an effective bully. He'd expose other kids' insecurities and tear them down without lifting a finger. It probably made it harder for teachers to do anything, and knowing Robert, the less Tenor did, the safer he felt picking on him."

Knowing Tenor, he'd probably taken it so Dad wouldn't pick on anyone else. Didn't mean Dad's behavior was excused, or that it hadn't affected Tenor long term.

"It's reading people," Mom continued, "that makes him charming. It's why he's so good at sales—when he can control his mouth," she muttered. "I was like you. Overlooked. Bookish. An older football player giving me attention? I didn't have a chance."

I grunted and slid open the cabinet the garbage was in. Dumping my uneaten pasta inside, I refused to think about how good Mae's lasagna would be right now.

I could see Mom's point. Wasn't that how I'd been with Brock? He had said the right things to seduce me, and then he had torn me down in a few words. But he had a stand-up job and, ugh, had played football in school. He'd given me attention and I'd continued going back.

"Like mother, like daughter," I said sullenly. "Brock probably would've left me if I had gotten pregnant too."

"You want to know why I never badmouthed your dad to you and why I encouraged a relationship between you two?"

Finally, I turned around. I hugged my arms around myself. "Why?"

"Other than because he wanted to be in your life when not many guys his age would've wanted that?" She gave me a pointed look. "Because he told me he didn't have his shit together and he didn't want to raise a kid who'd fail his or her way through school. He told me he'd get a job and make money, and someday, he could help financially, but he'd, in his words, 'be a shit dad.' "

"His self-awareness is impressive," I said impassively.

"I guess I thought so when I was seventeen. He'd at least said he'd sort of stick with me when my own parents hadn't."

I stared at the ceiling. None of this was Mom's fault. I might make Dad self-reflect, but not enough to keep from insulting Tenor last Sunday. "The thing is, I'm sick of guys like Dad. They'll tell me they're going to do better, treat me better, and then they don't."

She turned in her chair, crossed one leg over the other, and put her hands around her knee. "Is that what Tenor did?"

"Yes." I sniffed. "Sort of."

When she didn't speak, I dropped my arms and trudged back to the table. She'd also been messaging me to ask how I'd been doing since Sunday. When I had told her Tenor and I were over, she'd proposed dinner. I'd known she'd want to talk and I hadn't backed out. I might as well talk.

"He never really committed. I should've seen the pattern. Everything was on his terms, and I went along with it, oblivious."

"On his terms, or did you two just have similar interests?"

I scowled. "According to him, we don't have the same interests. He didn't bother coming to Bozeman to see how I live."

She rolled her lips in. "Okay," she said slowly. "So he'd come to Bozeman and you'd take him to your favorite bar?"

My frown deepened. "I don't have one."

"Your favorite hiking trail?"

I clamped my mouth shut.

"The movie theater that you don't go to because why pay that amount when you can just wait and watch the movie in pajamas? The coffee shop you don't read at because it's too loud? My house when I'm never home?"

"He didn't want to meet you guys in the first place."

"Ugh." A shudder went through her. "Meeting the parents is the worst part of dating."

"Is that why you broke things off with Daniel? He wanted you to meet his parents?" Did I date people like my mom? I didn't . . . Did I?

"He wanted to quit the trail and expected me to drop out too." She scoffed like I should understand how audacious the request was. "All that planning and he wanted me to quit."

Tenor would never let me leave a trail alone and injured.

My heart wrenched and I rubbed my sternum.

She pushed a lock of fine hair behind her ear. "Too bad Tenor didn't want to see your reading nook."

"I read in bed."

She lifted a brow.

Point taken. "It wasn't just that. He just never committed. I know it was new but, like, I felt something. Like we really had a connection. I was all in and he had one foot out the door the whole time."

"You two didn't date long."

"Felt like I'd been with him for forever. Like we were two old souls who'd finally found each other. And then he just calls it quits. Because of my dad. Nothing I could've done. He just dropped me." A hot tear rolled down my cheek. I swiped at it. "I felt less important to him than I ever did to the others."

"Oh, hon." She rose and enveloped me in a giant mom hug that nearly choked off my air supply. "I really am sorry. You should expect the best treatment from your partner, but I can't help but wonder how watching me date and being around your dad hasn't helped you. Lord knows, I don't weather any conflict in a relationship well."

"Dad was your first experience and you learned you couldn't count on him. Yet it's like you're still waiting on him."

Surprise mixed with dismay in her expression. "We're connected, and despite his rough edges, he's the only guy who hasn't asked me to change who I am. He just rolls with whatever I want." She leaned back. "But his hard personality made you too tolerant of assholes. If you think Tenor fits in that category, then I'll trust your intuition."

Tenor was *not* like Dad.

My dad hadn't given up on me.

# CHAPTER TWENTY-TWO

Ruby

It was almost closing time and there was no sign of Tenor. I only looked out the window and at the door to the lobby a million times. His pickup was in the same spot in the parking lot. He was here, like usual. Would he see me out to lock up like he always had before?

Or would he make Teller do it?

What was I hoping for?

I was afraid to answer.

I'd worn the black pleated skirt that drove Tenor crazy. I couldn't be the only one suffering.

What if he was unaffected? Would he see me and only picture my dad?

The mental torment was the worst. Lack of sleep also sucked. I hadn't been able to read. After I'd left Mom's place, I'd stopped at the bookstore and bought a few new books, mostly mystery and thrillers. Romance was not in the cards right now.

I finished cashing out just as the door opened.

My heart skyrocketed into my throat.

Tenor walked in and stopped, his solemn gaze on me. As drawn to him as I was, I had to force myself to look at him. My chest grew tight. His face was drawn. He wore the same oversized rust-colored polo and blue jeans. Same boots. And he looked as good as ever.

Longing opened up in my chest, but I sewed that damn tear shut.

*You deserve better.*

His words echoed through my head. Damn right I did. At one time, I had thought that was him. I'd get better for myself out of spite. Someday. When I pieced myself back together.

He shoved his hands in his pockets. "Hey."

"Hi." I put the tablet away and grabbed my purse. "It was a quiet night."

I hustled for the door, eager to get this uncomfortable interaction done with. Being around him only made me remember how good he could make me feel. Seeing him reminded me of everything I couldn't have through no fault of my own.

*You deserve better.*

I sure did. I deserved a guy who would stick around. Someone who wouldn't hold being me against me.

"Thanks for locking up." I breezed past him and pushed outside.

A wall of heat followed me out into the warm evening air. "Ruby."

My legs twitched to break into a run. But then my skirt would fly up and betray my plain black underwear. That picture wasn't exactly the strong-girl front I had to present.

I steeled myself and turned. "Yeah?"

Neither of us moved. Our gazes clashed. Two melancholy people. I couldn't even gloat that he seemed like he missed me. The thought just made me sad. He liked me but not enough.

Story of my damn life.

I had wanted to get this moment done with, but I was glued in place like I didn't want it to end.

"How are you doing?" he asked in that pleasing, deep timbre.

How was I doing? I wasn't sleeping. Food tasted like dust. The breakup made me see how bleak my social life was. I'd been reading nothing but murder stories. "Fine. You?" I asked more because it was expected. Not out of curiosity. Not because he looked like he'd gotten less sleep than me.

"I, uh . . . it's been rough."

His honesty shocked me. "Yeah?"

"I'm sorry."

My irritation roared back. "You said that."

He shook his head. "I might've been . . . I reacted harshly. About your dad."

My righteousness deflated—just a little. "I can only try to understand the shock you were in. Dad's mom was a real piece of work—not that that's an excuse. My grandparents never gave me details and they died before I got to middle school. He's still got an abrasive personality. Still . . . I love him. I take what I can get." My voice hitched on the last sentence. I clutched my purse to my chest. "But that's the only guy I'm going to settle for good enough with."

He flinched. "I couldn't get over my hurt." He let out

a dry laugh. "It's been two decades. Should be enough time."

Part of my resolve softened. "I don't know if there's a timeline."

"It's my shit to deal with. Not yours."

"A real couple would work through that kind of stuff."

His expression fell. "Yeah." He draped a hand around the back of his neck. "I can't take back what I said, but I don't want this to be the end of us."

Hope swirled to life in my stomach.

I smothered it.

He wanted take backs now? He could've asked for time to process what he was going through. Instead, he had ended it. "Even if you could get over who my dad is, I can't change our age difference."

"I don't want you to." He adjusted his glasses. The way his biceps bulged when he did that was just unfair.

Doubt was like an ever-present shadow. "Even if Dad was here right now, telling you you're a creeper for dating me? That you walked right into the nursery and plucked me out of the crib?"

The corner of his mouth curved up. "Even if he said that I'd been in middle school waiting for my girlfriend to be born."

A soft chuckle left me. Then reality sank in. I was not the same girl who let herself get jerked around. "You always kept a big part of yourself from me. With Dad, you just ended it." I gave him a helpless shrug. "How can I trust you not to end things again the next time you're upset? And then ask for another chance?" I shook my head, my sorrow hanging heavy on my shoulders.

Remorse rippled over his expression, furrowing his brow. "I've never been the one to end things."

Ouch. "Glad you saved it for me."

He winced. "Sorry, I meant that I was scared that you'd break up with me. That's how it's always ended."

"After how much I opened up to you, you thought I was just like the other girls?"

"Shit. No. I mean, yes, but it's my problem. It shouldn't have been yours." The crease in his forehead deepened. "I can earn your trust back."

"What if Katrina came to town? And seeing her made you wonder if I'd ever do the same to you?" His cheek twitched and I let out a bitter laugh. "You've already wondered that, haven't you?"

"I knew you wouldn't." When I shot him a flat stare, he looked away. "I worked through that fear. I'll do better. I'll be better."

He'd been the best. Until he hadn't been. I blinked. A tear rolled down my cheek. I swiped it away.

I didn't trust him.

Another tear skated down my face.

"Ruby." His mouth formed a troubled line and he stepped toward me.

I put a hand up.

He stopped. "I'll earn it back, but, Ruby . . . I have a lot to learn. I might be older but I'm not wiser. I haven't dated for over ten years."

The last time he'd been on a real date, I'd been in high school. He'd broken his streak and the world was wide freaking open to him right now. "I felt really special that you wanted to be with me." My throat grew thick and I hugged my purse tighter to myself. He could take his pick.

*I just don't know if this is what I want, Rubes. I need some time.* Brock's words rose from the depths of my mind.

"I still want to be with you," he said, his voice ragged.

"I . . . can't." I would not run into his arms after one *I'm sorry*. The sad fact was that he couldn't promise he wouldn't do it again. I'd been dumped by him once. Twice would just be cruel.

He exhaled and dropped his head. "Okay. I understand." His smile was tight but reassuring. "Will it bother you to have me see you out on Friday nights?"

He was giving me an out. I wouldn't have to see him again. He rarely went to the Bozeman site, and once I was done working the bar for the summer, I wouldn't have to come to Bourbon Canyon more than once or twice a year.

All I had to do was say no, it didn't bother me. I'd crack open the door to another chance. I would show up to work, knowing I'd get to see Tenor. The night would end with him. Maybe he'd try again. Maybe he'd ask me out. Maybe I'd say yes.

I deserved better.

Right now, it was too goddamn hard to convince myself of that. Tenor was in front of me, asking for another chance. It should be a dream come true. Instead, it felt like Groundhog Day.

"Yes, Tenor. It would be too hard."

All the hope drained from his features. He nodded. "I'll talk to Teller. Good night, Ruby."

I didn't look back as I walked to my car. I resolutely didn't check my rearview mirror as I drove off. And I waited until I hit the highway before I let the dam break on my tears.

Tenor

A pump on one of the fermenter tanks had gone out. We'd cleaned the seals, then replaced them, but to no avail. We needed a new pump. Until then, the tank was out of commission and all the mash inside had to be cleaned out.

"The delay shouldn't put us behind too bad," Teller said, pushing away from the tank. "Once we get the new pump installed, then we can clean it up and rock 'n' roll."

I checked the time. "I should get going."

His gaze was steady. "Ruby starts soon?"

Last week, she'd basically told me she didn't want to see me again. "Yeah." I wanted to be gone by then.

"You're not going to try with her again?"

I'd had to tell him so he or Tate or one of the girls could lock up after Ruby's shift. "I'm not going to stalk her, no."

"So that's it? You tried once and you're done?"

"Not sure what else I can do."

"I dunno. Something more. Did you apologize?"

"No, fucker. I didn't. I doubled down on how justified I was." I grabbed the clipboard with the lot numbers of the grain shipment we'd received. I'd been inputting them before we spotted the pump issue and stomped around Teller.

He spun as I went around him. "There's got to be another way."

"That's entering felony stalking territory." I pushed into the lobby. A group of tourists was forming at the front desk. I tucked my head down and beelined for the stairs.

Teller stayed on my heels and followed me all the way. "I'm not saying you should watch her through the window, jackass."

I tossed the clipboard on my desk. "There's not much else. She works and she's a homebody. So either I stare at her through her window—which, by the way, I wouldn't know how to find unless I checked the employee records for her address—or I linger outside her office. Either way, I abuse my position at Copper Summit, and I make her uncomfortable at her job." I dragged a hand through my hair. I needed a trim, but I didn't care to be asked about Ruby, and I would be. It was all the barber had talked about when I'd gotten a trim before the wedding.

We hadn't been spotted around town enough for people to yet notice the absence of Ruby-and-Tenor sightings. Soon enough though, someone would ask either me or one of my siblings and the thrilling news that we'd broken up would spread around town. Anyone who remembered Katrina's slander would speculate. I was still a nepo loser who played games and lacked independence. Sadder now, because I was older.

Teller's mouth formed a troubled line. "There's got to be something you can do."

Like I hadn't been trying to figure that out myself. "She said it herself. She can't change her age—which isn't an issue, but she won't believe me. And she can't change who her dad is—and he'll throw the age thing in my face."

He scratched the back of his neck. "Somehow you've

gotta get her to believe you. And you have to convince Bobby that her age is not an issue."

"I'm not fucking talking to him."

"Maybe not Bobby, but what about Robert Morgan?"

The corner of my mouth curled up. "Believe me. They're one and the same. That fucker can rot. I'm not begging him to date his daughter."

"You don't need to. Check the century on your calendar. You don't need his permission."

"For fuck's sake, Teller. I know all this. Don't you think I've been over and over what I can do?" I dropped into my chair. The wheels scratched on the hardwood floor. "I've got work to do."

He didn't budge. "I didn't peg you for a guy to give up so easily, but I should've."

I glared at him. He was trying to get under my skin, but he was an amateur compared to Ruby's dad.

"You shut down in front of Bobby for years, and then you shut down your entire dating life after Katrina. You're doing nothing but shutting down right now. Only this time, you're the one who hurt someone, and when 'I'm sorry' doesn't cut it, you give up."

"Jesus, Teller." He had no fucking clue what it'd been like.

"Bobby was in my class. Do you think I got nothing but compliments from the guy? Once he told me that I was only on the football team because of my last name."

Teller had been a good goddamn player. He could've gotten a college scholarship, but he hadn't been interested. "It was his go-to insult."

"No shit. The guy didn't have anything, so of course he hated us. We had parents who took in kids like him, but not him. He was being raised by grandparents who make your life look wild."

Fair.

"You know why that was all he said to me?" Teller propped his hands on the edge of my desk and leaned over. "Because I cornered him in the locker room and told him that if my family's name came out of his mouth one more damn time, I'd tie his tongue to the flagpole and let it flap in the wind. Tate was with me and he held the rope from the flagpole outside of the school."

"You know how Dad was about violence."

"Nothing wrong with bluffing."

I cocked a brow. "You weren't bluffing."

He only grinned. "My point is that you can tell them how you'll be treated. You know why Wendi took up with Scooter?" Teller's ex was selfish, so it likely hadn't taken much, but I shook my head. "Because I told her that I was helping Dad with working cattle and couldn't go on a wine tour in Napa Valley."

"Sounds like a vacation you'd hate."

"Every part of it, and I told her that. She still planned it. She got upset and told me I was a daddy's boy who couldn't think for himself."

I flinched. Those words had been thrown in my face too.

"I told her that she wasn't allowed to disrespect my family or me like that. So she cheated on me. Did you ever tell Bobby to stop?"

"What the hell do you think?"

"Did you do it in a way that would make him listen?"

"I'm not like you and Tate."

He chuffed. "Again, no shit." He sighed and pulled up

the chair across from the desk. "Did you ever think that's *why* Bobby and girls like Katrina targeted you?"

I gnawed on my bottom lip. "You think I made it easy for them? That they were justified?"

"I think you were afraid they were right. And I think you'd rather take it than risk ever behaving like them. You're not me and Tate. So lean into it. What about you drew Ruby to you?" He gestured to himself. "I can tell you that she was never interested in me. I wasn't into her either—FYI. Nor was she giving Tate googly eyes. Not one guy walked through here and got her undivided attention. But you did."

I tucked that info away. It likely wasn't real, but a small win was better than none. "I don't have it now. Little hard to win her back when she doesn't want me around, much less to touch her."

"Romance isn't all about touching. Nor is it fancy restaurants and impressing people you don't care about. Figure out what that is for you two and romance her."

"She doesn't want me."

"Is that what she said?"

"She can't trust me again."

"Sounds a whole lot like she's scared. You are too. Start there." He pushed out of his chair and swaggered out of my office like he'd just laid down the solution for world peace.

What the hell did I know about romance? Any time I had tried, it had blown up in my face.

Start with we're scared? Teller didn't know a goddamn thing—

*Is that what she said?*

No, she hadn't said she didn't want me anymore. She hadn't had to.

But what if . . . What if she could trust me again?

Just to humor Teller, what would earning that trust look like?

# CHAPTER TWENTY-THREE

Ruby

"Okay, how about this?" I aimed and clicked on the newest cocktail creation Wynter and Autumn had come up with for the fall menu in the tasting room. She was leaning on the counter behind it, half turned, with her long, pale hair down her back.

"I can't believe I'm modeling instead of Junie," she muttered.

Autumn stood behind me. "This is going to look so good," she said as I tabbed through different settings and took snapshots.

I adjusted the settings back to normal. "Your turn, Autumn."

She fluttered her hand over her hair. "Are you sure about this? I'm not a model."

"I can rattle off the stats of how much more engagement we get when I have Junie in the images, and thanks to Teller, I can tell you how much more there is when it's

Copper Summit royalty."

"Royalty," she scoffed. "I don't even work the bar anymore."

She might've been born a Kerrigan, married a James, but to Copper Summit customers, she was a Bailey. "I can blur you like I'm doing with Wynter."

Any edits with Teller made the fans go feral. I'd had so much fun responding to comments. They were still pouring in. If I had posted Tenor, with his soulful eyes behind his glasses? A cowboy nerd? We'd sell out.

Now I was grateful he hadn't wanted them shared. Otherwise, I'd be posting *Drink in the cowboy all you want. He'll be gone before you know it.*

Except he had tried coming back.

The space behind my sternum throbbed. Had I done the right thing, or had I condemned myself to a lifetime of pining for one man?

How could I trust him again? I'd been his gateway date. Either he'd shut himself back into bachelorhood for another ten years, or he'd come into the bar with his new fiancée and invite me to the wedding.

Before I could start spitting and snarling, I pasted on a bright smile. "I'll do whatever you're comfortable with, but I promise the images will be lovely. Wynter created the apple-muffin old-fashioned, and people will love seeing her with it. I think you should pose by yours."

She didn't look convinced. "I'm wearing a hoodie."

"Perfect for a drink you named 'campfire delight.' " The less photoshopped, the better. "You can approve any image I use."

"Have Gideon do it," Wynter suggested. "He'll say yes to them all."

Autumn scowled at her but then relaxed. "All right."

I got to work, using both my phone and camera to get photos. Teller walked in to ask Wynter about the spring campaigns she was working on and he got rooked into modeling too.

I was smiling and laughing when the first customers for the night showed up. Wynter and Autumn cleaned up the mess left behind from their mixology session while I took the new arrivals' orders.

Today had been nice. After the last Friday I'd worked when Tenor had stopped in, I hadn't been sure if I should keep picking up shifts, or if I should drop to just Wednesday evenings. Then other family members wouldn't have to work late to lock up.

How miserable was I?

My job was important to me, but if I had to move on to keep from going home and sobbing myself to sleep, then I would. I hadn't searched for any new positions yet though. My first step would be to give up the tasting room shifts.

I hadn't done that yet either. Without this extra side hustle, Wednesday and Friday nights would become just like any other night of the week. I'd crawl into bed, scroll for an hour, then prop up my book to read.

Mom's house was up for sale and she had her travel van ready to purchase when it sold. Soon I wouldn't even have my once-a-week plain pasta dinner with her.

Wild woman, right here. Who wouldn't want me?

The list had grown by one, and that one made it hard for me to breathe. Tears pricked behind my eyes. I turned my back to everything to take a quick inventory. My height worked for me. I could see how glassy my eyes were getting in the mirror behind the bottles. I blinked rapidly to banish the moisture.

Autumn stopped at my side. "We're taking off." She inspected my face. "Is there anything you need?"

Calling on that energy from earlier, I flashed another fake smile. "Nope. It's looking like a busy night." Tourists were pouring through town in the last weeks before school started.

"Sounds good." She turned to go, then spun back, her red hair flying. "Oh. There's a book under the cabinet for you."

A book? Why? More customers walked in and Autumn scurried out.

I worked for a couple of hours. The book had to wait. Just as I dropped a candied cherry into a bourbon lemonade, Cara walked in. She glanced round the room, a slight expression of distaste on her face.

No Brock.

What was she doing here alone?

She came to the counter and slid onto the stool at the corner of the bar. The one Tenor and I had—

Nope. Passing that stool a million times a shift had desensitized me to the memory of the passion we'd shared. Of how he'd declared he couldn't stay away from me.

Maybe I wasn't as immune as I thought.

"Hey, Cara. What can I get you?"

She gave me a demure smile. "You know what I like."

I held in my sigh and started on a mojito.

She propped her elbow on the countertop and rested her chin on her hand. "So? When are we going out, Rubes?"

I bit back the third—fourth?—fifth?—fake smile I'd flashed for the night. The last thing I felt like doing was humoring her. If I put her off, I'd be no better than my exes, stringing Cara along because I wasn't bold enough to face my feelings. I was too afraid of being hurtful like my dad. I could justify my response a million ways, but I was tired. My emotions were raw and my nerve endings exposed, left to the elements.

I pushed the glass in front of her. "Don't call me Rubes, please."

Her lips puckered as she dabbed the thin pink straw up and down. "It's just a nickname."

"I don't like it." I'd allow my dad to call me that, but only because he had never teased me about it. She had. "And I don't think it's a good idea."

"You don't think what is?"

"A forced friendship between us. You've been mean to me, Cara. I thought we were friends, but then you acted like I should be ashamed of my mom, where we lived, and myself."

Her jaw dropped open. "What are you talking about? I've always been nice to you."

"No, you haven't, and if you don't see how hurtful you're being, it's not my job to show you. My job is to serve you drinks."

"You mean this watered-down thing?"

I gave her a plain stare. She was proving my point.

She lifted her chin. "Why did you even come to my wedding? I could've used that spot for another guest."

I was done with Cara's bullshit. "You seemed to want me there, and I didn't want to hurt your feelings."

"And you're not now? We were friends." Her eyes flashed. "You were my best friend."

How could she talk like *I* had betrayed *her*? "Until you decided I wasn't." My volume was rising. I'd have to watch that. "You insulted my mom, my clothing, my athletic ability. You used me to make yourself feel better when I would've been that friend who built you up." Just like I would've been the girlfriend to show Tenor what he deserved. I was tired of being thrown away before I got the chance. "I don't want to give you the chance to take your unhappiness out on me again."

She drew back and real pain flashed through her eyes. Trouble in paradise? A little sympathy welled, but I couldn't waste more energy on her. I'd had enough of that in my life.

Only genuine relationships from here on out.

"I'm not unhappy." She swallowed hard, then slid off the stool. "See you around, I guess," she said and marched out of the bar.

While that hadn't been easy, it was done. One more person cut out of my life.

Tears pricked the backs of my eyes, always ready to spring forward lately. Didn't that sound pathetic?

I made it through the rest of my shift on autopilot. I glanced in the parking lot a million times, but Tenor's pickup never appeared. He was respecting my wishes.

Damn him.

If he hadn't, my resolve might have evaporated at the mere sight of him. The anger from the tennis fallout had faded. I was left with the hurt, and for some stupid reason, my heart thought he was the only one who could help me.

All the customers finally emptied out. Only Teller's pickup was in the lot. He often worked in his office or at the computer bank in the distillation room until he walked me out.

I sent off the nightly report, my heart wrenching like always when Tenor's name flashed up on the email. I opened the cupboard to stuff the tablet inside. A *Sense and Sensibility* book was in its place.

That's right. Autumn had said there was a book for me.

I eyed it. The *Sense and Sensibility* cover was a dust jacket. I narrowed my eyes and pulled the book out. As I peeled back the front flap, my lips parted and a soft gasp escaped.

A shirtless man holding a blaster was on the original cover, with some sort of spaceship as a backdrop.

I slammed the fake cover back in place, creasing it when I did.

Just then, the lobby door opened. My hopes jumped sky high, but Teller walked in.

"Oh. Hi." I hugged the book to my chest.

He cocked a brow. "Hey. Ready to lock up?"

I nodded, holding the book with one hand and grabbing my purse with the other. "Yes."

"How'd the night go?"

*I tried not to think of your brother and cut ties with an old frenemy.* "Good. It was busy, but mellow."

"Good to hear." He punched in the code and headed toward his pickup. I was parked on the opposite side of the lot. "Have a good night, Ruby."

"Yeah. You too." I started for my vehicle, but pivoted to Teller. "Hey, um. Don't wait for me. I have some messages to catch up on before I hit the road."

"Sure thing. Drive safe."

I scurried to my car and dove behind the wheel.

What the hell was this book about?

I knew who was behind it. But why had he left me a space marine romance novel?

I tossed the dust jacket onto the passenger seat with my purse and turned on the interior light.

I hadn't read this book yet. The side had brightly colored yellow tabs on certain pages. Had he annotated the book? I opened the inside cover. Bold handwriting was in the top left corner. **We're proof these scenes are realistic**.

My pulse hammered against my veins. If he'd highlighted sex scenes, I would climb out of my skin. I already dreamed of his touch at night, I didn't need to do it while lucid. Crying myself to sleep after masturbating to the memory of him wasn't on my breakup bingo card.

I found the first green highlighted passage. **"You're too important to give up on and I'm going to keep trying to earn your trust."**

I skimmed the material around the hero's dialogue. The heroine told him to fuck off. He worked for the enemy and she declared she would not be swayed by his good looks.

So not completely realistic. But the highlighted line hit home. I heard him reading the words in my head.

I swallowed and found the next tab.

**"Everything that's happened between us has meant something. You don't know what you mean to me, and that's my fault. I should've done better. I can do better."**

I blew out a hard breath and went to the next tab.

**"What's between us is bigger than our past."**

I blinked back tears. Was it, though? Or was he using his superpower of being sweet and intuitive to create a blank slate? And would we fill in that slate exactly the same way until we had the same falling out?

I sniffled. Another line caught my eye. He hadn't highlighted this one. It was part of the heroine's introspection.

**He doesn't realize words mean little to someone like me. The prettiest compliments can wield the harshest insults. Words can cut where a blade can't. They can cauterize old wounds but leave the ugliest of scars. His words weren't going to sway me. It had always been about action.**

I snapped the book shut. Tenor's attempt to connect with me was touching. If he had done it in person, I might've swooned. In the dark parking lot of Copper Summit after I'd finally stood up to Cara? His words meant little. They weren't even his words.

Tenor

The rack house was quiet. I could've been done a half hour ago, but I was taking my time. Being alone with nothing but rows of stacked, aging barrels was a form of solitude I needed.

I breathed in the smell of old wood and must with a nice undertone of bourbon: the angel's share of bourbon that had evaporated out.

I had been on edge since last weekend, but I'd heard nothing from Ruby. Last night, I had debated stopping in before I went to Billings for my game night, but I had passed. I had served the ball and she hadn't returned it.

I had another book highlighted and ready to go. I'd put another Jane Austen cover on it. *Emma*. The real book was a space romance. A fake facade on a fictional story to tell her my real feelings.

Nice fucking metaphor.

The exit door opened. Boots crunched against the concrete floor. I didn't bother to turn around, though the intrusion in my thoughts was welcome. If I stood here much longer, I'd sweat through my shirt. Natural fluctuations in temperature played through the ground and walls to help age the barrels. The heat in the summer would make the alcohol expand into the wood and absorb the characteristics of the oak. Then the cold winters would cause the spirits to contract, extracting all the flavor. That needed to happen for at least four years before whiskey was considered a bottled-in-bond bourbon. Just one of many specifications. Only I didn't have to stand out here for an entire cycle.

Teller rounded the corner, his eyes lighting up when he spotted me. "Those the ones?"

I had the tablet that would verify which oak barrels would become our special batch. Instead of doing a single-barrel line for the holidays, this year we were blending three barrels. "Yes."

After the barrels were taken by forklift to the main distillery, Teller and I would use the whiskey thief to extract amounts to blend. Then we'd work on a taste profile to give to Wynter. Sometimes, she joined us. Summer too. Tate sat out more and more every year as he got busier with his kids and the ranch.

"I'll get them hauled in." Teller propped his hands on his hips. "I forgot to tell you that Ruby left that book in the same spot for you."

I frowned. She was giving it back? What'd that mean? "Thanks."

"What's that all about? You two start some sort of book club?"

"Something like that."

"So you're talking?"

"I don't know." I started for the door. "I'll meet you inside."

Trotting across the parking lot, I managed not to sprint. The book was the only form of communication between us. I ducked into the lobby, waved at the college kid who was leading the tour until his semester started in Wyoming at the end of the month, and barged into the quiet tasting room.

I found the book in the same place I'd left it for her. The fake book wrap was still on it. Flipping the book open on the counter, I searched for some sort of message from Ruby.

My pulse jumped when I spotted a section highlighted in pink.

**He doesn't realize words mean little to someone like me. The prettiest compliments can wield the harshest insults. Words can cut where a blade can't. They can cauterize old wounds but leave the ugliest of scars. His words weren't going to sway me. It had always been about action.**

My gut twisted. Goddammit.

I rubbed between my eyes. Talking to her through passages in a romance novel had not been a success. She was not moved.

I blew out a breath and found another sentence in pink, spoken by the heroine. **"You were everything I wanted. I trusted you with my whole heart. And what did that get me? Thrown away. Like I was nothing but some space trash. Now you're trying**

**to claw me back? Maybe you shouldn't have ejected me in the first place."**

I closed my eyes and rubbed my forehead. I wanted Ruby back, but finding stupid sentences in romance novels wasn't how to do it. I had fucked up. She'd only seen my attempts as superficial dribble.

There was no way to turn back time. It was impossible to take back my words and learn my lesson before I jacked everything up.

She didn't trust me. I had hurt her and she didn't trust me.

*It had always been about action.*

Wasn't that what I had set out to do when we'd first started fake dating?

I shook my head.

When had we been fake? From our first kiss, we'd been real. I would quit denying that.

So what now?

No words. I couldn't abuse my position, and I couldn't follow her like a stalker.

So what'd that leave?

I paged through the rest of the book. About a quarter of the way from the end, more pink caught my eye.

**"Sometimes we can't outrun our past."**

Another nail in the coffin of my actions. I couldn't change how I had reacted.

So how did I face my past?

I pushed away from the counter and tossed the book in the trash, fake cover and all.

# CHAPTER TWENTY-FOUR

Ruby

**Tenor: Can we talk?**

Nope. I put my phone facedown and tried to concentrate on my computer screen. My office was on the second story and overlooked the wide, treed lot around the distillery. This location didn't have the character of the original distillery in Copper Summit. More trucks entered and pulled out of the lot, the barrelhouse looked like a standard warehouse and not a work of rustic art, but it was still pretty and peaceful.

I'd spent the last two weeks working in my office at Bozeman, on alert for any Bailey that wandered by. Since I had put in my notice at the tasting room and no longer picked up bar shifts, I hadn't had to worry as much.

I had foolishly thought that my heartbreak would heal faster if I wasn't going to Bourbon Canyon all the time.

I added a filter to an image of Teller's boots with a glass of bourbon superimposed over them. That sucked.

I tried another one. Both images faded with the glass looking overexposed. Ish.

Punching the keyboard, I tried several more. Ugh. None of them looked good.

What about another image?

Picture after picture scrolled by. The horizon beyond the pines around the Bourbon Canyon location. The sky with clouds and mountains in the distance. Almost looked like the outline of the peaks in Copper Summit's logo.

The picture I had taken of Tenor behind the bar the night he'd agreed to be my fake boyfriend flashed on the screen. His strong arms were braced on the countertop, his hips were kicked back, and his expression . . .

He looked at the camera with that tight jaw of his, smoldering emotion in his eyes. A heat reserved only for the person taking the picture.

Me.

He'd looked at me like that and he'd still ended things? I asked myself that every time I pulled up this image to refresh my heartbreak.

Now he wanted to talk. Had he seen the parts of the book I'd highlighted?

What had he thought?

I had gone to work last week, and the first damn thing I had done was look in the cupboard for a book. There'd been nothing. Twice he'd reached out. Twice I'd shunned him. He didn't like to be strung along either.

My eyes stung. I blinked rapidly. I would not cry.

My mind was made up. I had to live with the consequences.

Didn't I?

My phone buzzed again and I scrambled for it, my hopes catapulting upward for Tenor's name on my screen.

**Madison: Are you still open to a consult?**

Disappointment that it wasn't a text from Tenor gave way to curiosity. Wasn't Madison afraid her brother would get upset?

**Me: Yes. What are you thinking?**

**Madison: Meet me Saturday at 4 at Flat-landers.**

**Me: You sure it won't be an issue?**

I did not want to get on the bad side of a guy who seemed volatile.

**Madison: I already talked to Scooter. It's fine.**

Okay, then. Was news of my breakup with Tenor filtering through town? Now I was welcome at Flat-landers?

Didn't matter. I had plans for a Saturday night again. I'd take it.

**Me: See you then.**

Clicking away from the photo album, I turned my attention to the marketing campaign Wynter had sent me this morning for the holidays. I tapped out post after post. Tomorrow, I'd proof them and start scheduling.

My gaze continued to dip toward the clock. I could go home, to my quiet apartment, in five minutes. I'd spend my Friday night reading. Again. A psychological thriller—where the boyfriend was the killer. As if that'd change my mind. If Tenor showed up, announced he was a serial killer, and brandished a knife, I'd probably throw myself on it just to be close to him.

Finally, closing time. I shut down my computer and

pushed back just as Summer and Wynter appeared at the door.

"Hey, Ruby." Wynter sounded like she was trying to coax me out from under the car. Like I was nothing but a scared kitten and they weren't sure if I'd lash out or not.

Both of them entered, shutting the door behind them.

Wynter held her hands up, her expression instantly apologetic. "We're outside of work hours—you *do not* have to talk to me—but I wanted to see how you're doing and make sure this"—she wiggled her finger around the office—"is okay despite everything."

Part of me had hoped she'd leave the very real breakup alone, pretend like it had never happened, that I'd never dated her brother—for real. The other part had been hurt that she hadn't brought it up before. Just another sign of how easily I came and went from someone's life.

Words froze in my throat and I could only nod. "It's fine," I managed to croak after bobbing my head like my neck was a spring.

Sympathy filled Summer's face. She pulled out the chair across from me and perched on the edge, angling toward me. "Can we talk? Here, or we could go somewhere?"

First Tenor wanted to talk, and now his sisters did. Was this some sort of concerted effort?

We could not go to my apartment. I hadn't cleaned all weekend. My dishwasher mocked the pile of dishes by my sink. I went home, read thrillers about serial killers and stalkers, and cried myself to sleep.

"Here is fine." I folded my hands across my stomach

and grappled for my composure. Staying in an office setting might help keep me from breaking down. "But I don't know what you want to talk about."

I knew damn well what they were here for. Their brother, not me. Had I thought a couple of hours of brainstorming new drinks was anything more than a workday? These two were not my friends.

A fissure in my chest cracked wide open.

"He told us who your dad is," Summer said.

I scowled, my defensiveness rising, bringing a dose of anger with it. "Like I told Tenor, I can't change any of that. And you know what? I know exactly what Dad is like. He can be insulting. He can be a giant dick. Do I cut him off? For being such an asshole, he's one of the few men in my life who hasn't completely kicked me out of his life."

Except for the two times Tenor had tried to reach out. Three, if I counted his message today.

I expected more anger from the two sisters. After all, it had been Bobby Morgan who had been terrible to their loved one. Bobby Morgan who had teased him over his size, how he dressed, what his extracurriculars were. Bobby Morgan who had tried to make Tenor hate himself. And I'd paid for it.

They continued to study me with nothing but empathy.

"It's done." The hopelessness in my voice resonated through the office. I should quit talking, but it'd been a long week. "I can't change my age and I can't change the teenaged boy who knocked up my mom."

Nothing but understanding filled Summer's face. She folded her hands on her lap. "That's what we wanted to talk to you about. I don't think it's your age, necessarily."

Wynter nodded. "Or even your dad."

I snorted. "You were not there. It was definitely my dad."

Wynter tapped her chin. "Yes. But not in the way you think." She dug in her bag and withdrew the book Tenor had left me. The *Sense and Sensibility* dust jacket was on it.

Emotion filled my chest. Embarrassment? Sadness? Irritation? "Why do you have that?"

"I found it in the garbage," she said.

My heart sank. Right down to my toes. He'd thrown the book away? Because he'd seen what I had marked? What else had I been expecting?

Certainly not for him to dump the book, and then for his sister to find it.

"Getting teased so badly as a kid had an effect on him," Summer said, retrieving me from my ruminations. "We can't deny that. But part of why we think Bobby— your dad—was so hard on Tenor was because Tenor didn't change a damn thing. Tenor kept doing Tenor and that pissed your dad off."

Dad had thankfully dealt with whatever had caused that particular personality trait in him, but I didn't understand where they were going with this.

"But after Tenor's looks changed and girls started to notice him, he was different." Sadness laced Wynter's voice. "He tried to be the guy they wanted. Who they expected him to be."

"Very not Tenor," Summer said. "He'd take them on the dates they expected, he'd talk about football—which he gives zero fucks about—or bands—"

"If the singer isn't Junie, he doesn't care," Wynter interjected.

Summer nodded. "One time, I heard him mention a spreadsheet hack around a date and she scoffed, asking who the hell likes spreadsheets. He's never mentioned his love of Excel since."

"Anyone close to Tenor knows he loves Excel," Wynter said solemnly.

"And inventory systems," I said.

Summer gave me a heavy smile. "Yes. Then came Katrina."

"The fallout was bad." Wynter's fraught expression told me I'd hate what came next. "He hid all the best parts of himself, and their relationship was so superficial she never realized he lived at home."

I scrunched my face up. "How did she miss that?"

"She had a place in town and was always asking him to drag her to a bigger city or fly to one for concerts and *theater*." Summer said the last word with a pretentious tone. "She hated that he had standing nights each week when he couldn't do things with her. Our best guess is that she thought he was cheating on her."

Tenor would never.

Summer nodded like she'd heard my thoughts. "So when she found out that big ranch of his wasn't his alone and that he lived with his parents, she was pissed. On top of that, she learned he was leaving town for game nights with a bunch of dudes? She lost it."

"She waged a one-woman smear campaign on him," Wynter said. "After a few days, Teller found Tenor on his land, burning his Warhammer books. Apparently, he'd been in town nnd some guys had given him a hard time about what they'd heard. They thought it was funny. Everyone knew Katrina was superficial and just shy of batshit crazy, but she was gorgeous, so she got away with it, and suddenly Tenor was that middle school kid getting bullied all over again."

"That's awful." Though not a surprise. I'd pieced as much together.

Summer hooked her hands around her knees. "We aren't telling you that so you feel sorry for him. Or so you forgive how he's letting his past affect the very good thing you two had. We just wanted you to understand that it's not you, it's him."

Wynter nodded. "While we love our brother, he can overprotect himself."

"He built his house with the thought he wouldn't have a family," I said, empty. The signs had been there.

Summer sighed. "Yeah, we all figured. We're not here to lobby on his behalf. It's just that we understand the hurt you're feeling. The loves of our lives each did stupid stuff to protect themselves. They broke up with us to protect themselves."

I chewed the inside of my cheek. These ladies were everything I thought I would have to be to keep a guy. Smart, beautiful, and charismatic. They were the nicer versions of Cara that I assumed men like Brock wanted.

In my mind, I'd gotten dumped for the same reason I'd always been dumped. I wasn't enough. I wasn't worth the effort or the risk. So I'd walked. I'd walled myself off.

Now Summer and Wynter were telling me they'd had similar experiences with the men they were happily married to? "They broke up with you?"

"Ended it all," Wynter said.

I gnawed the sensitive flesh of my cheek. Yet Wynter and Myles were married with kids. Same with Summer and Jonah. They'd managed to weather the storms of their dating life. "How did you . . ." I blinked back tears, and my gaze skated away. Fear clogged my throat.

"We each took a risk," Summer said. "Because we thought they were worth it."

I cleared the growing lump out of my throat. "Did Tenor tell you how we started dating?" No surprise rose up inside me when they both nodded. "He said he was going to show me what I deserved in my dating life. Mission accomplished, I guess."

Summer leaned forward. "Unless you think he can be what you deserve."

And we were back to the beginning. I couldn't trust him to be what I deserved. I couldn't trust him with my heart.

***

**Me: What did you want to talk about?**

My curiosity had gotten the better of me this morning, but Tenor still hadn't answered. I'd texted him right before I'd left Bozeman. I had to take myself by surprise and just do it. I briefly thought about swinging by his house—not because I was desperate to see him—but he probably wouldn't be there.

Besides, it would've taken more courage than I had. I had wanted to go into my decision well informed, and just coming out and asking Tenor what he wanted was it.

It had seemed like a good plan. Until he hadn't replied for hours.

He was probably working.

I took a swig of my almost clear Malibu and Coke. Madison had gone in the storeroom to help Allen find more Malibu. Madison and I had been the only two in

Flatlanders at first, but a few more customers were populating the tables. It was early yet and I was on my second drink.

I held up my glass to the dim lights behind the bar. "Allen, do you realize how strong you make these? Coke is a lot cheaper than rum."

"You here to give business advice too, Rue?" He leaned in and smirked at my boobs. "I mean, Ruby."

"Eyes up here." I pointed my index finger and middle finger at my face. "My boobs don't have a mouth, but if you keep staring at them, they will bite you."

He grinned and it was just sly of sleazy. "Promise?"

I snickered. "I walked right into that one."

He laughed. "I appreciate nice tits. What can I say?"

Allen was one of the few men who could get away with being a little sleazy. Madison had introduced him as a cousin. Her brother was out of town, and she swore again he knew why I was here. She also mentioned that she might've asked him when he was drunk and he might not remember he'd said yes afterward, but the bar's books were getting too bad to ignore. His reputation was tanking the place. She hoped to remedy some of the damage via social media. I could help with that.

Madison breezed out of the back room and sat on the stool next to me. She adjusted her notebook and picked up her pen. "Sorry, where were we? Oh, the algorithm." She wrinkled her nose. "I don't think I'll ever understand that."

"It's an ever-changing thing, but the important part is that others spend a ton of time understanding it so you don't have to reinvent the wheel. Here's what I've gleaned." I happily geeked out on all things scroll feed and for-you-page related. I glossed over the different posts I'd tried, the types of videos that I'd found responded the best, and other variations I had tried over the eighteen months I'd worked at Copper Summit.

Allen placed a third drink in front of me with slightly more Coke than the last time.

"Just get comfortable with notes and spreadsheets. If you have someone who can design the shit out of a spreadsheet, it helps so much. Whatever I asked for, Tenor could—" My breath caught in my throat. My vision got all cloudy. I swiped at my eyes. Tears. Dammit.

"Everything okay, Ruby?" Madison asked softly.

No. It hadn't been okay for almost a month. All I got for trying to be true to myself was lingering heartbreak. "You ever fall in love with someone and then they hurt you and you want so badly to forgive them but you're scared?"

Her dark brows lifted the more I prattled.

I sucked down more of my drink. "Yeah. I'm pathetic."

"No." She sighed. "You're relatable."

"Really?" I sniffled and emptied the rest of my glass. The ice tinkled as I knocked it back. Madison had said the drinks were on the house. My second time getting free drinks.

The first time I'd been in this bar, Tenor had carried me out as soon as he'd realized I didn't like all the attention. I had only liked *his* attention.

More tears piled onto my eyelids. "I really fell for him, Madison. And I keep telling myself he's no different than the others, but what if I'm wrong? I feel wrong. I want to be wrong. But how do I know?"

She shook her head, interest and concern lighting

her eyes. "I have no idea what happened, but I'm the last one who should be giving relationship advice. My ex-husband cheated on me with someone I considered family."

"Oof—that sucks. Now you're out a husband and a friend."

Sadness darkened her brown eyes. "It's not like I have a well of friends."

I snorted a little too loud, thanks to the Malibu. "Right? I have none. Want to be my friend?"

Her smile was real but a little shy. "Sure, Ruby. I'll be your friend." The sadness lingered, like she thought that once the drinks wore off, I'd think differently.

She really was nice. The resting bitch face she had was admirable. Mine was a resting Snow White face and it hadn't served me well.

Through my third drink and part of a fourth, I poured my heart out to her. Tonight, she was my only friend. Wynter and Summer had promised nothing had changed, but I couldn't hang out with them and talk about my life when their brother had broken my heart.

What if I had broken his?

All the Coke and alcohol caught up with me, and thankfully, it was enough to distract me.

"I've gotta go pee." I wobbled to the bathroom. Shit. I was dizzy. Twice, I hit the sides of the stall, and if I had been sober, I might've gagged. Gross. Social media wasn't going to remodel the old, cramped bathrooms.

I squinted at the words scratched into the wooden stall door. **If you're reading this, blow him.**

I giggled and a sob came out. I couldn't blow him. I'd ruined it. Tenor had reached out in the sweetest way, and

I had retaliated by being a dick back. He'd trashed the book, and then he'd trashed me.

I had been too late.

I did not deserve him.

I cried and sniffled as I washed my hands. I zigzagged back out. Madison cast a furtive glance my way and did a double take. "Aw, Ruby."

She pulled me into a hug. Not only was she taller than me, she was strong as hell. I got crushed in her grip and I savored it.

"I'm sorry. Thank you for sharing with me." She sounded so formal.

I slid onto my stool and nearly careened off the other side. I righted myself and waited for my vision to settle.

Another Malibu and Coke was slid in front of me.

"Th-thanks." I reached for it, but Madison snatched it away.

She pushed it toward Allen and gave him a warning glare. "She's cut off. Give her a Coke."

"No," I pouted. I was freshly drunk, but I agreed with her. If he kept feeding me drinks, I'd keep drowning my sorrows and that was so unlike me. As it was, I was stuck in Flatlanders for hours until I sobered up. "The last time I got drunk, I crawled into Tenor's bed and got myself off."

Allen paused midpour.

Oops. I shouldn't have said that out loud.

"He was so sweet about it." Another sniffle squeaked out.

Madison rubbed my back.

Allen sidled in front of me to talk to Madison. "Can you guys sit in a booth or something? My dream lady's back in town and the crying girl is going to scare her away."

I was a girl and some other stranger was called a lady? *Fuck you, Allen.*

Madison scowled. "Dream lady?" She looked around.

I did too, squinting. A gorgeous woman wearing shorts that framed long damn legs and glossy blond hair pulled back in a high ponytail was leaning against the counter.

Madison sighed. "Really? *Her?*"

"She doesn't show up very often," Allen argued, eyeing the new arrival's legs. Should someone warn her about the way he ogled boobs? "One of these days, she's going home with me."

Madison rolled her eyes.

"Do you even know what her face looks like?" I asked him.

"I hate to break it to you, cuz," Madison said, "but unless you own a yacht club, she's not going home with you. Katrina aims high."

I sucked in a loud breath that turned heads my way. Including hers. "Katrina? Are you *that* Katrina?"

Of course she was beautiful. Gorgeous and sophisticated.

I hadn't tamed my hair and it frizzed out around my head. Dark circles ringed my eyes, and I had worn thick joggers even though it was in the high seventies outside.

Alarm filled Katrina's eyes, and she looked around, putting a dainty hand to her chest. "I'm Katrina, but I don't know if I'm who you're looking for."

Her gaze grew more frantic as I plopped off the stool, somehow managing to land on my feet. "Oh, you're her."

I had no idea, but my brain had taken the idea and run with it.

"Shit," Madison muttered. She grabbed her phone and hovered next to me.

"Do I know you?" Katrina side-eyed me with her perfect cat eye like I was a rabid skunk.

Between the two of us, yes, I was the smelly animal. I reeked of rum and sadness. She smelled expensive and sexy.

"You were so mean." I stomped my foot. Bad idea. The rum hit hard, and my balance sucked.

She drew back. "Sorry?"

"Tenor." When she blanched, I nodded, my hair bouncing. "He's the best man I've ever met but he couldn't trust me because of you, and then I couldn't trust him because of my dad and you."

Katrina's gaze darted around and she shifted her stance like she was going to run. "That was a long time ago, and I don't know who your dad is."

"You broke him. Because you're *mean*." My fuzzy mind grasped for a more articulate argument, but the tipsy part of my brain thought I'd nailed it.

Her eyes sparked. "He lied to me first."

Light speared through the bar as the door opened, but my focus was on Katrina. "I doubt that. You just assumed. You assumed you could strap yourself in for that Bailey money. You just never realized they worked for it."

She sucked in an indignant gasp. "That's not tr—"

"Shut it. You did enough talking, now someone gets to talk back. I don't care who you are, who your grandma is, or how goddamn pretty you are, I'm telling you off for him. He was too nice to do it."

She lifted her chin. "Does his mama still cook for him?"

"Yes," I hissed. "And it's *delicious*." I bared my teeth like I really was rabid. "And he still paints his models and plays Warhammer. And I read romance. And then at the end of the night, he reenacts the naughty scenes with me and it's *hot*."

Her expression flushed with shock and, if I wasn't mistaken, regret.

"He's so sweet," I continued and the tears were back. "He calls me Goldilocks because he wanted to show me everything that was just right. Everything I deserve in a relationship. But he doesn't realize that he's just right. He's everything I want and deserve, and I was too jaded because I have a shitty ex too."

The remorse in her eyes grew just before her gaze lifted over my shoulder. Relief and interest filled her face. Her lips curled up. "Is this little drunk girl yours? Have you started snagging them young so they don't complain about Mama's house?"

A growl left me and I balled my fists. I'd tear her luxurious locks out. "I'd take him if he lived in a barn. I'm not a superficial, greedy bi—"

"Goldilocks." A strong arm slipped around my waist. A finger tilted my chin up.

I had to be hallucinating. Hearing him in my drunk dreams. Feeling his strong hold around me. How strong were those drinks? But when I looked up, it was into his soft pecan eyes, glittering with affection. "Tenor?"

He studied me. "Am I really everything you want and deserve?"

A hot tear rolled down my cheek and he caught it with the pad of his thumb. "Yes."

"Good. Because I'm in love with you."

"I'm a little drunk," I whispered. He'd caught me yelling at his ex. He hadn't even looked her way. "Are you really here, or am I hallucinating?"

"I'm really here. Madison used your phone to call me."

I frowned. Was that why she had looked guilty when I came out of the bathroom? Or when I'd gotten in Katrina's face? Both? I'd thank her later. She'd given me the chance I thought I had lost. "I'm really sorry. The book was so thoughtful. It was perfect. Just like you."

"I'm not perfect, and you showed me that's okay. You were right. Words weren't enough. I have to show you I mean it."

Out of the corner of my eye, Katrina pushed her hair back and struck a sexy pose that'd dislocate my hip. "She's drunk and she's crazy."

"Enough, Katrina," he said, his voice hard but his attention only on me. "Like my girlfriend said, you've done enough talking."

She made a disgusted noise. "Your *girlfriend* doesn't know what she's talk—"

"Don't you dare insult my daughter or her boyfriend," said a man from behind me.

I frowned and spun, still in Tenor's hold. "Dad?"

# CHAPTER TWENTY-FIVE

Tenor

Ruby's blue eyes were wide and a little too glassy for my liking. The mass of curls around her head made me itch to bury my hands in them. She wasn't in a skirt, but in her cuffed sweatpants, she looked cute and cozy. Perfect for sitting on my couch to read a book and to strip off later.

Fuck, she was gorgeous. "Sorry I couldn't answer your text. Bob—Robert showed up on my doorstep. Sort of."

He'd confessed to hating the name Bobby, so I'd quit using it since he was earning a B-plus in not insulting me.

She glanced from me to her dad. "I don't understand."

Robert shrugged. "Thought maybe you'd answer the phone if I made nice with your boyfriend. I know I was a bastard to him, so I needed to talk to him anyway. He's easy enough to find and he agreed to meet me at his place."

Ruby still looked perplexed. "Did Mom tell you to?"

"She didn't have to," he said. "I asked her if she thought this guy would throw me on my ass, though. She said I deserved it."

Ruby glanced back and forth between us. "You're friends?"

"I doubt that'll ever happen," he said almost sadly. "I was pretty bad, Rubes." When I opened my mouth, he pointed at me. "I'm not going to quit calling her that. I'm her dad and I get to call her a nickname she hates."

As long as it wasn't meant to be derogatory, I wouldn't interfere. "That's up to her."

He nodded and met his daughter's stunned gaze. "All I care about is that he's good to you."

I doubted we'd be friends, but after talking with him, I was optimistic we could be amicable. He was loud and brash like Ruby had described, but I had learned a lot about that boy who had bullied me. "No, we're not friends. But he's apologized—"

She put her fingers on my lips. "He what now?"

"Apologized," I said around her finger. I flicked my tongue out.

She snatched her hand away but bit her lower lip, her gaze glued to my mouth. "I wouldn't do that. I don't know where this bar has been." She winced. "Sorry, Madison."

"Valid," Madison said. She handed Ruby's phone to her. "I called Tenor when you went to the bathroom. And then again when you confronted Katrina."

"I'm right here," Katrina snapped, but we all ignored her.

I cupped Ruby's face. "I'm not going to ask you to write your dad out of your life. We've talked about how things would work if you took me back, how we'd act around each other, how he'd be with our kids." I cut my warning gaze toward him. "Especially about nicknames."

Robert shrugged. He'd been fine with it.

Her lips parted. "Kids?"

"I know we only dated a couple of months, but there's no one like you, Ruby. I knew almost right away that you were it. You're my Goldilocks." I wrapped my hands around her waist. "I'll do anything you want. We can add on to the house. There's plenty of land, depending on how many kids you want."

Wonder filled her eyes. Then retribution filled her gaze. "You mean," she said loudly, "add on to the house you built with your own money from your *two* jobs? The one with the nice shop?"

I grinned at her, soaking in her militant pout.

Robert nodded. "Nice damn house."

Katrina let out a huff and stomped past us. "I only came here because there were no Baileys."

Light cut through the room as the door opened, then she was gone.

"You didn't care that she was here?" Ruby asked.

"She's been wanting to talk to me, but I keep deleting her messages. I haven't cared to see or speak to her. I quit being at her beck and call when she insulted me and my family."

Ruby's mouth curled into a sneer. "She probably heard you were back on the market and realized how much she'd fucked up. Her mistake is my win."

I feathered my thumb across her soft cheek. "You're amazing."

"I'm still a lot younger than you," she said in a ragged voice. The vulnerability was back.

"You're perfect. The only reason I'd talk to Katrina is to thank her for getting me to swear off dating. I didn't have to keep suffering through the wrong women."

She flattened her hands on my chest, but she turned her attention to her dad. "You're going to behave with him?"

"As long as he does right by you." He closed the distance between us, putting a hand on her shoulder. "Look, honey. I know exactly how I was when I was younger, and I know it wasn't right. I was an angry kid, and Tenor never fought back. He just took it and I kept giving it. Told myself I didn't respect him for it, but the truth is it pissed me off more. He was stronger than me. Nothing will take back how awful I was, but I've tried to be a better adult than I was a kid. Some days, I'm successful. Tenor and I—we've come to an understanding. You're important to both of us. And we're playing another match tomorrow."

"I'll still win," I said.

Robert sniffed, challenge in his eyes. "You can't win forever, Bailey."

I would. Out of spite. And I'd celebrate every win in front of him like an asshole.

I didn't have to worry about Robert anymore. He was part of my present because I got the very best of him in Ruby. He could no longer haunt me. Neither could Katrina. Her fucking dad could suck a rotten egg. If my school bully could accept me for his daughter, then the issue hadn't been me.

All the ghosts of my past had been put to rest. I didn't dread seeing them and I gave zero fucks what their opinions of me were. There was only one woman I cared about and I'd spend my life making her happy.

I'd indulge her reading habit—and her work ideas. "I love you, Ruby. I'll do anything for you." I took out my phone and pulled up one of Copper Summit's social media accounts. "But I need to prove it."

She glanced at the screen and did a double take. "Is that . . ." She let out a soft gasp.

"Yep." Thankfully, she'd sent the pictures of me to Wynter as examples of how she'd capture any employees who were willing to participate. Before Robert had arrived, I'd talked to Wynter. She'd posted the photo of me behind the drink I'd poured for Ruby. I hadn't looked yet, but I knew the post was there. For everyone to see and comment on. And oddly, I was only concerned that it pleased Ruby. Everyone else could fuck off.

"You posted this? For me?"

"Actions, not words. She's got more queued up for you to use."

"Oh, Tenor. I love you so much." She tucked herself into my side, holding the phone out. "This picture is my favorite." She giggled and peered closer. " 'Do I get one of those when I order an old-fashioned?' No way." She clicked out. "You know that book you left me? There's this shower scene . . ."

Ruby

I was plastered to Tenor when he carried me into the

house. My mind was foggy, but my body hummed. I clamped my legs around his hips.

He stopped at the island and kissed his way down my neck. "I thought I'd lost you forever."

"I was scared." I angled my head to make room for him. Why was I still dressed?

Why was he still dressed? I bunched up the fabric of his shirt to drag it over his head.

He straightened and gripped my wrists. "Not yet."

My buzz faded. "Why?"

He pressed a firm kiss to my mouth. "Because I'm going to feed you first."

We hadn't been together for almost a month, and he didn't want to have sex? "We're not going to . . ."

He gripped my hips and lifted me to the edge of the island. My legs were spread, putting the bulge of his erection right at my center. I groaned and rocked against it.

His pupils blew wide. "We're most definitely going to, but you're still drunk. And we should talk first."

Couldn't we talk after? Was he second-guessing himself? Now that he had me, he wondered what the urgency had been. Maybe seeing Katrina again—

He ground into me. "Get out of that pretty head of yours. I want to do this right. You're worth it."

That fissure in my heart closed completely. I cupped both sides of his face. "That book was so clever. I still have it."

His lips pulled down. "I threw it away. It was useless."

"Your sisters dug it out and talked to me about what you went through. They helped me see I wasn't being a doormat if we tried again."

He feathered a hand over my cheek. "They didn't tell me."

"Well, they brought me the book, and I read it last weekend. Good choice. You had to special order it, didn't you?"

He dipped his head. "I stayed up all night reading it to get it to you in time for your shift."

I wrapped my arms around his neck and planted a kiss on him. He stuffed his hands in my hair and devoured me. If we weren't going to have sex yet, I'd take this. We could make out for hours until I sobered up.

My stomach growled, and he pulled away. He swiped his thumb over my lower lip. "Food. Since you so valiantly defended Mama's cooking, I can throw her lasagna in."

I groaned. "I haven't had a good meal in weeks."

He smiled and made sure I was steady before retrieving a small pan from the fridge and tossing it into the oven. Then he took a glass from the cupboard and poured some water from the pitcher he kept in the fridge.

He stopped between my legs. "Here. Drink up."

"Allen pours them strong, but Madison cut me off." I gulped the whole glass down and set it beside me. "So. My dad?"

"I can tolerate him."

I brushed my hands over his shoulders, down his arms, and clasped his hands. "I really am sorry that my dad was your bully."

"Small world." He gently squeezed my fingers. "But it turns out I got the very best of him. Seeing him again made me face my past and reevaluate it. How I reacted and why."

"You did nothing wrong."

"I know." His brow furrowed. "I think I always felt like I did or that I should've done things differently. Like I should've done more, reacted like my brothers would've, and when I didn't, it meant I was the weak Bailey." He rolled a shoulder. "Instead, I'd rather he directed his meanness toward me than anyone else. I had my family. Others didn't. And it wasn't like I couldn't see the connection between him and my dating life, but after Katrina, I doubled down on being me. Yet somewhere in my brain, I was convinced nothing mattered. No one would really want me."

"I want you. If we do nothing but go to the jobs we enjoy and come home and read and paint models, I'll be so damn happy."

"I thought that was exactly the life you'd eventually run from. Somehow, I thought I wouldn't react appropriately and you'd leave." He lifted me off the counter and I hugged myself to him. He took me to the couch and sprawled over the cushions with me on top of him. Need swept through me. Being on top of his hard body made mine go haywire.

"I just need to soak you in." His hands roamed up and down my back. "I missed you."

"I couldn't read romance anymore."

He reached over to the coffee table and grabbed a book from a small stack I hadn't noticed. "I have some for you."

I pushed up, my hair tumbling over my shoulders. Without getting off him, I flipped through the books he had. Various space marine romances greeted me, including two others from the series of the first book I'd read at his house. He had tabs in each book.

"I can't believe you did all this." I selected a book and curled into the nook created by him and the back of the couch.

He plucked the book from my hands and opened it to a tabbed and highlighted page. " 'You were my everything, and I took you for granted.' "

"Tenor." I flattened my hand on his hard chest.

"I wanted to say so much to you, and I was afraid I wouldn't get the chance." He paged further into the book. " 'You've sucked me into your orbit and I don't want to be freed.' You'll have to excuse the space metaphors, but I wanted to get books that were relevant to us."

"I like them."

He flipped to another page. "If you like that, how about this one? 'You are my atmosphere, the very air I breathe.' "

"It's perfect."

He turned to a new page. " 'Do you want me on my knees for you? Because I will drop right now, honeybee. I will beg for you, but it'll come at a cost. I'll give you everything you want, but you'll come with my name on your lips. It'll be your sweet nectar on my tongue each time I have a craving. You will spread for me and you will need it. You will need me. But I'll be right there, on my knees and waiting for you.' "

Heat flushed through my veins and wicked under my skin. I scissored my legs, desperate to ease the ache between my thighs. "Oh god, Tenor. I'm not going to make it until after dinner."

"You'll make it." His deep voice was a rumble under my ear. "And I'll be right there, waiting for you. On my knees."

# CHAPTER TWENTY-SIX

Tenor

I stripped off her thick sweats, revealing each creamy inch of her thighs. The shower was running and the water was probably warm already.

Time had ticked by agonizingly slowly until dinner was done and dishes were cleaned up. I wasn't rushing her. By the time we'd been done eating, her eyes were no longer glassy, but her cheeks were flushed and her breath shallow. Each time she looked at me, a furnace roared hotter in her gaze. That wasn't from the alcohol. I hadn't had a drop and I felt the same.

I yanked every strip of clothing off her. She did the same to me. Our arms were getting tangled and we were dancing around to get each other naked.

She smiled at me and the damn sunrise was right here in my bedroom while outside the sun had set.

"You're mine, Goldilocks." I picked her up and stepped into my oversized shower. Carefully, I set her down, then dropped to my knees. Warm water hit my back. Her nipples were peaked and begging to be sucked.

Later. I needed a fast, hard connection with her, but I had to make sure she was ready.

She twined her fingers in my increasingly damp hair. "If I'm dreaming, don't wake me up."

"You're not dreaming, and I'll make you come so hard that you'll be sure of it." I hitched one of her legs over my shoulder and went right for her swollen clit.

"Tenor," she groaned.

Her salty-sweet scent surrounded me. I lavished her tight little bundle of nerves with attention, vowing to make up for the time we'd missed. A month might be a blink in a lifetime, but it had crawled by for an eternity.

Forever was what I wanted with this woman.

When it came to Ruby Casteel, I knew exactly what was in my heart. She was it. She was my endgame.

Sharp tugs on my hair massaged my scalp as I fluttered my tongue over her clit.

"Tenor. *Oh god*, Tenor."

She was close, but I couldn't let her come. Not yet. This first time between us, since we'd broken each other and pieced the other back together, I had to be inside her. I had to come with her.

Just as she arched her back, her hips making long, slow rolls against my face, I stopped and rose.

Water droplets danced on her eyelashes. Her eyes had gone hazy, filled with lust.

I claimed her mouth and lifted her. She automatically wrapped her legs around my waist. I adjusted my stance until my cock was at her hot entrance.

"I need you," she said against my mouth.

I thrust in and she called out. My hands were branding her ass, but she flexed her thighs to move along my length. "You're a greedy woman."

"When it comes to you." She gasped and rode me.

I put her back against the wall and took over, pumping in and out of her. I would slam into my climax in record time, but she was right there with me. Her soaked walls fisting me, milking me.

"Fuck, Ruby." I spread her legs wide and pounded into her. Each thrust scraped against her clit until my name rang off the bathroom wall.

Lightning raced down my spine, shooting through my dick. "Fuck!"

My legs shook as I came. I would not fall, but it took all my concentration to stay upright through the monster orgasm that rushed over me.

"Tenor!" Heat flooded between us.

Aftershocks ran through her and right into me. "Goddamn, Ruby. I'm so in love with you."

She blinked up at me, her expression dreamy. Satisfied. "You are?"

"Without a doubt."

"Good." She nipped at my lower lip. "Because I love you. And I really love what you do with that tongue."

"I'm never going to get enough of you."

"I used to think I'd never be enough."

"Oh, my little Goldilocks, you're so fucking perfect." I grinned and nipped and licked her lips before trailing kisses down her neck. My erection hadn't softened. I could take her again, but not like this. Gingerly, I untangled her limbs from me. When her feet hit the floor, I turned her around. First, I pressed one of her hands against the wall by her head, then the other.

"Stay right there."

She blinked over her shoulder at me. Water droplets cascaded down her soft skin. "What are you doing?"

"Remember that shower scene?"

Ruby

*Two months later . . .*

Tenor slammed the ball Dad had just returned. It skimmed over the net and the bounce wasn't high enough for Dad to get there in time.

Dad threw his hands in the air and waved his racket around. "Argh! You and those fucking net shots."

Tenor only flashed a smug grin and came over to high-five me. He was unrepentant when it came to tennis with Dad. We'd only played once last month when Tenor and I had gone to Helena. Today, Mom had driven her RV through Bourbon Canyon to meet up. Dad was keeping her rackets at his place, so he'd made the trip for a doubles match. He'd picked her up at the RV park to meet us.

Dad hadn't won one match yet with Tenor. I also

suspected Tenor had given up a couple sets just to let Dad think he had a chance.

"Good game, guys," Mom said, crossing to the net.

Tenor and I shook her hand, then Dad's. We went to our respective benches to close our gear back up in our bags. I shrugged into a black Copper Summit hoodie of Tenor's. It was warm from being draped over the bench in the sun and hung almost to my knees. I had worn leggings, but when the wind kicked up, there was a cool bite to it, promising winter was on the way.

The possessive glint Tenor got in his eye when he saw me in his hoodie would make it hard to take it off again. Unless he took it off. Which he could do any day he wanted. I had moved in with him at the end of last month.

I had meant to quit my extra shifts in the tasting room, but since I now had a handsome escort to and from the bar if the weather got bad, I kept them. He walked me out every Friday. Some nights, we didn't make it out of the parking lot before he was inside me.

God, I loved this man.

Dad hitched his bag over his shoulder. "Who's selling that obnoxious house by the golf course?"

"Cara," I said. I'd seen the for sale sign a couple of weeks ago. She hadn't come into Copper Summit again, and I hadn't cared.

Mom pulled a face. "I'm glad you don't have to run into her." She hooked her bag over her shoulder and slid her gaze toward Dad. Fondness filled her eyes. "Ready to go, Robert?"

"Whenever you are." He held his hand out and my heart crawled into my throat when Mom grasped it back.

"What is this?" I blinked at them.

Tenor slid an arm around my waist. I wasn't unhappy. Should I be? Confusion muddled my thoughts.

Dad turned sheepish, toeing the tip of his athletic shoe into the ground. "I figured if this guy could move past what happened between us, I'd shoot my shot with your mom."

My parents? Dating? "What about your travels?"

"I'm still doing them," she said, beaming at Dad. "We're taking it slow."

"You know how she gets sick of men," Dad said, like he'd never been happier his ex had been a player.

She nudged him. "I haven't gotten sick of you."

"You haven't lived with me yet," he retorted.

"I'll keep the van," she said lightly. "When you irritate me, I'll go to Banff for a week."

Dad just grinned. "As long as you come back."

My happiness broke free. My mom and I weren't star-crossed twins after all. "Good for you two." I stepped away from Tenor to give each of them a hug. Tenor gave them both a quick handshake. Then they were gone.

"My parents are dating," I said, my voice filled with awe. "Each other."

He took my tennis bag off my shoulder and tossed it in the back seat of the pickup with his. I was still staring in the direction my parents had driven off in. He returned to my side and handed me a book.

"What's this?"

"I have something to say. I hoped this was the right time."

With a perplexed smile, I flipped through the book. We'd been leaving each other notes in books since we'd reconnected. Mostly, we highlighted all the naughty parts we wanted to try.

I found the page with soft-green highlighter. I'd gotten a set with trendier ink. " 'Will you marry me?' " With a gasp, I jerked my head up.

He sank to one knee in his basketball shorts and baggy T-shirt. His loose shirts had remained the same. He claimed they felt better than tight stuff. And he'd still slouch, but only if he thought it put the other party at ease. He never diminished himself around me, my family, or his.

He brandished an open black velvet box. Inside, a perfectly square diamond ring in a platinum setting winked up at me.

"Oh my god." I put my hand to my mouth. "Oh my god!"

"Ruby Casteel, will you be my wife? You're the war gear stratagem to my unit. You're the denouement to my romance novel. Everything is just better with you."

Love bloomed so powerfully in my chest, I didn't know how I could love him more. But each day I did. I threw my arms around him. "Yes! Of course."

He caught me and lowered me onto his bent knee. "You've made me the happiest bastard in the world."

He helped me slip the ring on.

I admired it in the sunlight. "It's gorgeous. How did you know— Wynter." She had talked jewelry with me under the guise of a Valentine's Day promotional idea.

"She might've gotten me some details. Ready for your engagement party?"

I glanced around like people were going to pop out of the bushes. "Where?"

"At Copper Summit."

I pushed my hands through his hair. "Are you sure you're okay with how fast we're moving?"

I loved this man, but I'd give him the time he needed.

"I didn't make peace with your dad because we're nothing but a bourbon summer romance. We are forever. I'll make sure you want me that long."

"I'm going to want you even longer."

His grin went right to my chest, filling me up inside.

I kissed him. "Let's go party. Then take me home and paint me like one of your Warhammer models."

"I'll use my tongue."

———

Thank you for reading Tenor and Ruby's story. Did you know that Wilna finally talks Teller Bailey into doing the bachelor auction fundraiser? He's auctioning off the completion of one handyman project. Just so happens that Madison Townsend is left with a derelict bar that she needs to get open and making money. Only with her family history, there's no one she can trust to help. Then she hears about a certain bachelor from a family known for their bourbon and their values. Does she win the win in Bourbon Sunset?

If you liked the romance novel highlights, join Ruby and Tenor as they swap highlighted passages before their wedding in this bonus epilogue.

# ALSO BY WALKER ROSE

**Bourbon Canyon Series**

Bourbon Bachelor

Bourbon Lullaby

Bourbon Runaway

Bourbon Promises

Bourbon Harmony

Bourbon Summer

Bourbon Sunset